Clean Break

ABBY VEGAS

For my parents.

1

It is my firm belief that I wasn't always a miserable fuck-up. There are people I used to know who would disagree with me on this, and it's getting harder to remember what I was like before everything bad happened — but I was normal once, or close enough to pass for it. Then I was not-normal, and then I sort of vanished. For several years I was putting one foot in front of the other — existing, basically. But I was doing it in grand style.

Friends and acquaintances — well-meaning, mostly — questioned the wisdom of this unorthodox path I'd chosen. *Save your money,* they implored. *Stay in school. Think of the future.* And later: *Let us help you. You don't have to go through this alone.* But I did have to go through it alone, to the degree that I had to go through it at all. A clean break — one weighty blow, fracturing past from present — was the only way forward. There was no future to speak of, so living in the moment was my best-case scenario. Everyone I cared about was gone. In their place was a big pile of money, wholly inadequate in every way but one: it had to be spent.

And I'd had the nicest apartment! A corner unit in a brand-new high-rise building in Chelsea. With a doorman. A mailbox labeled with my name: *Lane Haviland. 22-H.* And a balcony — true, I'd never used it exactly as planned, but the sweeping southern views of the skyline and the Hudson River had made for some spectacular New York City sunsets. Sometimes, in my dreams, I still lived there.

Which reminds me of another thing I miss, I thought as I eyed the scummy interior of the subway car. Taxis. I'd had to take the subway to the LIRR just to get to the fucking B train from Forest Hills, and I still had a ways to go before I could get myself and my two overstuffed suitcases into my new apartment.

My gaze shifted to an old woman hunched over reading a tattered paperback. Buying books — that, too, had been a luxury, as were all the long, lazy afternoons spent reading them inside that glorious sun-drenched apartment. Whenever I got stir-crazy, I'd book a spare-no-expense trip — Prague and Budapest, Kyoto, a safari in Africa. How cool had *that* been, stepping off a plane in Nairobi and being whisked off to Tanzania to see elephants? I'd do it again in a heartbeat, especially if it meant I could escape this overheated subway car rumbling through the hinterlands of Brooklyn.

Of course the money couldn't last forever. I'd begun the downsizing process early, mindful of my dwindling bank balance and desperate to stretch whatever funds remained a little further. When my phone broke, I didn't buy a new one — instead I dropped thirty bucks on a prepaid flip-phone. These self-imposed austerity measures had bought me a few more months. But ever since I'd given up the apartment and jettisoned most of my belongings, each ensuing living situation had seemed more precarious. Like the cockroach-infested month-to-month studio sublet in the West Village. It could charitably have been called quaint, but I couldn't afford to keep it very long, not even after I caved to reality and found a job. Nothing serious — just dog walking, at first. Then I lucked into a catering gig with a few more hours and a boss who didn't suck.

But even working, cash flow remained a disaster, because living in New York on just shy of two hundred bucks a week is like trying to fill a bathtub with the drain wide open. And that's how I ended up couch-surfing — most recently at my ex-boyfriend's apartment in Forest Hills. His patience started wearing thin about two weeks ago.

Ding! That was the P.A. system in the subway car, followed by the oddly upbeat automated-voice announcement: *The last stop will be Brighton Beach.* Yesterday I'd visited there for the first time in my life. I'd met my new roommate, signed the lease, and made sure there really was a balcony as advertised.

I looked out the train-car window at the graffiti-covered buildings by the elevated tracks. Even in the blazing sunlight, the temperature had been well below freezing for several days and that somehow made everything look worse. Dreary. Brighton Beach was technically part of New York City, but at the moment it seemed far away from everything I'd ever known. Maybe that wasn't a bad thing.

It doesn't feel like home.

It doesn't have to be. Not for long.

Maybe. That plan — dropping off this mortal coil — wasn't set in stone. It never had been. But it was never far from my mind.

If I'd had someone to confide in, I'd have told them that the money issues had become way too intertwined with all my other problems, and as such I was tempted to throw them on the giant pulsating pile in the corner and ignore them entirely. Except there comes a point when you can't do that anymore and not be homeless.

Walking down Brighton Beach Avenue under the elevated tracks, I squinted against the cold, dry wind and yanked one of the suitcases over a troublesome curb. I still couldn't believe my luck, finding this sublet on Craigslist. I was getting the master suite in a three-bedroom apartment. The building was gleaming and modern — a little taste of luxury compared to the increasingly shabby apartments I'd been occupying of late. Since I hadn't had money for the deposit, I'd requested an advance from my boss, Randy, who'd handed it over without even asking me to sign anything. "I trust you," she'd insisted, and without consciously thinking too hard about it I knew that I would betray that trust. It wasn't a matter of if, just when. Nothing like a little self-loathing to make my downward spiral extra enjoyable.

I wondered which of the two roommates would be there to welcome me. I'd met Svetlana yesterday, but Rozaliya hadn't been there — she worked a lot, apparently. All the better. I wasn't interested in making friends. But the apartment door was locked, and no one seemed to be home. Svetlana wasn't answering texts or phone calls.

Shit. I dragged my suitcases down to the lobby and knocked on a glass door that said MANAGEMENT OFFICE. The woman working there was nice enough, but she hadn't heard anything about my arrival. No keys had been left.

I sighed. "Would you mind looking to see if Rozaliya's contact information is in your records? I only have Svetlana in my phone."

"Who?"

"Svetlana Grigoryeva. Penthouse Two."

She shook her head. "Penthouse Two is owned by an older couple. They're away. Overseas."

"I don't understand," I insisted. "I was inside the apartment yesterday. Svetlana showed it to me."

"Well, they're away," she repeated. "They had someone coming in to water the plants every few days. I wonder, I wonder if…" She trailed off.

Suddenly I felt lightheaded. My knees wobbled and the nice lady asked me if I wanted to sit down. "I gave her a deposit," I whispered. "Eight hundred dollars."

"I don't know what to tell you." She had a pained look on her face. "Can you cancel the payment?"

"It was a cashier's check." I had a receipt, somewhere in the two suitcases that held all my worldly possessions. Was Svetlana even her real name? I felt like I might throw up.

The nice lady brought me water to drink in a paper cup. She helped me find the bank's customer service number, and she stood by anxiously as I called to report the stolen check. Then she showed me on her phone where the nearest police precinct was, because I'd need to file a report. She offered to hold my luggage for me. She wished me good luck. I'd need it.

2

I arrived at the Sixtieth Precinct all breathless and agitated, but the uniformed cop manning the front desk seemed in no particular hurry to fight crime. "Wait there," he grunted, and he gestured to a long wooden bench. "An officer'll call you in a few."

I sank down onto the bench and grieved for the loss of my smartphone. How on earth had people dealt with discomfort and ennui before portable screens? There wasn't even a magazine to thumb through — just pamphlets for affordable cosmetic dentistry, in English and Russian, featuring grinning models with preternaturally square white teeth. The overhead fluorescent lights buzzed. I checked my flip-phone, but no one had called or texted me. Fucking Svetlana.

Eons passed, children were born and men died and still no one called my name. Just as my ass was going completely numb, a powerfully-built man in street-clothes came up by the desk. A gold badge hung on his shirt pocket.

"Haviland," he announced, and I stood up. He was holding a Dunkin' Donuts coffee cup, and at the sight of the logo my stomach grumbled audibly. "I'm Detective Jarrett." He didn't offer a handshake, just waved me through a small gate and then led me through a maze of cubicles. His back was impossibly wide at the shoulders, tapering down to a trim waist, and his blue dress shirt was stretched tightly over everything in a manner that suggested he might be wearing a superhero costume underneath.

"Have a seat," he sighed, pointing to a folding metal chair by his desk.

Over the din of the precinct office, I recounted my humiliating story while Detective Jarrett nodded and sniffed and took notes on a steno pad. He didn't seem particularly shocked at Svetlana's treachery, although he did raise an eyebrow at the amount she'd stolen. "Eight hundred bucks," he repeated, shaking his head. "That's a lot of money."

"Yeah." I assumed he was commiserating. I was wrong.

"Why'd you give it over to a stranger you met on Craigslist?" He leaned back in his swivel-chair and stared at me with close-set eyes.

"I was too trusting," I admitted. Inwardly I fumed at his knee-jerk victim-blaming. "You know how it is in New York. You find an affordable apartment, you snap it up right away."

He shrugged his meaty shoulders. He had one of those thick bodybuilder necks and a close-cropped military-style haircut. Big hands with fingers that looked like sausage links. He closed the pad and held up the phony lease I'd signed. "This is evidence. It stays with me. You need a copy?"

"I guess so."

He got up and came back a minute later to hand me a photocopy. Then, without sitting down, he glanced over at a calendar taped to the wall. "Come back tomorrow afternoon to pick up the report. Sorry you had to go through this, Miss…" He trailed off rather than attempt to remember my name.

I sat there stupefied. "Is that it? I mean — is that all?"

He frowned. "Do you have anything else you'd like to tell me?"

I felt my face flush. "Aren't you going to find this woman and get my money back?"

He snorted. I just stared at him, so he sat back down and looked at me levelly. "Miss, I'll tell you right now, you're not getting your money back unless the bank refunds it. You said you called that in, right?"

"Yeah. They said once I have a police report it takes sixty to ninety days for a decision." My voice was tinged with desperation, but Detective Jarrett just nodded. A rational part of me knew that it was pointless to blame the messenger.

"Look, I'm not naïve," I stammered. I know you can't drop everything to go looking for this…this person. But can't you — I don't know, put it into the computer and see if it matches other crimes? I bet she's scammed other people."

He scratched his nose. "I will be referring your case to the Fraud Unit," he replied. "And you're right, she's probably done this before." I felt one last desperate stab of hope. "But listen, Miss Haviland. Focus your energy on the bank." He rubbed one eyelid with his thumb, then leaned back in his swivel-chair until it groaned in protest. "As far as Svetlana's concerned, your money's already gone."

I gritted my teeth. To his credit, Detective Jarrett didn't seem to be particularly enjoying this part of his job — at least not in the typical jaded New York cop schadenfreude way you'd expect. I could detect a glimmer of beaten-down sympathy in his eyes. I swallowed. "Can I ask you a question?" Why did my voice sound so unnaturally high-pitched?

He glanced longingly at his computer screen. "Absolutely."

"Can you help me with—" I paused and looked down at the paper in my lap. "Look, I signed this lease. I'm pretty sure it's bullshit, but I don't know if — I mean, I don't know what the protocol is in this type of situation…"

"That's not my role. It's a civil matter."

I felt a lump forming in my throat. "Right."

He took the paper from me and looked down at it. "It's a phony lease. What's your question?"

The floodgates opened. Hot tears began to trickle down my cheeks. Detective Jarrett looked pained. "I'm really sorry," I choke-gasped. "I just — I honestly don't know what to do." Great heaving sobs. Right in the middle of the Sixtieth Precinct. No one seemed to notice or care that I was having a breakdown, which was oddly reassuring.

"Do you have any friends or a family member you can call?"

"N-no." Another shuddering sob. God, this was so embarrassing.

"Here. Have some water." I took the mini bottled spring water he offered and sipped. *Deep breaths.*

"Tissue?" He held out a box.

"Thanks." I grabbed a handful of tissues and scrubbed at my face. My breathing was returning to normal. Then I hiccupped, which made me feel even more like a prize jackass if that was indeed possible.

"I can refer you to an agency that may be able to help out with the housing situation," Detective Jarrett said, enunciating *the housing situation* slowly and carefully as though its mere mention might cause me to spontaneously combust.

"I don't need—"

"It's just an option. You can decide later whether you want to pursue it." His words had the ring of a well-practiced spiel. I wondered how many hard-luck cases came through here every day.

He offered me a business card: *New York City Department of Housing Preservation and Development.* "Thank you," I mumbled, and I stood up. "Really — thanks. I'm sorry. I know you probably have—"

"Wait a sec," he snapped. I looked dumbly at him; he was dialing his desk-phone. He pointed at the chair and motioned for me to sit down, so I did. "Yeah, this is Detective Jarrett with the Sixtieth Precinct," he stated authoritatively. "Who am I speaking with? Okay. I'm here with a woman. She signed a lease yesterday. Got scammed." He went silent for a moment. "The lease is on your letterhead." He fidgeted with his pen. "She lost her money. Says she spoke with a Svetlana Grigoryeva. You know Svetlana?"

I blew my nose, then wrung the tissues into a sodden mass while I hung on every word of the conversation.

"Yeah, well, if you see her, give me a call." He checked his watch. "Listen, maybe you can do me a favor. Miss Haviland here, she needs a place to stay for a couple of days 'til she…" His eyes met mine. "Regroups." I sat up straighter. "You think you can do that?…I'd certainly appreciate it." He drummed his sausage-link fingers. "Okay. Right. Thank you very much."

He hung up and scribbled something on his pad. "All right, Miss Haviland. Brighton Realty Management. Tell 'em I sent you." He tore off the page and handed it to me along with his card.

I was rendered momentarily speechless. "Thank you — really — thank you so much. I mean it. You're awesome."

"You're welcome, and goodbye, Miss Haviland."

Sitting on the train on my way back to Brighton Beach, I considered my options. It was pretty clear that they were pathetic. Detective Jarrett's suggestion to call a family member had stung especially hard since I had no family, but the fact that I had no friends I could call for help might have been even more depressing.

My stomach growled again, insistently, and I ignored it. *Later.* First I needed to make sure I didn't spend the night sleeping on a park bench. I walked the few blocks to the address Detective Jarrett had given me, which was tucked away in the back of the ground floor of a red-brick complex on Brighton 14th Street. I knocked timidly on the door of Brighton Realty Management. No answer. I knocked louder, then tried the door. It opened into a dark, shabby office that positively reeked of cigarette smoke. An older woman sat at the single desk, which had a computer with the world's grimiest keyboard, an overflowing ashtray, and several stacks of manila folders and papers.

"Yes?" She looked me up and down through Coke-bottle glasses. Her gray hair looked like a Brillo pad and her sweater-set had definitely originated in the Reagan administration.

"Hi. I'm Lane Haviland." I forced myself to smile and offered my hand, which she regarded as though it were a turd. She finally reached out and gave it a limp, cursory shake.

"What do you want?" Thick Russian accent.

"Yes, well, actually." I suddenly felt out-of-breath. "I just came from the Sixtieth Precinct." Blank stare. "The police station." At this piece of news, she glared at me. I stumbled on. "I — Detective

Jarrett said I should come here. I think he called. Did he speak to you?"

"Have seat." She motioned to a small swivel-chair upholstered in stained gray cloth and I sat down. Then she yanked a drawer open and rummaged around in it.

"Excuse me, I didn't catch your name," I said lamely.

She shot me an icy look. "I am Mrs. Pasternak." The desk drawer slammed shut. She took a cigarette out of a pack and lit it. Then she took a long drag and regarded me stonily.

"Well, Mrs. Pasternak, I really do appreciate your taking the time to — to see me." The cigarette smoke was making me feel lightheaded. Perhaps now wasn't the best time to broach the subject of smoke-free workplace laws in New York State.

"I talked with police." She waved her cigarette in the air dismissively. "Heard about your money. Too bad. Lousy criminals." Smoke swirled around her as she took another drag. I coughed.

"I don't want trouble," she continued. "You need place to stay, for a few days?" I nodded. "There is unit." She reached for a binder on a tottering shelf. "On West End Avenue. Few blocks away." She flipped the binder open, then pointed with her cigarette to a floor plan that had been photocopied so many times that the numbers in the room's dimensions were too blurry to read. "Studio apartment." She slammed the binder shut and stared at me. "You will take it?"

"Um — sure," I replied. She gave a curt nod. "How can I ever thank you?"

She crushed the cigarette into the overfull ashtray. "Monthly rent on unit is one thousand fifty dollars," she rasped. "You have job, yes?"

I didn't know how to respond to this — statement? Proposal? — without seeming ungrateful — or worse, souring the deal. "It sounds promising," I said, and I plastered a vapid smile onto my face. "May I see the apartment?"

She opened up a flat metal box, fished around in it, and handed me a set of two keys. "On West End Avenue," she repeated, and she wrote down an address on the back of a business card. "Basement Unit C."

The stretch of West End Avenue in Brighton Beach where Mrs. Pasternak had directed me was derelict and depressing in the thin midafternoon sunlight, a far cry from the gracious prewar buildings that lined its Manhattan namesake. But as ominous as "Basement Unit C" sounded, it still beat a park bench, probably. I tried to hold this thought in my mind, along with some measure of gratitude, as I turned the key in the lock of a rundown building's lobby.

A staircase led down to a cinderblock-walled basement hallway. It was darker than I would have liked, industrial and slightly grubby, but at least it didn't look rat-infested. Everything smelled strongly of disinfectant. A rough humming noise emanated from one end of the corridor — the boiler, I assumed. The first door I saw was labeled COMPACTOR ROOM; the second, LAUNDRY. Below that, an OUT OF ORDER sign had been affixed to the door with duct tape.

At one end of the hallway were two doors, facing each other. Sure enough, one said BOILER ROOM and the other was blank and padlocked from the outside. I headed back in the opposite direction and found one last door, shrouded partially in darkness thanks to a broken light bulb. The label said SUPER, and in faded, peeling stenciled paint was a large "C".

I rang the buzzer. It sounded inside, but there was no answer. The door was locked. I inserted the second key, turned it experimentally, and pushed the door open a crack. I half-expected to come face-to-face with a vicious attack-dog guarding a meth-lab, but inside it was dark and quiet.

I fumbled around on the wall until I found a light switch. A single naked bulb illuminated the empty apartment — what little there was of it. Indeed it looked more like a prison cell than a living space, with the same cinder-block walls as the adjacent corridor and a too-low, claustrophobic drop ceiling that had seen better days.

I took a step inside. At first I'd assumed the place was windowless, but once my eyes adjusted to the dim light I spied a small window set high in the wall facing the street, placing it just below ground-level. The glass was so filthy I couldn't see through it, but something was on the other side blocking the daylight — a sheet of plywood, maybe? I couldn't tell.

A Manny Pacquaio poster was taped to the wall. I peeked behind it to see if it was hiding a bloodstain, then opened a set of louver-doors expecting to find a closet. Inside was a midget kitchen — dorm-sized fridge, a single electric-coil burner, and a very small sink. Bracing myself for the worst, I peeked inside the fridge, but it was clean, and empty except for an Aquafina water-bottle. Behind a second door was the world's smallest bathroom with a surprisingly mildew-free shower-stall, along with a toilet and sink jammed in at uncomfortable-looking angles.

"Okay, okay," I murmured out loud, a little breathlessly. It wasn't the Taj Mahal, and I'd have laughed at this get-up in the halcyon days when money was plentiful. But in light of current circumstances, it actually seemed like it could work, at least for the next couple of days until I got something better. I dug out my phone and opened it — zero bars. Of course; it was a fucking basement. So I trudged back upstairs into the lobby.

No one answered the phone at Brighton Realty, so I left a voicemail for Mrs. Pasternak. Then it was time to retrieve my meager possessions. Lugging everything several blocks and then down to the basement sapped what was left of my energy, so I sat down on one of the two suitcases that held the accumulation of my life's detritus and looked around the bare room.

I had no creature comforts. That had been intentional — as my moneyed life had wound down, I'd gotten rid of pretty much everything in the realm of material possessions. There had been a practical reason for this: moving between short-term sublets is easier and less expensive when you can just pick up and go. But I won't lie: another part of it was — well, at the time it had *felt* spiritual. A farewell to the material world as the cash dwindled away. Very Zen. But now I was more broke than ever and I didn't have a bed to sleep on. And I wasn't dead yet.

I was contemplating that last matter in a somewhat gruesome fashion when I heard a knock at the door.

3

"Who is it?" I called out. I didn't feel remotely ready to accept visitors, but I supposed there were worse scenarios — the Brooklyn Boiler Room Killer. Or my landlady.

"You in there?" It was a man's voice. Muffled.

"Yes?"

"Maintenance. For Lane Haviland." He pronounced it *Have-eee-land.* "Open door, please." Heavy Russian accent.

Well, he knew my name. At least I wouldn't have the life strangled out of me anonymously. I opened the door to see two men standing there. I wouldn't say they seemed hostile. More like bordering-on-annoyed.

"You are Lane?" The guy doing the talking was holding a red toolbox. He had a creased, weathered face, close-cropped hair, and a shiny gold front tooth. I tried not to stare at it.

"Yeah," I replied. "What's up?"

"'Scuse me." He pushed past me into the apartment. I gaped at him. Well, what did I expect — white-glove service? Still, it was more than a little off-putting to be shoved aside by a creepy-ass Russian guy with a gold front tooth as he waltzed into my space uninvited. I turned to the second man, who was tall and lean with shaggy jet-black hair. His face was chiseled and pale with a beak of a nose and a stern expression.

13

"Well, come on in," I told him.

He grunted and slunk past me to join his companion at the sink. Then he took a flashlight out of the toolbox and said something in Russian: *"Ty chto? Ahuyel."*[1] It sounded harsh, accusatory, but what the hell did I know? Maybe that's just what Russian sounded like.

The guy with the gold tooth turned to face me. "Landlord sent us. To connect sink to water."

"Oh. Well. Thanks for coming out on such short notice." Good thing I'd done such a thorough inspection of the place.

The gold-toothed man leered at me. His nose was an explosion of broken capillaries, and the rest of his teeth weren't looking so hot. The tall guy, who was younger — in his thirties, probably — was peering up into the sink base from a crouched position. When he leaned back over the toolbox I spied a scar running down the side of his face. I hadn't noticed it before; it was the angle of the light hitting him that revealed a pale line that started on his forehead, skipped over his left eye and picked up again on his cheek, snaking down towards his jawline.

There had to be an interesting story there. I indulged my fascination with the macabre a moment longer and wondered what the hell had happened to this guy as I watched him pluck a wrench from the toolbox. Then he wedged his lanky frame into the sink base as far as it would go, all gawky and long-limbed, and suddenly I felt like the World's Biggest Asshole. Why was I cataloging everyone's faults? *For fuck's sake, they're just doing their job. Relax.*

The two men clanged around under the sink, alternately muttering and snapping at each other in Russian. I let my guard down and decided to test my wildly hopeful hypothesis regarding cell-phone coverage and the apartment's lone window. It wouldn't be good for light or a view, but I was hopeful that I could get one bar of coverage — enough to send and receive texts, anyway — if I placed my phone up there.

---

[1] Translations in Appendix I.

I dragged one of the suitcases over to the window-well and laid it down flat, then stepped on top of it and held my flip-phone as close to the window as I could without touching anything. And it worked! One bar of coverage. The window-well would require a thorough scrubbing with some highly caustic substance before it was fit to touch with bare hands, but I allowed myself to revel in this small victory. I'd be slightly more connected to the outside world, as little as I sometimes liked it.

The sound of running water jolted me back to reality. The two men were packing up their tools, so I walked over to rejoin them. Gold-Tooth turned off the faucet, then leered at me. "Okay?"

"Sure." I nodded stiffly. "Thanks. Is the bathroom water hooked up?"

He grunted an affirmative and glanced around the room. "You have furniture coming?"

"No, this is it." I jammed my hands in my pockets.

"No bed?" Gold-Tooth was incredulous. "You sleep where, on floor?"

I walked over to the door and pulled it open. "Thanks again," I snapped.

Scar-Face, who already had his toolbox in hand, slunk past me wordlessly and lumbered through the doorway. Gold-Tooth stayed, and smirked. "You need job, honey?" His eyes, bloodshot and rheumy and generally disgusting, traveled down the length of my figure. "I can maybe help you out."

"Nope." I looked him straight in the eye and he grinned. I felt everything I'd ever eaten rise up in the back of my throat.

"You sure?"

He took a step towards me, and then suddenly he was *way* too close. Hair-standing-up-on-the-back-of-my-neck close. And I was standing against the wall. "Back off!" I shouted, and my voice sounded oddly loud and hoarse echoing around the concrete room.

He stepped back, still grinning, and shook his head. "Excitable girl."

"*Cho blya?*" Scar-Face had suddenly reappeared in the doorway. He glared down at me, then at Gold-Tooth. There was

15

fury in his eyes. My heart was beating way too fast. More than anything, I wanted a locked door between me and everyone else in the world, starting with these two.

Gold-Tooth shot Scar-Face an annoyed glance, then shifted his gaze to me. "Rent is due Friday. Don't be late, okay, honey?" He sniffed. "Call if you need anything." He took one more look around, then walked out.

I shut the door and locked it. What now? Maybe it was time to invest in some pepper spray. Or figure out a way to get out of this hole. I checked my phone for texts from Randy — nothing. I already owed her money that I couldn't possibly pay back.

I sat down on the suitcase and considered my options. Helping Randy with the catering gigs was okay, but I didn't see that getting me out of this predicament in any reasonable amount of time. And even once I got my police report, the bank would doubtless take its sweet time deciding whether it should refund my money. If I was going to get out of this dump and repay Randy — in that order — I'd need a real job. Under normal circumstances I'd have recoiled in horror at the prospect. But nothing re-aligns your priorities like a creepy Russian Don Juannabe breathing down your neck.

I glanced down at the suitcase I was sitting on. My old smartphone's screen was cracked, and its data contract had been an early casualty of the downsizing — but it worked okay in places with free WiFi. And I still had the charger.

I looked around the apartment. Manny Pacquaio stared back from his poster, menacing, ready and willing to punch someone in the face. The day wasn't over yet. I got up and rummaged around in the suitcase until I found the defunct smartphone. Then I grabbed my flip-phone off the windowsill and headed out the door.

Half an hour later, I had two job leads thanks to Craigslist. The first was a medical receptionist at a Physical Therapy clinic in Brighton Beach. It seemed unlikely that I'd get the job, but it was geographically desirable and the hourly pay was decent, so I emailed them my pathetic résumé and hoped for the best.

The second job was less straightforward — a part-time

Personal Assistant for a "busy professional" in Manhattan. The ad was worded vaguely, which made me wonder whether it was a thinly-veiled advertisement for a sex worker, but I responded with an earnest inquiry. Then I stared at the ruined phone's screen a little longer before stuffing it into my bag and heading back to West End Avenue.

4

Should you ever need a reason to crave death's cold embrace, try sleeping on a pile of folded clothes on a bare concrete floor. Every muscle and bone in my body ached terribly by morning.

The water pressure in the shower was sub-par, but I wasn't about to ask Mr. Gold-Tooth Creep to come fix it. So I dried off with my one and only towel, got dressed, and sat down on one of the suitcases.

Money. I needed it desperately, whether I stayed in this dump of an apartment or not. Even if I managed to find a cheaper and less depressing living situation, I'd need to pay rent. And eat, at some point. But the rent was more pressing. I tried not to think about my running negative balances with Randy and the landlady. Those were hanging over my head, circling like vultures.

I grabbed both phones and headed upstairs, towards the light, towards the free WiFi, and found an unprotected signal a couple of blocks away. Okay, not my proudest moment. But the Personal Assistant lady had emailed me back! She wanted to interview me this afternoon.

Back at the apartment, I stripped down to my underwear and flung open the previously-unopened suitcase — the one with marginally-nicer clothes inside — and changed into a charcoal sweater, black skirt, and opaque black tights. Then I added a chunky vintage necklace to dress things up and realized that I didn't have a full-length mirror. Well, nobody wants a personal assistant who looks like the Walking Dead; I dug out my makeup kit and headed for the bathroom.

My sister Charlotte used to joke that I was Jane Bennet — the comelier older sister from *Pride and Prejudice*. Which was bullshit, but being two and a half years older than her I was past the awkward early teen years when she'd started to become hyper-aware of her looks. I'd shed the braces and the acne and the worst of my adolescent insecurity just as she was entering into the thick of that madness.

"You got the big boobs and the better hair," Charlotte had frequently wailed, but I disagreed — on the hair, at least. My straight dark-blonde hair was boring. Charlotte's wild auburn ringlets had been higher maintenance, but they'd also been enchanting. Blessed — or cursed, depending on your viewpoint, with a porcelain complexion, she'd barely tolerated our mother's constant nagging about sunscreen and hats. "You never make *Lane* wear a hat unless we're at the beach!" she'd cry out, and then she'd make a show of stomping back to her room to fetch something with a nice wide brim. And she'd got the big blue eyes. My brown eyes were utterly ordinary, unless my tenth-grade boyfriend, who'd called them "soulful," had been on to something. I doubted it.

Living dangerously, I let my thoughts linger a little longer on my sister. Had she been lying when she'd insisted I was prettier? No, but she'd been wrong. At sixteen, Charlotte was like a young Jessica Chastain who hadn't grown into her looks yet — all pale and luminous, a waiflike beauty. Another few years and she'd have been stunning. If only she'd lived.

Whatever. It doesn't matter. I dug around in my zippered cosmetics bag for concealer. Convincing a rich Upper East Side lady that I was serious about this job over the phone was one thing; making that happen in person was quite another. I needed to look — well, not-desperate. That was a start.

A little over an hour later, I climbed up out of the subway in

19

Manhattan, determined to get myself hired as a Personal Assistant for one Mrs. Cynthia Waldrop. Walking through my prospective employer's neighborhood, I experienced a pang of envy. Not because the houses were gorgeous and close to Central Park — they were — but because the people who dwelled there would never need to count the loose change in the bottom of their handbags as I'd had to do this morning.

I'd largely ignored the real-estate bubble during my period of self-imposed exile, but I was aware that plenty of Manhattan and Brooklyn neighborhoods had torpedoed past wealthy and gone straight to ostentatious. This particular stretch of 74th Street between Park and Madison Avenues seemed to ooze money — some of it old New York family money, if I had to guess, but most of it was newer. Wall Street money, investment bank money, hedge fund money. Rich asshole money. And I needed to lay claim to some of it.

I checked my teeth in a parked car's side-view mirror — they were clean — and climbed the steps to Cynthia Waldrop's front door. Then I smoothed out my sweater, took a deep breath, plastered an enthusiastic smile on my face, and rang the bell.

The blonde woman who answered the door looked like she was in her mid-forties. She was well-dressed, well-preserved, and a little flustered. "Are you Lane?" she asked.

"Yes, I'm Lane Haviland." I offered my hand and she shook it.

"Cynthia Waldrop. Please come in."

I took in the graceful foyer — exquisitely-framed minimalist art on the walls, a Mission-style occasional table with a vase of fresh flowers. Good! Money to burn.

"I'm just feeling very overwhelmed," she fretted as she took my coat. It was a strange way to begin a job interview, especially considering that the front door was still hanging open behind me, filling the foyer with freezing-cold air.

"Should I shut this?" I asked.

Cynthia poked her head out from the closet. "Oh! Yes. Please. Everything's just been so crazy today," she said, rolling her eyes conspiratorially.

"If it's not a great time, I could—" I swallowed. "Come back."

Shit! Why had I offered that up? My empty stomach growled.

"Oh, no no no no no," she insisted, and she waved me farther inside. "This is *important.* I need to delegate." She looked down at her hardwood floor as she said this; she seemed to be talking mostly to herself. Then she looked up with an odd smile. "Sit down and let's talk."

I perched on the edge of a club chair and clasped my hands in my lap. "You have a lovely home," I offered.

"Thanks. It's a *bear* to keep up with." She crossed one leg over the other. I took in her hair (professional blowout), her clothes (expensive, perfectly tailored) and her nails (beautifully manicured). "Hence my need for an assistant."

I nodded, and she stared at me. An awkward moment passed. "What types of duties are you planning to delegate?" I finally asked, just to move the conversation forward.

"Well, we just bought a beach house in East Hampton," she began. "My problem is that I get overwhelmed by all the options and decisions I need to make, and then the decorator gets mad at me and threatens to back-burner everything, and then it's just…" She waved her hands around in the air. "It gets too crazy. It eats into my other priorities."

"I see." So she wanted someone to run interference with her bossy interior decorator. I could do that.

"I'm just trying to do it *all,*" Cynthia said without a hint of irony. "I do a ton of volunteer work. And taking care of my husband, my kids — both houses. And just try having a social life!" She rolled her eyes again and I nodded and smiled with what I hoped looked like sincere empathy.

"How old are your kids?" I asked.

"Thirteen and eleven." She glanced down at her lap. "Magda — our nanny — she's been with us for years. The kids absolutely adore her." She nodded as she said it, head bobbing up and down. "Anyway, I've been told to get professional help" — again, not a speck of self-deprecating humor here — "and that's where you come in, Lane, if it's a good match. I need—" She paused dramatically. "I need to clone myself, basically, but barring that I need someone on my side. Someone smart, who knows my taste.

Someone who's really good with details and can think on their feet. Most of all, I need someone I can trust completely."

"Okay. So if I'm understanding you correctly, it sounds like you want to delegate some of the noisier details to an assistant. So you can shift some of that focus to the things that really matter most to you."

Cynthia nodded slowly.

"And it also seems like you have a very definite — I'll just say leadership style," I went on, "where you don't want to abdicate responsibility on key decisions." Cynthia shook her head emphatically: *no.* "Someone on your team," I parroted, "like you said, who gets your taste, knows what you like. Someone who can make an informed preliminary decision and winnow the choices down to something manageable."

Now Cynthia's face lit up. "Yes, you get it. That's it." She sat up straighter. "It's like you read my mind. Exactly."

So Cynthia Waldrop wanted a lackey for twenty hours a week. Who could blame her? I could serve as her part-time buffer against reality, although in the interests of getting hired I was vastly overstating my direct dealings with it. The rest of the interview was more of the same baloney, and half an hour later I left the Waldrops' townhouse feeling like I'd done well.

Halfway down the block, I called Randy to warn her of the impending reference-check. She didn't seem upset that I was looking for additional work, which was a minor relief. Assuming Randy gave me a good recommendation and the background check came back clean — no reason why it shouldn't, considering that the bad stuff was protected by HIPAA confidentiality rules — I'd be making $15 an hour as Cynthia Waldrop's personal assistant and generating some positive cash flow.

Perhaps the tide had finally turned in my favor.

Then again, maybe not. I called the Department of Housing and learned that all they could offer me was a bed at the homeless Women's Shelter in the Bronx. Any hopes I'd had of escaping Brighton Beach quickly and painlessly were slipping away.

5

At least I still had my catering job. Assembling miniature sandwiches for a bridal shower the following afternoon wasn't exactly thrilling, but it served as a distraction from the money-anxiety that continued to gnaw at my consciousness.

I'd picked up my police report, so at least there was a theoretical hope of getting my money refunded. But I still hadn't heard back from Cynthia. There was nothing to do but cool my jets, hope for a miracle, and earn whatever money I could at Catering by Miranda.

Randy emerged from the walk-in freezer and glanced over my work table with a discerning eye. Did she seem cooler than usual towards me? I hoped my job search wasn't pissing her off.

Finally, she cleared her throat. "You're awfully quiet today, Lane."

"Sorry. I'm a little undercaffeinated." I hadn't had money for coffee earlier, and now I had a headache.

"Well, nice work on the sandwiches." Inspection finished, Randy gave me an approving nod. She was tiny. Five foot one and probably under a hundred pounds, all wiry strength — she'd been doing yoga since before it was cool. She'd once told me offhand that she started every morning at four o'clock so she could get both her meditation and her full complement of poses in.

"Hey," I ventured. "Have you gotten any calls checking references?"

"Not yet." She was busy wrangling a piece of plastic wrap over a tray.

Great. I peeled off my food safety gloves and threw them in the trash. "I fully intend to pay you back the money you loaned me." Jesus. I hadn't planned on saying that, but there it was. The elephant in the room. It wasn't going to sit there and be ignored, even if I was an ingrate and a fraud.

Randy turned to face me. "I know. How's the new place?"

"...Unexpected," I managed.

"That good, huh?" If she only knew. My stomach was doing gymnastics again.

"This Personal Assistant thing," I blurted out. "If I get it — and that's a very big 'if' — it's only twenty hours a week. It doesn't mean I want to quit working here."

Randy shrugged. "All right. Let's see what happens."

I spent another horrid night on the floor of my apartment. Sometime after two in the morning, I made an executive decision to use the nuclear option and try for a cash advance on my one remaining credit card. I'd kept it as a hedge in case I decided to drive a ZipCar off a cliff, *Thelma and Louise*-style, but my circumstances were turning out different than anticipated.

Borrowing money wasn't part of the plan. Getting to zero was. My mind seemed to treasure these hours on the cold hard floor, never hesitating to remind me of my failures. But I already owed money to Randy, and that's how I finally justified it to myself. I'd rather die in debt to a faceless corporation than disappoint the one person who might actually show up at my funeral.

When morning finally came, I ignored my rumbling stomach and headed up the stairs. It didn't take long to find a WiFi signal. I'd continued to scour the want-ads and Craigslist for employment opportunities. But there was no news to report. My job inquiries were like the rest of my life — going nowhere.

Ten minutes later I stared unblinking at the screen of the Chase Bank ATM:

TRANSACTION DENIED. CONTACT YOUR INSTITUTION.

A cold calm settled over me. I pushed through the glass doors and inside the bank proper, joined the line, and awaited my fate. I already knew what they'd tell me, though. Because it was the truth. Of course they'd yanked my card. Of course I was a bad credit risk. I wasn't even sure I wanted to continue living.

I left the bank and walked aimlessly for a while, ending up on the frigid, windy boardwalk. I was racking my brain for ideas, but they didn't come. I was well and truly hosed. Insolvent.

Observing the sparse crowd on the boardwalk wasn't helping. Watching people go about their daily business was giving me the impression — probably inaccurate — that everyone but me had their shit together. As if every person holding a Starbucks cup or staring down at a smartphone was, by definition, a responsible and successful adult. Not like me.

I was so tired of worrying about money.

I sat on a bench and gazed out at the water. I thought about scissors. And femoral arteries. Acting on impulse. Balconies. *You don't need one, you know. You could just jump off a bridge.* The bank needed sixty days minimum to make a decision on my check refund. If I could screw my courage to the sticking place, maybe I wouldn't last that long.

I turned my attention to an outdoor café. Of course the chairs and tables were stacked up, empty — it was way too cold to eat outside — but it was safe to assume that they were serving food indoors. How lovely it would feel to sit down and place an order! My traitorous stomach rumbled anew: whatever I'd last eaten wasn't holding me.

I had nothing. My life was shit.

I heaved myself up off the bench. Time to face the music — or rather, face the fact that the music had stopped. Only I was the moron still standing.

* * * *

Brighton Realty Management was just as depressing the second time around. Mrs. Pasternak was there, seated inside her permanent cloud of cigarette smoke. "I'm here to discuss my rent," I began, once pleasantries had been offered and not reciprocated.

"Hm."

She continued to regard me curiously, so I plowed on: "I don't have it. I'm so sorry about this. When I first came in here I thought I'd be able to scrape something together—"

"Hah." She took another long drag and twisted her features into something that resembled a smile as she exhaled. I shut my mouth. Had I said something riotously funny? Smiling Mrs. Pasternak was unsettling. But soon enough she was back to business. "No worries about rent this month, honey." She stubbed out her cigarette. "Already paid."

"What?" I was thoroughly confused.

She finished stubbing, and without pause reached for a mostly-full pack of Benson & Hedges. "Already paid," she repeated loudly, as though this were an illuminating new fact she was adding to our discussion.

"Who paid it?" I blurted out, then instantly regretted it. Who's to say that this wasn't a fortunate accounting blip? I was looking the proverbial gift-horse in the mouth. Stupid!

Mrs. Pasternak took a long drag on her fresh cigarette, exhaled slowly, and chortled. "Really, *blyats,* you do not need to pretend innocent for me. Viktor stopped by this morning and paid. In full." She gave me a pointed look.

"Viktor?" She nodded exactly once. "I — I don't..." For the second time this morning, my stomach lurched around uncomfortably. I couldn't form a sentence. Mrs. Pasternak took another puff and watched me flounder.

I took a deep breath to steady myself. "Who is Viktor?" I managed. *Please, God, not the guy with the gold tooth.*

She shrugged. "Handyman. Is tall skinny man with big nose. I sent him over two days ago."

I couldn't hide my astonishment. "Why would he...?"

She made a funny kind of half-snort. "You are crazy girl, I

26

think," she said, tapping her cigarette into the full ashtray. "Here is your lease. Is month-to-month. Read it and sign."

And with that, I sensed, our conversation was over.

Panic. That's what was churning through my head as I walked back towards my apartment. If this Viktor guy had paid my rent, he'd no doubt expect payment in return — something I was not prepared to give. But what were my alternatives?

Somehow I got through the lobby and down the stairs, only to narrowly avoid colliding with a piece of furniture sitting in front of my apartment door.

I stared at it: a futon. Well, at least I had someplace comfortable to sit as I contemplated this final twist in my horrifying downward spiral. I dragged the futon inside my apartment, then shut the door and turned the flimsy lock. *He probably has the key*, I realized, and I shoved the futon forward until it blocked the door. Then I sat down, head in my hands, and considered my options.

There were no two ways about it — I'd have to leave. That much was clear. But where could I go? *Think.*

I could leave the city, seek my lack-of-fortune elsewhere. Sure, I felt like I had unfinished business here, but I didn't want to conduct it from the Women's Shelter. Asking Randy wasn't an option; she shared her alcove studio with her mother, whose health was in decline — senile dementia? Alzheimer's? Dammit, I hadn't asked her about her mom lately; I was a terrible person.

I was so absorbed in my own misery that I barely heard the knock at the door. A soft three taps. Then three more, slightly louder. My heart leaped up to the back of my throat and froze there. *What if it was Viktor?* Jesus, that didn't take long. I instinctively looked around the room for a means of escape, but of course there was none.

Two more dull thuds on the door echoed through the apartment. "Hey," came a deep, muffled voice. I sat deathly still. "Are you there?"

He had a Russian accent.

"Go away," I called out, more tremulously than I would have

liked. Silence. My heart pounded in my chest. My breathing was too fast, too short. My eyes darted to the window-well. Could I text 911?

"Miss." It was the voice from the hallway again, quiet but firm. "Please, I will not hurt you."

"Why should I believe you?" I called out. My voice wasn't quavering; that was good, wasn't it?

Silence from the other side. Seconds ticked by. "I promise I will not touch you," he finally said, sounding vaguely annoyed. "Please," he repeated. "Open up."

Well, if this was it then I'd just have to go down fighting. I pulled the futon out of the way, gathered up my courage, and opened the door.

There stood Viktor. "Hello." Damn, his voice was deep.

"What do you want?" My nerves were fried to a crisp, and I judged him absurdly calm considering the circumstances.

"I came to check you are okay."

I most certainly was not. His eyes darted past me and into the apartment's interior. He was taller than I remembered: he'd have had to duck to get through the doorway, not that I was about to invite him inside.

"Did you pay my rent?" I asked him.

"Yes," he replied, and his eyes met mine. They were a steely blue-gray.

"What about the futon?" I gestured towards it. "Did you bring that over here too?"

He gave a short nod. "Tenant moved out. She left it."

I looked around. Nothing to see here; same grim cinderblock-lined hallway with the broken fluorescent lights overhead. My heartbeat, at least, had slowed to a rate more compatible with life. I still half-expected Viktor to get fresh and try to wheedle his way inside, but he just stood there, arms crossed over his midsection, looking uncomfortable. Which was a relief, in a way. I'd been so twitchy the past few days that I'd started to feel like an alien life form. Here was a horribly awkward kindred spirit at last.

"Well, thank you," I mumbled, crossing my own arms in front of me. "Thanks a lot. That was very — very kind of you. I appreciate it."

He nodded. "I must go," he mumbled.

"I intend to pay you back," I blurted out. "The rent, I mean."

"Yes. When you can."

The panicky feeling returned. "Look, I don't know what you expect—"

"I expect nothing," he interjected sharply.

Don't antagonize him! my better judgment warned, but I felt more clarity was needed. "Your friend with the gold tooth—"

"Sergey?" His expression had turned darker. Impatient.

"He... he seemed to want to, like, date me or something." Assault, date, whatever.

A trace of a smile played across his thin lips. "You want to date Sergey?"

"No. I mean, I'm sure he..." Why was I suddenly searching for Sergey's redeeming qualities? "I'm not interested."

He tilted his head in acknowledgment, but didn't say anything further. I couldn't figure out this guy's angle. At least he didn't seem to actively want to snap me in half, now that we'd cleared up that whole Sergey business. And his nose wasn't *that* big.

"Okay." I felt my shoulders relax a bit. "Thanks again, Viktor."

I locked the door behind him. Then I plopped down on the futon, stared up at the drop-ceiling, and let my mind wander. Predictably, it made a beeline for skeptical territory: why would a handyman loan a total stranger a thousand bucks? It was a legitimate question, but lying there listening to the radiator knock and hiss wasn't giving me any insights into Viktor's motivations. For now he was a puzzlement. But being in a decent bed for the first time in days felt glorious, and before long I fell asleep.

6

I awakened to a text from Cynthia Waldrop:

You're hired! Start Monday chez moi 9am?

Sounds great, I texted back, grateful that my monthly MetroCard was still in business for another week and a half. Later, I found a ten dollar bill in the pocket of a pair of jeans, so I could eat — provided I wasn't stressing over my mounting debt. Mrs. Pasternak hadn't mentioned a security deposit for the apartment, but I was certain she'd want one sooner or later.

My Personal Assistant career began with a thud Monday morning. Cynthia was in an agitated state, fretting that she simply did not *have time* to brief me on the ins and outs of whatever crisis she was currently in the middle of. Instead, she directed me upstairs to her office on the second floor, to organize files on her laptop computer. Which was near-impossible to do without any sort of context. At least it was a soothing place to sit, with soft chartreuse-painted walls and assorted tasteful tchotchkes that looked like they'd been purchased as a set from Anthropologie.

That was Day One. On Day Two, she took me shopping at Bloomingdale's. "So you can get an idea of my taste," she explained. I didn't mind getting paid to tag along shopping.

Things got testy when Cynthia disappeared into a changing room and asked me to go get her a pair of slacks in the next larger size. She ended up not buying them, but her mood changed — she was no longer happy-go-lucky Cynthia. Now she was moody, chip-on-her-shoulder Cynthia. I gave her a little more space and breathed a silent sigh of relief when we moved on to the shoe department. But she'd gone quiet. Too quiet.

"I am not a size fourteen," Cynthia muttered to me in Accessories.

"These designers and their sizes," I commiserated. "They're never consistent from one brand to the next."

"But I. Am not. A size. Fourteen." She said it through clenched teeth. And she wasn't being funny.

"You're not," I immediately agreed. What had I done wrong? *Stay employed!*

Cynthia glared at me, then exhaled loudly through her nose and continued looking at scarves. She didn't mention the slacks or her pants-size again. And neither did I.

By Day Three, Cynthia's mood had improved to an almost disturbing degree. She couldn't stop giggling over some video of a hamster on YouTube. "Do you see?" she shrieked as she thrust her iPad under my nose. "It's eating a tiny cheeseburger!" Mercifully, her jubilation lasted long enough for her to dispatch me to the interior decorator's office to discuss plans for the beach house. "Just take pictures of anything that looks good," she instructed.

I was almost afraid to tell her I didn't have a smartphone, but I was even more afraid to withhold this information. So I took a deep breath, dug out my flip-phone, and told her the truth.

Cynthia looked puzzled. "How can you not have a smartphone?"

"I don't know," I confessed. "I used to have one, but it broke. I guess I didn't use the smartphone features enough to miss them." That last part wasn't true, but I didn't want Cynthia to know how penniless and desperate I was.

She flared her nostrils. "Well, you'll need one if you're going to be my assistant." I must have looked lost, because she added,

"I'll look into it," then shooed me out the door. "Just have Dante take pictures and email them to me," she trilled, already looking down at something on her iPad screen.

Dante. Pictures. All righty then.

The man who greeted me at the interior decorator's office was about my height, with fabulous salt-and-pepper wavy hair. He was wearing a designer t-shirt and jeans that probably cost six hundred dollars. He was also barefoot.

I cleared my throat. "I'm Lane Haviland. Cynthia's new assistant." He looked at me over the top of his wire-rimmed glasses. "Are you Dante?"

"That's me," he sighed, and he indicated a folder marked WALDROP GREAT-ROOM on a large table. "I've got the revised sketches."

I moved closer so I could examine the sketches. "They're gorgeous," I whispered. A high-ceilinged great-room with vast windows was illustrated beautifully, with swatches of fabric clipped to the sides of the board. I wanted to step into the picture and have someone bring me a gin and tonic. "Cynthia's gonna love this."

"You think?" Okay, Dante was pissed off.

"I do." I took a step back and looked at him. "Is something wrong?"

"No. No, nothing's wrong." He flipped the folder shut. "Do you have sign-off authority on these?"

"I'm not sure what you mean."

"Do you, Lake, have Mrs. Waldrop's blessing to tell us to go ahead with this?"

"It's Lane," I corrected him. "And Mrs. Waldrop told me to take pictures of what you showed me today. Except my phone is broken, so I was hoping you could—"

"Yeah. That. That's what's wrong." Dante leaned on the edge of the conference table and glared at me.

"Did I do something to offend you?" I was genuinely confused.

"You? No. But you're the third Personal Assistant Mrs. Waldrop's sent us in the past six weeks. We've redone this room — I don't know, five times? She has a vision that's difficult to articulate."

My mouth had gone dry. "I see."

"Sorry I didn't get your name right," he mumbled. "If you last more than a week and a half, I'll learn it."

I ignored his sass and reopened the folder. "What's been her issue with the concepts so far?"

"Beats the hell out of me. She keeps saying it's not quite right and we should keep trying." He used air-quotes on *keep trying*.

"Okay, forget about taking pictures," I told him. "I'm going to bring these sketches back to Mrs. Waldrop. I'll get you a yes-or-no answer by Friday." My mind raced. "No, Monday. Monday at the latest."

Dante stared at me. "Seriously?"

"Seriously."

He sniffed. "It's your funeral."

It was cause for celebration when I realized I was on track to make it through the week without getting fired from either one of my part-time jobs. Randy seemed happy enough to see me Thursday afternoon, and I was doing my part to keep Cynthia on an even keel. Viktor hadn't come knocking on my door demanding an immediate loan repayment. I wasn't sure what I was even expecting from him — neighborly visits? But he didn't make an appearance, and neither, thankfully, did Sergey.

By the time Day Five with Cynthia rolled around, I was cautiously optimistic about the type of hand-holding she was going to require. Not that I was thrilled about providing it — getting her to commit one way or another to various elements of her great-room's design plan was like trying to nail Jell-O to the wall. But just because she was annoying and difficult didn't make her impossible. And after listening to her tell the story of every piece of antique furniture she'd ever owned, I realized that she just wanted someone to talk to.

So we talked. About feature walls and functional zones. Traffic flow — *very* important, according to Cynthia and some home design blog she followed. The pros and cons of wainscoting, even though it wasn't in the plans. Pendant-lights versus a chandelier over the dining table. Window treatments could *not* be "too foofy." She was deeply conflicted about wall sconces.

Our discussions went off the rails a few times — Cynthia was inclined to disappear down Internet discussion-board rabbit holes frequented by others like her. That's when I started setting a timer to alert us when we'd been on a single topic for more than ten minutes. I also scheduled a ten-minute break for every hour she spent on decision-making, and I used this time to draw up a road-map of whatever we'd be looking at next. Somehow I was helping Cynthia pull her life together despite having thoroughly fucked up my own, and by Friday afternoon Cynthia was in a good place with everything except a console table and two fabric swatches.

"I can't believe we got through all that." She actually seemed a little dejected.

Quick! Distract her. "This calls for a celebration," I announced, and I tidied up the desk. "Can I fix you a cup of tea?"

"Sure. I have something for you. I'll be down in a sec." Cynthia puttered around her office while I padded downstairs to the kitchen. There I found Magda, whom I'd seen only in passing, and two sandy-blond-haired kids in school uniforms sitting at the breakfast-bar. Magda was busy setting out an after-school snack of yogurt and sunflower seeds.

"Hi, I'm Lane. You must be Magda."

Magda gave me a broad grin. "It's a pleasure to meet you." She was plump and matronly, with a Spanish accent and a warm countenance. Her mostly-gray hair was pulled into a tight bun. "And may I introduce Miss Emily and Mr. Mason?"

I turned to the kids, who looked me over none too enthusiastically. "Hi there," I said, and they mumbled greetings in return as I reached for the tea kettle.

"Did you and Mrs. Cynthia get all your work done?" Magda asked, and I immediately felt panic creep in. *Why — what do you know?* I wanted to ask. But then Magda caught my eye and I realized she was just making conversation.

"I think so." I took a cup down from the cupboard and opened up a hinged wooden box. Cynthia's tea stash was nothing short of exquisite — all luxury brands, beautifully packaged. I'd savored a cup earlier, along with a couple of lemon cookies.

"Lane!" Cynthia arrived in the kitchen and gave each kid a perfunctory air-kiss. "You've met everyone? Good. I have a credit card for you."

"Pardon me?" The kids had finished eating and were starting to drift upstairs. I'd been staring at the leftover sunflower seeds.

"A credit card. It's on my account but it has your name on it." Cynthia plunked a MasterCard down on the counter. "So you can pay for work-related things."

The shiny new credit card said *Lane Haviland*. What a beautiful thing. Beautiful and potentially disastrous. I looked questioningly at Magda.

"I have one too," she said. "Always taking the kids here, there — taxis, food. Who needs to walk around with a lot of cash?" She swiped the bowl of sunflower seeds off the counter and offered it to me. I took a handful.

"Of course. You're right." I popped a few sunflower seeds in my mouth. *Do not abuse this privilege,* I cautioned myself.

"Oh, and before I forget," Cynthia said. She handed one white envelope to Magda and another to me. "Friday is payday."

Payday meant I could finally get my hands on the fried chicken dinner I'd been craving from The Palace, a takeout joint under the elevated tracks on Brighton Beach Avenue. I ate all I could, stashed the leftovers in the fridge, and flopped onto the futon. And I brooded.

That's your problem. You can't let yourself be happy. Well, what was there, really, to be happy about? I'd temporarily staved off homelessness. I was not currently starving or sleeping on the floor. I still owed money all over the place, and I was bound to disappoint Randy and Viktor. Even if I could manage to pay them both back, it would take months if not years. And that was assuming I could successfully juggle two part-time jobs.

Stop. Just stop thinking. I got up and killed the light, and the room slid into darkness apart from a fluorescent-lit sliver under the front door. I felt my way back to the futon, lay down on my side, and squeezed my eyes shut.

A credit card. With my name on it.

Don't fuck it up. She trusts you.

Why would anyone trust me? I don't even trust myself.

The radiator hissed and knocked. Someone on an upper floor threw a bag of trash noisily down the chute. None of it did anything to quiet the mental hailstorm raining down — past events, accumulated failures. No shortage of those. They piled up and melted, flooding my thoughts. My mind was determined to do cannonballs into that roaring river.

Attempted suicide.

Not really. I only wanted to quiet the noises in my head.

With scissors, though? In your leg, buried to the hilt?

I shuddered at the memory. Blood everywhere, and people shouting in my face. The overwhelming feeling that I'd messed up.

Messed up how, exactly — by not having better aim?

No. It was a spur-of-the-moment thing. A regrettable decision.

Hindsight. Femoral artery or get the fuck out.

I got up and wrapped myself tightly in my winter coat. Then I lay back down and did my best to think about nothing at all. A void.

Nothing's ever gonna change, though. You know it won't.

Maybe not.

You can't raise the dead.

This is normally when the tears would have started, but I wasn't going there tonight. Yes, I was a failure. Yes, everything was fucked up. But I just couldn't spare the energy to throw myself against that particular brick wall. Not tonight.

Maybe tomorrow.

Eventually I drifted off to sleep.

* * * *

Saturday morning I schlepped to Flatbush and bought a comforter and a pillow on clearance at Target. I came back to Brighton Beach and found Viktor at my front door installing a deadbolt lock. Absorbed in his project, he seemed unaware that I was standing ten feet away.

"Hi," I ventured, and he practically jumped out of his skin. "Sorry, I didn't mean to startle you."

"It's okay." Viktor looked… well, he looked ashen. Even by abysmally low winter-in-New-York-City standards, the guy was pale.

"Did Mrs. Pasternak send you?" I asked him. "To install the lock?"

He shook his head. "No. I had some time today." He dug around in the front pocket of his work coveralls, took out a key, and handed it over to me with a conspiratorial glance. "I have the other one. Not Sergey."

I accepted the key; my head was buzzing with questions. "Thanks." Why was he being so nice?

"It's no problem." He used one foot to flip the lid of the toolbox closed. His jet-black hair was messy, sticking out in all directions. Had it been a long night for Viktor? He noticed me looking at him and a ghost of a smile passed over his face. Darkly handsome, I decided. And probably not a serial killer.

"Do you want something to drink?" I asked. "I mean, sorry… all I have is water."

"Sure." He stepped aside so I could pass. Then he followed me in, ducking his head smoothly under the too-low door frame. He tried the deadbolt while I wriggled out of my coat and tossed it on top of the Target shopping bag, silently berating myself for my failure at every single one of the domestic arts. Broke or not, it wouldn't have been unreasonable to procure a single wire coat-hanger somewhere in my travels.

Viktor lingered by the door, long arms crossed over his chest, and glanced around the room. It hadn't changed materially since his last visit. I opened the midget-sized cupboard, took a clean disposable coffee-cup from my stash, and filled it with cold water from the tap.

"You're going to have to stop going on and on like this, Viktor," I warned as I handed him the cup. "You talk too much. I can hardly get a word in edgewise."

He took a drink. There was an uncomfortable silence and I realized my lame attempt at humor had missed its mark entirely. He cleared his throat. "My English, it's not good," he mumbled.

I tried to think of something encouraging to say. "It's way better than my decorating." I pointed out the Manny Pacquaio poster as evidence.

He looked at the poster for a too-long moment. Tumbleweeds.

"Hey, Viktor, would you like me to help you with your English?" From the look on his face, you'd think I'd just spontaneously birthed triplets. "I mean, if you want. You're being really nice to me and I swear I'm going to pay you back. But in the meantime I'd like to thank you. For helping me out." Shit, I was babbling. This was coming out all wrong.

"Okay."

Now it was my turn to be surprised. "Yeah?"

"Yeah, sure."

So vocabulary would be Priority One. I took a deep breath. "Great."

"I must go," he murmured, pulling out his phone.

"Well, text me when you want to start," I told him. "Here." I scribbled my number on a scrap of paper and handed it over.

He looked down at the paper. "Thank you." Then, once again: "I must go."

"Bye, Viktor."

7

Sunday I slept in, only to be roused by the *ping* of my phone in the window-well. I wondered if Viktor was ready to start his English lessons, but it was a text from Cynthia.

Call me ASAP plz!

Panic curdled in the pit of my stomach: Was I being fired already? I pulled on some yoga pants and a hoodie and jogged upstairs to call Cynthia, who picked up on the first ring.

"Oh, thank God," she breathed. "I don't know what I'm going to do. Magda might quit."

Relief! "Oh, gosh." I ground my sneaker against a smashed cigarette-butt on the lobby's grimy linoleum floor. "Is everything okay?"

"No." I heard Cynthia blow her nose. "Magda has some family... *issues*... at home. In the Dominican Republic. Someone's sick."

"That's terrible," I replied, trying for an appropriate level of gravitas in my voice.

"I need you here, Lane." Cynthia sniffed. "I need support right now while I figure this out. Can you come?"

"I'm on my way."

I'd thought Cynthia was acting histrionic over the phone, but with a live audience in front of her she was well-nigh inconsolable. "This is such a bad time for this to happen!" she wailed as she accepted the cup of Gyokuro Imperial Green Tea I'd prepared for her.

"You do have a lot on your plate right now," I agreed. Putting aside the fact that most of it was total bullshit, Cynthia's calendar *was* pretty full. I clasped my hands in my lap and waited for her to collect her thoughts.

"I mean, I know most of this isn't, like, life or death," Cynthia muttered, swiping over-aggressively through her calendar on the iPad balanced in her lap. "But just when I was starting to get organized! Making the puzzle pieces fit together. Thanks to you," she added, smiling weakly in my direction.

"Tell me how I can help," I offered. "Should I call the staffing agency first thing tomorrow morning? I'm sure they can set up interviews for a replacement. Interim replacement, I mean," I added out of loyalty to Magda.

Cynthia stared into space and chewed on her cuticle. "I guess so. Sure. But…" She trailed off mid-sentence.

I peered back, this time with genuine interest. Of course this was all about her; Cynthia Waldrop wasn't the type of person to give a shit about her kids' nanny's sick *abuela* or whatever tragedy was currently unfolding in the Dominican Republic. If her Google Calendar was any indication, she preferred charitable causes that involved gala masquerade balls. "I just wasn't thrilled with the staffing agency in our last go-round," she finally mumbled. "It's tedious. Meeting people, *talking* to them." Agreed. "And Magda thinks she's coming back. She just doesn't know exactly when."

"I see." I wondered whether this mini-therapy session would be considered billable hours. My stomach was starting to anticipate its next meal, maybe a toasted bagel with butter from the Korean deli down on Lexington Avenue. Coffee, swirled with sugar and extra cream.

"Actually," Cynthia said, snapping me out of my melted-butter carbo-fantasy, "I just had the best idea!" She flashed me a dazzling-white smile. "Lane, it's perfect. I don't know why I

didn't think of it before. You should do it. You should help with
the kids while Magda's away!"

Well, this was unexpected. And worrisome. What kind of
person hands their kids over to the care of a stranger who happens
to be a quasi-suicidal fuck-up? I had no concept of how to take
responsibility for myself, much less two children. But I had to take
Cynthia up on her offer. The hourly rate would be slightly less,
but there would be a lot more hours — and with an anticipated
six hundred bucks a week cash I could finally start getting out of
the hole I'd dug myself into.

Predictably, telling Randy was the hardest part. I dialed her
number and closed my eyes while the phone rang on the other
side of the ether, hoping to get sent to voicemail. No such luck.

"What's up, Lane?" Randy sounded tired. I felt like such a jerk.

"Cynthia wants me to go full-time," I blurted out. "I—
I'm sorry."

"Don't be sorry." An awkward moment of silence. "Good for
you, Lane. I had a feeling you were moving up in the world."

"Will you be okay, though? Without me?" At least I could feel
some of the tension in my shoulders releasing.

"I'll muddle through somehow," Randy reassured me. "Don't
be a stranger."

The following morning I began my career as a professional
nanny-slash-personal-assistant. And I couldn't quite believe my
luck, because Cynthia's kids were far easier to cope with than
Cynthia herself. Sure they were spoiled rotten, but frankly I'd
have been shocked if that weren't the case.

Both kids had come fully equipped with iPhones, and at the
moment they were pecking away at their screens in the back seat
of a taxi bound for swim lessons on the Upper West Side. We
inched along through crosstown traffic.

"Got any homework today?" I addressed Mason; Emily
was absorbed in some all-encompassing eighth-grade-girl

texting drama.

"I have homework every day," Mason replied. He gave me the most morose look I'd ever seen.

"If you need help, let me know," I offered. He rolled his eyes, shook his head and went back to his phone.

More good news: I'd been given an iPhone to use for work. It was a three-year-old model, probably excavated from Cynthia's kitchen junk drawer. "I just can't have you using that flip-phone," she'd informed me crisply while coiling her hair into a bun for Hot Yoga. "Now you can access my calendar, my contacts, e-mail, everything — wherever you go!"

Lucky me! At the moment, Cynthia was at home, prepping to attend a formal dinner party at the home of her husband's boss.

"You have my mom's old phone." Mason again.

"Yeah, wasn't that nice of her?" I put the phone down and made eye contact, setting a good example. "Sure beats my old flip-phone."

"Why's it so old? Can't you buy a new one?" He seemed genuinely curious.

Emily punched him in the arm without looking up from her phone. "Shut *up,*" she whispered.

"No, it's okay, he asked an honest question. No hitting," I added as an afterthought; Emily rolled her eyes. "I had a smartphone, but it broke. I switched to the flip-phone because it was cheaper."

Mason cocked his head in contemplation; *cheap* was an abstract concept for him. "Are you poor?"

Emily nudged him in the ribs.

"Poor? I don't know," I stalled. "I mean, I guess it depends who you compare me to. Poor is sort of a relative term." In truth, I was battling near-constant anxiety over my still-unpaid security deposit that Mrs. Pasternak would probably demand any day now. And I hadn't started paying Randy or Viktor back. Not yet.

We arrived at the West Side Aquatic Club before Mason could form a response to my bullshit answer, and he and Emily got out of the cab while I swiped Cynthia's card to pay the driver. They waited patiently for me on the sidewalk and I silently offered up thanks for the stage of life they were currently in. Imagine toddlers running into the street, or babies in diapers! That would have been a total disaster, and I congratulated myself on averting it. Then I got out of the cab just in time to hear Emily say to her brother: "Of *course* she's poor, stupid."

Well, Emily was right. But I was working as hard as I could to dig myself out. I spent the week shuttling the kids between school and activities, dealing with Cynthia's inevitable crisis-du-jour, and getting myself situated in Brooklyn.

That last one was harder than anticipated. I was starting to suspect that my apartment was too crappy to require a security deposit — I still hadn't heard anything from Mrs. Pasternak on that front. Still, I was doing my best to turn it into a more habitable space. I'd cleaned it top to bottom, for one. And even though I was setting aside most of my money for necessities — next month's rent, a weekly MetroCard, debt payments, and the minimum food required to survive — I'd picked up some basic kitchen items from the Dollar Store and a couple of lamps from Goodwill. I'd also salvaged a prize from a sidewalk trash heap — a large industrial wooden spool that had once held cable or wire. It was now a slightly wobbly coffee table.

My diet was entirely ramen noodle-based. The Manny Pacquaio poster was gone. The radiator still clanged and hissed, especially when I was trying to fall asleep. But I was usually so tired by the end of the day that the noise faded into the background.

It was good enough, this apartment. Not perfect. I missed the sun. But every time I came inside and locked the deadbolt, I felt safe — and for now, that was everything.

My days with the Waldrops started blending together at the seams. Each morning I arrived in Manhattan impossibly early and schlepped the kids to school, then returned to Chez Waldrop to devote my full attention to whatever Cynthia happened to be obsessing over. I saw Mr. Waldrop in passing a few times, but he seemed to leave for work early and come home late.

Viktor hadn't texted me yet about the English lessons, and I kind of wished he would. Saving up the first payment on my debt was hard enough without feeling like a total deadbeat in every aspect of my life. Such was my thought process as I examined my ragged thumbnail against Cynthia's honed-granite countertop.

"Cappuccino?" Cynthia was enthralled, at the moment, with her expensive new espresso machine.

"I would love a cappuccino right now," I replied. Cynthia fiddled around with a nozzle and I decided to push my luck. "Is now a good time to talk window treatments?"

"Ugh! You had to bring *that* up!" She frowned and set the cup down under the nozzle just as it began to sputter. "I mean, she measured the windows two months ago, right? Now she has to re-measure them! Who does that? Honestly!"

"I know, it's so frustrating. Thanks," I added, accepting the cup. Part of me couldn't believe I was actually having this conversation. The cappuccino helped, though. I won't lie.

"Let's talk about the kids," Cynthia said. She took a sip of her double espresso.

"They're great." I felt like I was about to be unmasked as a huge fraud.

"You like spending time with them?" she prodded.

"Yes. I mean, they're so mature." Cynthia beamed, so I continued down that track. "They're really creative." I assumed that Cynthia was one of those mothers who just wanted to hear about how wonderful her kids were, all the live-long day.

"I worry about them," she confessed. "It's a hard place to grow up, the city."

I murmured my agreement, thinking about the homeless guy we'd walked by the previous day en route to a Dunkin' Donuts on Lexington Avenue.

"Everything is so competitive at school, with their friends," she continued. "It's hard to keep a sense of perspective. You know?"

"They seem pretty grounded," I said carefully. "They're not

the least bit spoiled," I added. *Liar.*

"I'm so glad you think so." Cynthia shot me an I-have-a-secret look. "Do you know that Emily's best friend — her whole family! — they just flew down to the Caymans on a private jet."

I felt my eyes go wide with disbelief.

"Yes! For Christmas," Cynthia whispered. I'd never seen her so thrilled. "The mom was live-Instagramming the whole thing. It's absurd." She sat back and awaited my reaction.

"Instagrammed it. Huh." I wrinkled my nose at Cynthia, who nodded her agreement: *Tacky.* Then she drained her espresso and segued into window treatments. Just like that. Absurd.

I was buying ramen noodles in a mini-mart on West End Avenue that evening when my flip-phone chimed. Nobody besides Randy and Cynthia had texted me in weeks. It was just a number — no name attached — so it wasn't from anyone in my contacts. I peeked anyway.

sorry so busy.still need help with english.viktor

The way he'd signed his text-message made me smile; I couldn't help it. I paid for a few packs of shrimp-flavored noodles. Then I walked outside and texted him back:

Happy to help. Name a date and time.

As I turned towards home, the phone chimed again.

Now ?

It was just a text — a one-word text — but for some reason I felt sweaty inside my coat.

Well, why not? My social calendar wasn't exactly bursting at the seams.

Sure. I'm on my way home.

Texting on that flip-phone really did take forever. By the time I closed the phone and started home again, a light snow had begun to fall, and even Brighton Beach looked kind of pretty.

8

Viktor arrived at my apartment not long after I did, bundled up in a leather jacket. A few snowflakes were melting in his hair, which was damp and pushed back from his face. *You'll catch your death of cold,* I thought automatically. My mother's daughter.

"For you." He handed me a six-pack of Budweiser.

"Thanks." I took out two beers and stashed the rest in the empty fridge while he took his coat off. Underneath he was wearing a dark gray sweater and black jeans. Silently I approved of his color palette.

"So what do you want to learn first?" I asked as I filled a pot with water and set it on the burner.

He looked surprised. "I have choice?"

"Yes, you have a choice." I held up two ramen noodle packages. "Like for dinner. Shrimp, or shrimp?"

He smiled, barely. His cheeks were still pink from the cold and for some reason that put me at ease.

"Seriously, you want some ramen noodles? I've got plenty." He nodded, so I grabbed two bowls out of the cupboard and displayed them with a flourish.

"You went shopping," Viktor said. "Good."

"Yeah, I even have lamps now. And spoons." I held up two.

"Okay." A real smile this time. He was the most relaxed I'd

ever seen him.

"I'll cook," I declared. "Let's talk about English."

Viktor walked over to the wall next to the futon and lowered himself to the floor. He stretched his long legs out in front of him.

"You can sit on the futon," I called, absorbed in unwrapping the noodles. When I didn't hear a response, I glanced over my shoulder. He was still sitting on the floor, leaning back against the wall, eyes closed. Weird. I hummed to myself and emptied the seasoning packets into each bowl.

A few minutes later, both bowls were billowing fragrant MSG-laced steam. I carried one of them over to Viktor. He'd opened his eyes, but otherwise hadn't moved. That Viktor, always the life of the party. "So. What do you want to learn?" I handed him the noodles, along with utensils and a wad of napkins I'd swiped from the mini-mart. Then, since he didn't seem likely to move from his spot on the floor, I rolled the wooden spool over, retrieved my food, and settled myself on the floor opposite him.

Viktor set everything down on the table slowly, carefully. Then he leaned back and stared up at the ceiling. His Adam's apple was very pronounced. "I must think," he murmured. I waited patiently. "All right." He directed his imperturbable gaze at me. "Would, could, should. Please explain."

"Would, could, should?" I repeated dumbly.

"Yes. I am often confused." He cracked open his beer.

"Would, could, should," I chanted to myself. I opened my beer. "Cheers," I offered, holding up the can.

He looked uneasy, but touched his can to mine and took a drink.

"Don't you drink toasts in Russia?" I asked. I was buying time. This would-could-should business was dreadful.

"With vodka." His voice was very deep.

"Just vodka? Nothing else?"

"Cognac, maybe. Not beer. Maybe that is American custom." He took a swallow.

"Okay, so in Russia you *could* drink a toast with a beer…" I ventured. "But…*would* you do it? No." I smiled triumphantly. "*Could* means you're able — you can. But *would* means you

47

actually will. Sort of. If conditions are met." The more I explained it, the less sense it made — to me, at least.

He set his beer down on the floor beside him. "Maybe it's good for me to learn more American customs."

"Well, are you planning on staying?" Good Lord, I was flirting with this man.

"Staying where?" Holy Mother of God, he was flirting back. I felt my face flush. Maybe the lighting was sufficiently bad that he wouldn't be able to tell.

I felt his eyes on me, so I picked up my fork. "Does that help? I mean, with would and could?" *Please don't ask me about* should. *I can't handle the pressure.*

"Yes." He picked up his fork too, and I summoned the courage to look him in the eye again. He looked the same — no, he looked different, but not creepy-different. There was a little mischief in his face. I hadn't seen it before.

He broke the silence first. "Let's eat."

Later, while washing dishes and tidying up, I allowed myself the luxury of a little futurecasting. For once I felt positive about a guy I'd met, and that hadn't happened in a very long time. I wasn't at all sure I was going to be any good at teaching English to this guy. But I had to admit it: I sort of liked him.

Viktor had been circumspect about his background, saying only that he'd recently arrived in the country and he knew "a little" English. Most of the time, he seemed to understand me just fine, except when I caught myself using the type of idiomatic speech favored by kids — principally those blasted Waldrop children.

Did he want to learn more technical terms for his job, I'd asked? *Sure.* Was his job basically handyman-type stuff? *Um-hmm.* Whenever I tried to dig deeper, Viktor clammed up.

So I'd downshifted into less-personal territory. We'd practiced some conversational English, going from "Hello, how are you?" to "I'm fine, thank you, and yourself?" Then we'd gone through some typical responses: Fine, Good, Great. "Can't complain" probably carried more subtextual baggage than the others, I told him, although when Viktor asked why, I couldn't explain it.

"A lot of it is tone. The way you say something. Like sarcasm. Is there sarcasm in Russia?" Oh God, that was a dumb question.

"No. Sarcasm is not allowed in Russia." Another swig of beer, another sly glance at me. I'd felt myself flush again. Then we'd gone over words that might prove useful to him: hammer, nails, drill, paint, wrench, hinges. I'd pantomimed some of these actions, to Viktor's apparent amusement. *Spackle* and *grout* were more difficult to explain, requiring an extremely awkward field trip to the bathroom.

It was the strangest evening. But I'd genuinely enjoyed his company. He'd left shortly after ten, with a promise to text me soon to set up our next lesson. *He's funny,* I thought as I crawled under my comforter. *Easy to look at. And maybe smarter than he lets on.*

The next day started more groggily than usual — I wouldn't call it a hangover, exactly, but I guess that's what it was. No malingering, though: Cynthia was headed for a half-day yoga retreat on Long Island, and she wasn't getting there without a great deal of emotional support.

"I look like a sausage in these leggings," she wailed the moment I walked through the front door. "They're practically see-through on my ass. Look!"

I bent down to investigate.

"This is the biggest size they came in," she declared. Was this an apology? An accusation? Maybe both.

I stood up. "Well, I wouldn't call it a disaster. But maybe these aren't the leggings for you. Come on." I made for the bedroom.

She scurried after me. "I'm a whale!"

"You are so *not* a whale." I dug around in a dresser drawer for an alternative. "How about these?" I held up a pair of black stretchy pants in a slightly looser style.

She stuck out her lower lip. "I don't really like those so much."

"Are they better or worse than the ones you're wearing now?"

Cynthia heaved a persecuted sigh, so I pressed on: "Better?"

She squeezed her eyes shut and nodded. I tossed the pants onto the velvet-upholstered bench at the foot of her bed as she began to peel the offending tights off.

"I like this warm-up jacket too," I said, plucking a two-toned hoodie from the activewear rack of her vast walk-in closet. "It elongates everything."

Cynthia was staring at the mirror transfixed, both hands clutching her outer thighs in a death-grip. "If I could just chop these off with an axe," she hissed. "You know?"

"I know, I hate those," I replied. She tore her eyes away from her reflection to give me an incredulous look. "I have them too," I reassured her, and she visibly relaxed.

"What size are you?" Cynthia asked me, and even though her tone was casual I felt like it was a trap.

"Six, I guess." It had been so long since I'd been clothes-shopping. For myself, anyway. I wondered if Viktor had noticed the complete lack of effort I was putting into my appearance lately.

"Fuck. I'd kill to be a six again." I had a feeling she meant it literally. *Find a way out of this.*

"What does Fabrizio recommend?" Fabrizio was Cynthia's personal trainer, a chiseled-from-granite specimen hailing from somewhere in Eastern Europe.

"Fabrizio says the outer thighs are the last thing to go." Cynthia grabbed the looser yoga pants and yanked them on. "Fabrizio says, 'Don't quit before the miracle happens.'"

I chuckled. "That's pretty good."

"The advice, or the Eurotrash accent?" She was twisting her neck as far as it would go to see how her ass looked in the looser pants.

"Both." I handed her the warm-up jacket. "Car's waiting downstairs."

With Cynthia packed off to yoga, I plunged into my latest assignment — cleaning out and organizing her packed-to-the-rafters closets. I'd correctly surmised that this task would be easier without Cynthia present, and I was making decent progress when my iPhone chirped at eleven-thirty.

It was a text from Cynthia:

PICKUP MASON FROM SCHOOL ASAP.

No explanation followed. I dashed out the door.

The Weatherly School's main office sat at the top of a flight of stairs, and I was completely out of breath when I arrived. Mason was sitting on a polished wooden bench, his uniform rumpled and dirty. He was holding an ice pack against one eye.

"Mason!" I gasped. "Are you okay?"

"I'm fine," he mumbled. He stood up and hefted his backpack over one shoulder. "Let's go."

"Wait, what happened?" I looked around for a responsible adult. An older woman with perfectly-coiffed silver hair materialized. She was wearing a long tartan plaid skirt and a sweater-set — and pearls!

She cleared her throat. Full-on Dolores Umbridge. "Young Mr. Waldrop was fighting with a schoolmate. The headmaster has sent him home for the day." She pursed her lips. "And you are...?"

"I'm Lane. I'm filling in for, you know, um, Magda. The nanny." My mouth had gone bone-dry. "Mrs. Waldrop said she submitted the paperwork for me to pick up the kids. I've been picking them up after school for a, um, for a couple of weeks."

"I see." She leaned over and checked something on her computer. "Your name?"

"Lane Haviland." I tucked a flyaway strand of hair behind my ear and stood up a little straighter. I hadn't felt this flummoxed since — well, since I'd been asked to explain *would, could,* and *should* at the drop of a dime.

"Yes, all right. You're free to go." She gave me a polite nod.

"Wait," I protested. "His head. Mason, are you okay?"

Mason stared at his feet and scowled.

"The school nurse has examined him," the school-lady chirped. "She recommended the ice pack."

"Right. Will the principal, um, contact Mr. and Mrs.

Waldrop later?"

She stared me down over the top of her reading glasses. *"Headmaster* Marschalk will be following up with his parents later today, I expect." She shifted her gaze to Mason, who looked even more miserable than before.

"Right." I suspected that Cynthia would want more information about what had happened, but I didn't feel like it was my place to demand it here and now. Mason was drifting towards the office door, clearly desperate to take his leave. I took a deep breath. "Okay. Come on, buddy, let's go."

Mason stayed silent on the cab ride home. I resisted the urge to press him for details, but I did insist on taking a closer look at his eye, which was badly swollen and starting to discolor underneath and around the lid. Once I'd finished my examination, he retreated to the other side of the taxi's back seat and stared out the window.

When the cab turned onto 74th street, I spoke up. "I think we're gonna need to have the doctor take a look at that eye, Mason."

He didn't acknowledge me, so I placed a call to the family doctor, who agreed to come by the house in an hour to take a look. ("A concierge medical practice," Cynthia had told me with a straight face, "is basically the only way to go.") Calls to Cynthia went right to voicemail, so I texted her a quick update. She texted back immediately:

HORRIFIED! PLZ CONFISCATE HIS PHONE ASAP!!!!

I looked over at Mason. He was still staring out the window.

"She wants you to take my phone, doesn't she?" he mumbled.

"Yeah."

"Well, fuck," he replied.

I was sure my jaw was on the floor of the taxicab as I watched Mason dig out his phone. He tossed it over.

"Is your mother okay with that language?" I asked him.

He didn't answer.

Deprived of his phone, Mason sat at the Waldrops' kitchen

breakfast-bar, elbows splayed out on the counter, a fresh ice-pack clutched to his eye. The silence in the empty house felt oppressive: I could actually hear the seconds ticking by on the wall-clock.

"It's a lot of excitement for one day," I remarked. "I think I could use a glass of chocolate milk."

Is it possible to roll one's single good eye? This kid was so not-buying-it. Nevertheless, I hunted around in the door of Cynthia's SubZero until I found milk and chocolate syrup.

"And straws," I pronounced. More eye-rollery from Mason. I poured and mixed two glasses, and set one down in front of him. "Cheers." I clinked my glass on his, which he hadn't touched.

He finally reached for the glass. "What are we drinking to?"

I hadn't expected that question. "To better days."

He shook his head, but at least he took a sip.

"Do you want to talk about it?"

"Not really," he mumbled.

"Okay. You don't have to get into it now if you don't want to."

"Thanks." He drummed his fingers on the countertop and gazed off into the distance with his one working eye.

"Your mom and dad are going to want to know what happened, though."

"They won't understand," he muttered. "They never do."

"What makes you say that?"

Silence. I waited a bit, even cocked my head at him expectantly, but he was done talking. That cemented my opinion: he was a smart kid.

"Okay. Doctor'll be here soon. Why don't you wash your hands and face?" I cleaned up the dishes and Mason dragged himself off to the powder-room. My phone pinged again. Cynthia, texting.

PLZ SEND FULL DETAILS OF THIS EVENT TO DR. HOYT. CONTACT INFO IS IN MY ADDRESS BOOK.

Was there any parenting function Cynthia wasn't comfortable delegating to me? At least both kids had been weaned by the time I'd entered the picture. I tried to remember the name of the doctor who was making the house call. I was pretty sure it wasn't Hoyt. "Mason?" I called out.

"Yeah." He emerged from the powder room holding a hand-towel.

"Who is…" I squinted down at my phone. "Who is Dr. Hoyt?"

"That's my psychiatrist."

Fantastic.

9

I kept careful watch over Mason for the rest of the afternoon, checking on his eye periodically while he stared at a dog-eared book in his lap — *One Universe: At Home in the Cosmos,* by Neil deGrasse Tyson. I made a few half-hearted attempts at conversation, but Mason was resolute in his silence.

One universe, though. I had to smile at that. Because there's always that person in every group therapy session who talks about the universe as though it's their personal benefactor, and they its hapless ward. Life is a reality TV show: the universe is sitting there slack-jawed on the celestial sofa, deciding who gets voted off every week.

"My dream was to marry Janelle, but the universe had other plans." (Some dope at Silver Hill Hospital.)

"I wouldn't say I set out to be a bulimic rage-aholic, but that's what the universe decided. Maybe it had to happen." (Profoundly annoying chick in the psychiatric unit, The Haven at Westchester.)

"Every day I have to get down on my knees and ask myself: Why am I fighting so hard against the universe?" (Sad-eyed longtimer at the National Council of Jewish Women's Tuesday Bereavement Support Group.)

All these fucking people mired in their grief: I didn't want to turn into one of them. So I stopped. Years ago. The introspection, the analysis, the endless *talking*. None of it ever helped me move on. You know what helped? Drugs. The legal kind, mostly. Also culling people out of my life — I was exceptionally good at that. Not to minimize what had happened; it sucked. It shattered me into a million pieces. But at least I knew when I was done talking about it.

Maybe that's why I'm okay with the basement apartment, I thought as I finally heard Cynthia coming through the front door. My interaction with the universe had become so minimal that living as a troglodyte hadn't materially changed anything.

I fully expected to have to talk Cynthia down from the ledge regarding Mason's school troubles, but she seemed outwardly unconcerned upon her return home, even when I related to her that Mason had refused to reveal details on what had happened.

"Fighting at school." She shook her head and gave herself a generous pour of white wine. "He knows how I feel about this. Brad will handle it."

"Okay." Well, what was I supposed to say? Brad was Cynthia's husband. We hadn't even been properly introduced. Not that I could blame him for making himself scarce — Cynthia's mood swings were starting to haunt my every waking hour. I never knew who I was talking to until it was too late: cold and detached Cynthia? Or the neurotic, needy mess I'd tended to this morning?

"I need to talk to you about something," she suddenly implored. "In private. Want some wine?"

"No thanks." I followed her into the TV room; she closed the door.

"This is just between us," she began. "I've been thinking about it a lot and I need your help but it has to be a hundred and ten percent private."

"Sure."

She took a deep breath. "I'm suspicious. Of Brad. I think he's having an affair."

No. No no no. "Really?"

She dropped her voice low. "He's been coming home late all the time. He's blaming work, but when I call him — in his office, on his cellphone — he doesn't pick up."

"I see." I fumbled around for something logical to say. "Maybe a private detective—"

Cynthia shook her head vigorously. "No. I'm not at that point yet."

I had to tread carefully. "I understand that you feel suspicious," I said, and Cynthia took a gulp of wine. "It's just that I don't have any experience with… in this area."

"I trust you." Cynthia looked beseeching. "For now I just want you to keep your eyes open. Can you do that for me?"

Eyes open? I'd never even spoken to the man. "Yes, of course—"

"And look at some things." I must have given her a quizzical look, because she continued: "Nothing crazy, just, like, Facebook — that sort of thing. Sometimes old flames reconnect there. It happened to a friend of mine. I need a fresh pair of eyes on this."

"I don't have a Facebook account," I mumbled apologetically. And I sure as hell wasn't going to create one.

"You can use mine," Cynthia assured me. "Be a neutral third party. Tell me whether I'm being ridiculous."

You're being ridiculous. "Sure."

"I knew I could count on you! Lane, you're the best."

Please, God, never let me owe anyone this much money again so I can just tell my crazy boss to stuff it. Amen.

As I trotted down the Waldrops' front stoop and into the cold night, I felt like I'd just navigated the Bermuda Triangle only to emerge into whitewater rapids that might or might not sweep me over Niagara Falls. It occurred to me that Cynthia's paranoia was overflowing into my mental space and creating whole new ludicrous levels of crazy. *Just deal with your own shit,* I warned myself, and then I realized that it might help to talk to a normal person, even if just to remember what that felt like.

I couldn't recall the last time I'd willingly initiated social interaction with a fellow human being, so it wasn't altogether surprising that the only contacts in my flip-phone were Cynthia,

Randy, and Viktor. I scrolled down to Viktor's name and hovered my thumb over the "Select" button. Would it be weird if I texted him randomly, asking to hang out? Yes. Too soon. I tried Randy instead. Texting had always been her preferred method of contact.

You around? I have some $$ to pay you back.

Her reply came in right away:

Hey stranger. Sure, come by the kitchen. I'm just finishing up.

I shoved the phone back in my bag and headed for the downtown 6 train.

Randy was alone and finishing cleanup when I arrived. The prep-tables and fixtures and floor were spotless, just like she'd always insisted I leave them at quitting-time.

"There she is!" Randy called out when she saw me. "What brings you down here?"

"Just wanted to say hi. And give you this." I handed her two twenties and a ten with a yellow sticky-note upon which I'd scrawled today's date and my remaining balance.

"Thanks." Randy glanced at the note and nodded approvingly.

"It's not much…" I stammered. My throat had suddenly gone dry. "Things are a little tight financially right now."

"It's all right. I know you're good for it."

"Yeah." I jammed my hands into my coat pockets so I wouldn't fidget with them. "Thanks for having faith in me."

"Of course. You okay?"

"Yep." Compared to what?

"Good. Walk me out."

I shuffled along and waited while Randy locked the front door. Outside on the sidewalk, she winced at the biting cold and wound her scarf twice around her neck. "So I've got to know," she said. "What's it like being a personal assistant?"

"It's different than I expected." My breath formed little visible puffs in the cold dry air. "You know, rich people. Rich people problems."

Randy smiled. "Are you keeping the world safe for Cynthia

Waldrop, or safe *from* her?"

I smiled back. "Both. It's kind of a rollercoaster."

"Good. Might as well have fun."

Sure. Fun. "What if I don't like rollercoasters?"

"Oh, well then it's a total nightmare. Sorry," she chuckled, and I had to laugh.

"It's good to see you, Randy."

"Likewise. There's something different about you. Better."

"Really?"

"Yeah." She leaped over a crosswalk slush-puddle. "You look more alive. Maybe it's best to mix things up. New challenges and all that crap."

I thought about it. I knew she was referring to my career change-up, but for some reason my thoughts turned to Viktor.

Randy cleared her throat in the silence. "That's what they say, anyway."

I snapped back to reality. "Who's *they?*"

"I don't know," she sighed. "A bunch of bastards, probably."

I hadn't realized how much I'd missed Randy. We both stopped at the stairs leading down to the subway. I shifted my weight from one leg to the other as if that could keep the cold at bay, but it wasn't working. My toes were going numb. "I'll text you next week? Figure out a good time to come by... to make the next payment, I mean." Suddenly everything felt awkward again. As much as I'd craved social interaction earlier, now I was longing to be alone in my apartment. Preferably with the door bolted.

"Of course, Lane. Payment or not. Just text me." She surprised me with a hug, which left me standing there with a lump in my throat.

"Thanks, Randy."

By the end of my second week as the Waldrops' interim nanny I was barely half a step above roadkill, emotionally speaking. Subsisting on a pack of Twizzlers for two straight days hadn't helped, in hindsight. In any case, I was out of clean underwear. My building's laundry room remained shuttered, so Saturday morning found me sitting inside a dreary coin-op laundromat on Corbin Place.

I watched my clothes tumble around in the dryer and rubbed the sleep out of my eyes. With my luck, Cynthia was certain to call or text with some new emergency, summoning me to Manhattan in the middle of my laundry cycle to discuss the latest developments in backyard pool decking materials. But the phone stayed silent, and I was done by nine-thirty.

I left the warmth of the laundromat hugging my overstuffed basket of clean laundry tight to my chest. Then I turned the corner of Hampton Avenue and saw Sergey approaching. *Oh, crap.* I tried to slink by him unnoticed, but his voice rang out behind me: "Hey."

I walked faster. But then I felt a hand clap down on my shoulder. I turned around, making sure to keep the laundry basket between us, to see Sergey grinning triumphantly. It disturbed me to notice that his gold tooth was actually glinting in the morning sunlight.

"Hello." His grip on my shoulder tightened ever-so-slightly. "It is Lane, yes?"

"Yeah." I took a step backwards. Sergey miraculously took the hint and let my shoulder slip from his grasp. I didn't recognize the two guys he was with. They looked me over with scant interest and returned to their cigarettes and conversation.

"How is it going?" He flicked his cigarette butt into the gutter.

"Fine." As long as he kept a respectful distance.

"Everything is okay in apartment?" He leaned in a little closer. His breath smelled foul. Vaguely boozy.

"It's fine. I gotta go." I turned and hurried away, heart pounding in my chest.

"See you soon," he called after me.

I really, truly hoped not.

Normally, I didn't feel safe until I was inside my apartment with the deadbolt locked — and my chance encounter with Sergey had multiplied that feeling a thousandfold. I leaned against the door until my heart rate slowed to normal. Was this how things were going to be, in Brighton Beach? Fleeing Cynthia and her insanity, only to end up hiding from Sergey and his unwelcome attention.

Suddenly I felt way too hot, and I noticed that the radiator was emitting a steady hiss of steam punctuated with louder bursts and sharp clangs. Not normal.

I dug out my flip-phone and texted Viktor:

Hey Viktor, my apartment is crazy hot. Radiator broken. How's your day going?

I grabbed my bag and headed up to the lobby to ensure the text got sent and await his response. It didn't take long:

Coming

He was a man of few words. But he was also a man of action. I put away my phone and took out Cynthia's. Might as well catch up on her calendar during the downtime.

Twenty minutes later, Viktor showed up, toolbox in hand. Boy, was I happy to see him!

"Hey," I said. I put Cynthia's phone away.

His icy-blue eyes met mine. "New phone?"

"It's my boss's," I explained, mortified. "Mine's still the same old…crappy as ever."

He gave a short nod and headed downstairs. Awkward! Why did I feel like I owed him an explanation for this? Well, he *had* fronted me a thousand bucks, and I hadn't even started paying him back yet. I followed him down to the basement.

My apartment was now a sauna, minus the cedar paneling and hairy naked men. I pulled off my sweater and dropped it on the futon. My tank top was sticking to my midsection, and not in a particularly attractive way, but now certainly wasn't the time to dig around in suitcases for something more flattering.

Viktor was standing over the radiator, frowning down at it. "What's wrong?" I asked him.

"I think problem is with boiler." He turned and strode out the door. I followed behind him, fanning myself with a Chinese takeout menu, and watched him fiddle with a keyring at the boiler room door. Then he disappeared inside.

A minute later, he called out from inside the boiler room: "It's still going like before? Your radiator?"

I ran back and checked. "Yeah. Full steam." What a waste of a good pun.

A loud *clunk* sounded from inside the boiler room. Then a soft thud, followed by another, louder, more complex series of clunks. Then a shout: *"Gavno!"* I could guess roughly what that meant.

Finally, Viktor emerged from the boiler room. The top half of his coveralls were off, hanging around his waist. A dark gray t-shirt clung wetly to his chest, and his long, lean, muscular arms were covered in bluish-black tattoos — some pictures, some text. Cyrillic, from the looks of it. I swallowed and tried hard not to stare.

"I must call plumber," he said, a little breathlessly. He ran one hand through his now-damp hair, pushing it out of his face. "Boiler is busted. This will affect whole building." I must have been staring stupidly at him, because he added, "Excuse me," and pushed past me, gently but purposefully, to return to my apartment.

I shuffled after him and peeked in the open door. He was wrenching something into position on the radiator. It was still emitting steam, although not as forcefully as before. Then he dug around in his coveralls pocket and noticed me standing there. "There is cell signal down here?" he asked.

"No." I looked everywhere except at his tattoos. He hurried out the door, frowning at his phone, and I heard his footfalls going upstairs. Then I sank down on the futon and resumed fanning myself with the Chinese takeout menu.

A few hours later, after I'd had a two-Twizzler lunch followed by the world's most necessary nap, I heard a soft knock at the door. "Viktor?" I called out hopefully.

"Yes."

I opened the door. His coveralls were back on, not that I could unsee what I'd already seen. Thought about. Okay, obsessed over. "Come on in."

"Boiler is fixed. I must look at radiator." He rubbed his eyes. Had this been his day off?

"Go ahead. I have something for you."

A puzzled look crossed his face, but he walked over to the radiator. I took two twenty dollar bills and two fives out of my wallet. Once he'd finished, he turned around and I handed him the cash. He stared down at the money, his brows knit in confusion.

"I'm paying you back," I said. "This is just the first installment."

"No rush." He started to hand the money back to me and I pushed his hand back gently. His skin felt very warm.

"It's important to me." My voice sounded thin. He looked back down at the money in his hand, then at me. His eyes had the same icy-blue intensity as earlier. What was he thinking? Could he sense how attracted I was to him?

"You will continue to teach me English?" A sly smile was forming on his face as he slipped the cash into his pocket.

"Count on it." My words came out as little more than a whisper.

He took my hand in his and turned it over, examining it. He ran one thumb over my palm.

"You had money, once," he said. His eyes met mine and I felt something. Like a small jolt of electricity.

"True." I withdrew my hand.

The half-smile on Viktor's face suggested he was satisfied to get that nugget of information out of me. Meanwhile, I felt like I was teetering on the edge of the high diving board atop Mount Doom.

Just ask him. The worst he can say is no.

"Would you like to stay for dinner?" My heart was thundering in my chest.

"Yes." Viktor looked down at me with that same half-smile and I realized how close we were standing. Pretty close, it turns out.

"Don't you want to know what we're having?" I asked.
"No."

Viktor went out on a beer run, so I tidied up my possessions. That took all of thirty seconds. Then I sat down on the futon. My apartment had cooled down; I had not. Why was I suddenly so into this guy?

Well, he'd been kind to me, for one. And: intelligence. Despite the language barrier, I could tell there was a light on upstairs. He was tall. Good looking. And *okay,* the tattoos. Tattooed guys were crazy-sexy, as long as they weren't hipsters or members of the Aryan Brotherhood. In that order.

You're being foolish. There it was, my better judgment. I was well accustomed to ignoring it, but something about my apartment — its isolation? — was suddenly making me feel like I'd stumbled into a trap. No one could hear me scream down here.

A serial killer would have murdered you already. That notion came courtesy of the same part of my mind that fetishized bridges and balconies and razor-blades. Why did it always come down to my mother versus Sylvia Plath? I wondered if my attraction to Viktor was just another self-destructive impulse. Not that I was feeling suicidal at the moment, but it had been laying there so long. So patiently.

There was a knock at the door and I twitched. Whatever was happening between me and Viktor, it was about to move past flirting. I got up and checked my reflection in the bathroom mirror. A little flushed, a little frazzled, but I looked okay. I looked — I could hardly believe it. I looked happy.

10

For all my fevered anticipation, dinner commenced in a sedate, almost prim fashion. Viktor was sitting on the floor with his back resting against the wall. His work boots, which I hadn't noticed before, seemed enormous, and his forearms were resting comfortably on his bent knees as he studied the label on his bottle of Budweiser. A few locks of black hair had fallen down over his forehead, which made him look younger.

I placed two steaming bowls of ramen noodles on the wobbly table, then sat down cross-legged. Viktor's eyes followed my every move as I shifted into position, trying to make myself comfortable on the floor.

"*Spasiba,*" he said. "That is Russian for thank you."

I acknowledged him with a bow of my head. "You're very welcome."

He took a bite of noodles. "Something new?"

"Chicken flavor."

"It's good."

"Well, *spasiba* to you too." Suddenly I felt very shy. We ate in companionable silence for a time. I was aware that I'd wanted to jump this guy's bones quite recently, but now that he was sitting in front of me with those giant boots, the whole situation just felt weird. Complicated.

"I have some information on the Could, Would, and Should front," I finally said.

He smiled down into his noodles but didn't say anything.

"Do you want to hear the official explanation?" I asked. "Or did I do a Google search for nothing?"

"Please, tell me everything." His eyes twinkled and he took another drink of beer.

"Well, they're auxiliary verbs. Um, auxiliary means they help with something." I wiped my mouth with a napkin. "*Could* is ability. *Would* is desire. And *should* is a moral imperative. From the Latin root *debere,* which is duty or obligation."

Viktor nodded solemnly and swallowed what he'd been chewing. "Perfectly clear," he said, and he took another drink of beer. "Thank you," he added, and gifted me with another shy smile. Ugh! That angular face! So severe, and yet it softened around the edges when he smiled — *really* smiled, with crinkles at the corners of his eyes. He had to know exactly what he was doing to me. Elevating my pulse to dangerous levels.

"So tell me," he said, setting the bowl down. "What is story of Lane?"

"My story?" My first impulse was to stall him. I hated the story of Lane. "I have to warn you, it's not the least bit interesting."

He shrugged. "No obligation to tell."

"You were right," I admitted. "I used to have money. Not a lot, but enough, I guess. Now I don't."

Viktor nodded gravely. He was looking at me as though this was the most interesting thing he'd heard all day. Maybe it was.

I looked up at the ugly drop-ceiling. "It's not an especially exciting story. I didn't lose it all at once on, like, a poker game. Or drugs. I just spent it. Because I wanted to." I indicated the four walls of the cramped room. "And here I am."

He sipped his beer and gave me a contemplative look. "Sounds like one small part of much larger story."

"Most stories are." I shifted my weight again; my foot was falling asleep.

"I will clean up." Viktor whisked both bowls away before I could protest. He moved fast, for such a big guy. I pushed myself up onto the futon and shook my numbed-out foot while Viktor put the dishes into the sink. Then I limped and lurched to the kitchen to provide assistance and moral support, not that two adults could simultaneously occupy my kitchen unless they were joined somehow. Perhaps that could be arranged.

Jesus! Calm yourself, woman.

"I noticed your ink," I blurted out.

Viktor shut off the faucet but didn't turn around. I wondered if he'd even heard me.

"I mean, I really like your tattoos." I was balancing on one leg, trying to shake the pins and needles out of my foot. I was pretty sure I looked like an idiot.

He finally turned and looked down at me. The severity had returned to his features — not angry, but guarded. "When did you see?"

"When you came out of the boiler room."

A flash of understanding crossed his face, and he seemed to relax a bit. I sat down on the futon, then patted the space next to me. After a moment's hesitation Viktor sat down, leaving some personal space between us. Truly, this man was the anti-Sergey.

I picked up my half-finished beer and realized that I was, once again, very close to Viktor. He smelled of cigarette smoke and the leather jacket and something else I couldn't identify — aftershave? Cologne? The combination was heady. Lord, was I ever in trouble.

"The tattoos," he said. "They are from another time in my life."

"It's okay if you don't want to talk about it." God knows he'd given me that courtesy.

"No, it's okay." He was steepling his fingers, which were long and tapered, delicate — like an artist, or a musician. Then he turned to me, his expression serious. "I was in prison. In Russia. For almost six years."

"Oh." I had no halfway-intelligent response to this. My better judgment was nodding smugly, but I disregarded it. Viktor wasn't the only person on this futon who'd been locked up.

He looked at me another moment, then pulled up one sleeve to his elbow, revealing a bluish-black band of ink encircling his forearm just above the wrist. From there, two large chain links plus a third, broken link threaded up the inside of his arm. Cyrillic lettering was etched above and below them.

I stared at the words. What did they say? And why had he been sent to prison?

"They all have different meanings," he murmured.

"The words?"

"The objects. In prison, each tattoo is, like..." He paused, searching. "Statement. About myself."

"I had no idea." I wanted to know more. Those blue eyes were holding fast to mine while I spoke. Studying me, taking in my reaction.

"Other prisoners understand this," he continued. "The tattoos are...common language."

I traced my fingertip over the manacle around his forearm, across the chain links. "What does this one mean?"

"Five years in prison." He looked like he was about to say more, but then he pulled his sleeve back down.

"I'm sorry you had to go through that," I said lamely.

"It's fine."

I had to suppress a smile at that. *Fine* had been one of my favorite words in the depths of hell. *I'm fine,* I'd insisted; never mind the fact that I was under a 72-hour involuntary hold in a locked mental ward.

"I wasn't completely honest with you earlier," I told him. "My family was in a car accident and I guess I lost my mind."

Viktor looked quizzically at me. An already-awkward moment had just become infinitely more so. Well, I'd started down this path. "My parents and my sister. They were coming to visit me at school and this truck, it — it crashed into their car and it killed them."

Viktor didn't say anything. He wore a pained expression.

"I fell apart," I went on. "I left school. I just — I don't know. I checked out." I chanced a look at Viktor. He was still looking at me intently.

"I'm sorry," he said. He looked like he meant it.

There was a pause. But not an overly uncomfortable one.

"I am not sure what this means, *checked out*," he finally said.

"Me neither." I clasped my hands together; this was hard. "Reality. I guess I couldn't face it for a while."

Viktor nodded. I looked at the scar on the side of his face. It didn't seem so bad, close up. "I still don't. Want to face it, I mean." I swallowed. "The story of Lane is pretty pathetic." And then I felt them — hot tears, welling up behind my eyes. I tried to blink them back, but of course that was pointless, so I wiped my eyes over-aggressively, like Cynthia on her iPad, and hoped for the wave to pass. At least I hadn't been seized by horrible choking sobs.

Viktor spoke up softly: "You are very hard on yourself." He reached over and clasped my hand in his.

"Probably," I whispered.

He leaned in and peered up at me. He couldn't have been more non-threatening if he'd been a puppy. "You okay?"

"Yeah." He was so close. He'd never been this close. I felt myself stiffen. "I'm sorry," I told him. "I — it's weird for me." I looked down at my hands. How could I possibly explain to him what a mess I'd become?

Viktor sat back up, but he didn't seem inclined to run screaming. "Maybe you have advice for me," he said.

"Advice?"

"Yes." His voice was buttery-soft. "I would like to kiss you, but not sure if I should."

"You definitely should," I told him. "It's a moral imperative."

He smiled, and then he leaned in and kissed me — the softest, slightest brush of his lips on mine. It made me tingle everywhere.

Yes. More. I moved in closer. Viktor cupped one hand behind my ear and drew me closer and kissed me again, a proper kiss this time, and he did it so slowly and tenderly I thought I might swoon. When he stopped, I looked up to find his eyes locked onto mine. They were hooded, hungry. But also searching. Questioning.

"Keep going," I whispered, and his expression turned wolfish. Now he was off the leash. More demanding, insistent, but still he took his time, giving due respect to all the spaces in between. I let myself relax into the futon cushion: *Keep going.* He shifted closer, cradling my head in both hands as he kissed and nuzzled me. His stubble felt rough. The effect was intoxicating. I could feel myself slipping deeper under his spell — a needy warmth was rising up from deep within me. *Shit, that was fast.* He was good at this. I didn't want him to stop. And if he moved his attentions down to my neck, I wouldn't be able to tell him to.

That last thought knocked around inside my head for a moment too long. I felt myself withdraw. To his credit, Viktor didn't push it. "You okay?" he whispered.

"I don't know," I whispered back. "I think — I think we should stop."

He sat up stiffly. "I'm sorry," I said. "I'm very attracted to you. I can't explain it." Did anything I was saying make sense, even? "I just can't rush."

"It's okay." He ran a hand through his hair, which was still disheveled. "I should go." He stood up.

I stood up too. "I'm sorry. For sending mixed signals."

"No need." He cocked one eyebrow at me as he shrugged into his jacket. Devastating.

What the hell was my problem, anyway?

"I'll text you tomorrow," I said.

"Good." He leaned in and kissed my cheek, a quick peck. "Thank you for dinner." And with that, he was gone.

Sunday was a crack-of-dawn wakeup call. Cynthia had arranged for me to take the kids to church. She was busy organizing a school fundraiser, and Brad was in Las Vegas playing golf. Must be nice, I thought as I dragged myself from bed with the comforter wrapped tightly around me, burrito-style. I was grateful for the work, but I wouldn't have refused a weekend trip to Vegas with zero responsibilities.

I yanked open the fridge to grab my customary bottle of chilled tap water, only to find a bottle of dark green juice. The label said *NAKED* — the brand name — and below that, *Kale Blazer*. The bottlecap had *Drink Me* hand-scrawled on it with a Sharpie.

I shook the bottle, cracked it open, and took a sip. Not bad. Not good, either, but at least it had a gingery tang to mask the overwhelming kale flavor.

I texted Viktor from the Q train:

Thanks for the juice. :)

He didn't text back right away. I leaned my head back against the graffiti-scratched window, closed my eyes, and thought of Viktor's kisses. A very nice way to end the evening. And he hadn't seemed shocked by my crazy history. But that whole prison thing was a little unnerving. And I was letting him inside the barricades even though I barely knew him at all.

Once I got to the Waldrops' house, Cynthia was nowhere to be found, so I roused both kids from their beds to get them fed and dressed. "I can't believe you're taking us to church," Emily grumbled. "Can't we just do brunch and call it a day?"

"We won't tell Mom," Mason added, looking extra-pitiful. I suspected that Cynthia still had possession of his phone, and possibly his Xbox.

I ignored their pleas. "Do you guys know how to work this espresso machine?" I was longing for a coffee, but the gleaming chrome pipes and dials were beyond intimidating. The kids had no idea, of course; why would they? So I pulled out the bottle of Kale Blazer and finished it, to a chorus of *ewwwwwws* from both children. "It's good for you," I admonished, and then I gagged.

All three of us survived church. "You have a playdate at Brooke's," I reminded Emily, checking the address on Cynthia's phone as we walked north on Park Avenue.

"I know. And it's not called a playdate," Emily snapped. "It's hanging out."

"Oh. *Pardonnez-moi.*"

She rolled her eyes. "Don't you think I'm too old to need a nanny?"

"It's not my decision," I told her. "Have you brought it up with your mom?"

71

Emily heaved the world's most persecuted sigh. Then she hurried ahead of me and Mason so she could pretend she was walking the last few blocks to Brooke's by herself.

"Your sister," I told Mason, "is remarkably haughty this morning."

"If you say so." Mason was back to his I-don't-care monotone. At least he was talking.

Five milliseconds after Emily disappeared through the front door of Brooke's exquisite town-house, Mason was ready to crawl back into bed. "Can we go home now?" he whined.

"We just came from home." That earned me a murderous glare. "Let's take the long way, at least. Walk with me through Central Park."

"Whatever."

Central Park was sunny and cold, and mostly empty except for dog-walkers and hardcore joggers. "Some guy got killed near here when a tree branch fell on his head," Mason announced, looking up at the trees' bare branches. "Heavy snow. A hidden hazard."

"Sheesh," I replied. "That's random."

"Yeah."

We watched a man walk by with a beautiful German Shepherd. "Did you ever have pets?" I asked.

"Nope." Mason picked up a stick and tossed it up towards a towering boulder. "My dad's allergic."

"Oh. That's too bad." I picked up a pebble and chucked it in the same direction. It bounced off a rock outcropping and clattered back onto the paved pathway.

"How about you?" Mason asked. "Do you have a dog?"

"Me? Nah. It's a life goal, but I'm not there yet. Not even close."

Mason squinted at me. "Where do you live?"

"Brighton Beach, at the moment. That's in Brooklyn."

"I know where it is." He picked up another stick and lobbed it hard, into a tree trunk.

"Ever been there?"

"Nope." He was absorbed in his search for more sticks. "Magda took us to the Aquarium once, in Coney Island. That's near Brighton Beach, right?"

I nodded. "Not far at all."

"So I've been close. But no cigar." He threw another stick, this one spinning, boomerang-style.

"Hey, that one went pretty far!" I offered him a fist-bump. He obliged.

"So," Mason sighed, "Can we go home now?"

"We seem to be headed in that general direction."

We ambled on together.

By the time I remembered to check my phone, I was bone-tired and headed back to Brooklyn. Sure enough, Viktor had texted me:

:)

I looked for more texts from him, but there weren't any. Well, he wasn't the most talkative guy in person; I shouldn't expect Shakespeare's sonnets via text message. I texted back:

When can I see you again?

No immediate response.

I snapped the phone shut, leaned my head against the side of the subway car, and let my eyelids slide down at last. Rest; leave it alone. Either Viktor would want to see me again or he wouldn't.

Could, would, should.

I hoped he would.

11

Monday was another early morning wake-up call. I showered, got dressed, and plodded up the stairs to West End Avenue, where the air seemed somehow colder than usual in the pre-dawn gloom. A freezing wind whipped against my face and an empty plastic grocery-bag was blowing across the street and up an invisible wind-tunnel.

I headed for the subway holding one gloved hand over my exposed face for warmth and wishing I had a scarf. Half a block later, I caved in and gave myself permission to go to the Starbucks on Brighton Beach Avenue, even if only to smell the aroma of coffee brewing.

Quite a few sleepy commuters were already waiting to place their orders, so I walked to the end of the line, closed my eyes, and inhaled deeply. That roasted coffee bean smell — the best! I wondered if the change at the bottom of my purse would cover the $1.75 I'd need for a coffee. Probably not. And even if it did, spending it thusly would be irresponsible.

That hadn't ever stopped me before.

"Miss Haviland?" I blinked my eyes open to see a familiar face. The cop from the precinct. What was his name again?

"Mike Jarrett. Remember me?" He had a day's beard growth and he was wearing a suit that didn't fit him very well. Probably because his shoulders were vast steppes of muscle.

"Yes, Detective Jarrett. Good to see you."

"Likewise."

The line inched forward. I looked up, down, sideways, and finally at Detective Jarrett, who was staring at me. "How's it going for ya?" he inquired.

I took a deep breath. "It's going." Another half-step-shuffle forward. Lord, this was taking forever. "I'm really grateful for your help and all."

He waved away my thanks. "Looks like you decided to stay in the neighborhood after all."

"Yeah." I gave him a rueful smile. "Keeping busy."

He scratched his head. "Brighton Realty got you a place?"

"Yeah, over on West End. You're up," I told him, motioning towards the barista.

He gave me a curious look. "Let me buy you a cup of coffee."

"I don't want to be late for work," I protested.

"Five minutes," he said. "C'mon. What do you want?"

The barista tapped her fingers on the register and stared me down, clearly annoyed with both of us. People behind us in line were becoming agitated.

"I, uh, a caramel latté, I guess. Grande," I added hastily.

"Two grande caramel lattés," he pronounced, handing over a crisp twenty. "And a slice of that marble loaf." He shot me a triumphant grin. Advantage, Detective Jarrett.

"So where were we," he remarked as he sat down. "West End Avenue?"

"Yup." I took a sip of coffee. Mother of God, it was good.

He removed the slice of cake from its wrapper and set it down carefully on a napkin. "I'm a little surprised to hear that. A nice young lady living down there all by yourself."

He and Sergey should form a support group. "It's not The Waldorf. I manage."

"Sixty-one West End?" He tore off a piece of cake and popped it into his mouth.

"Yeah. How'd you know that?"

He took a sip of coffee. "Part of an ongoing investigation. The

75

owners have several buildings around here. I've been looking into it since our last talk. I've gotta say, they're a little shady. Up to no good."

"Oh." I was wholly absorbed in my latté love affair. Would it have been greedy to order an even-more-colossal Venti size? Yes, I decided. I'd shown remarkable restraint.

"There's some organized crime in this area," Detective Jarrett continued. "Russians. Ukrainians." He gave me a meaningful look and took a bite of marble-loaf.

"I don't know who owns the building," I told him. "I'm sort of focused on other things right now."

"I get it." He gave me a crooked grin.

"I have a question," I said.

"Ask away."

"I thought you were more of a Dunkin' Donuts kind of guy. What's with this sudden defection to Starbucks?"

"Very perceptive." He took another drink of coffee. "I'm actually a consistent fan of both establishments. As an officer of the law, I wouldn't want to be seen as playing favorites."

"Is that diplomacy or strategy?"

"You're a clever one." His mouth curved into a smile, revealing two dimples. "Listen, Lane. Is it all right if I call you Lane?"

"Sure."

"I like you. You've got moxie. But be careful with these people. They're dangerous and you're vulnerable."

I thought of Mrs. Pasternak and fought to suppress a smile. "I'm sorry, I must have missed something. Who are 'these people'?"

He shifted in his chair. "Something goes on in the neighborhood, I usually hear about it. And I hear you've been hanging around with a low-level enforcer in your spare time."

Viktor? I grasped around for some scrap of composure while Detective Jarrett observed me silently. Suddenly I felt uncomfortable, and my better judgment reminded me who I was talking to. *Maybe he's just doing his job.* But this was Starbucks — not a police interrogation room. And I hadn't done anything wrong.

"How is what I do in my spare time any of your business?" I finally managed to say.

He wiped his hands with a paper napkin. "It's not. Unless you're fraternizing with known gang members and criminals, in which case I owe you fair warning about who you're getting involved with."

Well, *that* was a disturbance in the fucking Force. I turned it over in my mind as I stood in a crammed-full Manhattan-bound subway car. Viktor, an enforcer? It seemed a bit much. Sure, he'd been evasive on details about his current situation, but I'd chalked that up to shyness, or embarrassment. Surely he wasn't — couldn't be — a low-life. Sergey, sure. Not Viktor.

But that whole Russian prison thing. What was the story there? My phone pinged. I dug it out and found a text from Viktor:

hey, professor higgins? ready for next lesson?

I stared down at the screen for a long moment. Then I flipped the phone shut without responding.

I was out of breath, ten minutes late, and deep into the challenging mental exercise of justifying to myself why an essentially decent person might spend six years locked up in a Russian prison as I turned my key in the Waldrops' front door. The house was empty. A note from Cynthia was sitting on the front hall console table.

I took the kids to school. PLZ DO Facebook project. Already logged in @ desk. Check text for instructions.

I dug out the iPhone. Sure enough, she had texted me:

Look 4 suspicious patterns! On Wall, in Favorites, Places...etc.

I dragged myself upstairs to Cynthia's desk and sat down to the moment I'd been dreading all weekend. What could Brad's Facebook profile reveal about his secret life, such as it was? I started by clicking through his Favorites.

Movies: *Caddyshack, The Godfather, The Magnificent Seven.* Okay, moving on.

Music: Jimmy Buffett. Two other bands I hadn't heard of.

Books: *The Six Sigma Way*. Seriously, Brad?

None of this was useful, so I moved on to Brad's biographical info, or at least the Facebook-sanitized version he'd chosen to present to the world. He'd graduated from Yale, played in a lacrosse club with a bunch of other square-jawed jocks, and earned his MBA from NYU. I yawned and scrolled through his timeline, noting check-ins at various fashionable Manhattan restaurants. Most recently, he'd visited a celebrity chef's Las Vegas steakhouse and checked in at a couple of golf courses. There were a few 'likes' and sparse commentary on his posts, but I saw no obvious attention from any one female friend in particular. No, Brad seemed like every other investment banker I'd ever met: rich, white, entitled, stultifyingly bland, and more than likely a complete douchebag. But nothing in his Facebook life suggested that he was violating his marriage vows.

In fact, the whole thing was making me uncomfortable. It felt perilously close to stalking, and I was reminded of why I'd deleted my own Facebook profile years before — fake friendships, fake lives, everyone up in your business.

I wondered if Viktor had a page.

Mercifully, that train of thought was cut short by Cynthia's arrival home. "I'm really sorry I was late," I began pre-emptively, but she shushed me and pulled up a chair.

"What did you find?"

"I found nothing suspicious." This was the God's-honest truth.

Cynthia's eyes widened. "Really?"

"Yes. Unless there's someone in particular you want me to look at. I mean, there isn't a lot of activity, really, to go on," I added, and instantly regretted it.

"There isn't. You're right." Her brows furrowed in thought. "I wish I had his password," she whispered.

"No, you don't."

"I need to install Facebook on your phone," she said. I must have looked confused. "So you can log in as me. Keep tabs on Brad's page, see if anything unusual happens."

"Okay, let's do that later." I stood up. "I want to finish the closet clean-out." Cynthia nodded, still lost in thought. "Do you need anything from your closets before I go in there and make a mess?"

She made a face. "The only things that fit me are my fat clothes!"

"That can't be true." We weren't at the point where I intuitively understood what she meant by 'fat clothes,' but I had the sinking feeling we were about to go there.

"It *is* true." She hefted herself out of the chair and motioned me to follow her to her dressing room. "I'm up seven pounds since Christmas and I'm just disgusted with myself."

"The post-holiday season is rough," I agreed.

No response. *Quick, she's slipping into her Dark Place!* "Do you want to see what I've done with the closets so far?" I was dreading the emotional fallout of this discussion, but I might as well get credit for being enthusiastic now that doom was imminent.

"I guess so." Morose Cynthia spoke in a monotone, not unlike morose Mason.

"Okay. Prepare to be amazed."

And amazed she was, to the degree that it's possible to amaze a Kardashian-level self-absorbed crazy woman with basic closet organization skills and near-total sycophancy. Cynthia was now the proud owner of an "aspirational" rod in her closet, home to several pairs of too-snug trousers that I'd convinced her she'd be wearing by summer. So in some sense, I'd merely kicked that can down the road. At least I'd have my debts paid off by then.

Cynthia went off to mope by herself and I realized I still hadn't responded to Viktor. Why was I running away from him? We'd been alone together on more than one occasion and I'd never felt the least bit threatened. Maybe Detective Jarrett was lumping Viktor in unfairly with Sergey.

I texted Viktor:

I'm ready for our next lesson whenever you are.

As usual, he didn't respond right away. So I went about my

business and picked up both kids at school. Then, as the three of us headed to Mason's psychiatrist's office, Viktor texted me back:

Thursday night?

Yes, I texted back. *8pm.*

OK

I caught myself smiling. Then I pressed my lips together as I tried, and failed, to push the lingering worries from my mind.

Emily and I dropped Mason off. Then we headed back to Chez Waldrop together. "My brother's a total psycho," Emily told me cheerfully. When I didn't react, she added: "He sees that doctor twice a week and he has to take antidepressants."

"Everyone has problems," I mumbled. My least favorite subject by far. "How was school?"

"It was okay. Brooke made Honor Roll. I didn't."

I shrugged. "As long as you're trying your best."

"Who texted you before?" Emily's tone was too bright, too casual. I gave her a side-eye and she blinked innocently.

"No one important," I told her.

"Liar, liar, pants on fire," Emily replied in a sing-song voice. Then she darted in front of me. "Race you to hot chocolate!" She sprinted ahead and disappeared through the door of a Starbucks. I shrugged and followed her inside.

With Emily deposited at Chez Waldrop, I headed back to the shrink's office to wait for Mason. The bronze plaque on the waiting-room door was inscribed *Emmanuel Hoyt, M.D., Child & Adolescent Psychiatry.* Solid; respectable. Could he be one of the better ones? I hoped so, for Mason's sake. I steeled myself and pulled the door open, gave the receptionist a polite nod, and sat down on a minimalist modern sofa.

"Can I get you anything?" the receptionist asked me. I must have given her a blank look. "Water, tea?"

"No thanks." It took every ounce of self-restraint I had not to request a Xanax.

I shut my eyes.

"As time passes, Lane, your grief will change its size

and shape."

So said Dr. Ulrich — the last psychiatrist I'd visited and the only one who was worth a tinker's damn. He'd been remarkably open to my idea of not wasting my time or his with weekly appointments. All I'd wanted from him was a Prozac prescription with twelve months of refills, no questions asked. He hadn't argued.

"I have one request," he'd told me as he scribbled something on the prescription pad on his desk — *Give the crazy girl her crazy pills.* In Latin, perhaps.

"I'm listening." Not group therapy. Anything but that.

"Promise me you will consider what I just said. About grief." He set his pen down and looked at me steadily, his large hands clasped loosely in front of him.

"That it will change size? I mean, shape?" I tried not to stare at the already-written prescription. So tantalizingly close!

"Size *and* shape. Right now it's a tsunami and you're running for higher ground. It's a matter of survival. Would you agree?"

I nodded. I knew what was good for me.

"I can tell you that it won't always be like this. Grief. It changes. It won't be today. Or tomorrow. But one day you'll wake up and your grief will have taken another form. I want you to be open to that possibility. Think about it from time to time." He ripped the prescription off the pad. "Will you do that?"

"Yes." I'd have signed a pact with the Devil himself in exchange for a year's worth of antidepressants.

And in some sense, I'd done exactly that, because no matter how hard I tried to forget the good doctor's advice, I couldn't quite excavate the seed he'd planted in my head. Maybe some part of me had actually trusted him, or perhaps my state of mind had been so precarious that I'd been overly suggestible. Whatever the reason, every so often — once a week, maybe — I'd think about my grief, and what form it was taking today. These thoughts came out of nowhere, and they went nowhere until I did what he'd told me:

Today my grief is a spiderweb, invisible from most angles but sticky and horrible, so whatever you do, don't walk into it face-first.

Today my grief is a cold, damp basement, so quiet and vaguely threatening that I want to run away.

Today my grief is the schoolyard bully, cruel and smirking, pointing and poking at my many weaknesses, real and imagined.

Was it working, this months-long mental exercise? I couldn't know. But I was still here, and that had to count for something.

I caught the receptionist's eye. "Will Mason be done soon?"

"Here he is," she said with a broad smile, and I turned to see Mason standing before me, a scowl on his face, hands stuffed in his pockets. *He's embarrassed,* I thought. He shouldn't be. If only he knew.

I stood up. "Ready, buddy?"

He slunk wordlessly towards the door. I picked up his backpack and followed him out.

12

The familiar tap on my door came at just after eight o'clock Thursday night. There stood Viktor, holding a bottle of wine. Two small white butterfly bandages were plastered across a nasty-looking cut on his forehead.

I motioned him inside. "What happened to you?"

"Nothing. Just a pipe. Accident." He handed me the wine and shrugged off his coat. I didn't even try to pretend I wasn't inspecting him. I spied a bruise on his cheekbone, and the knuckles on his right hand were raw and scraped.

"Big pipe," I remarked.

He didn't take the bait. "Wine?"

"Sure." While Viktor opened the bottle with his pocketknife corkscrew, I took two juice glasses from the cabinet. "Sorry, these are all I have."

"It's fine." His voice was very soft. He poured me some wine.

"You give a generous pour, bartender." I took a sip. "This is good," I pronounced. "It just needs to come to room temperature."

"I have present for you," Viktor said. He produced a small black cylinder from his pocket. When I looked at him quizzically, he took a few long strides over to the boarded-up window and set it down carefully in the window-well. "Bluetooth speaker." He did something on his phone. Moments later, music began to drift through the room — some sleek electronica-pop song I'd never heard.

"Nice." I leaned back against the cinderblock wall and chanced a bonus look at Viktor. God, his eyes! I wanted to drown in them. "It's good to see you again."

He scratched the back of his neck. "I'm sorry, I am bad at texting." I watched his lips as he took a drink of wine. I wanted very much to kiss them.

"Viktor. I need to ask you a question."

"Okay." There was that blank look again: His face, even bruised and battered, was inscrutable.

"Are you in the Russian Mafia?"

He held my gaze. "Mafia is Italian."

"Okay, Professor. The Russian version of the mafia."

"Why do you ask this?"

Here we go. "Someone I know, here in the neighborhood. He warned me about a Russian criminal element. He said they own this building and they're" — I used air quotes — 'up to no good.'"

Viktor drained his glass of wine.

"I just need to know if you're part of it. Whatever it is," I said. Was the room getting warmer? I felt sweaty.

"Okay," Viktor sighed, "Let us talk about work." He took the bottle of wine and motioned for me to come sit with him. As usual, on the floor. What was it with Viktor and sitting on the goddamn floor? Whatever. I plopped myself down and held out my empty glass for a refill.

"Thanks for the music," I told him. "It's nice."

"You're welcome." He took a sip of wine. "Tell me about your job then."

I opened my mouth to object, then thought better of it. A little wine and conversation might loosen him up a little, make him more willing to discuss non-plumbing-related matters. Besides, Cynthia and her first-world problems made for good storytelling. I described the endless stream of personal trainers, Chinese herbalists, and interior decorators who paraded through her life. Her weekly mosaic of appointments: The Fung Shui expert, the

84

naturopath, the Math Coach who was so sought-after among the private-school-moms set that he interviewed prospective clients instead of the other way around.

"Today she tasked me with finding a Gluten Consultant to address her son's behavioral issues," I sighed.

Viktor chuckled. "Will it help him behave?"

"I have no idea. Probably not."

"Americans, you are ridiculous." He got up to use the bathroom.

"Hey, we're not all as grotesque as Cynthia," I called out loudly. I was feeling the effects of the wine, so I heaved myself up and filled both glasses with water at the kitchen sink. When Viktor came back, I pounced. "Your turn."

He lowered himself to the floor and leaned back against the wall, gazing at me steadily. "I work for guy named Roman." That prominent Adam's apple, there it was again. I tried not to stare at it.

"And what do you do for Roman?"

"Mostly, help with building maintenance." He indicated the apartment's four walls. "Tenants call, I come fix things. Take garbage from trash room. Check gas lines, boilers. Very glamorous." He took a sip of water.

"Anything else?"

"Sometimes, yes."

"Like what?"

He shook his head, but he was working to suppress a smile. *Aha!*

"Why do you ask?" he said. "If you believe that you already know the answer."

"To confirm that what I believe is true. Is this Roman guy a criminal?"

Viktor shrugged. "I have never asked him this question."

"Oh, come on. You know if he is or he isn't."

"What did your friend say? 'Up to no good'?"

"Yeah. He's not my friend," I added.

"He is partly correct. Some of the activities are legitimate, some...maybe not."

"Are you involved with any of the—" I paused, searching for a diplomatic way to phrase it. For some reason, the only word I could think of was *shenanigans,* and that sounded stupid.

"He is my boss," Viktor said before I could think of anything. "He tells me 'Do this,' I do it. Does not mean I always agree with him." He stretched out his long legs, which looked nice in the dark jeans he was wearing. "It's like you," he added, studying me. "Finding world famous gluten expert."

Ouch. Was he calling me a hypocrite? Well, he wasn't wrong. "Your face," I said. "Are those cuts and bruises from something illegal? Something Roman told you to do?"

Viktor touched the bandage on his forehead. "Why is this important?" he asked.

"Because it's incredibly dangerous, for one."

"It's not so dangerous." I shot him a you-must-think-I'm-an-idiot look. "Lane. Please understand. I have very boring life. Mostly I fix toilets. I am at bottom of heap."

Heap. There was a word I hadn't heard in a long time. "So why don't you get a different job?"

"Because it's difficult, with my history. This is — how do you say it? This is new start."

Well, that I could understand. And I was prepared to put aside — temporarily — my reservations about any new start that involved working for a Russian crime boss. But just then *Hey Jude* started playing, which is a drop-everything moment in my books.

"I love this song!" I piped up.

"It's good," Viktor agreed. He looked relieved. Probably because he was no longer being interrogated.

I got to my feet as gracefully as I could — not very gracefully, thanks to the wine — and held out one hand to him. "Dance with me?" He looked at me with disbelief. And didn't move from the floor. "Come on, I don't have all night." I wiggled my fingers.

He shook his head but stood up in one impossibly smooth motion. Then he took my hand, wrapping his other arm around me to pull me close. He still had that cigarette-leather-cologne scent — it couldn't be aftershave, I decided; he looked like he hadn't shaved in a couple of days. There wasn't really enough room to dance, but we swayed to the music as the cramped space allowed.

"Why do you love this song?" he murmured.

"Summer camp." I rested my cheek on his chest and closed my eyes. My left hand was on his shoulder. He felt so tall and solid. Strong.

"Summer camp." It sounded like he was forming those words on his lips for the first time. "Tell me, what happened at summer camp?"

I smiled into his shirt. "Oh, the usual stuff."

His fingers traced a trail on my back, sending the most delightful shivers up my spine. Maybe the wine had gone to my head and upended what was left of my good sense, but I felt carefree. Happy. And just like that, exactly that fast — the moment I recognized and named it — it slid away as quickly as it had come. The universe was laughing at me: *Nope! You don't get to have that anymore.*

I stopped swaying. My mind was a jumble of thoughts, pleasant and unpleasant, light and darkness. Why couldn't I enjoy a song without being plagued by the Grim Fucking Reaper?

"What." Viktor's voice was low, concerned. His thumb brushed my wet cheek. But I was a coward; I couldn't look at him. I turned away.

"I'm sorry," I whispered. I scrubbed at my tears with the back of one hand. I wanted none of it, this inconvenient freshly-surfaced grief, but I knew from experience that it couldn't just be willed away. So I turned to face Viktor, who looked appropriately worried and probably wanted nothing more to do with me. I wouldn't have blamed him. "I don't know why I'm so emotional all of a sudden," I lied, my voice wavering.

Viktor took a step towards me, and it took every ounce of self-control I had not to back away. "Stop this," he murmured, and he touched my lower lip with one finger. I realized I'd been biting it, hard.

"Sorry," I whispered again, and a sob hitched in my throat. I must look a sight. "You can go if you want," I added pointlessly, because who in their right mind would choose to stay? But Viktor stayed. He took my tear-stained mess of a face in his hands and brushed a stray lock of hair from my face. He waited there a moment while I managed to resume a normal breathing pattern to the 47th chorus of *na-na-na-na's*.

"Music," he finally said, "is the shorthand of emotion."

"...What?" Where the fuck did he come up with these things?

"It's Tolstoy." Of course it was. As usual, he made no sense.

"You're full of surprises, aren't you?" I asked, and in response he leaned down and kissed me, softly at first until my toes curled. Then I reached up and pulled him closer with greedy hands. His fingers moved up the back of my neck, then into my hair, and he pulled me even closer, nuzzling my ear before moving down one side of my neck — oh God, my Kryptonite! His lips, his tongue, his stubble, his breath, even the tip of his nose. My knees were going weak. *Yes.* I wanted more. *Needed* more.

The music cut out then, and an obnoxious marimba ringtone blared through the speaker. "Shit, sorry," Viktor whispered as he disentangled himself from me. He dug his phone out of his pocket, glanced down at the screen, and took the call. *"Privet."*

Great. More cloak-and-dagger Russian conversations that couldn't be eavesdropped on. I smoothed my disheveled hair and wondered how he managed to get a signal down here.

"Shas budu." Viktor shoved his phone back in his pocket. No more a chatterbox in Russian than in English. He took my hands in his. Those hands! The things they could do to me. *Should* do to me. I was still in a state where anything Viktor suggested would have seemed like a good plan, up to and including upside-down tantric sex.

"It's work. I must go." Viktor's hooded eyes ran down my body appreciatively before returning to my face. Why was it so sexy when he did it? Sergey had done the same thing and I'd nearly puked.

"Good night," I whispered. "Be careful."

To his credit, he kissed me one more time before he left.

I couldn't get Viktor out of my mind that night. No wonder,

since I went to bed moody and frustrated. It didn't help the following morning when I found another surprise bottle of Naked juice in my fridge. This one was carrot-based, and it tasted marginally better than the kale concoction. He must have sneaked it in when I was using the bathroom — crafty.

Jammed into the subway on my overlong commute, I allowed myself to imagine what might have happened if Viktor's phone hadn't rung. The thought alone was tantalizing. How could he be having this effect on me? It was like I'd been bewitched, and moreover I was loving every second of it.

He wasn't like anyone I'd dated before. None of the half-dozen men I'd slept with over the past few years had been particularly memorable. They'd been decent company when I was in the mood, and easy to forget about when I wasn't. They'd faded away quietly, each one in turn. I'd been disciplined about deleting them from my phone contacts.

At least I didn't sweep up any innocent bystanders in my tsunami of grief. I clung to that thought as I bounded up the subway steps to a frigid 77th Street sunrise. And to be fair, I thought, wrapping my newly-acquired knitted scarf around my neck and chin, none of them had seemed any more interested than I was in a meaningful or monogamous relationship. Now I was close to hooking up — was that the correct phrase? — with an ex-con Tolstoy-quoting Russian handyman. Telling him all my secrets. How could this possibly end well?

13

The kids' school drop-off went smoothly, but once I returned to Chez Waldrop my day turned confusing. I was having a great deal of difficulty determining whether Cynthia was in a remarkably good mood or headed towards full-blown mania. She swooped into the kitchen wearing a quilted silk kimono and a radiant smile.

"Guess what I'm planning?" she gushed, rather breathlessly for someone who'd just rolled out of bed.

"Ooh, what?" I put the last breakfast plate in the dishwasher and gave her my full attention.

"London! A family trip this spring!"

"Wow! What dates are you thinking?"

"April sixteenth to the twentieth. Brad says he can sneak away from work. We'll celebrate Mason's birthday!" She dropped her voice to a stage-whisper: "And do some shopping."

I grinned. It did sound fun, plus it was easy to summon enthusiasm imagining Cynthia a continent away. "Shall I look into flights and hotels for you guys? You have that nutritionist appointment at ten," I reminded her.

"Oh! I have to get ready." She twisted her engagement ring — a sizable rock — around her pinky. Her ring finger was currently "too fat," she'd told me. "Would you? Find some flights, hotels, transport?" I could hear the beginnings of a *faux* British accent in

Cynthia's speech. It seemed appropriate in some strange way.

"Of course."

She started to leave, then turned back with a hangdog expression: she wanted something.

"Come with me to the nutritionist?" Now she was using a high-pitched little-girl voice.

"Sure, I'll come." Dear God.

"Thanks! You can write down everything he says." Cynthia sailed upstairs to get dressed.

At least I didn't have to wipe her ass for her. Not yet.

Later that afternoon, I waited outside the Weatherly School holding a two-week menu printout from Hugh the nutritionist (he preferred the term "Food Coach.") He'd specified menus, preparation instructions, portion sizes, and to-the-minute feeding times that seemed more suited to an exotic zoo animal than a human being. "We're in this diet neck-deep," Cynthia had informed me, a little ominously.

Mason trotted down the school's front steps. "Hey, buddy!" I held my hand out for him to shake, which he did, reluctantly. "Your sister has field hockey practice," I told him. "We're going to the store."

"Oh gee willikers," he said as I clapped him on the shoulder and steered him down the sidewalk. He continued in a robotic voice: "What fun we shall have. I can't believe I get to go to the store. Lucky me." This kid cracked me up! Why wasn't he in the Drama Club or something? I made a mental note to ask Cynthia about changing up his extracurricular activities in a way that wouldn't challenge her maternal authority.

We strolled uptown, towards the Fairway on 86th Street, and I hazarded an attempt at conversation. "How's school?"

"Fine."

"I heard from your mom you're going to London for your birthday."

Mason grinned — the first real smile I'd seen from him since the confiscation of his Xbox. "Yeah."

"Any thoughts on stuff you'd like to do there?" I asked. He stared down at his shoes, which were both untied. "I'm doing some of the planning," I clarified. "I can make anything happen. Show tickets, tours, you name it."

"I don't know." He kept looking down at his feet as we walked. He was avoiding stepping on the cracks, which was difficult in some places where the pavement was crumbling. "I don't really know anything about England," he finally sighed. His shoulders drooped under the weight of his backpack.

"How about I find you some options, and we'll talk about it in a few days?"

"My dad," he said suddenly. "I want to do something in London with my dad."

"You got it."

The next few days were consumed by a flurry of cooking and portioning out food. Cynthia's new diet consisted mostly of poached skinless chicken breast, sweet potatoes, and steamed green vegetables, and everything had to be refrigerated in color-coded plastic boxes. Cynthia may not have needed a Personal Assistant for much apart from containing her emotional outbursts when she first hired me, but I wasn't lacking for things to do anymore.

As Wednesday wound down, Cynthia had a private Reiki session upstairs while I was tasked with purging her kitchen of forbidden foods. "I just know I'll have a moment of weakness overnight," she'd told me, and she'd given me *carte blanche* to deposit any potentially dangerous goodies into a heavy black trash bag.

"Should I throw these out?" I held up a half-full box of Mallomars for Mason and Emily, who were doing their homework at the kitchen counter.

"Mom's downfall," Emily replied. "She'll be looking for those in a few days."

I looked to Mason for confirmation; he nodded gravely. I pitched the cookies into the trash and tried not to think about

CLEAN BREAK

ramen noodles. What a fucking waste.

"I want to go to Harrods, in London," Emily announced. "And Harvey Nichols."

"Odds are, your wish will be granted, my dear." As I threw away an almost-empty bottle of chocolate syrup, my flip-phone chirped; I dug it out of my jeans pocket.

"You're still using that old thing?" Emily was incredulous. "I thought my mom gave you an iPhone!"

"She very generously gave me the *use* of an iPhone, for work. I continue to use this ancient relic" — I gave Emily a pointed look — "for personal matters." I opened the phone to see who the text was from. Viktor.

Off work soon?

In half an hour, I texted back.

"Is that a text from your boyfriend?" Emily had a devilish grin on her face.

"Don't be ridiculous." I pulled open the pantry shelves in search of more contraband. "Flax-seed chips. These look dangerous and they probably don't even taste good."

"What's his name?" Emily demanded.

I chose to ignore her. Then, inconveniently, my phone chirped again.

"Well?" Emily smirked. "Aren't you gonna look?"

"Don't you have homework to do?" I opened the phone. Viktor again:

Text me your location. I will pick you up.

"Ooooh, what's it say?" Emily jumped down from her stool and walked over. "Come on, what's it say?"

I took a step away from her. "Don't be cheeky, Emily. That's British for rude."

"I know." She leaned over. Then, softly: "What's it say?"

"Emily!" Mason stabbed his pencil into the pages of his spiral notebook so hard the point snapped off. "I can't concentrate on my homework when you're blabbering about boys all the time!"

"Calm your tits, you little crying baby." Emily hoisted herself back onto the stool and looked levelly at me.

"Emily, that was inappropriate," I snapped. "You may go to

93

your room."

"Whatever." She flounced off. Mason took his leave as well, slouching away in the opposite direction. Clearly I was reaching Expert Level in this whole "taking care of the kids" enterprise.

"Okay. Where were we?" Now I was talking to myself in the empty kitchen. "Flax chips." I threw them in the trash and picked up a bag of miniature marshmallows. Then I remembered Viktor's text. Why would he want to pick me up here? The thought of Viktor-in-Manhattan was intriguing; I'd always considered him a permanent Brighton Beach fixture, which I now realized was silly. I texted him Cynthia's street address. Then I dragged myself upstairs to do my damn job.

The music blasting in Emily's room was loud enough to render my repeated knocks on her door inaudible, so I let myself in. Emily was lying on her bed, slumped into a pile of decorative pillows, texting furiously on her phone. She gave me a passing glance, then reflexively rolled her eyes. "What."

I turned the music down on her Sonos speaker and pulled a haphazard pile of sweaters off her desk chair. They felt impossibly soft. Cashmere, probably. The closet was a holy overstuffed mess, so I set the sweaters down atop a wicker laundry basket. "I wanted to talk to you. Mind if I sit down?"

She shrugged without looking away from her phone, so I sat on the hard plastic swivel-chair.

"Emily, please put your phone down." This earned me another, even-more-pronounced eye roll, but she tossed the phone onto her bedside table and crossed her arms in a huff.

"What just happened in the kitchen?" I asked. Emily was stone-faced. "With Mason," I added. "I think your words hurt him more than you might realize."

Emily heaved a great sigh. "It's not my fault he's a freak."

"What do you mean?"

She shook her head. I waited.

"It's just—" Her phone chimed; her eyes darted towards it, then back at me.

"Give the phone a rest. Finish your thought."

She grunted in annoyance. "It's like I said. He's a freak. At school he's like a total embarrassment."

"All right. Can you give me an example?"

She studied her glitter-polished fingernails. "Like, he's always getting into fights with boys in his grade. And sometimes the older boys too. He doesn't have any friends. He eats lunch at a table by himself. Every day!" She gnawed on a cuticle. "He's, like, abnormal." Her phone chimed again and she shot a desperate look in its direction.

"Okay." I was trying to process this new information; it felt like uncharted territory, even though it didn't really surprise me. I plumbed the ether for some wise Mary Poppins advice, but nothing sprang immediately to mind.

"Is that it?" Emily didn't even try to hide her annoyance.

"...I think so. Just — Emily." I forced myself to make, and hold, eye contact with her. "Try to be kind to your brother. I know it's hard sometimes. But honestly," I floundered on, "If what you're saying is true, then he really needs your support right now. He needs you as an ally."

Emily's phone chimed again, and again, and again.

"Will you try to do that?" I asked. "Be an ally to your brother?" The phone chimed twice more while I was finishing my sentence.

"Fine," she groaned. "Can I please check my phone now?"

After that it was a mad dash through Chez Waldrop to track Mason down, make sure he was okay, and say goodbye for the evening. I found him curled up on a leather couch in the darkened TV room, playing Minecraft on his laptop, more or less oblivious to my comings and goings.

Outside it was dark, and Viktor was nowhere in sight. My hand automatically went for my phone to check for texts, but then I heard a car door slam and looked up to see Viktor walking around the front of a double-parked car. He looked happy to see me. Also unshaven.

"Nice car," I said. And it was. A late-model BMW, black,

polished to a high shine. It gleamed under the streetlights.

He leaned down and kissed me on the cheek. "Hi."

"Hi." I felt thrilled and totally thrown off-center by that kiss. So casual — like a boyfriend. And his stubble brushed my cheek for the briefest moment, which made my head spin.

Oblivious to my internal flailing, Viktor proceeded to open the car's passenger-side door for me. So gallant. I slid into the leather bucket-seat with a little sigh of pleasure — he'd turned the seat-heat on! He settled in and started the engine, then looked over at me. *"Pristegnis."* He had a devastatingly handsome smirk on his face and I was losing what was left of my mind. "That is Russian for 'fasten your seat belt.'"

I buckled up. "Where are we going?"

"New Jersey." He pulled out into traffic. "For dinner. That is all I will say. The rest is surprise."

A surprise. Pray I wasn't under-dressed. I settled in and watched Viktor drive. He was good at navigating the city traffic. Fearless. You had to be, to drive here, even in an old junker. Driving a fancy car like this through city traffic took balls of steel.

I glanced at the center console screen, which showed the song playing on the car stereo — some kind of modern electronic alt-rock, totally unfamiliar to me. Were Viktor's musical tastes eclectic, or was I just hopelessly behind the times when it came to music? I couldn't remember the last time I'd listened to the radio, and my iTunes collection had fallen off my list of possessions somewhere along the line. Maybe it was still out there, somewhere in The Cloud, protected behind long-ago-abandoned usernames and passwords.

"Is this your car?" I asked.

"No." He checked his blind spot. "Boss's car."

"You're brave, driving it in this traffic." As if on cue, a yellow taxi cut us off.

"Less scary than subway." Viktor pulled around the offending cab and we sailed through a yellow light.

"So you're not gonna tell me where we're going? Beyond this mysterious New Jersey business, which sounds pretty horrifying, by the way."

Viktor shook his head. His face was dimly lit by the dashboard and the occasional streetlight. It had a different quality here than I was used to seeing, angular and unshaven and undeniably sexy. Neon signs and people and buildings flashed by behind him. He looked alive, determined. Also amused, maybe, at my ramblings. I could hope.

"Not even one little clue?" I begged, studying his face in profile. The right side of his face was beautiful, unscathed. What was the story with that scar?

He gave me a mock-stern glance before turning his attention back to the road. "You must learn patience, Lane." Little crinkles formed in the corner of his eye when he smiled. Honest confession: I could have sat there and stared at his profile for hours.

Miraculously, traffic wasn't terrible. Viktor drove us crosstown through a Central Park transverse and then up the West Side Highway. Before long we were on the upper deck of the George Washington Bridge. "It's beautiful," I murmured, admiring the lit-up cables and towers. The Hudson River drifted below, inky-black in contrast with all the glittering electric lights.

"I agree." Viktor sounded relaxed. I loved the sound of his voice — deep, baritone. Like black velvet.

"You like driving, don't you?"

He cocked his head to one side. "Never thought of it."

"Well, I can tell you're enjoying yourself."

"I think I am enjoying company." He shot me a goofy grin. I hoped the car was dark enough to hide my suddenly-flushed face. I felt like a teenager and made a mental note to ask Emily for tips on how to talk to cute boys.

"I must make quick stop before dinner," Viktor said as we circled down the exit-ramp. "It will be quick," he repeated as he swung the car into a deserted industrial park and pulled to a stop next to a small building. A rusted sign was leaning against one wall: Palisades Towing and Auto Body.

"I will lock car," he said. He caught my eye, so I nodded my acknowledgment. "Two minutes." The car chirped as he locked it with the key fob. Then he disappeared into the building.

Well, this was sketchy. I looked around at an overflowing dumpster and some scraggly bushes. Would Viktor emerge in a hail of gunfire? I drummed my fingers on the center armrest and tried not to think about Detective Jarrett's advice. Seconds ticked by. Then the door locks sprung open. Thank God it was Viktor, shoving something into his inside coat pocket and sliding smoothly into the driver's seat.

He started the car. "Ready for dinner?"

"Yeah." I was glad to leave the creepy parking lot behind us. "What was that about?"

"Work."

14

We pulled into the parking lot of something called Mitsuwa Marketplace — a low, boxy building. Viktor walked around and opened my door. Parting with the seat-heat was such sweet sorrow. "Where are we?" I asked him.

"I told you, surprise." He took my hand and we walked towards Mitsuwa in the chilly night air. I was beginning to suspect it was a supermarket. At least I didn't have to worry about being under-dressed. Inside, everything was Asian. Even the produce, stacked in neat rows, featured exotic fruits and vegetables: lychee nuts, bok choy, ginger root. But unlike the cramped Asian markets I'd visited occasionally in New York, this place was huge. Modern. Spotless.

Viktor walked me towards the rear of the store, past stands selling sushi and soft-serve ice cream, and stopped in front of a crowded stand. "Here," he said, and he gave my hand a squeeze.

I looked up at the sign. "Santouka?"

He looked down sideways at me. "Ramen noodles. Real ones."

I had to laugh. "You brought me all the way to New Jersey to eat ramen noodles?"

"Yesss," he drawled, dragging out the syllable, trying for an American-style accent. He was adorable. "Do you trust me to choose?" He jerked his chin towards a display case with plastic models of noodle bowls.

"Sure." Might as well trust him on this too. I was neck-deep already. That's definitely how it felt.

Ten minutes later, we were seated at a blond wood table in the bright central seating area, drinking Japanese beer and waiting for the two steaming bowls to cool. Apart from the name, this ramen bore little resemblance to what I'd been living on for the past several weeks. "Um. This is insanely good," I admitted. "Still too hot to eat."

Viktor picked up a pink-and-white-swirled wafer from his tray, broke it into a few pieces, and added them to his bowl.

"What is that?" I asked. "It's so pretty."

"*Naruto*. It's good."

I picked up my own pink-and-white wafer and sniffed it, then took an experimental nibble. I wasn't about to admit that I'd thought it was a cookie. It tasted salty. I dropped it into the soup and swirled it around with my chopsticks. "You seem to know a lot about Japanese food," I said.

"A little," he replied. "I come here when I am in neighborhood."

"I'll have to re-form my opinion of New Jersey based on this store." I took a small bite of the soft-cooked egg floating on top of the soup. Absolute heaven!

Viktor just smiled at me and started eating. He was wearing a dark gray button-down shirt with the sleeves rolled up almost to his elbows. I spied tattoos on both forearms. *Hot.*

"You know, your English is really improving," I ventured. "I'd love to take credit, but I've done absolutely nothing since our first lesson."

"Not true." He leaned back in his chair, all loose and lanky-limbed. "You talk, it sounds nice. Like music."

"If you say so." I smiled at him over my chopsticks.

"I say so." If Viktor was trying to seduce me over dinner at a food court, it was totally working. I felt self-conscious at the extent of my goggly-eyed adoration, but I couldn't tear my gaze away as he ate. He still seemed too thin; his face was severe, all planes and angles. Yet something about the whole package — his height, the mop of black hair that refused to behave, those clear blue eyes — it all worked together. He even looked good chewing. How many people can lay claim to that?

"I had to cook five chicken breasts and four sweet potatoes today," I remarked, mostly to wrench my mind away from lustful thoughts about the man sitting across the table. "Cynthia's on this strict new diet."

Viktor wiped his mouth with a napkin and regarded me appraisingly. "You like your job?"

"Not really," I admitted. "Well, sometimes. I'm planning this fabulous family trip to London. But a lot of it is just wearying." I took a bite of roast pork, which was eyes-rolling-back-in-my-head delicious. "I always feel like Cynthia might go crazy at any second. That's a concern. She's not exactly stable."

"And her children?" Viktor asked. I'd briefly mentioned my nanny duties to him the other night while telling him Cynthia-stories.

"The kids, they're...something." I wasn't sure how I felt about them. Sure, they were annoying at times, and I worried about Mason. But I also felt protective of him, and I resented his parents' near-complete abdication of his day-to-day care. He deserved better, surely. As would any child.

"You care for them," Viktor murmured, jarring me out of my thoughts. He was studying my face with his usual serene stare.

"Yeah. Not the smartest move, huh? They're basically raising themselves, plus they have me." I finished my beer and wondered why a red flag had just gone up in my head. Was it Viktor's sudden interest in the Waldrop children? *He knows where you work now,* my better judgment warned. *Could be a kidnapper.*

Jesus. The serial-killer career was a bust, so now he's branching out. "Why are you asking about the kids?"

"No reason." Viktor glanced at his phone. "I must go back. Work."

"You work late hours." Just call me Captain Obvious.

"Yes." He stood up and offered me his hand. "First, one more surprise."

* * * *

The surprise was a cream-filled *yaki* cake, possibly even better than the ramen that preceded it. Viktor and I each devoured one on the way home to Brooklyn.

"God, that was amazing." I licked a drop of custard off my thumb.

"We will keep it secret from your boss," Viktor deadpanned as we merged onto Ocean Parkway.

"Don't remind me. There's a storm coming." I yawned and felt a deep desperation to think about anything else besides having to get up early for work tomorrow. We passed a slowpoke Toyota, then returned to the center lane. "Do you think," I mused aloud, "That there's a middle ground? Between living and dying?" That thought had been knocking around in my head lately and I wanted a second opinion.

Viktor seemed to consider it and I was treated to another dashboard-lit view of his profile. "Interesting question," he finally said. A cop-out fit for a shrink. Just add 'What do *you* think?' for full therapeutic value. "Existing," he finally murmured, and he glanced briefly at me before turning his gaze back to the road.

"Good answer." At least it rang true. I'd occupied that particular center lane myself for some time now. I'd only recently opened myself up to the possibility of merging back. He wasn't a kidnapper, he was a Russian philosopher.

"Door to door service," Viktor announced as he turned onto West End Avenue. We stopped in front of my building.

"You'll spoil me," I warned when he walked me to my building's front door.

"I am gentleman." He opened the lobby door and motioned me inside.

At my apartment door, I turned to face him. "Thank you, Viktor, for dinner. For everything." I reached around and hugged him tighter than I'd intended to.

He hugged me back. Tight. "You're welcome," he whispered. I let go reluctantly. "This is for you." He produced a small USB thumb-drive from his coat pocket and handed it to me.

"What's on it?"

He leaned down and kissed me gently, letting his gaze linger a moment, a smile playing on his lips. "Find out."

Okay, so the USB thumb-drive would be my undoing. I was desperate to know its contents, I had nothing to plug it into, and I was alone with Cynthia's MacBook most days at work. But Cynthia was on a protein-fueled productivity rampage and had me running around all day Thursday doing errands. Which was fortunate because it gave me time to reflect on what a terrible idea it would have been to look at unknown files on her laptop. What if it was porn? Or a virus, or something else I didn't even know about?

But! It could also be a digital love letter. As unlikely as that seemed, I couldn't evict the thought from my head, and by mid-afternoon I was annoyed with myself for getting so moony-eyed over a guy and his crumbs of attention. I texted Randy:

Can I drop by later?

She texted right back:

Anytime after 6 babe. I'm at home.

A little after seven, I exited the downtown 6 train at 23rd Street and stuffed Cynthia's phone into my bag. Currently onscreen were Google search results for *connect USB drive directly to an iPhone.* Apparently this was possible with a degree in electrical engineering and a bunch of equipment, but it wasn't going to be happening for me anytime soon.

I headed east towards Randy's walk-up and pondered my next step. Maybe I could try Randy's laptop. The public library had a branch in Brighton Beach, and that was a place to start if I couldn't think of anything else. Just as I was about to press the buzzer, Randy came tiptoeing down the stairs, bundled up in an extraordinarily puffy down coat I'd never seen before.

"Hey, Michelin Man," I called softly.

She put one finger to her lips and beckoned me to follow her out onto the sidewalk. "Mom's having a moment," she muttered once we were outside.

I stopped walking. "Is now a bad time?" I suddenly felt petty and small, obsessing over thumb-drives when Randy's mother was so ill.

"Don't be silly. I need a break."

"Are you sure?" I looked back towards her building.

"Lane, come *on*, it's freezing," she hissed. "My neighbor came by to sit with her and watch *Jeopardy*. She'll be fine."

We found refuge from the cold in a Greek diner on First Avenue. I sat down and rubbed my hands together to warm them up while Randy extricated herself from the jacket.

"First things first." I dug a fifty dollar bill from my bag and handed it over.

Randy accepted it and scanned the laminated menu. "Work good?"

"As good as can be expected." I pushed my menu to one side. "How's business?"

"Pfft. Boring, who cares." She glanced at me. "What's on your mind? You seem downright antsy."

I wondered where the hell to even begin. The waiter appeared and I ordered coffee. Randy got tea and a toasted bagel.

"Well?" She leaned forward. "Don't leave me hanging."

"It's...kind of hard to explain." I tried to think of a way to describe my romantic entanglement that didn't sound pathetic.

"Is it a guy?" She peered at me over the top of her water glass. I tried to keep a poker-face, but I felt my mouth twitch involuntarily and then Randy nearly choked. "Oh my God! Lane, tell!"

"It's nothing," I insisted. "In fact, I feel silly for being all moony-eyed over him." But the story of Viktor spilled out. Abridged version: I omitted the part about him being an ex-con, choosing instead to focus on his smoking-hot body — what I'd seen of it, anyway — and his tendency to bestow me with small yet thoughtful gifts.

"He sounds sweet," Randy said. "And Russian. I do love a man with a sexy accent."

"I have to say, his is pretty thick." I couldn't keep the smirk off my face.

"Lane! Awful." She threw a crumpled napkin at me. "Do you have a picture?"

"No. That's strange, isn't it?" I sipped my coffee and felt guilty about telling Randy a whitewashed version of events, especially since I knew I could trust her. Some small but important part of me felt broken in this regard.

She drummed her fingers on the table. "It could be a good sign if he's not taking selfies all the live-long day. A couple of weeks ago I matched up with a guy on Tinder. Super cute. We got coffee, I had high hopes for a minute, and then he sent me a picture of his dick."

"Unsolicited, I take it?" I asked, and Randy rolled her eyes. "I hope it was a Congressman."

"Anyway. Your guy sounds swell." She gave me a fist-bump. "Keep me posted."

"Scout's honor."

Well, at least she approved of Viktor's better attributes. And focusing on the positive, for once in my life, was a refreshing change of pace. But I felt like I'd told Randy a lie of omission, and I couldn't quite shake the feeling of disappointment in myself on the subway ride home.

15

The next day I set two goals for myself: Focus on work and stop obsessing over the stupid thumb-drive. Cynthia was already headed for the gym by the time I returned from morning school drop-off, but she'd left me a note approving the London itinerary.

I bought the plane tickets, then booked an "executive" Mercedes to meet the Waldrops at the airport and whisk them off to their suite at the Mandarin Oriental Hyde Park. Satisfied with my progress, I glanced at my dwindling To-Do list, which included Mason/Dad activities. Shit. I'd asked Cynthia about Brad's London availability twice, and she'd put me off. I resolved to get his email address so I could initiate a direct discussion about London. I was preparing to tackle dinner reservations when a text came in from Cynthia:

Can u bring my lunch 2 the gym? AM STARVING 2 DEATH!!!

Sure, I texted back.

And a protein bar, she texted.

I cringed — Cynthia's favorite protein bars were not on her extremely depressing list of "legal" between-meal snacks. But she was with her trainer! Was Fabrizio putting her through a killer Arnold Schwarzenegger-level workout? And was it even my place to enforce her dietary restrictions? I hoped not, and took one last longing glance at the USB port before heading downstairs.

* * * *

As it turned out, I didn't need to ask Cynthia for Brad's email address. When I returned from my lunch-delivery errand, there was an email from Brad in my inbox.

Subject: Birthday.

Message:

Get Cynthia a Birkin Bag for her birthday.

Regards,

H. Bradley Waldrop, CFA.

No "Please." No "Thank you." No "Hi Lane." Not even a cursory "I know we haven't had a chance to meet properly, but I wanted to express my profound gratitude for your efforts to help my son through his struggle with major depression."

"Fuck," I muttered to the empty room.

At least I had a day off coming. And great merciful heavens, the Brighton Beach library had computers for public use! I sat down, pushed the USB drive into the slot, and waited. Then the window popped up. It was a long, scrolling list of MP3 files.

"It's a playlist!" I squeaked, then clamped one hand over my mouth in mortification when I realized I'd said it out loud. A mustachioed old man in a tweed hat shot me a stern look.

I took out my old smartphone with the cracked screen. Today I was carting around three phones, in case my sanity was ever in question. All I had to do was copy the files onto the broken phone, pay my rent, and do my laundry. Then I'd be done with reality for a while. I couldn't help lingering at the library, though. I spent some time prowling through the biographies, but ended up checking out the first *Harry Potter* book. I'd only read it a hundred times.

I made the briefest of pit-stops at my apartment, then hoofed it to Brighton Realty Management in the cold, leaving my basket of dirty clothes in the hallway outside lest Mrs. Pasternak find it objectionable. As it was, she looked none too thrilled to see me when I entered her smoky domain.

"Good afternoon," I greeted her, bracing myself against the

wall of odor emanating from her smoke-infused upholstery. "I'm here to pay my rent."

"Huh." She was wearing her usual sweater set and sour expression.

"I'd like an invoice and a receipt, please," I said, taking out the money I'd squirreled away all month long.

She eyed my wad of cash, then swung her gaze back to meet mine. "So Viktor's not paying your rent anymore."

I deliberately ignored this statement. She yanked open a desk-drawer and fished out a paper form, then began filling it out with a ballpoint pen. It was one of those old-fashioned triplicate things, with a white original and two copies — one pink, one yellow. "I don't understand what you girls think you're getting with that one," she muttered. *Girls?* "He's a *zek.*"

I stayed silent while she clacked something into her computer. Then she took a rubber stamp from the side of her desk blotter and pounded it down on an ink-pad. Once on the white copy: *Thunk!* Again on the pink sheet: *Clunk!* And one final smackdown on the yellow sheet, which she tore off and handed to me while avoiding eye-contact.

"Invoice is on printer," she grunted, motioning towards a copier/printer/fax combo-unit sitting on a wheeled cart by the door.

"Thank you so much."

"You're welcome. *Suka blyats.*"

Suka blyats. Had I heard that one before? It was worth asking Viktor about, I mused on the way home from the laundromat in the freezing spit-rain, although I could guess roughly what it meant. More importantly, what on Earth was a *zek?* And who were these unfortunate girls — emphasis on plural — that Mrs. Pasternak had alluded to?

Whatever. I allowed myself to feel some small measure of pride at having paid my rent with money I'd earned myself. That was a first, for me, and it deserved to be celebrated. With Viktor. By the time he came over, I was already on the road to tipsy-ville.

"Spaghetti with marinara sauce," I announced, rather grandly for a meal consisting of three shelf-stable ingredients from the Dollar Store plus a box of "red Italian table wine" that I'd already cracked open.

"Smells good." Viktor was wearing a dark blue crewneck sweater and inky-black jeans. His hair was wet from the freezing rain and I noticed that he'd shaved for the occasion.

"This is a celebration." I filled a juice-glass with wine, then handed it to him along with a $50 bill — another payment on my debt. I'd texted him the news that I'd paid the next month's rent; that had been too big not to share.

"It's not necessary. But thank you." His icy-blue eyes twinkled as he touched his glass to mine and took a drink.

I divided the pasta into two bowls and stirred the sauce in the pot on the stove. "May I offer you some fake Parmesan cheese from a can on your spaghetti, sir?"

"No. Thank you." Viktor picked up the speaker, which was playing the music he'd given me. Once I'd listened to the first few songs on Shuffle, I'd realized it was the same playlist he'd had going in the car. Lots of ghostly synthesizer-infused alt-rock interspersed with some older stuff, mostly British. Including *Hey Jude,* naturally.

"You broke big boss lady's phone?" Viktor's deep voice interrupted my inner monologue. The look on his face was somewhere between alarmed and amused. Like everything else about him, I found it very attractive.

"That's my old phone. Cynthia wouldn't be caught dead with an Android." I finished stirring the sauce and moved towards him. *Courage.* He reached out with both hands and pulled me close, then looked down and locked his eyes onto mine, whereupon I practically melted into a puddle of goo.

"What you need," he murmured, "is more phones."

I privately admired his lips. On the thin side, but very talented. Then I remembered Mrs. Pasternak's *coup de grâce.*

"Hey Viktor. What does *suka blyats* mean?"

"Bozhe moy." He turned me around and steered me towards the pasta bowls. "First let's eat."

* * * *

"Where did you hear this — *suka blyats?*" Viktor seemed wholly absorbed in his meal, staring at his fork as he twirled strands around the tines inexpertly. We were sitting on the floor, as usual.

"At the landlord's," I replied, taking a bite. "Mrs. Pasternak's really warming up to me. We're gonna be best friends soon. I think we'll go to Ladies' Night at Tatiana's and get smashed on vodka shots together."

Viktor didn't raise his head, but his eyes came up to meet mine. He finished chewing and swallowed, then took a drink of wine and cleared his throat. "What she said to you... it is not polite."

I knew it. "What's the translation?"

He shook his head, holding one hand over his mouth, curled into a fist. "I can't say it! It's bad." For a second he looked almost boyish.

"I can take it. I swear. I guarantee you I've been called worse in English."

"I will think about it." Viktor took another drink of wine, never taking his eyes off me.

"Okay," I sighed. "I'll ask Yulia down at the bakery next time I'm there." Yulia was about a hundred and fifty years old.

He smirked. "Watch out, you may get punched in face."

"Next question. What's a *zek?*"

Now his brow furrowed in confusion. "Pasternak said this to you?"

"Yes, but I believe she was referring to you." I took a bite of spaghetti. This fake Parmesan-in-a-can was hitting the spot.

"This I can tell you." He wiped his mouth with a paper napkin. "*Zek* means a prison inmate, in Russian. Convict."

"So she doesn't like you either."

Viktor acknowledged me with a tilt of his head, but he didn't comment.

"What, aren't you annoyed that she's talking shit about you?" I felt semi-outraged on his behalf.

"She is not wrong." His tone was light, but there was an intensity in his eyes that hadn't been there a moment ago.

"Why were you in prison?" Oops, I just went there. This was the wine talking, I was certain. Viktor gave me a surprised look. "I'm sorry, that was a rude question," I whispered.

"Not rude. Unexpected." The song ended and a new one began during the silence that followed. "I stole something," he finally said.

"Oh." Not the best news ever, but I felt relieved that it wasn't something worse. The music played on. Haunted electronica. I couldn't quite make out the lyrics.

"Music was something we did not have in prison," he said, studying me. "And books. It's nice in here with some music."

"You made me a playlist." I kept to myself the part about this being the most romantic thing anyone had ever done for me. "Thank you. It's lovely."

He nodded and wolfed down another bite of spaghetti. I felt certain he was wholly unaware that his cheekbones were perfect. "Damn. You were hungry," I remarked, and he nodded — still chewing. He was so cute. "So what did you do for six years if you didn't have books or music? Crossword puzzles?" I stretched my legs out so they wouldn't fall asleep and took a gulp of wine. *You're drinking too much,* my better judgment warned. I ignored it.

"Work." He pressed his napkin to his mouth. "Most of that time I was at labor camp."

"What kind of work?" I was being pushy, but I didn't care. My curiosity was piqued.

"Cutting trees, mostly."

Whoa. "They let you have an axe? In prison?"

He took another bite. His eyes had that faraway look again. *Stop interrogating the man, for God's sake.* But then he met my gaze.

"For work, yes. We also used saws. And..." He looked up at the ceiling. *Kuvalda.* Don't know English word."

"Well, they must have thought you were trustworthy." I reached for my wine on auto-pilot, but forced myself to sip it a little more slowly. Viktor looked at me with faint amusement and didn't say anything. I felt that creeping curiosity return. What had he stolen? And why?

So ask. I was trying to think of a delicate way to route the conversation backwards when he set his fork down. "So much gluten." He patted his stomach through his sweater as though it had swelled into a grotesque potbelly, even though it looked flat as always. "I think it's possible we will behave very badly tonight."

"That's the general idea." Oh hey, the wine was talking again! I hoped I wasn't blushing too much and set about clearing away the dishes. Standing at the sink, I felt a pang of doubt. How well did I even know this guy? Sure, he was handsome — but everything I knew about him reeked of danger. And that was just what he'd told me — what about everything I didn't know?

Girls. Why was that bothering me so much? Why should promiscuity matter more than, say, a six-year stint in a Russian prison?

I turned around to see Viktor standing a few feet away, his face half in shadow. I hadn't even heard him move.

"Hey," I said, and I hugged my arms around my middle.

He took a step towards me, and I felt myself flinch. "You okay?" he murmured, looking down at me.

"No, not exactly." I swallowed, too aware of his proximity. "Suddenly I feel like I hardly know you at all."

He leaned against the wall and glanced down at the floor. I took a deep breath. Now or never. "Do you date a lot of girls?"

"Counting you?" he asked me, and I nodded. "One."

"But Mrs. Pasternak said—"

"Mrs. Pasternak is *spletnitsa.* I don't know it in English." He took out his phone and typed something in. "Busy-body?" he read aloud, and I nodded again. "So why do you believe her?" he asked me. "She calls you *suka blyats.* I know it's not true."

"You still haven't translated that," I reminded him.

"You're right." He swayed himself upright and closed the remaining distance between us in one smooth motion. I didn't flinch when he took both my hands in his. His palms felt warm. "The other night," he said in a low voice. "When my phone rang."

"Yes?" My heart was hammering away in my chest.

He drew me a bit closer, then lowered his head so his mouth was by my ear. "I could not stop thinking about you after."

"Really?" Okay, that came out way shriller than I'd intended.

"Really." He brought his head back and I was sure he'd kiss me, but he just held my gaze. A smile played at the corners of his mouth. "You find this hard to believe?"

"No. I don't know," I confessed.

His hands found my waist and gently drew me in closer. "You must know what you do to me, Lane." He leaned close to my ear again. "Keep me awake at night." His breath was hot. He nuzzled at my neck and I could feel the dam crumbling. "Always teasing, hot and cold."

"That's...accurate," I mumbled. "I'm sorry if I—"

"No. Don't be sorry." He cupped my face in his hands. "If you're afraid of me, it's no good." His fingers felt warm and gentle on my skin, and I turned my head to kiss them.

"You're right," I admitted. "I *am* afraid. I don't know what I want."

"I know what I want." His eyes locked onto mine and I felt a jolt of desire between my legs. *Fuck yes. I want it too. Why can't I go for it?*

"What if..." I was finding it hard to form a coherent thought. The physical sensations were overwhelming and we weren't even doing anything naughty yet. "What if I want to stop?"

"Then you tell me stop." His thumbs brushed behind my ears.

"You'll stop if I tell you?" My heart was pounding again.

"I will. I promise."

And I believed him.

I wasn't the least bit surprised that Viktor knew exactly what he was doing. Or that he was fine with going slowly. In fact, he seemed to enjoy every second of our evening on the futon, even those interstitial bits that previous partners had blown through at top speed.

"What is this?" he asked, running his lips and fingers over the curve of my hip.

"What?" I craned my neck. I couldn't see anything.

"*Murashki.*" He kissed the quivering skin on my waist and

smiled down at it. And then I understood.

"Gooseflesh," I told him. "Or goose bumps." Then he gave me a wicked grin and nibbled at me until I shrieked for mercy.

"Not fair," I gasped, pulling my shirt back down over my midriff protectively.

"Yes, fair," he murmured into my neck. "You said stop. I stopped."

True — Viktor was a man of his word. I wouldn't have objected to a mad dash to copulation with ripped-off clothes flung to all four corners of the room, but he seemed more interested in a mutual seduction by micro-degrees. I'd never been with a man who worshiped every inch of me like Viktor did, homing in on pleasure centers I wasn't even aware of and taking his sweet time there.

Those magic fingers! They were everywhere, slowly driving me mad. I pressed up against him appreciatively. Then he pulled off my shirt and kissed the sensitive skin on my neck until I groaned and reached for his belt buckle. "Not yet," he whispered, so I settled for pulling his sweater up over his head. His physique: hot damn! It was even better than I'd imagined — lean and muscular, with bluish-black tattoos on his chest and back as well as both arms. I didn't even try to pretend I wasn't staring at them.

"Want a picture?" he murmured. He tossed his balled-up sweater on the floor and held both arms out with a smirk.

I swallowed. "I hope I'm not making you feel self-conscious. You look amazing."

He dropped his arms and hovered over me, his eyes traveling from my cleavage up to my face. "So do you."

I touched his shoulder. "Someday I'm gonna want to know what they all mean."

He answered by unhooking my bra and moving his hand up under my breast while he nibbled and nipped at my neck. I felt myself surrender another inch and closed my eyes. I could hear the wind whipping rain up against the plywood blocking the window.

"Do you have protection?" I finally whispered when I could take no more.

"Yes." He tugged my underpants off and I didn't try to stop him. "But first you."

Viktor stayed most of the night, taking his leave in the predawn darkness.

"Too early," I objected sleepily. "Where are you going?"

"Rego Park," he whispered, and he pulled his sweater down over his head. He leaned down and kissed me. "It's just work. Go back to sleep."

It was still raining and windy outside, judging from the *pitter-pat* noises coming in waves on the plywood. The futon mattress was still warm where Viktor had slept. I rolled over onto my side and tried not to think about what "work" might involve. Handyman duties, or fisticuffs? Drudgery or malfeasance? The deadbolt clicked softly as he locked it from the outside hallway. I closed my eyes but I could not go back to sleep.

16

I replayed that night of passion in my head about a thousand different ways on Sunday. A text from Viktor came in before noon:

Hey.you sleep late?

I smiled: he was thinking of me too. *Whenever possible,* I texted back, and then I promptly took a nap. It was too cold and rainy to leave the apartment anyway.

Monday morning was the usual slap in the face from reality. A text from Cynthia arrived as I emerged from the 77th street subway station:

PLZ BRING ME A SHOT OF WHEAT GRASS JUICE!

Well, this was new. No doubt a recommendation from Hugh — the nonstop chicken breasts and raw kale smoothies had to be getting as tedious for Cynthia as they were for me. I detoured into a health food store on Lexington Avenue.

Cynthia met me at the front door of her townhouse, dressed for the gym. She grabbed the tiny paper cup of juice and gulped it down. "Antioxidants," she said breathlessly. "My body craves them now."

"I hate to ambush you first thing in the morning," I ventured as I hung up my coat. "I wanted to ask you about Mason and getting him into some extracurricular activities at school."

Cynthia cocked her head at me. "Mason's on probation. The Headmaster thinks he needs fewer extracurriculars, not more of them."

"Oh." It sounded so final.

"Mason knows what behaviors are expected of him at school," Cynthia quipped, checking her left eyebrow in the hallway mirror. "Right now he's not anywhere close to living up to those expectations."

"Yeah, I was hoping I could talk with you about that."

Cynthia was still peering into the mirror, now with a renewed focus on her upper lip. "Can you book me an appointment with Radhika?"

"Sure." Radhika was a waxing specialist at the day spa Cynthia frequented, very in-demand.

"Thanks." She air-kissed me and sailed out the door.

I dropped the kids off at school and used the walk home to compose an email to Brad in my head. I was loath to do anything that might be construed as a challenge to Cynthia and Brad's authority in the parenting department, but my desperation to see Mason happy trumped everything else at the moment. By the time I got back to an empty Chez Waldrop, I was ready to type it up.

Subject: Birkin Bag + Fun stuff in London

Dear Mr. Waldrop,

I've placed your name on the waiting list for the Birkin Bag (in Etrusque) at Hermès. Expected delivery date is in two weeks. I will follow up.

Mason told me that he'd like to spend some time with you in London. Shall I schedule both of you for a lunch out? Maybe a West End show (age appropriate), or is there something else you might have in mind? Please let me know. Thank you!

- Lane

I'd just hit "Send" when another text arrived from Cynthia:

PLZ TEXT HUGH TELL HIM I LOST 3 LBS!!!!!!!

I rolled my eyes. If she was texting me, then why couldn't she text Hugh the good news herself? I felt a headache coming on and went downstairs to look for some Advil. As I rifled through the medicine cabinet, another text from Cynthia popped up:

HI HAVE U TEXTED HUGH YET???????

Not yet, I texted back. I could actually feel the pounding in my head getting more intense. *Do you want me to call you?*

CAN'T TALK-ON TREADMILL-INTERVALS!! DON'T SEND THAT TEXT 2 HUGH YET THNX!

I shook three bright-blue Advil gelcaps out into the palm of my hand and stared at them. The iPhone, lying on the side of the sink, remained mute for the moment, yet its very presence mocked the life choices that had gotten me to this point. I shook my head: Whatever psychodrama Cynthia was having with her nutritionist, for now it was not my problem. I swallowed the pills with a handful of water from the tap, grabbed the phone, and stalked upstairs to finish my To-Do List.

As much as I hated the short winter days, I was glad when the overcast sky finally darkened — it meant I could leave Cynthia's house, and her madness, and, God help me, her kids — behind.

My flip-phone chimed as I trotted down the Waldrops' front stoop. Who would call me? It was an unknown number, from a Brooklyn/Queens area-code. Could it be Viktor, calling from a payphone? I took the call.

"Lane Haviland?" The caller, whoever he was, was shouting over some seriously chaotic background-noise. "It's Detective Mike Jarrett from the Sixtieth Precinct."

"Oh. Hi." I crossed the street mid-block and dodged a wrong-way bicyclist.

"I've got an update on your case. Can you come down to the precinct?"

"Now?"

He paused and I heard yelling in the background. "Is now a good time for you?"

"Yeah, I'm leaving work."

The F train to Coney Island was miserable and overcrowded and depressing, not unlike the scene inside the Sixtieth Precinct.

Detective Jarrett greeted me at the front desk, square-jawed and overly-muscular as ever. I wondered if his neck was actually thicker than his head and decided it was an optical illusion as he led me past the chaos of the cubicles and into a small room with a conference table and chairs. "Have a seat," he told me, and he closed the door.

I walked over to the table and ran my fingertip over its rough surface. It was scarred and rutted, probably more authentic than the distressed-wood floors Cynthia was currently evaluating for her beach house. "Is this where you interrogate suspects?"

"Sometimes. Right now it's just a room where we can have some privacy." He dropped two thick folders onto the table and gestured towards a chair. "Please."

I wriggled out of my coat and sat down.

Detective Jarrett settled himself into the chair opposite me and pulled it in. He shot me a tired smile. "Thank you for coming in," he pronounced, opening the top folder and shuffling through its contents. "We got a break in your case." He glanced up at me. "A suspect was arrested on a drug charge in Manhattan."

"Good. Throw the book at her." I stretched out my legs under the table.

"Let's not get ahead of ourselves." He started placing photos on the table in front of me, evenly spaced, six in all. "This is a photo line-up. I need you to tell me if any of these ladies look like the individual who scammed you."

All the pictures were mug-shots — blonde-haired women of roughly the same age. I immediately spotted Svetlana. "This one." I tapped my finger on her photo.

"You sure?"

"Yep. I'd never forget that face." I could almost hear the wheels of justice grinding. "Will I get my money back?"

He gathered up the photos. "It's theoretically possible. If I were a gambling man, I wouldn't bet on it."

"Will she go to jail?"

"I don't know. She's a junkie." He frowned down at a paper in his folder. "She'll probably plead out, get probation, time served." His eyes met mine. "I hate to be the bearer of bad news," he added, and his features softened into a sad smile.

"It's not your fault." I rubbed my aching forehead. What a long, draining day it had been! More than anything, I wanted to go home and sleep it off.

"How's your pal Viktor?" Detective Jarrett tapped his pen on the table. He showed no sign of ending our meeting or getting up out of his chair.

"What do you mean, 'my pal Viktor'?" I knew even as the words came out of my mouth that I sounded like a petulant teenager, but what the hell?

"I mean, is it getting serious?" Jarrett gave me a knowing look, then pushed the Svetlana folder to one side. The other folder remained on the table in front of him.

I considered his question. "That's really none of your business."

He didn't react to that — he just opened the folder, took out a photograph, and slid it across the table to me. "You know this guy?"

The man in the photo was white and heavyset, middle-aged, dressed in a nice suit. He had close-trimmed gray hair and wore an annoyed expression. He looked like he was getting into or out of a car.

"Nope. I've never seen this guy in my life." I smiled and slid the picture back to Detective Jarrett. A small triumph.

He met my gaze. "That's Roman Maksimov. He's kind of a big deal over in Brighton Beach."

At the name *Roman*, I felt my breath catch in my throat. But if Detective Jarrett noticed, he didn't mention it. Instead, he continued: "Your friend Viktor works for him." He leaned back in his chair and looked me over with a practiced, calm expression. And he waited. I tried staring back at him, only to discover that I wasn't nearly as comfortable with long silent periods as he seemed to be.

"I recall that you mentioned he was up to no good." At least I remembered to use ironic air-quotes.

"Yep. Still true." Detective Jarrett drummed his fingers lightly on the table. "Roman Maksimov, though." Now his brow was worried. "You really don't want to end up on his bad side. Couple of weeks ago I got a call." He returned to the folder and shuffled through its contents. "E.R., here on Coney Island. Gentleman was in pretty bad shape. He'd been assaulted." He pushed another photo towards me.

I looked at the picture and immediately regretted it. Holy crap! It was a man lying in a hospital bed, his face a distorted bloody pulp. Both eyes were swollen shut, black and blue and purple, and his lower lip looked like it had been sewn together with Frankenstein-stitches. I pushed the picture away. "Why would you show me this?"

"He owed Maksimov some money. Apparently he wasn't paying it back quickly enough."

"How awful." I eyed the closed door. Could I just leave now?

"Off the record," Detective Jarrett continued, "Roman's gang beat the shit out of him and left him bleeding on the sidewalk."

I clenched my hands into fists so I wouldn't pick at my cuticles and tried not to think about Viktor's bruises and cuts and scraped knuckles from two weeks ago. More silence from Detective Jarrett's side of the table. Damn, he was good at this. "What about…what about *on* the record?" I finally asked, just to fill the leaden silence.

"Nobody wanted to talk to me on the record. Strange how that works."

I took a deep, steadying breath. "What happened to him? This guy. At the hospital."

"He's recovering. Doctor told me he may lose the sight in one eye permanently. Too soon to tell."

"That's horrible."

"Yeah." He leaned towards me. "Strangest thing, though — he's not pressing charges. He made a sworn statement that he got jumped by three men he didn't recognize. He can't describe how they looked. Has no earthly idea why the whole thing happened."

I swallowed.

"Your boyfriend Viktor was one of the low-lifes who did it."

Oh God, no. "Who ever said he was my boyfriend?"

Detective Jarrett shrugged. "He's gonna get arrested. If not for this, then it'll be something else. That's how it goes with these guys. They're a dime a dozen. They all end up at Green Haven, or deported. Or dead."

"Green Haven?" It sounded like a retirement home.

"It's a correctional facility. Upstate."

"Oh."

He cocked his head to one side. "I could really use your help, Lane. With my investigation."

"You can't be serious. I don't know a thing about Roman... whatever his name is."

"And yet you're close to Viktor," he countered softly, and I didn't have it in me to issue any more denials. "Even if he's not your boyfriend. You two talk, you spend time together."

I swallowed. "He doesn't talk about any of this stuff."

The detective gave me an understanding nod and leaned forward across the table. "Do you know what a confidential informant is?"

"No." My stomach chose this moment to start doing abdominal-cavity backflips.

"It's a way you can help with a police investigation." Detective Jarrett's voice was absurdly calm. "Just by talking with me once in a while. Sharing information, anything you might hear." I stared at him. "As the name suggests, it's confidential. No one would have to know."

"I don't — I'm not really comfortable with that." I glanced at the still-shut door. "And not so long ago you were warning me not to get too close to Viktor."

"True." He flicked a speck of dust off the table. "But it's clear to me that you've made your decision and it's not in line with my advice." I bristled at that. "Hey, don't take offense. How old are you — twenty-six? You're a big girl. You can make your own choices."

"I know." How did he know my age? I hadn't liked this conversation to begin with; now I was starting to feel like the walls were closing in.

"You'd get paid for your participation," he said in a low voice. I could feel his eyes on me. "You'd only ever talk with me, Lane.

It would be one hundred percent between us."

"I'll think about it," I mumbled, and Detective Jarrett gave me an approving, almost affectionate nod as I stood up to leave.

"Good girl." He patted me on the shoulder.

I couldn't get out of there fast enough.

As I walked away from the precinct I felt dirty, disgusted, but mostly just numb. A thick mental fog had descended on me by the time I boarded the train for the short ride home to Brighton Beach. I found myself staring at the other passengers, most of whom seemed absorbed in their phone screens. A few were sleeping, their heads leaning against the walls and windows of the subway car. It was probably for the best that no one took notice of me — New York straphangers don't take kindly to being stared at. I blinked and shifted my gaze down to the dirty floor.

Viktor's being "up to no good" wasn't exactly new information — I'd known he was working for Roman, and I'd known he'd been in some sort of physical altercation when I'd seen his bruises and cuts. But somehow I'd written it off — as what, mischief? Surely I must have realized that there was a person on the other side of that fight. *Three against one.* I shook my head but I couldn't block out the image etched in my mind. That poor man! Lying in the hospital bed, he'd barely looked human — his face like meat at a butcher shop. All bloody and broken.

I looked down at my hands. They were shaking. My thoughts shifted to Detective Jarrett and his offer. Being his "confidential informant." Every instinct I had screamed *no.* And it wasn't just the snitch factor, or the way Detective Jarrett had made me feel trapped and uncomfortable in that room. That had been intentional.

He was just doing his job.

Who — Detective Jarrett? Or Viktor?

So now it was back to Viktor again. I couldn't deny that I had feelings for him. He wasn't a choir-boy; I knew that. But was he the violent monster Detective Jarrett had described? Something here didn't add up.

My phone pinged. It was a text, from Viktor:

Hey can I see you tomorrow?

Sorry I can't, I texted back.

The train rumbled on, the metal wheels screeching and groaning against the tracks. I missed Charlotte, and not just for all the usual reasons. She would have known what to do.

17

I should have endured a restless night after all that mess, but the truth is I slept like a baby. Not even the possibility of a boyfriend with violent tendencies — the same fellow who possessed the spare key to my apartment — could stop me from passing out cold on the futon for several hours.

When morning came, I made my own To Do list: Contact Randy. Get a second opinion on this. Clearly I couldn't trust my own judgment — I was way too close.

We need to talk, I texted Randy when I got off the subway in Manhattan. *ASAP. Man trouble.*

Lunch? God, she was such a good friend!

I'll come to you, I texted. Surely I could come up with some excuse to keep Cynthia at bay for a couple of hours.

By lunchtime, I was sitting across the table from Randy at our usual diner, fiddling with a spoon and wondering how the hell I was going to explain everything.

"Lane, Earth to Laney." Randy muttered. "Have you tried the Black and White milkshake here? It's heaven." She offered me a spare straw.

"Thanks, I'm not hungry." I realized I was chewing my lip so

I forced myself to stop and took a deep breath. "I'm having trouble figuring out where to begin."

"At the beginning?" Randy took a long draught of the milkshake and closed her eyes to savor it. "God, you have no idea what you're missing."

"So I should just tell you the whole story? Like so much word-vomit?"

She set her glass down and pushed a stray curl away from her face. "I wouldn't have used that exact phrase, but yes. Leave nothing out."

So I told her the complete story of Viktor — his past and present, along with Detective Jarrett's warnings and caveats regarding Roman Maksimov's gang. By the time I finished with Jarrett's proposal to use me as a confidential informant, Randy's eyes were wide as saucers. I could tell she was riveted because she'd forgotten all about her precious milkshake.

"Lane. Holy shitbuckets."

"I know." I twisted the unused straw around my index finger and watched the tip turn pink.

"Ew, stop that, I can't look at it." She brushed the straw to one side. "This could actually be serious."

"Yes, which is why I'm asking for your advice." I clasped my hands in front of me on the table lest I be tempted by stray cuticles or other nervous habit triggers.

Randy sat back in her seat and blew a deep breath out through puffed cheeks. "We need to put our heads together on this. What's up with your boss? She okay for the moment?"

"She's fine." As far as Cynthia knew, I was at the dentist's having a very painful toothache looked at, after which I would do her grocery shopping at the Union Square Whole Foods. The best part about this particular lie was that I could turn my phone off for a couple of hours.

"Good." Randy twisted around in her seat, pulling on one shoulder as if to wrench it into position. "Torticollis," she explained, waving away further inquiry. "So on the one hand, this guy Viktor is awesome, according to your own personal first-hand experience."

"Yeah." He really was, I thought miserably.

"And on the other hand, this cop — pardon me, *detective* — is telling you that Viktor is, in fact, not awesome, that he's a low-life thug and the whole affair can only end in misery. Right?"

"Yeah. But—"

"Shh. I'm deductive reasoning." Randy pursed her lips. "Are you sure Viktor's as wonderful as you say? From one-on-one interactions. Like, would you be having doubts about him even if Detective what's-his-name weren't part of the picture?"

I thought about it. "Sometimes I wonder what his angle is. He plays his cards close."

"What do you really know about him? What's his last name?"

"I don't know," I admitted. How weird was that?

"What's his favorite movie?" Randy asked me. "Does he get along with his mother?" I shrugged my shoulders. "Do you know anything intimate about him?"

"He's uncircumcised," I said, and Randy gave me a withering look. "Sorry. I should definitely ask him some of this stuff."

"Has he ever pushed you around? Shown a violent side?"

I shook my head slowly. "Never."

"I still don't like it. The company you keep and all that. Plus he went to prison! How many excuses are you gonna make for this guy?"

"Maybe there's a logical explanation," I said. "It's within the realm of possibility that Detective Jarrett has his own agenda."

"It's also within the realm of possibility that you're grasping at straws," Randy pointed out, and I gave her a reluctant nod. "But you have a point. Detective Asshole might be lying. I'm not a huge fan of cops."

That made me sit up and listen. I didn't exactly have a warm and fuzzy feeling about Jarrett, but 'Detective Asshole' might have been a little harsh. "Why don't you like cops?"

"That's a topic for another day." She sucked down the last drop of her milkshake. "The story doesn't relate directly to this situation." Suddenly I wished I had more time with Randy. I wanted to pick her brain, talk about something besides me and my problems. Reciprocate her friendship instead of depending on her all the time.

I took a deep breath. "You've given me a lot to think about."

"Just be careful, Lane," Randy urged me. "You might be getting mixed up with something dangerous. And I'm not just talking about Viktor. Cops are — well, they're not always on the up and up. I'm worried about you."

"I'll be careful." I felt like a twelve-year-old, but I knew Randy was just being cautious. "Seriously. I promise."

"Good. Keep me posted."

I turned on my phone to find three texts from Cynthia. She'd successfully picked up both kids from school and she needed me at the gym at exactly four-thirty, with mini-meal number five from Hugh's menu in hand. Her final text was the show-stopper: *PLZ CONFIRM U GOT THIS!!!!!!!*

I texted her my confirmation and a quick apology that the dentist's appointment had gone overlong. Fortunately, she had no questions regarding the specifics of my toothache. There was, however, a puzzling text from Mason:

what time was your dentist appointment?

I wasn't sure what to make of this question. *1 pm,* I texted back. *WRONG,* he replied.

My heartbeat quickened. Could the kid be on to me? He certainly paid more attention to things than his mother tended to, but how would he know I'd lied? As I pondered my response, another text from him popped up:

it was at Tooth-Hurty!

I stared down at the phone for a long moment and then burst out laughing in the middle of the produce section at Whole Foods. *GROAN!* I texted back, and then, with a big stupid grin on my face, my thoughts shifted to Viktor. I debated back and forth with myself for a few minutes before ultimately deciding that mind-blowing sex trumped caution. I texted him from the legumes section:

Plans changed. You still around tonight?

Five minutes later he texted back:

For you always. 8?

His response sent a little shiver of anticipation up my spine. Then I felt slightly ashamed about being so excited, followed by a pang of postfeminist guilt over feeling ashamed. I put my phone away and scolded myself: *Get a grip.* I had plenty of time to get to the bottom of Viktor's story later. In the meantime, Cynthia's groceries weren't going to buy themselves.

I arrived home to find a vase of red roses waiting outside my apartment door. I picked up the card. They were from Detective Jarrett, with a note: *Thinking of you. Call me?*

Okay, now he'd crossed the line into creepy territory. Had I unwittingly sent him a signal I was...*interested* in what he was offering? And even if I had, how on earth did a bouquet of roses tie in with any of that? This gesture seemed quasi-romantic. I stared at the roses with a sinking feeling in my stomach. Then I placed the vase on the wooden spool.

At eight o'clock sharp, I opened the door to Viktor, who was holding a telltale flat box in one hand and a small bottle in the other.

"Pizza and vodka?" I asked.

"Believe it or not, they are good together." He hung up his jacket on a newly-installed hook by the door. Music was playing softly through the Bluetooth speaker, and he nodded at it approvingly.

"I believe it." The bottle was frosty cold, as though it had come straight from the freezer. I peeked inside the box. Ham pizza! He couldn't possibly have bad intentions. I took down two juice glasses, two plates, and a handful of napkins. "You pour. You're the expert."

He complied, twisting the cap open in one smooth motion. The bottle made a clinking noise on the rim of each glass. "We can drink toast?"

"Yeah." I raised my glass. "To getting to know each other better." At that he gave me a tight smile, but he touched his glass to mine and drank it down. I, on the other hand, tried a small swallow only to splutter and choke on it.

"It is real Russian vodka," Viktor said, unable to hide his amusement.

"Goes down smooth," I rasped, reaching for a napkin.

"Take your time. Savor it." He looked like he was trying very hard not to laugh. I moved to slap the side of his arm but he was too fast — he ducked away, then encircled me in his arms from behind. "Amateur," he whispered in my ear. He nuzzled my neck; his breath felt hot. Predictably, my knees went weak.

"No way," I protested, wiggling away from him. "First we eat. And we need to talk about some things."

Viktor looked momentarily crestfallen, but he picked up the pizza box and walked over to the coffee table, where he set it down next to the roses and lowered himself to the floor. I couldn't help but notice how gracefully he did it. Did he have a secret yoga practice? I forced myself to stop staring like a lunatic and sat myself down.

"I want to get to know you better," I began, and I took a bite of pizza. God, it was delicious.

Viktor shifted position on the floor. He glanced from the rose bouquet to me with an irritatingly neutral expression. "There is not much to tell you. Like I said, my life is boring."

"Where do you live?"

He seemed momentarily caught off guard by this question, but he recovered quickly. "I rent room in house. Brighton Tenth Street. It's shared with five other guys."

"The room is shared?"

He gave me a sardonic smile then, full-on eyebrows, devilishly handsome. "House is shared. I have small room."

"Can I visit sometime?" I knew I was pushing it. But I needed to figure him out.

He shrugged. "It's no place to bring date. Is bachelor pad." He folded a piece of pizza in half, New York style, and took a large bite.

I switched tactics. "What about your family? Where are they now?"

He met my gaze. "Back home." Then he took another bite of

pizza. Totally nonchalant, just eating his dinner as though this were a discussion about the weather.

"Are your parents alive?" I couldn't deny that this subject was of particular interest to me.

"Yes." His voice was a little softer around the edges now.

"Do you talk, often?"

"No. We are not close." I waited, borrowing a tactic from Detective Jarrett, and Viktor stretched out his legs in front of him before continuing. "They don't approve of my job, my life choices. After prison...it was clear."

"Sorry," I whispered.

Now he had an amused expression. "It's okay. You want to know me better. So ask."

I felt unnerved by his blasé attitude towards my mini-inquisition, but I decided to assume he was being sincere. "What's your last name?"

"Kozlov."

"Your age?"

"Thirty-four. You're sure you don't work for CIA?"

"Any brothers or sisters?"

He nodded. "One sister. She is eight years older."

I wondered what she looked like. "What does she do?"

He leaned back against the wall. "Musician. Plays clarinet in orchestra. She's really good."

"What were you doing for work before you went to prison?"

"Same thing I do now, more or less."

Not good news. I took another gulp of vodka. "And when you got out? What happened then?"

"I could not return to same job as before."

"Why?"

He paused. "They did not want me back."

"Because you'd gone to prison?"

"They said I was no good. How do you say it? Damaged." He took another drink.

I put that aside for the moment. "You told me you stole something that didn't belong to you and that's why you went to prison." He nodded. "What was it?"

He shook his head. "Can't tell you."

"Why not?"

"I can't."

"That's not fair," I pointed out.

He looked at me for a moment, then stood up. I wondered if he meant to leave, but he just walked over to the kitchen and took the vodka bottle out of the freezer.

"I will answer more questions on one condition." He poured himself another drink.

"What?" I drained my glass and held it out for more. He refilled it with a satisfied smirk.

"You must take your clothes off."

Well, I had to hand it to Viktor — he knew how to take an amateur interrogation and run it utterly off the rails. Lying in his embrace on the futon, naked as the day we were born, I could barely remember my own name. At least the lights were dimmed down as low as they would go, and we had the blanket to cover us, so I could hope to regain some measure of equanimity.

"You had questions for me," Viktor murmured. He moved his mouth over my neck and down to my bare shoulder. His lips and his tongue were exquisitely soft.

"Yes," I managed to whisper. The too-sweet aroma of Detective Jarrett's roses had drifted over to where we lay, reminding me of the doubts I had about both him and Viktor. But if I'd been too close to the situation earlier today to be an impartial judge of Viktor's character, now I might as well give myself up for lost. I could feel the warmth of his body, taut and barely touching my backside, and all I wanted was to snuggle in closer. For now I decided to resist that urge.

"So ask." One of his hands slipped around my ribcage. His fingertips moved up under my breast, tracing a shivering path. This was so not fair.

"I hope it's not too personal a question," I began. His hand moved south, tracing a shape on my stomach, and it took real effort to not think about where else I wanted those magic fingers to go. I turned to face him. "How did you get that scar on your face?"

He shifted position. "A fight. In prison."

"You say it so matter-of-factly." I turned on my other side and ran my fingers down his chest, over a tattoo of an onion-domed church.

"It is matter of fact." He smiled up at the ceiling, then at me.

"How could someone do that to you? To anyone?"

"That's how it is," he answered softly. "Prison, what is word…" I brushed a lock of hair off his forehead. "Brutal. It's brutal place."

I didn't have any intelligent response to that. So I kissed his shoulder, which was inked with a sailing ship.

"This guy," Viktor continued. "He had toothbrush handle with razor blade inside. He hated me. Don't know why. I kept to myself, always."

"So he slashed your face?" I felt a lump form in my throat.

"Yes." Viktor rolled onto his side and faced me. His expression was thoughtful. Concerned. Was he worried about what I'd think of him?

"Weren't you scared?" I whispered. "I don't see how anyone could cope with — with being attacked, like that."

Viktor ran one hand down past my waist and slid it over the curve of my hip before answering. "Of course I was afraid. Not everyone survives there."

"How did you survive it?" I asked, and he looked at me quizzically. "The attack. The guy who stabbed you."

"I fought. I won." His expression had hardened. "You don't want to know details," he added in a softer voice.

I got his meaning. "And then what? Did they extend your sentence?"

"Ninety days in punishment cell. Solitary." He swallowed and I noticed his Adam's apple doing its thing. "After that nobody bothered me."

"Did they…did they take care of you? I mean medically. You must have been a mess."

Viktor smiled up at the ceiling. "You worry about strange things." Then he turned and reached for me again. His hands felt so warm. "There was guy, former medic in the Russian army. He

133

fixed me up. I healed. No more career as fashion model though."

"It sounds so — business as usual. Did this stuff happen all the time?"

"Yes. I am glad to be out." His hand roved from my arm to my breast, which he cupped gently before stroking it. "For a lot of reasons." He met my gaze.

"Me too," I whispered. And then he moved in closer.

The sound of mumbled nonsense-words stirred me from sleep, and I blinked my eyes open in the darkness. I could feel Viktor lying next to me.

"Nyet," he grunted. *"Ne nado."*

"Viktor?" I fumbled around for the light switch and turned it on. He was lying on his back with his eyes closed. There was a sheen of sweat on his face and chest. "Are you awake?" I whispered.

He twitched. *"Ne nado,"* he mumbled again. His breath was coming faster now and his expression was pained.

"Viktor, wake up," I whispered. "You're having a bad dream." I was tempted to tap his shoulder or gently shake him awake, but I didn't want to frighten him needlessly. Wasn't there a protocol for how to safely wake someone up from a nightmare? Or was that Night Terrors? And how the fuck was I supposed to know which was which? "Viktor," I repeated, this time at a conversational volume. "Wake up."

"Pozhalsta." This came out as a strangled cry. He was gripping the blanket so hard that his knuckles were white. *"Ya ne ponimayu."* He was breathing harder now.

"Please, wake up. You're freaking me out." I reached over and patted his hand, and suddenly he sat bolt upright. His eyes were open, unfocused, and I couldn't tell if he saw me, or if he was even registering my presence or anything else in front of him. His face looked a fright. I withdrew from him, pulling the blanket up around myself protectively.

"Viktor? Are you okay?" My heart was pounding hard in my chest. He didn't respond; he didn't even look at me. He lurched out of bed and stumbled naked towards the bathroom, pulling the door shut behind him. Horrible retching noises followed.

Oh, God — this was all my fault! I'd asked him about those awful things, things he'd rather forget. Made him relive horrible events just to satisfy my morbid curiosity. Stupid! I pulled on a shirt and a pair of yoga pants and tidied up the room, spreading the pillow and blanket back into place on the futon. I folded Viktor's clothes into a neat pile and left them by the bathroom door. Then, desperate for something constructive to do, I put some water on the stove to heat for tea.

The bathroom door stayed shut. After several minutes had passed, I tapped on it. "Hey Viktor? You okay in there?"

The toilet flushed. At least he was alive. I heard the water running in the sink. "Your clothes are here by the door," I called softly. No answer. My water was boiling, so I walked over to the kitchen and made tea — two cups. I heard the bathroom door open and shut.

I was dumping three packets of sugar into my tea — and wondering if a fourth would be necessary — when Viktor emerged from the bathroom. He'd dressed, and his hair was damp and slicked back. He looked pale. Shaken.

"Hi." I held out a mug of tea, but he shook his head.

"I used your mouthwash," he said, without making eye contact.

"That's fine. Are you okay?"

"Yeah." He picked up his belt and his coat and looked around the room awkwardly before finally glancing at me. Then he looked down at the floor. "I must go."

"I'm so sorry," I managed to whisper. But he was already out the door.

18

"I think you should be aware that I *don't* need a nanny." Emily was using her most imperious voice in the back seat of the taxi. Her thumbs flew over her phone-screen in a blur as she speed-texted.

"So you've said." I really wasn't in the mood to go head-to-head with her this early in the morning. Viktor's awkward departure had plagued my thoughts for two days. And I still hadn't heard back from him, despite having texted him twice to ask if he was all right.

"And?" Emily demanded.

"And I have responded to you thusly: Talk to your parents." She tore her eyes away from her phone for as long as it took to roll them, then it was back to the texts. I gazed out the window. Gray clouds had settled over Manhattan, and the trees lining Fifth Avenue were waving bare branches in the wind. We were headed south towards Tiffany's, where Emily would choose a tasteful Bat Mitzvah gift for her friend.

"I mean, I'm way too old," Emily continued. "All the kids in my class are allowed to walk to and from school by themselves."

"Really? I usually see them getting dropped off by their drivers right by the front door." I looked at Emily, who immediately assumed a cute-guilty expression: Oops, you caught me lying! Tee-hee!

"That's just because it's winter. And that's another thing," Emily pouted. "We don't even have a driver. It's embarrassing."

"I could take up a collection." I was tired of this conversation, tired of my job, tired of 95 percent of my life. And I was worried about Viktor. *Damaged* — that word had stayed with me these last two days. So had his nightmare and its aftermath. I needed to talk to him.

But first I had to navigate my way through Tiffany's with a spoiled thirteen-year-old. I hadn't cared about jewelry even back when I'd had money to waste, but the gems and precious metals under glass display cases were nonetheless enticing in their own sparkling way. They weren't just rings and necklaces — they were a lifestyle. A highly aspirational one, in my case.

"La-ane!" Emily's voice interrupted my reverie.

I hurried over. "What?" I asked in a deliberately understated voice, as if to communicate to nearby salespeople that I, at least, understood the importance of a proper tone for speaking aloud at Tiffany's.

"This! This is the necklace Alanna said she wanted." Emily pressed her finger down on the glass display case, indicating the chunky silver necklace below.

"That's an exceptionally beautiful piece." The saleslady's cool voice startled me; she had silently materialized before us, all willowy understated class. Impeccably groomed, yet subdued relative to her clientele. She reminded me of the velvet forms that the jewelry rested upon. She removed the necklace from the display case and set it out for Emily to examine.

"I know I saw J-Law wearing this on the red carpet," Emily murmured. She reached out and touched it reverently.

"Good eye," the saleslady said. This whole outing was suddenly making me nauseated.

"What does it cost?" I asked. Cynthia had given us a budget — a ridiculously large one, but at least there was a theoretical limit to how much she was willing to spend on jewelry for a middle schooler.

"This piece is priced at seven-fifty." The saleslady smiled

ABBY VEGAS

benignly down at me, then at Emily. No hard sell here. Part of their strategy was making customers feel honored to be buying their tasteful crap.

"Good, we'll take it," Emily announced brightly. "I want it in one of those blue Tiffany boxes. With the white ribbon."

"Of course." The saleslady took my proffered credit card. I kept my opinion to myself, as usual.

On the taxi ride home, Emily renewed her anti-nanny campaign in earnest. "I'm really responsible," she informed me as she set the shopping bag between us on the seat, and I wondered if her argument would stand up to solid cross-examination. But before I could answer, my flip-phone chimed. Viktor? I dug through my bag to find it. Yes! It was a text from him:

I am ok.sorry.

Relief washed over me: At least he wasn't at the bottom of the Gowanus Canal.

"Your boyfriend's texting you again." Emily's voice had taken on a teasing quality. For once I didn't mind.

I'm glad, I texted back, then thought better of it and texted again: *no reason to be sorry.* Then I snapped the phone shut with a satisfying *thwap.*

"Is he?" Emily prodded. "Your boyfriend, I mean."

"That's none of your beeswax."

"Come *on!* Nobody ever tells me anything."

"I'm your mother's employee," I pointed out. "It would be inappropriate to talk about it. And besides, you never tell me anything either."

"I told you about Mason and his psycho-weirdo reputation," she countered.

"You did. Any news there?" I was trying to appear casual.

"No," Emily groused. "He's still a psycho."

"I don't like you using that word," I told her. "I hope you're supportive of him when you can be." That earned me another eyeroll.

"Brooke has a boyfriend," Emily said suddenly. "Connor. He's

138

in our grade at school."

"Hmmm." Where was she going with this?

"They've had a crush on each other forever. Now they're starting to, like, you know."

"Actually, I don't know," I admitted.

"You know, like...sex."

Shit. "They're having sex?"

"Sort of." Emily narrowed her eyes. "Like, not all the way."

Ugh. Oral? Did I even want to know? Not really. But it was like a train wreck and I couldn't look away. "They're your age? Thirteen?"

"Connor's fourteen. He was red-shirted." I had no idea what that meant and I didn't care. "He's super cute," Emily added with a face usually reserved for puppies and boy-bands.

What could I say to her? That thirteen was way too young for sex, even part-of-the-way? That they should use protection? That Emily still had her American Girl dolls displayed in her bedroom, and blowjobs don't mesh well with lifeless glass eyes gazing down upon you? Mercifully, the taxi arrived at Chez Waldrop just then, and I paid the fare while Emily got out and bounded up the front steps to ring the bell.

"Hey Emily," I called. "Responsible teenager."

She turned back. "What?"

I held up the iconic robin's-egg-blue Tiffany's shopping bag. "You left this in the back of the taxi."

Cynthia decided to drop Emily off at Alanna's Bat Mitzvah herself, leaving me and Mason alone in the house. I cleaned out Cynthia and Brad's master bathroom as instructed, marveling at all the never-used cosmetics and toiletries I had to dispose of. Amongst the rejects, an unopened bottle of L'Occitane massage oil caught my eye; I felt a pang of regret over the wasted Mallomars and slipped it into my bag. But once that work was done, the house felt impossibly dreary. I knocked on Mason's bedroom door but got no answer. "I know you're in there," I called. I tried the door, but it was locked. "Open up."

The lock clicked open from the inside but the door stayed closed. I waited an appropriate length of time before I opened it a crack and peeked in. Mason was in bed with his iPad, stony-faced. Four large Bloomingdale's shopping bags lay by the foot of his bed, filled with new clothes.

"New spring wardrobe?" I asked him.

"Whatever." Mason tapped and swiped on the iPad with determined purpose.

"Can I interest you in a snack? Some hot chocolate, perchance?" Mason sometimes liked it when I used old-timey words in casual conversation.

"There's nothing to eat except Mom's gross diet food," he grumbled without taking his eyes from the screen.

I walked over and tousled his hair. "Nothing's stopping us from hitting the diner, though."

He yanked his head away. "I'm really busy."

"They have hot chocolate with whipped cream," I reminded him. And waited.

He kept pecking away at whatever he was doing, but finally looked up from his screen. "You're not gonna leave me alone, are you?"

"Nope." I grinned down at him, arms akimbo.

"Fine, let's go."

"That's the spirit."

"I take it shopping with your mom wasn't awesome, then?" I stole a French fry from Mason's plate.

"She's barely tolerable." He dipped a fry in ketchup and popped it in his mouth.

Privately, I agreed. "Well, the worst part's over. Having some nice new clothes isn't the worst fate imaginable."

He rolled his eyes. Was that a Waldrop trademark? "They're all preppy. Lame."

"Hmmm." I felt like I'd been saying that word a lot lately. It felt stupid and non-committal.

"It's like she's dressing me up as someone else. Someone not like me." Mason seemed to be growing more miserable by the second.

"I wish I knew what to say," I confessed. Still lame, but at least it was the truth. Mason shrugged and stared down at his plate. My heart ached for him.

"Your mother loves you," I told him. "I see your doubtful expression and I challenge you to dig a little deeper. It's possible for her to love you even if she doesn't fully understand or appreciate you."

He sniffed and ran a finger down the side of his water-glass. "It counts for something," I insisted. My parents and my sister were suddenly foremost in my mind and I reflexively pushed them away before I got over-emotional.

"You look weird all of a sudden," Mason grumbled. Eleven-year-old boys are not known for their tact.

"I was just — never mind. I was thinking about my parents," I added hastily when he gave me a questioning look.

"What does your dad do for a living?" Mason asked.

I floundered about for an answer. "He ran a small blimp-repair shop."

Mason shot me a doubtful look as he nibbled on a fry. "Do you all get along?"

"Usually, but not always. Everyone has problems with their parents. Some more than others."

He narrowed his eyes. "A blimp-repair shop couldn't be small. Are you lying?"

"Just making sure you're paying attention." I managed a faint smile. "He was an engineer."

"Is he retired?"

"He's gone." I was desperate to change the subject. "With respect to the preppy clothes, may I remind you that you attend prep school."

Mason scowled at that, so I snatched two more fries from his plate. "Your mom probably just wants you to fit in. Which is also not the worst thing in the world."

"Do *you* fit in?" This kid had been in therapy a long time. He knew all the standard follow-up questions.

"I guess not. Not really."

"See? And you're cool."

"I don't know about that." But I was secretly pleased he thought so.

On the packed subway ride home, I could feel my stomach twisting itself into a knot over Mason. Poor kid! If only I could reassure him into infinity that his parents loved him, whether it was true or not. No child his age should have to doubt it.

For once I didn't fight it when my parents drifted into my consciousness. Had they loved us? Yes they had, unequivocally, in different ways. Mom had worried over everything and Dad had been the counterbalance — solid, calm, easygoing.

I smiled when I remembered how Dad had taught me to drive stick-shift in our old Honda. It had taken so many tries — and nerves of steel — but I'd finally gotten the hang of it. Much less successful were his attempts to teach me euchre. "Never trump your partner's ace, Laney," he'd say with a wink and a nod, staying patient even when I kept making the same mistakes one game after another. Charlotte was the fast learner — mathematics and probability came easily. She'd been so smart. And sweet-natured, like Dad.

I took after my mother, and we were worriers. *You worry about strange things,* Viktor had said, and he'd been right. Mom would slide into these weird dissociative loops where she'd fret over the least likely shit. "Cautionary tales," my sister and I called them privately. The neighbors were expecting a new baby? Well, then by all means let's talk about an umbilical cord accident that happened thirty years ago and a thousand miles away. Whatever route a conversation took, Mom would find a way to connect it with a story of something terrible that had happened — usually to someone she'd known personally. Maybe it was her way of inoculating herself against fate. Showing respect for the risk and unpredictability of life — as though bearing witness to others' suffering might steer her and her loved ones away from danger. I couldn't argue with that impulse, even if I hadn't understood it at the time. But in the end, it didn't save any of us.

Sunday rolled around, and my thoughts turned to Viktor. I was surprised at how much I missed being with him. But I also wondered if he needed some space after what had happened. I stretched out on the futon, looked around the cramped apartment, and realized that Detective Jarrett's roses probably would have lasted longer if I'd bothered to add water to the vase. Their wilting presence still gave me an unsettled feeling. I threw them in the trash.

By mid-morning, reality had collided with my desire to stay in bed all day. I collected my basket of dirty laundry — the one constant in my life aside from Cynthia's texts — and headed out into the chilly day.

My route to and from the laundromat, which never varied, took me past the corner of Brighton Seventh Street and Neptune Avenue — an unremarkable intersection that had a pharmacy and a T-Mobile store. A few men were exiting a double-parked car in front of a building with "Islamic Center" signage in English and Arabic, so I stopped to let them pass. Then I saw that Viktor was among them.

He was hard to miss — the tallest of the group, and easily the best-looking. He was dressed smartly, in dark trousers and an overcoat, and he was clean-shaven. His usually-shaggy black hair was combed back and gelled into submission. He closed the back door of the gleaming black BMW that two older men had just exited, and I recognized one of them as Roman Maksimov.

My heart skipped a beat and I instinctively looked away. I'd have turned around and walked in the other direction but I was afraid that would draw more attention. So I bowed my head, hugged the basket to my chest, and started to walk around the car.

And then, because my timing has always been and will always be terrible, Roman Maksimov barked something in Russian at Viktor, who started walking back towards the BMW. Without meaning to, I looked up at him, and our eyes met for the briefest moment before I continued on my way. There was no recognition in his eyes. I read the signal loud and clear: just keep walking.

At the laundromat, I watched my clothes tumble around in the washer and brooded over what had just happened. There wasn't a lot of new information here — I'd already known what Viktor did for a living. Still, seeing him in that element was unsettling. He'd seemed almost like a different man — cold. Dangerous, even. Detective Jarrett's accusations rankled at the edges of my consciousness like a houseguest who's overstayed his welcome.

Once my laundry was done, I ventured out to the Dollar Store to buy food — ramen noodles — plus I splurged on a pack of Yodels for stress-eating. Then I stopped at the produce market, where I got a bunch of green onions and a half-dozen eggs so I wouldn't drop dead from a vitamin deficiency.

As I walked home down Brighton Beach Avenue, a text came in from Cynthia:

Did u make brown rice? Can't find it

Immediately followed by:

HELLLPPPPP I'm having a total carb craving attack!!

Safe in Brooklyn where no one of importance would see me, I rolled my eyes. *Center shelf of fridge,* I texted back. *In single-serving containers.*

OK remind me 2 tell u about summer camp 2morrow!!

"Oh, fuck off," I muttered. To Cynthia, I texted: *Sure.* I could actually feel my mood turning blacker. Hunching against the cold and wind, I slouched towards home.

19

The last person I expected to see in the lobby of my building was Viktor, but there he was, wearing his coveralls and tinkering with one of the tenants' mailboxes.

"Hi." I scooted around him so as not to trip over his toolbox.

"Lane." He stopped what he was doing and smiled broadly at me. It felt odd after what had happened earlier. "Are you busy now?"

"Just coming home. You want some ramen?"

"Yes. Thank you." He picked up his toolbox and followed me down the stairs.

"Were you waiting for me up there?" I asked. "Because I wasn't aware that we were still on speaking terms." I unlocked my door and motioned for him to come inside, giving him a half-cocked smile as I did so.

"I wanted to talk," he said haltingly, looking around the room and then at me. "In private."

"Well, it doesn't get much more private than this." I hung up my coat and rubbed my hands together to get the cold out. Viktor just stood there looking uncomfortable. I pushed my hands into my pockets. "Do you want to sit down?"

He shook his head. "I'm sorry," he said, looking down at me. "For what happened before. On street."

"Okay, apology accepted," I told him. He gave me a confused look. "Viktor, you're freaking me out. I know who you work for. You don't want your boss to know we're..." I paused, unsure of how to word it. "Together."

"This does not upset you?"

I crossed my arms over my chest. "Maybe a little bit. Mostly I'm just worried about you."

He raked a hand through his hair, which had begun to break loose from its gelled coiffure. "The other night. I am sorry...you saw that."

"I'm not sorry," I replied. He shot me a disbelieving look. "We don't have to talk about it if you don't want to," I added. "It's fine."

Viktor looked around the apartment again. He seemed downright twitchy. "It's difficult to talk about," he finally said.

I sat down on the futon and motioned for him to join me. He hesitated, but came and sat down. "I have the same nightmare at least twice a week," I told him. "It sucks. Do you want to know what it is?"

"If you want to tell." He didn't sound wildly enthusiastic.

"I get a call. There's been a bad accident. My parents and my sister have been hurt."

Viktor blinked. He didn't say anything.

"In the dream," I continued, "I try to go to them. I think: if I could just get to the hospital, be with them, everything will be okay. But I can't. There's always some reason I can't get there in time."

Viktor pressed his lips together. "What reason?"

"It varies." I took a deep, steadying breath. "Sometimes my car won't start. Or I get lost while I'm driving to the hospital. I lose control of the car and it goes off the road — that's a fun one. Or sometimes there's a person who blocks my way, who won't let me go for whatever reason." I swallowed. "Sometimes I get to the hospital but I can't find them. I walk down endless corridors but it's never the right place. They're somewhere else. In a different wing. Or at another hospital — I came to the wrong place entirely."

Viktor was gazing down at the floor. When he looked back at me, his expression had softened. "And I always feel the same way," I went on. "Panicked. Rushed — desperate. Because I know exactly what will happen if I fail."

"You have this dream twice, every week?" Viktor asked me. He moved his hand onto mine and squeezed it softly.

"Just about," I sighed. My eyes were moist, but for once I wasn't bawling.

Those long fingers stayed curled around mine. "You blame yourself for what happened."

"Yeah, maybe. On some level."

His brow creased in puzzlement. "Why?"

"They were coming to see me," I reminded him. "They'd still be alive if they hadn't come."

"But it's not your fault," he said.

"I've been told it's not a healthy way to think." I'd been over this so many times with so many shrinks it felt like déjà-vu.

Now Viktor was gazing down at our intertwined hands. He raised my hand to his lips and kissed it. "I am not giver of advice," he murmured.

"Yes. I like that in a man."

He arched an eyebrow at me. "If you must experience such regret over the past, then at least make sure it's your own decisions."

I contemplated that for a moment. "So are you going to quit your shitty dangerous job and run away with me to an island paradise, like the song in your playlist?"

He laughed. "Quit your shitty dangerous job," he repeated, mimicking me. His American accent wasn't bad. "Not yet," he said, and he squeezed my hand again.

"But soon?" Some distant, half-sane part of me really wanted closure on this. Without thinking, I reached up and touched his chin. There it was — the beginnings of stubble. He just couldn't stay clean-shaven very long.

"Soon." His lips curved back into a smile and he moved in for a kiss.

* * * *

147

Viktor didn't stay the night, which wasn't a shock. I assumed he was still gun-shy after the awkward puking-in-my-toilet incident. I texted him the following morning:

Missed waking up with you today. xoxo

Standing on the lurching Q train and staring at my sent text, it occurred to me that I was sliding over the edge into foolishness. X's and O's — really? I stuffed the phone into my bag and resolved to act less pathetic in the future.

Neither of the Waldrop children was running on all cylinders that morning, so they were too sleepy to object much to my getting them to school on time. Once I got back to the house, I headed for the kitchen, hoping to get started on Cynthia's food preparation for the next three days: poached chicken breast, egg whites, brown rice, and some gross green-vegetable medley. I was so involved in mentally optimizing the food-prep that I almost missed Cynthia sitting at the counter in a disheveled heap. Her hair was a rat's nest and she was still wearing the previous night's makeup.

Oh, God. Approach with caution. "Good morning," I ventured, setting my bag down.

"Hey." Cynthia's voice was rough. As I got closer, I detected the aroma of stale cigarette-smoke. Her eyes remained shut.

"Hey, you okay?" I asked. "You want a coffee or something?"

"Just water." Cynthia laid her cheek down on the cold countertop while I filled a glass with bottled water from the fridge. I set it down in front of her, whereupon she heaved herself back to a seated position and opened bloodshot eyes. "I've got a rotten hangover," she mumbled.

"Oh. The worst." I had no idea what I was supposed to say.

"My friend Nadia came over last night for wine and sympathy," Cynthia added. "I guess it got out of hand."

"I think we've all been there," I said.

She looked momentarily surprised at that, then winced as she swallowed a bit of water. Her skin was duller than I'd ever seen it, with a greenish hue. "Why don't you go rest in bed?" I offered. "I can keep busy down here. Food prep. And I can research the kids' summer camps if you want."

"Food prep. Dear God." Cynthia rubbed her eyes.

"Sorry to mention food."

"No, it's just, you know." She looked around the kitchen and heaved a sigh. "I totally fucked up my food plan. I must have drank, like—" She looked up while she did the calculations in her head. "A bottle and a half of wine? No, that can't be right."

"It happens."

"Then we got into the potato chips." She winced again and ran a hand through her hair.

"Well, that's not so bad." I felt a vortex of dread forming in the pit of my stomach.

"And a ton of cheese. And oh my God, the cigarettes."

"Ouch."

"I feel so disgusting right now. Disgusted with myself." Cynthia hissed out that last bit with a good measure of self-loathing — something I recognized.

"What can I do?" I wasn't sure I wanted to know the answer, but I felt compelled to ask.

Cynthia tossed her phone onto the counter. "Handle any incoming stuff," she said. "I'm gonna try to sleep it off."

"Sure, no problem. I'll check on you later."

"And cancel my workout. Tell Fabrizio I'm sick." She hugged her robe tighter around herself. "Text Hugh because he'll expect to hear from me — same deal, 'kay? I'm sick with a virus."

"Sure." The trainer and the food coach. Keep them at bay.

"Thanks." She shuffled towards the stairs. "You're a doll."

Once the chicken breasts were poaching in organic broth, I texted Fabrizio and Hugh separately regarding Cynthia's sudden-onset viral illness. I wasn't sure if the two were comparing notes or even knew about each other, but I didn't want to rock the boat needlessly and risk Cynthia's wrath. Hugh texted back a disinterested "K," but Fabrizio wasn't buying it:

Tell her to get her ass down here now!

She's resting in bed, I replied. *I can't disturb her.* I waited, half-amused, to see his reply, but none came, so I abandoned Cynthia's phone and checked my flip-phone. There was a text from Viktor:

missed you too.next time i will stay

Progress! He was coming back around; a little patience was all it took. I poured some broth into a saucepan to sauté the horrible vegetable concoction and tried to suppress my gag reflex as I broke apart a bunch of raw broccoli. The doorbell rang as I was smashing a clove of Red Killarney garlic with the side of a chef's knife.

"Yes?" I hurried to the door and yanked it open before whoever it was could ring the bell again and wake up Cynthia. There stood Fabrizio, wearing sweatpants and a hoodie and a stony expression.

"Where is she?" he demanded.

"She's asleep," I whispered. He snorted and walked past me into the foyer uninvited. "Hey!" I whispered fiercely. It was freezing outside, so I closed the front door. "What do you think you're doing?"

"Where's Cynthia?" Fabrizio glanced up the stairs.

"I wouldn't go up there if I were you," I warned, dropping the pretense of whispering. "She's in bad shape."

"Yeah, I know." Fabrizio turned to face me. "A virus, right?"

"Uh huh." Lying to Fabrizio's face was a mite more difficult than texting him Cynthia's nonsense.

"Right." Fabrizio looked up the stairs again and I maintained my best poker face. "You sticking with that story?"

I crossed my arms over my chest and tried to stare him down. Then he pulled out his phone. "Cynthia drunk-texted me last night. She told me all about the wine, the cheese, the junk food." He handed me the phone with the text conversation loaded; I braved a look. It was very bad indeed.

"Well. This is awkward." I handed his phone back.

"You're running interference for Cynthia now?" He pocketed the phone and gave me a withering look that I absolutely deserved.

"What do you expect me to do?" I whispered.

His eyes went wide. "Get it together, woman, that's what I expect you to do!"

Now I shot a wary glance up the stairs. "I am not her babysitter," I hissed through clenched teeth. "And I'm not her mother. She's a grown woman."

"Yeah," Fabrizio replied softly. "And if she doesn't lose this weight, I lose my job. I wouldn't be surprised if she tells you to hit the road too."

I blinked. "That's ridiculous."

He shook his head. "When Cynthia's pissed off, she fires the help. I'm emailing her workout schedule for the week. Make sure she shows up and follows the directions for non-gym days. She's committed to this and I will see her through."

He turned to go, and I lingered there a moment before returning to the kitchen and the artisanal garlic.

I spent the remainder of my workday in an agitated state. It was emotionally exhausting to about-face between pooh-poohing Fabrizio's doomsday scenario and imagining myself penniless and unemployed. A foreboding silence reigned within the Waldrop house — I didn't dare make a sound lest I disturb the sleeping Cynthia. By the time I left to pick Mason up from school, she'd begun to shuffle around upstairs.

On my way to school, I got a text from Randy:

Come see me after work! I need updates on your boyfriend like a fat kid needs pie.

I had to smile as I tapped in my reply. It was nice to know someone cared.

Yes. Same time/place?

Same Bat Time! Same Bat Channel!

I grinned again and shoved my phone into my bag as I rounded the corner. Mason was walking down the school's front steps, shoelaces flopping untied as usual. Just as he reached the sidewalk, a burly red-headed boy behind him kicked him in the back of his knee joint, sending him tumbling face-down onto the pavement.

"Mason!" My heart dropped into my stomach. I raced over and knelt down beside him. "Are you okay?"

He picked himself up. "I'm fine," he scowled, looking down at his hands. His palms were scraped and bloody where he'd broken the fall, and one trouser-leg was torn. I popped back up to standing and looked around for the red-headed bully, but he'd disappeared into the milling crowd. That little fucker!

"Come on," Mason mumbled, staring down at the sidewalk as he tugged on my arm. I was still looking around for the perp. "Come *on*," Mason repeated, and when I looked at him his cheeks were pink with embarrassment and his eyes were brimming with tears. So I tore my gaze away from the crowd, with regret, and followed Mason home.

"I swear to God I'm gonna pound that fucking kid into the ground when I find him," I told Randy later at the diner. "I don't care if he's twelve. He has it coming."

Randy nodded sympathetically and poured half her milkshake into an extra glass she'd procured. "He sounds like a nasty piece of work. Red-headed child, you say?"

"Yeah."

She sniffed. "Unsurprising."

"You know what really chaps my ass? Cynthia! She doesn't give a shit. I told her what happened and she started complaining about what a pain it is to order new school uniform pants for Mason." I stabbed a straw into my half of the milkshake and stared down at it.

"Not a single fuck was given," Randy mused. "That's rough. At least your parents should have your back."

"At the very least." I rubbed my neck; a stress-knot had started to form there. "She said she'd 'bring it up with Brad.' Maybe I'm getting over-involved in this." I took a sip of the milkshake. It tasted overly sweet. I pushed it away.

"What over-involved? He's getting bullied. Bullies suck and your outrage is justified." Randy took another long draught of the shake. "But you don't appreciate a good black-and-white milkshake. True story."

I drummed my fingers on the table and looked around the diner to make sure no one I recognized was nearby. "I'm researching summer camps now. Maybe I can find one that lasts a full three months and forbids parent visitation."

"On Mars," Randy added, and that finally made me chuckle. "Come on, Laney, I'm dying to know what's up with your Russian mystery man. Viktor." She pronounced it *Veek-torr*.

"He's had some ups and downs." I sketched a vague outline of what had happened with his nightmare, leaving out the humiliating details while getting the story across.

"Bad memories suck." Randy shifted impatiently in her chair.

"There's more." I told her about the awkward incident on the street when we'd pretended we didn't know each other in front of Roman Maksimov.

"Okay, that bothers me," Randy said. "I don't want to say 'I told you so,' but doesn't it raise a giant red flag?"

I shrugged. I knew she was right, but my better judgment was currently exiled to a gulag in Siberia.

Randy narrowed her eyes. "Where'd you say you were when that happened?"

"Neptune Avenue. Old big-shot Maksimov was getting out of his shiny new car. Going into the Islamic Center, of all places."

"The Islamic Center," Randy repeated. Her brows were furrowed in thought. "Why would a Russian mafia guy want to go in there?"

"I don't know. Community relations?" My mind was wandering to desperate, pathetic places. "I'm starting to wonder if a confident and liberated woman should be okay with a guy who'll only meet her alone in an out-of-the-way location."

"Yes, you *should* be wondering that. Do you think," she said, "that there's a terrorist connection? Organized crime plus radicalized Muslims?"

"Radicalized?" I snorted. "You watch too much TV."

"True." She chewed her lip. "But this particular sub-set of Muslims is consorting with someone we already know is a criminal." She shot me a provocative look.

"I seriously doubt it." I rubbed my eyes; the long and draining day was catching up with me. "Listen, I gotta get back to Brooklyn before I collapse."

"You're working hard," Randy observed. "Good for you,

Laney."

"That reminds me." I pulled two twenties and a ten out of my wallet. "Payback."

Randy took the money. "Excellent. And I'd like you to introduce me to Viktor."

"Why?"

"Clearly you're smitten. I want to see him with my own two eyes."

"Judge him, you mean?" Now I sounded like a twelve-year-old.

She shot me a stern look. "Never you mind."

20

As luck would have it, I found a use for the massage oil a few nights later at my apartment. Viktor was lying face-down on my futon, clad only in his boxer shorts while I straddled him. "Your tattoos are almost unspeakably sexy," I confessed as I kneaded his shoulders.

"Mmm." Viktor's eyes stayed closed, but he smiled. His face looked uncharacteristically relaxed. Working my way down his shoulder blades, I craned my neck to examine the tattoo of a many-sailed tall ship on the side of his shoulder. It was slightly sharper around the edges than the others — well, less blurred — though it had the same blue-black ink color. I continued kneading my way down his spine, using both my thumbs to work around the vertebrae. "Feels good," he rumbled, and I scooted my knees down so I could put more weight into it. My eyes were drawn to a tattoo of the setting sun with birds flying over the horizon. I stared at it while I worked at his trim lower back. All bone and tendon and muscle. I was working on what felt like a knot at the base of his spine when he inhaled sharply.

"Did I hurt you?" I stilled my hands for a moment.

"No," he breathed, and he flipped over and reached out to pull me in towards him. "Perfect," he whispered, and he drew me down close for a chaste kiss. Too chaste. My greedy hands crept up his bare chest of their own accord and he chuckled.

"Laugh it up," I shot back, running my fingers down to his taut stomach. There was something about almost-naked Viktor in my bed that made me want to freeze time. Well, not *something* about it; more like the totality of the experience. I could be happy here forever. My fingers traced a well-defined pectoral muscle inked with a five-pointed star. Below it were three words: *Dum Spiro Spero.* "I still don't know what most of these mean, you know."

He smiled up at the ceiling. "Laney, Laney, please explain-ey," he chanted softly, and when I thumped him on the arm he laughed. He looked relaxed. Happy. Almost like another person entirely from the tense, severe Viktor who appeared every time his phone buzzed with "work," as he called it.

"All right," he sighed, and turned over to face me again, eyes hooded, his fingers trailing down my bare arm. "Which one?"

"The sailboat."

He reached down for the comforter and drew it up over both of us with one smooth motion. I hadn't realized I was chilly, but the warm blanket felt delicious. "Sailboat. This means I lead roaming life. Don't stay in one place very long." His hand rested on my hip.

"It looks clearer than the others," I observed. "Less blurry."

His palm began a circling motion on my hip, warm and slow. "That was my first. I did not choose it myself."

"What do you mean?" Most of my energy was being spent on resisting the urge to climb on top of him again.

"I was not at labor camp entire time in prison," he said. His hand had moved down from my hip to the back of my thigh, and it was mesmerizing. "First eighteen months were in Moscow. For questioning."

I was unsure what to make of this new information. Eighteen months seemed like an awfully long time to be held for questioning. "Was it better there? Better than the camp, I mean?"

"No. Worse. Lie on other side." I turned my back to him. "Good." He began working on my shoulders. It felt tingly, heavenly, and I let out a little sigh of pleasure. "At first," he continued, "When police picked me up, they had very high hopes for me." His thumbs worked over a knot in my shoulder and I thought I might die of bliss. "They thought I knew everything. A lot more than I actually knew."

"So — *ahhh*," — the knot finally surrendered — "So they questioned you?"

"Yes."

"Why did it take so long? Did you cooperate?"

He took his time answering. "In Russia, you must understand — it's different. Police there, they are very persuasive. In time I told everything."

"And that took eighteen months?" Whatever Viktor was doing to my trapezius muscle had to be illegal. I gritted my teeth and arched towards him.

He chuckled. "No, was sooner. Maybe six months. But by that time, they liked me so much it's another year before they're finished with me. How do you say it? That's how they roll." He laid on an American accent for that last bit. It was convincing. His hands had moved down past my shoulder blades and I was melting into a puddle of goo.

Viktor touched my shoulder. "Lie on stomach," he whispered. I complied and felt him straddle me as I'd done to him earlier. He rubbed some oil between his hands and ran them up and down the back of my ribcage, warming the skin there. "Arms out," he murmured, and I felt myself relax another tenth of a degree.

"This guy, Ignaty. My interrogator in Moscow." Viktor worked his fingers around a muscle in my back and dug in gently. "We became close, in a way. He…" Viktor paused for a moment, then resumed kneading. "He arranged ship tattoo."

"Um. Is that a good thing?" I wondered aloud. "Having someone else arrange it?"

"It was kindness." Viktor's palms flattened and moved over the area of my back he'd just finished with. "He knew where I was going. Wanted me to fit in so I wouldn't get my throat cut."

"Sounds like someone you'd bring home to Mother," I said dreamily.

Viktor chuckled. "He brought in professional to do it. Pyotr did the rest. A guy at the camp."

My eyes slid open. Of course; how else would he have acquired prison tats? "How?"

"You really want to know?" Viktor had moved down to my lower back, where his thumbs were pressing the flesh around my spine. The feeling was indescribable.

"Yes."

"It's sharpened guitar string on electric shaver." I winced inwardly at the thought of it. "For ink, you burn heel of boot. Then mix soot with urine." All right, that detail was perhaps superfluous. "It wasn't clean. There was risk of infections. Septicemia." He continued working down my back. "Hepatitis and AIDS." My breath caught in my throat. "I got tested after I got out. Was negative. I was lucky." He lowered his head down close to mine. "You still think they're sexy?"

"Yes." I could feel him hovering over me and it was exciting in every sense of the word. "The manner by which the tattoos were acquired does not negate their aesthetic appeal."

"Is very open-minded of you." He reached under the futon and grabbed the box of condoms. Then he lowered his head down to mine again. "You relaxed?"

"I am putty in your hands," I said through a wide smile as I felt his body, warm and taut and heavy, pressing down on top of mine.

The next few days passed quickly. As worried as I'd been about Cynthia and her tendency towards all-or-nothing thinking, at least she seemed to be back on the wagon. She ate the food I prepared, setting alarms on her phone with military precision. Her workouts occupied most of her mornings, exactly as Fabrizio prescribed, and she'd even added in a late-afternoon meditation session to get her through what she'd started calling her "problem time."

If Mason was suffering at school, he showed no sign of it. In fact, he seemed cheerier than usual, bantering back and forth with me during after-school homework time. He found my hopelessness with math especially amusing.

"Is this Common Core?" I asked him. Cynthia's suburban Facebook pals had been ranting about that lately, posting petitions and memes and all manner of lazy click-based outrage.

"I dunno. It's just how they teach it." He reached for a carrot stick and I privately rejoiced that he was choosing to eat a vegetable.

I heard footsteps echo on the staircase and Cynthia floated into the kitchen. She was wearing a yoga ensemble and flip-flops; her face was the picture of serenity. Already I liked this meditation business. "Lane. A word?"

"Sure." I dried my hands on a dish towel and followed her into the living room. "What's up?"

Cynthia perched herself on the edge of a Danish modern chair and motioned for me to take a seat. "Summer camps," she said, and looked at me expectantly.

"Yes, Emily's all set." I'd enrolled her in a four-week session at the same horseback-riding and field-hockey camp she'd attended last year up in the Berkshires.

"I'm not talking about Emily," Cynthia replied, and there was an edgy tone to her voice that made me sit up a little straighter. "It's Mason. I told you to find sports camps and instead I got this." She picked up a printout from the table. "Computer programming camp."

"It's more than just programming," I said. "It's video game development and design, and robotics. I thought it might suit him. I thought—"

"You aren't doing what I asked," Cynthia interrupted.

I felt my face flush. "I apologize," I said carefully. "My intention was to find a good fit for Mason. I wouldn't dream of undermining you."

"Brad wants Mason to play lacrosse." Cynthia might as well have been quoting Scripture.

"I understand."

"What if I don't want to play lacrosse?" Mason demanded. Cynthia and I both looked up to see him standing in the doorway.

"Honey, your father and I—"

"I don't want to play lacrosse," Mason repeated, and he set his jaw stubbornly. "I'm not going to sports camp."

"We'll talk about it later," Cynthia snapped. She stood up and shot me an accusatory look.

"Now or later, my answer's still the same," Mason muttered. *Let it go,* I silently begged him.

"Why, Mason? Why do you have to make everything so difficult all the time?" Cynthia's cheeks were flushed. Mason responded with a shrug and slouched off. Cynthia retreated upstairs, muttering to herself.

Fabrizio's words echoed in my head: *When Cynthia's pissed off, she fires the help.*

What had I done?

On Friday night Viktor arrived at my door holding a large paper bag that I suspected was takeout. Before he could take his coat off, I caught him in a hug and buried my face in his sweater.

"Thank you," he murmured, returning the hug. "I feel welcome." When I didn't reply, he looked down at me with concern. "Bad week?"

"I'm stressed out at work," I confessed. "Cynthia's pissed off at me."

"Must be her diet," he chuckled, kissing the top of my head. "Come, we will have feast tonight."

"What did you bring?" I asked him. "It smells good."

"Russian food. From Primorski." The food was delicious — dumplings and spiced meat and vodka. It was very romantic, apart from the fact that Cynthia had decided to live-text me her Spartan dinner, sending me multiple photos of depressing food with frowny-face weeping emojis.

Once we'd eaten our fill, Viktor insisted on putting away the leftovers and taking out the trash himself. I brushed my teeth. When I emerged from the bathroom, Viktor put away his phone and walked towards me.

"Promise me something?" I asked him.

"What." That deep voice. I'd decided it was an aphrodisiac.

"Stay with me tonight," I told him. "All night."

"Okay."

This time it wasn't Viktor's voice that woke me up — it was his arm. A sudden jerky movement jolted me out of my spiced-dumpling dreamscape.

"Viktor?" I whispered. I didn't reach for the light switch, I just waited in the darkness. His movements had stopped but his breathing was ragged. I placed a hand on his bare shoulder and he twitched.

"*Ya veryu tebe.*" His voice was low, shaking. Then it dropped to a whisper. "*Ya tebe doveryayu.*" He let out a choked sob. "*Ignaty. Pozhalsta.*"

Ignaty — the interrogator! And *pozhalsta.* He'd said that same word last time. What the fuck did it mean? Was it even possible to Google Russian words without knowing the Cyrillic alphabet? "Viktor, it's just a dream, wake up," I urged, and I felt him jerk upright. He sounded like he was gasping for air. "You're okay, it's just a bad dream," I repeated, and I fumbled for the light switch and turned it on.

Viktor was sitting up in bed, the comforter thrown to one side, his face a mix of panic and confusion. He glanced at me and looked quickly away.

"Are you okay?" I was afraid to touch him; he looked like he'd just arrived from another planet.

He nodded, still looking away. His hair was sticking out in all directions. At least he hadn't puked. You could call it progress.

"Will you stay?" I asked him.

He finally turned to look at me. "The lights. Keep them on?"

"Yeah." I scooted over to make space for him on the futon, but he got up and pulled on his boxers, which had been lying on the floor in a heap with his clothes. Then he lowered himself to his customary seated position on the floor with his back against the wall.

I peered at him. "Are you coming back to bed?"

"Not now." He closed his eyes and pressed his lips together. My mind reeled with curiosity, but I resisted the urge to question him. Instead I lay back, closed my eyes, and tried to go back to sleep. Which, incredibly, must have happened — because when I opened my eyes again it was quarter past five in the morning.

"Viktor?" There he was, lying on the floor, curled up against the wall. Still wearing only his boxers, sleeping peacefully from the looks of things — despite the chilly temperature inside the apartment. I rolled out of bed, naked, and dragged the comforter over to where he lay on the floor. I draped it gently over him and he let out a little sigh of pleasure in his sleep. I felt a smile spread across my face.

It was Saturday; I didn't have to leave for work until after seven. I lowered myself to the floor and scooted up in front of Viktor until we were roughly in a spooning position. Then I tucked the edge of the blanket around me and snuggled back against his warm, strong body, feeling his chest expand and contract with slow breaths. It wasn't long before one tattooed arm draped lazily over me. His fingers found my bare midriff and crept across it, moving slowly up my stomach.

"Good morning," I whispered through a smile.

He kissed my neck. "How long have you been here? On floor," he murmured, his voice still foggy with sleep.

"Not long."

"Is not comfortable for you." His hand traveled south now, rounding my butt. He gave it a gentle squeeze. "Sorry about last night."

"You have nothing to apologize for."

He didn't respond, but his hand continued its slow exploration and moved over to my hip — not aggressive, just curious. His fingertips brushed over the scar on my thigh. It was the absence of feeling I noticed, on the severed nerve endings. I didn't flinch. "What did Ignaty do to you?" I couldn't believe I'd dared to ask him that.

"He did his job," Viktor whispered. When I didn't respond, he nuzzled my neck again.

"That's half an answer," I told him, and his fingers slid over my scar once more.

"He wanted information. Sometimes—" He paused. "Torture.

CLEAN BREAK

Other times, kindness. They go together," he added cryptically. "I have tried to forget about it."

"Bad memories suck," I said. As usual, Randy had nailed it.

He chuckled. "Yes. You have any good ones?"

I snuggled into his arms and thought about it. "Sure."

"Please, share." He brushed my hair off my neck and nuzzled the skin behind my ear. Shivers! How could he expect me to think straight when he pulled such shenanigans?

"Summer on Block Island," I blurted out, before I could think better of it. "I was, I don't know — twelve years old?"

Viktor withdrew from his nuzzling and pulled me in close. "Keep going," he murmured.

"Charlotte." I swallowed. "She was nine or ten, I guess." I couldn't believe I was talking about this. "We spent the afternoon at the beach with Mom and Dad. It wasn't crowded. Just a few families. It was hot. We'd jump in the water every so often, to cool off." I could almost hear the waves crashing, smell the salt air.

"Mmm. I like it."

"We'd just eaten dinner," I went on. "Sandwiches out of a cooler, probably. Devil Dogs for dessert. It was just so simple, so good." My voice trailed off. A lump was forming in my throat — par for the course.

"Is good memory," Viktor rumbled, and he pulled me in closer.

"I'm not done," I protested. "After dinner, me and Charlotte took our bikes and went to New Harbor. A mile away, maybe less."

"Without your parents?" Viktor's hands were warm against my skin.

"No parents. Just us. We wanted to see the sunset." I closed my eyes and saw it so clearly: Riding our bikes — legs pumping furiously, flip-flops precarious. The cooling island air rippling over my skin, which was so tanned after a few weeks on Block Island that Mom'd had a conniption fit about my lifetime risk of melanoma. Coasting side-by-side down the road into New Harbor and dropping our bikes down in the dirt. Charlotte's laughter, tinkling like glass. Standing together and looking out at

163

the boats anchored there, squinting at the bright orange sun as it sank slowly but inevitably over the western horizon.

"I never imagined a world without her," I said.

"Your world was better with her here." Viktor gave me a gentle squeeze.

"She made me a better person," I admitted. "I didn't know that until she was gone. Then it was too late." I flipped myself over to face him. My throat hurt from trying not to cry. He kissed my forehead and I let out a great shuddering sigh. "You must think I'm pathetic," I whispered. "Getting so upset about this all these years later."

He pulled me close. "If you believe that, you don't know me at all."

We lay there quietly for a few minutes. Just having him close to me felt good. "Maybe a part of me died with Charlotte," I said suddenly.

"What part?"

I thought about it. "The best part. The soft, squishy part."

Viktor hoisted himself up onto his elbow. "When I got out of prison," he said, "Was my sister who helped me most."

"Really? The clarinet player?" Talking to him was like peeling away the layers of an onion.

"Yes." His eyes met mine and I couldn't look away.

"How did she help?" I whispered.

"She listened to me. We talked. She knew me." He looked lost in thought. "She maybe helped me get closer to person I was, before."

"Prison changed you," I murmured.

"Yes. If not I'd be dead." He sounded defensive, which was understandable.

"You're lucky to have her then," I told him, and he nodded, still deep in thought. "What's your favorite movie?" I asked him, out of nowhere.

"Hm." He relaxed visibly. *"Bullitt."*

"What's that?"

"My favorite movie," he answered. "Steve McQueen." Still it didn't ring a bell. "What is your favorite?"

"Harry Potter and the Prisoner of Azkaban," I told him without hesitation.

"I have not seen that one." He stroked my hair.

"Why are you helping me?" I whispered. "I mean why did you help me at first, with the rent money. And the futon."

"Why not?"

"You didn't even know me," I pointed out.

"I could not let you sleep on floor," he said. "It's too cold. Too hard."

"Yet that doesn't stop you from sleeping here by choice when there's a perfectly good futon a few feet away."

"With beautiful naked girl in it," he added, and I felt a pang of smug contentment at his flattery despite myself.

"So why would you choose to suffer?" I pressed.

It took him a moment to answer. "Bad habit. Sometimes suffering brings strange comfort. You might be familiar with this."

He had me. In every way. "How about a quickie before work?" I whispered.

"A quickie," he repeated, and then he sprang to standing, all catlike grace in only his boxers. I started getting awkwardly to my feet, then shrieked and giggled when he scooped me up and carried me back to the futon.

21

My subway ride into Manhattan was pleasantly uncrowded. I sat there basking in the glory of having two seats all to myself until I remembered to Google Viktor's twice-spoken Russian word. *No results for 'pohlzasta,'* Google chided me, and instead showed results for some municipality in Brazil.

Had I used the wrong spelling? I frowned down at Cynthia's phone and cleared the search field. Then I pecked in *polzhasta.* Paydirt! I got a short list of basic Russian phrases for travelers. And there it was, halfway down the list: It meant *please.* Mystery solved.

Ignaty. Polzhasta. The subway car was heated and I was bundled up in my winter coat, but I shivered nonetheless. Everything about this Ignaty fellow creeped me out. *My interrogator in Moscow.* Eighteen months! *We became close.* I bet. The tattoo he'd "arranged." *It was kindness. So I wouldn't get my throat cut.* Viktor was fucked up, well and truly. Maybe that's why we got along so swimmingly well together.

Enough doom and gloom. This morning on the floor! Again I'd wanted to freeze time forever, the second time that urge had come to me while I was curled up with Viktor. The fact that I'd voluntarily conversed in depth with someone about Haviland family memories was frankly shocking, but Viktor had an unusual effect on me. A realization dawned: I felt safe with him.

Attention Dr. Ulrich. Today my grief is like a whale. It can lay low, be down deep. Then it comes up for air. Happy now?

I was hoping to speak with Cynthia — I wanted to smooth things over after the summer-camp-planning fiasco — but when I arrived at Chez Waldrop, she was running out the door to a Rise'n'Shine yoga class. The kids were sleeping in. My first instinct was to check the fridge, to make sure there were adequate meals to get Cynthia through the next 48 hours. As I fumbled with the plastic containers, I heard a deep voice.

"Hello." Right behind me! I turned around to see Brad Waldrop sitting at the counter.

"Oh, Mr. Waldrop! Sorry, I didn't see you there." He was wearing pajamas and a bathrobe and holding a coffee mug. The Saturday *Wall Street Journal* was spread out in front of him.

"I hope I didn't scare you." He regarded me amusedly over the top rim of his reading-glasses.

"No, no, no, not at all. No." My heartbeat was slowly returning to normal. Brad raised a doubtful eyebrow. "Okay, yes, you scared me." I let out a nervous laugh. Why did this man intimidate me so much? And furthermore, why was I acting like a goddamn idiot? He looked older in person than he did on Facebook. Distinguished, square-jawed, very captain-of-industry in his silk pajamas. I knew they were silk because I'd picked them up at Saks Fifth Avenue a couple of weeks ago. They cost more than I made in a week.

Brad set down his glasses and folded the Off Duty section of the paper. "Can I make you a cup of coffee?" he asked. My eyes snapped to the gleaming, complicated espresso machine. How to respond? I bit my lip. "That looks like a yes," he said, and he stood up.

"Oh, no, Mr. Waldrop. Please don't get up on my account," I stammered as he walked around to my side of the counter. "I should be getting *you* coffee."

He ignored my bumbling protestations and scooped beans

into one of the machine's compartments. "How could you make me coffee?" he asked. "You don't know how to work this thing."

I was momentarily speechless. "That's true." How did he know?

"I know," he said, grabbing a clean mug and placing it under the dispenser, "Because nobody can. I must have massacred ten pounds of beans figuring it out." He turned a dial and the machine commenced the noisy business of grinding. I watched, impressed, as he went through the rest of the process, finally adding hot water to the espresso to make a more American-style cup of coffee, which he handed to me.

"Thanks," I said, and took a sip. "This hits the spot."

He gathered up the newspaper sections. "You want any of this before I recycle it? The puzzle?"

"No thanks. Actually," I ventured, summoning up my courage, "I was hoping to touch base with you on Mason."

"Yes?" He stood there holding the newspaper.

"Well, Mason wanted to spend time with you in London," I said. "I could schedule you two for something fun together, like maybe dinner. Or a West End musical."

"Ah. Yes." One hand went to his chin. He rubbed it thoughtfully. He hadn't shaven yet. I automatically thought of Viktor.

"I don't mean to put you on the spot, Mr. Waldrop. You don't have to answer right now."

"You know what? Book it." He flashed me a million-watt smile. I'd never seen such perfect white teeth. "Thanks, Lane."

"Thank *you*, Mr. Waldrop."

Brad disappeared shortly thereafter without saying goodbye, leaving me alone with both kids. I instructed them to email Magda — she was still stuck in the D.R., according to Cynthia — and procured two high-priced London theater tickets over the Internet. Then I got breakfast started.

"You're booked for a show in London," I told Mason. "Your dad's psyched to be taking you."

Mason's whole face brightened for a moment, then turned suspicious. "I've never seen Dad get psyched about anything.

Except maybe golf."

"He has a point," Emily muttered through a mouthful of cereal. She had *Teen Vogue* open on the counter in front of her.

"Well, believe it," I told them. "They're great seats." I'd booked *Matilda* — it was kid-friendly, and topical. Perhaps Brad would have an epiphany moment and get a goddamn fucking clue.

Emily's friend Isabella arrived for a playdate at noon, and the two girls made a beeline for Emily's room. The door slammed shut and the sounds of a Taylor Swift song wafted out into the hallway. Mason and I exchanged a look.

"Can I ask you some for technical help?" I dug around in my pocket for Viktor's USB drive. "I need to get some songs onto my iPhone."

Mason examined the USB drive. "Can't you use your flip-phone for that? Plug it into a cassette tape player or something?"

"Funny." I followed him into his room and watched him launch iTunes on his MacBook. "Thanks, though. I had them on my old phone but it's not holding a charge anymore."

Mason turned around in his swivel-chair and looked at me with disbelief. "Are you telling me that you have an even older phone than that piece of shit Motorola thing?"

"Language," I warned.

"Sorry." He swiveled back towards his laptop and stuck the USB drive into a slot on the side. "Whoever gave you this should just use Spotify." He typed something in and dragged some files into a folder on the desktop.

"Look at you, schooling me on iTunes," I observed.

"Yeah, I'm pretty nasty at that," he replied. I gave him a look. "Nasty means I'm good at it." He plugged my iPhone into a cable on his desk. "Thanks," he added. "For sticking up for me on summer camp. With my parents."

"You're welcome." I studied a Doctor Who poster on the wall. "Think they'll come around?"

"I'm applying pressure. I'm doing well in school. Staying out of trouble."

"I'm glad," I said. "I never doubted you could do it if you

tried."

He bobbed his head. "They don't understand me, but I understand them. If I got kicked out of school, Mom would die of shame."

"Don't say that," I told him. "Don't say she'd die."

Mason swiveled back around to face me, a peculiar look on his face. "Okay," he drawled. "She'd be positively mortified."

I managed a small smile.

"All done." He stood up and handed me the phone and the USB drive. "They're in the Music app," he added.

"Thanks." I felt strange, like something had changed between us. "That was…"

"Clutch," he supplied. I had no idea what that meant.

"Whatever happens with camp, Mason, I know you're a great kid. I believe in you."

He rolled his eyes. "Let's not get emotional."

Sunday was cold and rainy — miserable weather, perfect for doing as little as possible. I sat alone in the laundromat on Neptune Avenue, my mind a blissful blank, and watched my clothes tumble around in the dryer. But my peace couldn't possibly last. A text popped up from Cynthia:

OMG there is PEANUT BUTTER in the PANTRY!!!!!!

Dear God. *Throw it away,* I texted back. *Stay strong.*

TOO LATE!!! LOL

A moment later, she texted me a series of pig emojis along with a photo attachment: a jar of peanut butter with a tablespoon stuck in it.

I considered my next move. One thing was certain: Cynthia alone with a half-eaten jar of peanut butter was going to require U.N. Secretary-General level diplomacy. Were her texts a break for freedom, or a cry for help? Should I call, or continue texting her?

Just as I'd made the decision to call and talk her down from the ledge, the laundromat door squeaked open and Detective Jarrett walked in.

"Lane. Fancy meeting you here."

"Hey, Detective." I felt wholly unprepared to deal with him right now. "What brings you out on such a fine day?"

"Just going for a walk around the neighborhood." He brushed some rain droplets off his green and white New York Jets jacket. "Mind if I sit down?"

I gave him a noncommittal shrug and glanced down at my phone. Cynthia hadn't texted anything further. The one time a series of frantic texts from her would have helped me, she chose radio silence.

Jarrett lowered himself down into a white plastic lawn-chair, one of several scattered around the laundromat. "You okay?"

"I'm fine." I thought about the dead roses in my trashcan and wondered how best to address that whole situation. Thanking him would only encourage more attention. At the same time, I didn't want to start World War Three. Maybe it was best to say nothing at all.

Detective Jarrett drummed his fingers on his knees. "Have you given any more thought to our conversation at the precinct?"

"Not really." I stared at my clothes as they tumbled around in the dryer. Why did being in the same room as this guy make me feel so uneasy? "I don't think I'm the person you're looking for."

"I'm sorry to hear that, Lane. I thought we could help each other out."

"Is that how you see it?" I asked him. "Because the idea of secretly informing on my friend kind of makes my skin crawl." Even as the words spilled out of my mouth, I wondered if I was taking out all my other frustrations on him. He *was* just doing his job. "Sorry to be so blunt," I added.

He leaned in a little closer, elbows resting on his knees. "I understand your hesitation," he murmured, and he smiled at me, almost like a friend might do. I felt another pang of doubt. Was I being unreasonable? My instincts had led me down questionable paths before. But I could count the number of people I trusted in this world on one hand — twice — and still have a thumb to spare. I couldn't betray Viktor.

Detective Jarrett cleared his throat, interrupting my reverie. "I have some news that might interest you." He shifted his chair slightly closer to mine, causing the hair on the back of my neck to stand at attention. "Your boyfriend got arrested last night."

My blood froze. "Viktor?"

"Viktor," he confirmed.

"What for?" I asked him. My voice sounded strangled.

"As I told you, he was up to no good."

"You're not gonna tell me?" I demanded, and the Detective smiled almost imperceptibly. "Now you're just being an asshole." My voice was shaking. He'd come in here to taunt me.

"Strong words, Lane." Jarrett remained gratingly calm. "Now you have a decision to make. You can do the right thing, which is all I've been asking. Or you can start planning weekend trips up to Green Haven. Visit Viktor in prison. Deposit some money in his commissary account."

Could he *be* any more condescending? "Fuck you," I snarled. "You don't know anything about me."

He snort-laughed. "I know exactly what you're about. And I can see that you and I have nothing more to discuss." I didn't acknowledge him. "See you around, Lane." He headed for the door.

Part of me wanted to run after him and demand more information, but I managed to resist that urge, just barely. Yanking out my flip-phone, I texted Viktor:

Are you okay? Pls text me back when you see this.

Seconds ticked by, then a minute. No response. I tried calling him, but it went straight to voicemail.

I texted him again:

I heard you're in trouble and I'm worried. Call or text me ASAP.

My iPhone chimed and I jumped. Cynthia again:

Ate half the jar. Am now throwing it AWAY!!!!!

My stomach churned. I couldn't muster much enthusiasm for dealing with Cynthia right now, but at the same time I couldn't exactly ignore her. *Glad u contained the damage,* I texted back. Then I switched to Safari and Googled *arrested in NYC*, adding a silent prayer that Cynthia wasn't monitoring my web-browsing history through her mobile account. The NYC.gov website helpfully

CLEAN BREAK

informed me that you can call 311 for information on anyone who's been arrested in the last 24 to 48 hours.

With trembling fingers, I dialed the phone.

Ten minutes later, still alone in the laundromat, I started to text Randy, then changed my mind and called her. I needed to hear a human voice that wasn't Detective Jarrett's.

She picked up on the third ring. "Lane?" She sounded sleepy.

"Yeah, it's me. Viktor got arrested. I don't know what to do."

"Shit. What for?"

"I don't know. He's 'in custody pending arraignment.' It's like a bail hearing." I could hear the panic mounting in my voice. "That's all the information 311 could give me. I haven't heard anything from him directly."

"Lane, listen to me. I'm not saying you don't have every right to freak out, but I want you to sit down and take a deep breath."

I sat down on one of the plastic lawn-chairs. "What can I do?"

"I'm thinking. Can you go to the courthouse, physically? Where is it?"

"They said it's on Queens Boulevard. Near Kew Gardens." I gnawed on a fingernail. "I hate this! Not knowing. I feel like a dupe." My boyfriend was turning out to be a scumbag. "I'm scared I messed up," I whispered, and having said it I felt even worse, because I knew Viktor had to be in worse shape than I was at the moment. All the lectures I'd given Emily on empathy-for-those-less-fortunate were circling the karmic drain.

"Lane, did you do anything illegal for him? With him?" Randy's voice was sharp, worried.

"No." I felt a gigantic lump forming in my throat. "I don't expect you to understand this. I'm not sure I understand it myself."

Randy went silent for a moment, and that's when the dam burst. Hot tears trickled down my cheeks. The Story of Lane, Part Two: The Fucking Cycle Continues.

"Shit. You love him." It wasn't a question. I couldn't even respond coherently.

173

* * * *

In the end, I didn't go to the courthouse. I gathered up my clean laundry and what little remained of my self-respect and I went home, where I stared at my debt repayment schedule and tried to imagine what it might feel like to zero it out. If I stopped paying Viktor and put all the money towards Randy — and didn't eat too much — I could be paid up in a few weeks. I'd be skinny, and almost-solvent, and I could plan my escape from this troglodyte dump. Move into someone's spare bedroom in an anonymous Queens mid-rise while I saved up enough money to pay Viktor back.

And deposit it into his commissary account at Green Haven? If jamming a meat-thermometer into my ear had been a reliable way to get Detective Jarrett out of my head, I'd have seriously considered doing it.

At five o'clock, I dragged myself out for a walk around the neighborhood and hoped I didn't look too much like the walking wounded. Outwardly, at least; inside, my mind was racing at a mile a minute, mostly churning through self-flagellating angst. At least the rain had stopped.

Just as I walked by a shawarma restaurant with its heavenly smells wafting out onto the sidewalk, my phone buzzed. Randy. As much as I didn't want to take the call, I knew I had to. I didn't want her to worry about me.

"Hey." I was surprised at how calm my voice sounded, compared to the chaotic thoughts knocking around inside my head.

"I'm checking on you to make sure you're not wallowing overmuch in self-pity."

I let my gaze wander across the street at a red neon CHECKS CASHED - WE BUY GOLD! sign. "I'd say I'm wallowing an entirely appropriate amount."

"Any word yet?"

"No." My fingers were turning numb from the cold. "I'm a fool, you know."

"You're way too hard on yourself is what you are."

I sighed. "It's nice of you to say so."

"I mean it, Lane. Don't beat yourself up about this. Just forget about him. He's not worth it."

I had to snort at that last bit. "Roger that. You sound like a diplomat in the Foreign Service."

"It's one of my many hidden talents. I can also ride a unicycle."

I blinked back fresh tears. "Thanks, Randy."

At nine-thirty that night, my flip-phone pinged from its hopeful perch in the window-well. It was a text from Viktor.

Sorry I am ok

Four words. I felt at once relieved and angry and wildly curious. Four words, threatening to rouse my mind to its previous cacophonous state. He was okay. What did that mean? He was alive. If he had his phone, he was obviously no longer behind bars. Was he in trouble? Out on bail? Charged with some horrible violent crime?

Truly, I didn't know how to respond. I stood there looking at his text for a long time. Then, finally, I flipped the phone shut.

22

I forced myself to wear a neutral face for work on Monday. *Just hold it together,* I repeated to myself on the ride into Manhattan. My guts were still roiling — I hadn't eaten much in the last 24 hours — but I was determined to act professional, or at least what passed for it in Cynthia's world.

An unread Viktor text from last night taunted me steadily. I finally looked at it:

Need to see you

Lovely. Great. I shoved the phone back into my bag without responding, then thought better of it and pulled the phone back out.

This week is hectic.

Passive-aggressive, my conscience needled at me. I bulldozed past that thought and reasoned that I needed time and space to figure things out. And, possibly, consort with the enemy.

Cynthia was still in bed when I returned from the kids' school drop-off, which was unusual. I tiptoed up the stairs and knocked on her bedroom door.

"Mmmmmmmmfffff." An extremely muffled groan.

"Everything all right?" I called through the door. Silence. Was it a medical emergency? Breaking a chicken-breast fast with half a jar of peanut butter couldn't be without risk. Maybe Cynthia's gallbladder had finally exploded.

Finally, when I was about to give up, I heard her muffled voice again: "Come in."

I took a tentative peek inside and saw a heap of blankets on the bed. I tiptoed closer.

"I'monrobation." Her voice was coming from inside the blanket-heap.

"What?"

"I'm. On. *Probation!*" Cynthia's bedraggled head emerged. She looked so different without her hair and makeup done — less conventionally pretty, more human.

"Did you get arrested?" Please no. One was enough.

"Lane." Cynthia cocked her head and looked at me as though I'd just sprouted tentacles. "Don't be ridiculous."

"Oh. Well, good." I sat down on a mustard-colored Louis XIV-style ottoman.

Cynthia heaved a great sigh. "It's Hugh. He put me on probation after my weigh-in."

"The food coach." I still felt like I wasn't firing on all cylinders.

"Yes." She flopped backwards onto a pair of Euro-sized square pillows with six-hundred-thread-count Egyptian cotton shams. "The best in the city. Hugh works with winners. He doesn't waste time with people who are only halfway committed."

I shifted my weight. This ottoman had better be an antique; it was uncomfortable as hell. "Was it the peanut butter?"

"No. The wine, the cheese, et cetera." Cynthia rolled over onto her side. "The peanut butter hadn't even happened yet."

"So you're on probation." Frankly, I felt kind of like I was on probation myself. I was sure I still hadn't heard the last of the summer camp debacle.

"Yes," Cynthia pouted. "I confessed everything and I begged him to give me another chance." I tried to get more comfortable; this ottoman was officially the worst thing ever. "I had to, Lane! He knows. He knows everything. You should see his before-and-after portfolio!"

I stood up. "So what are we waiting for? Fabrizio's expecting you at the gym in fifteen minutes. Come on."

Cynthia rolled out of bed with a groan. And she complained steadily until I shut the front door behind her. But she went.

I spent most of the day prepping Cynthia's food and playing Tetris with her schedule, signing her up for as many group exercise classes as I possibly could around the naturopathic doctor and acupuncture appointments that had suddenly begun to populate her calendar. Her next appointment with Hugh was the following week, so we had some time to reverse the effects of the peanut butter binge through SoulCycle and clean living.

Later, I shepherded Mason to his after-school shrink appointment. Emily was at Brooke's. The house was empty at four o'clock and I could delay the inevitable no longer. I flipped my phone open and scrolled through the Received Calls log. Stopping at the number with the 718 area code, I took a deep breath and pressed the CALL button.

"Jarrett here." He sounded busy, or pissed-off. Perhaps both.

"It's Lane Haviland, Detective." I swallowed.

There was a pause, and an odd, staticky noise coming from the other end of the line — as though he were fumbling with something. "Okay," he finally said. "I'm frankly a little surprised to hear from you."

"I wanted to tell you that I'm sorry," I blurted out. Like ripping duct-tape off my genitals while cartwheeling off the high diving board. "For my behavior. I was kind of a jerk." I offered up silent thanks that he couldn't see my face flush tomato-red over the phone.

"Well, I accept your apology." More rustling and static on the phone. Then: "I'm not the type to hold a grudge."

"That's very evolved of you." I hoped that didn't come across as bitchy, because I meant it as a sincere compliment. Someday my brain would catch up with my mouth, but today was not that day. I pressed on. "Will you have coffee with me tomorrow?"

"Uh, what?" Finally, Detective Jarrett was speechless.

CLEAN BREAK

"Coffee," I repeated. "An elixir made from magical beans. It prevents more frequent workplace homicides."

"Hey, she's smart *and* sassy." More crackling and moving around on the other end of the line. "Sure, I'd love to."

"We can meet in Manhattan," I told him with much more confidence than I was feeling. "Dutch treat."

The East Midtown coffee shop I'd picked to meet with Detective Jarrett was cavernous and sparsely populated by seven-thirty in the evening — perfect for a clandestine encounter. Not that I believed I was being followed, but everyone seemed to know everyone else in Brighton Beach, and I already had enough problems.

I arrived early in hopes of getting there first, but Detective Jarrett was already seated at a booth in the far corner. He stood up to greet me and I kept a polite distance, shaking his hand and sliding onto the bench opposite him. "Thanks for coming out here, Detective," I said. "It's much more comfortable for me."

He sat down and tilted his head in acknowledgment. "I understand. Call me Mike."

I preferred not to, but I nodded. Suddenly this felt like a scene from a Regency period-drama: everything about it was stiff and forced and uncomfortable. "You must see a lot of crazy stuff in your line of work," I remarked, pushing my menu to the side unopened.

He scanned his menu. "Some days are crazier than others. Full moons tend to bring out the real weirdos, let me tell you."

Suddenly I felt warm. I pressed both palms against the table and slowed down my breathing: *In. Out. Easy.* The two texts Viktor had sent me earlier today, asking to meet, were not what I wanted to be thinking about. And yet here they were, foremost in my mind.

"I hope you're not being too hard on yourself." Detective Jarrett closed his menu. "Many criminals — most criminals — are master manipulators."

Was that what Viktor was? A master manipulator? I didn't say it out loud, but my lack-of-a-poker-face must have betrayed me. "Hey now," Jarrett said softly, and he placed his large hand on top of mine and gave it a squeeze. Our eyes met — his were gray, and set close together. "We don't have to talk about Viktor." At least he'd dropped 'your boyfriend' from his sneering lexicon.

"No." I took a deep breath and looked across the table, focusing my full attention on Detective Jarrett. "Let's talk about Viktor."

"You had coffee with Detective Asshole?" Randy was barely keeping it to a stage-whisper at our usual diner on First Avenue.

"Don't call him that. I needed to talk to him."

"And you think this is a smart move because…?"

"Don't worry, we met in Manhattan. There's no possible way Roman Maksimov will find out I was consorting with the po-po. And we went Dutch."

"God forbid he should spring three-fifty for the standard Lane Haviland dinner, the bagel and coffee. Also the standard Lane Haviland breakfast and lunch." Randy pursed her lips in motherly disapproval, calling to mind Viktor and his bottles of Naked juice.

"I'm in enough debt already," I insisted, and Randy stuck her tongue out at me. "Well, I *am.*"

"And you're paying it back. Ahead of schedule, even." I'd given her $100 cash when I arrived.

"I'm trying."

"So," Randy said, setting her water glass to one side. "What have we learned from The Detective Formerly Known as Asshole?"

I let that slide. "Maksimov has a lot of irons in the fire," I began. "He has strong ties to the old country, but he's also branching out, getting local. One of his closest associates just got indicted for Medicare fraud," I said conversationally. "Apparently it's a very lucrative business these days — like a cash machine spitting out free money, if you can find a doctor who's okay with committing a Federal offense."

"That's...shitty," Randy said. "Was it Viktor?"

"No. Viktor's very low-level in the organization. Our Detective confirmed that."

"Okay. What'd he get arrested for, then?"

"You're never gonna believe this." I looked around to make sure no one nearby was listening. "Advancing prostitution." Just saying the words made my stomach lurch.

"What?" Randy choked on her water.

"A bunch of guys who work for Maksimov got arrested in some raid by the vice squad. At a residence in Rego Park. They also rescued a bunch of Russian and Ukrainian girls who'd been trafficked in. You okay?"

Randy nodded, wide-eyed, still wheezing as she coughed up the last drops of water that had gone down the wrong pipe. She motioned with one hand for me to continue.

"They had to let them all go," I went on. "Because the D.A. didn't bring charges right away. Something about the evidence. But Detective Jarrett thinks it'll move forward."

"You seem oddly okay with this," she rasped, and blinked watery eyes. "Please tell me you're not okay with this."

"Oh, I'm perfectly okay with it," I told her. "I don't have to waste another second of my time hemming and hawing. Viktor and I are finished."

"What about that whole confidential snitch thing?" Randy asked. "Does Detective Jarrett's offer still stand?"

"Yeah, he mentioned it," I mumbled. "My answer hasn't changed." As pissed off as I was at Viktor, my integrity was still too new for me to put it up for sale.

Randy sighed. "You really okay, Lane? This sounds tough. You had feelings for Viktor, even if he turned out to be a schmuck."

"It blows," I admitted. "But what choice do I have? I can't stay with him."

"No, you definitely can't." Randy looked somber. "How are you gonna break the bad news?"

"This weekend. Quick and painless." I drained my cup of coffee.

"Stay strong, hon." Randy looked as miserable as I felt.

"Why so glum?" I asked her.

She seemed surprised at the question. "Because he hurt you. Thus I want to strangle him."

The next three days were a struggle. Keeping Viktor at bay was the least of my troubles: *Let's catch up this weekend,* I suggested via text message, and when he agreed, I tried to let myself feel relief. It was for the best. We never would have made it as a couple. It was a nice fantasy for a while, but what did we really have in common?

Except suddenly I'd become a lousy liar, even when it came to the lies I told myself. Right below the brave face I wore for Cynthia and the kids I was already grieving for the end of this friendship. Relationship. Whatever it had been, once. Or still was.

I texted Randy during a moment of weakness waiting for Mason after school:

What if there's a reasonable explanation?

She texted back in twenty seconds:

There is no reasonable explanation.

And she was right. I *knew* she was right. I'd fallen into a self-destructive pattern with this guy, making excuses for him. What kind of a person advances prostitution, or has anything to do with prostitution in the first place? The only reason I held onto any hope at all was the incredibly slim chance that Detective Jarrett was wrong, or lying.

Late Friday afternoon, I lingered at Chez Waldrop longer than I absolutely had to. Cynthia was helping Mason with his French homework in the kitchen, so I wandered up to Emily's room. Taylor Swift was playing, but not as loud as usual. I knocked on the door.

"Come in," Emily called. And then: "Lane. You look sad." She put her phone down and patted the space next to her on the bed.

I sat down and looked around at the pink-painted walls. Emily was allowed to hang up posters of her choice as long as they were framed and matted to Cynthia's standards. "I guess I could use a pick-me-up," I conceded. "Although you and your brother almost always make me smile."

"Really?" She bit her lip. Brace-face.

"Yes, really. You're great kids." I picked up a stuffed unicorn. She was still a kid in so many ways, despite her teenage bluster. "I'm off this weekend, you know."

"Yeah. Our cousins are visiting. And my aunt and uncle." She puffed up her cheeks and exhaled slowly.

"Should be fun. Right? The Boston Waldrops." I gave her a smile that was probably unconvincing.

"Lane, do you..." Emily started over. "I mean, do you want to come over? And just, like, hang out? My cousins are crazy. It'll be so much fun."

A lump was forming in my throat. "No thank you, sweetie," I told her, and I leaned in for a hug. "But it's lovely of you to ask."

At eleven on Saturday morning, Viktor came knocking, prompt as ever. I steeled myself as I opened the door.

"Hey." He was looking handsome in jeans and a dark gray T-shirt with an Adidas warm-up jacket.

"Aren't you cold?" I blurted out.

"It's warm outside," he replied with a smile, and handed me a brown paper bag. I set it down on the counter unopened and turned to face him. But I didn't know how to start, so I just stood there.

"Coffee?" he asked, and motioned to the bag. "I already had mine."

I nodded; coffee couldn't possibly make the situation worse. He lifted out a cup and handed it to me. "Cream and extra sugar for Lane, like melted ice cream. There is also bagel. Cream cheese and smoked sable."

Smoked sable! I had to break up with him before I proposed marriage. "What happened last weekend?" I said, a little more stiffly than I'd have liked.

He looked down at the floor. "I got arrested." At least he respected me enough not to lie outright.

"What for?" I asked, and our eyes met, and I could tell that he knew that I knew. Because I'm always so great with the poker-face.

"Lane," he began, and I backed away, because even the thought of what had happened made me feel sick. I knew that if I let him touch me I'd want to forgive him and I'd hate myself for even entertaining that possibility.

"Just tell me," I said. "I want to hear it from you, in your own words."

"You already know," he said evenly, and I felt a tiny spark of hope inside of me flicker and die. "Advancing prostitution. It was mistake," he added, holding eye contact with me. "Police let us go. No charges."

"I don't care if they pressed charges!" I yelled. "You think I give a shit about that? Really?" Tears ran down my cheeks and I didn't even care.

"Because it was bullshit," Viktor said quietly, pleadingly. "I was in wrong place at wrong time."

"And the girls? From Russia and Ukraine? The cops took them out of there. Were they also in the wrong place at the wrong time?" I choked back a sob and turned away, burying my face in my hands. This was too humiliating.

"They — listen. I was there on business," he said softly, and I turned around and shot him a brief, murderous look. "Not that kind of business," he added. "Just regular stuff."

"I'm afraid to ask about the regular stuff," I hissed. "Why would a self-respecting person be involved with any of this? On *any* level?" Now my voice was shaking.

"I'm telling you the truth," he pleaded, then he shook his head. "I don't expect you to understand."

"Well, guess what? I don't understand! Mission fucking accomplished!"

He nodded grimly, and stared down at the floor.

"I had real feelings for you, Viktor. That's the worst part. None of this makes any sense." His icy-blue eyes met mine but he didn't speak. "It's true," I said. "Look at you. *You* don't make sense. I can't think of a scenario where the man I know, the man I trusted and confided in, would be okay with any of this. I guess I misjudged you."

Viktor shook his head, arms folded in front of him. "I'm sorry," he finally said.

"Sorry for what you did, or sorry for getting caught?" He didn't take the bait, so of course I pushed harder. "Are you sorry we ever met?"

That seemed to catch him by surprise. "Are you?"

"I asked you first." Okay, not my proudest moment.

He ran one long-fingered hand over his mouth and shook his head again, looking up, then down, taking his time to find the words. I grabbed a tissue and blew my nose. He was taking way too long to answer this question.

Finally he met my gaze. "Lane, please listen. I could never be sorry I met you."

I nodded, unable to speak. My throat hurt, and so did my entire face. Fresh tears were streaming down my cheeks. I turned away so I wouldn't have to watch him go.

23

"He's the first guy I've liked in years, and he's a low-life and a liar." I grabbed another homemade chocolate chip cookie and shoved it into my mouth before Randy could take the plate away. I was due back uptown in twenty minutes, but that didn't seem like any reason not to extend my lunchtime pity-party a bit longer.

"It's profoundly unfair," Randy scowled.

I slumped down in my chair and brushed cookie crumbs off my skirt. "Well, I don't know what I was thinking. I mean, a normal, well-adjusted guy would see me and run screaming in the opposite direction."

"That's ridiculous."

"Is it? My life is a train wreck, remember." I checked the time on my phone. "And now I have to go back uptown and deal with everyone else's bullshit."

"I'm sorry he turned out to be a pig, Laney." Randy ran a hand through her curls. "And never doubt that I'm on your side. But you're being way too hard on yourself about this."

"Sure." I stood up and pulled my coat on.

"Lane." Randy planted herself in front of me so I couldn't ignore her. "I'm being serious now. It was an error in judgment. You still deserve to be happy."

"An error in judgment is going on a date with a guy who texts you a dick-pic afterwards. I fell in love with a pimp." I buttoned up my coat. "At least grant me the indulgence of a little self-loathing."

Randy shook her head, forever stubborn. "Sometimes we give people the benefit of the doubt whether they deserve it or not. Do you really want to go through your life believing the worst about everybody?"

I shrugged. "You gave me the benefit of the doubt."

"And I've never regretted it." She grabbed my hat from the table, reached up, and pulled it onto my head at a cockeyed angle.

"That reminds me — I'm almost all paid up." I dug a $50 out of my bag for her.

She took the cash and surprised me with a bear-hug. "Just promise you won't stop coming to see me once you're back in the black."

"You won't get rid of me that easily."

She finally let go. "Take care of yourself, Lane."

By the time the weekend rolled around, I decided I was done wallowing in self-pity. I could only take so much insanity, and Cynthia was supplying it in endless amounts. Not that I could blame her; she seemed legitimately hungry, and she hadn't strayed one inch from Hugh's prescribed menu. As tired as I was of cooking chicken breasts for her, she must be doubly sick of eating them with lemon-water at every meal.

Sunday was about fifteen degrees warmer than usual, so I dropped off my clean laundry at home and took a walk around Brighton Beach. The breeze was cool on my face — not cold — and it felt like a precious gift after such a long winter. Since I was in no hurry to get home, I detoured down a side-street I hadn't explored before, and I noticed that several single-family houses there were adorned with multiple satellite dishes. I puzzled over one yellow house with no fewer than six dishes affixed to the roof eaves. How many could one family possibly need? That's when it hit me: it wasn't for a family. The house was subdivided into tiny apartments. Illegal ones, probably.

I stood there and studied the house with renewed interest. Six satellite dishes — one for each bedroom? The monthly rent on each room couldn't possibly be as much as what I was paying Mrs. Pasternak.

I resumed walking. Forward: it was the only way to go. My mind raced with the possibilities of what I could do with an extra couple of hundred bucks a month. Finish paying off debts, for one. Eat something besides ramen noodles for dinner. Buy a monthly MetroCard instead of a weekly one to realize even more savings. Then take over the world!

I arrived home with feelers out on three possible Craigslist leads. The matter was far from settled — more research would be necessary, and the thought of sharing my living space with housemates made my stomach churn. But part of me was already mentally bidding farewell to my sourpuss landlady and Sergey the creep. The fact that I wouldn't have to worry about running into Viktor anymore — well, that was good too. Right?

"Lane? Lane! I can't move my arms." Cynthia, recently returned from the gym, was lying flat on her back on the sofa. I abandoned the cup of green tea I'd been fixing her and hurried to her side. "Help me up," she implored.

I grasped her by the shoulders and pulled her awkwardly to a sitting position.

"Do you think maybe Fabrizio needs to cool it a little with the weights?" I asked.

"This is how I'm gonna get the results I want." Cynthia rotated her shoulder slowly and grimaced. "Fabrizio says my body will get used to it."

"If you say so." Probably best not to ask what kind of results Cynthia wanted. "Your face definitely looks thinner."

"Really?" She suddenly looked as happy as a normal person might have been if, say, World Peace had been achieved.

"Yeah, your cheekbones are way more defined. It's working."

"Good." Her smile faded and she flopped back against the sofa-pillows with a melancholy sigh.

Shit. "How about that tea?"

"I haven't seen Brad in three days," Cynthia said suddenly.

I clasped my hands in my lap. "Why's that?"

She shrugged. "He says he's busy at work." Her eyes met mine. "Have you seen anything suspicious on his Facebook?"

"I haven't." Brad's Facebook page had been silent for two weeks. "He doesn't seem very active on there."

"I know." She chewed her lip. "It's just — it's worrisome."

I nodded sympathetically. "I'm sorry I'm not much help," I told her. I didn't know what else to say; I couldn't exactly commiserate and share my own man-troubles. Or could I? "I just broke up with my boyfriend," I said before I could think better of it.

"You have a boyfriend?" Cynthia perked right up.

"*Had* a boyfriend." I stood up. "Past tense. I'll get you that tea."

"No, I'll come with you." She stood and wobbled towards the kitchen on unsteady legs. "Make yourself a cup and we'll chat."

I couldn't know whether confiding in Cynthia about my ruined love life was the right call professionally speaking, but at the very least it got her into a slightly less perilous headspace where Brad was concerned. I supplied few details, saying only that Viktor had started out promising but ended up not being who I expected. That only intrigued her further.

"Of course I want to hear the whole story," she said. "But not before you're ready to share it with me." Then she limped upstairs, leaving me to round up the kids and make sure they did their homework.

The trouble was that even though Viktor was out of the picture, his existence was still managing to complicate my life. The moment I'd decided to move out of my apartment, stuff had started to break; at the moment, the water pressure in the shower was dreadfully low, and the refrigerator light was out. I'd considered raising a ruckus, but ultimately decided I could live with it — I didn't want to risk Sergey coming over as Mr. Fix-It. *And forget about Viktor,* I told myself sternly. I forbade myself from even thinking about texting him.

* * * *

189

"I'm scoping out a new place," I told Randy that night. I'd stopped by to say hello on my way home.

"Good, Lane! Onward and upward." Randy had finished cleaning the prep tables and was sweeping the floor. I dropped the mop-bucket into the industrial-sized sink.

"Literally upward," I agreed as I turned on the hot water tap. "One room I'm looking at is on the third floor of a shared house. I think it actually has a window. That's my top prospect at the moment." I sloshed some detergent into the bucket and watched it foam.

"There are others?"

"One, so far. Seems shady though. I think this guy is renting out bedrooms by the night and the week as well as the month."

"Ew." Randy wrinkled her nose.

"Yeah, I think I'll give that one a pass." I turned off the water and heaved the bucket out of the sink and onto the floor.

"Do you feel safe where you are now? Because if you don't, you can crash on my air mattress until you find a new place." Randy stowed the broom and saw me mopping. "You don't have to do that," she added.

"I don't mind. Work clears my head." I thought about Randy's offer. "And thanks, but I feel safe enough. As much as I want to get out of there, for obvious reasons."

"Viktor?"

"Yeah, but he's just the tip of the iceberg. The landlady hates me and the other handyman is even more of a creep. Viktor still has the only other keys to my deadbolt lock, because God forbid Sergey gets in."

"Viktor still has the keys to your apartment?" Randy didn't even try to hide her disapproval.

"What's the alternative?" I shoved the mop under one of the prep tables and pushed it around on the floor. "Like I said, the only other handyman is a total letch. He thinks he's Rico Suavé." The last thing I needed was to come home late at night and find Sergey lying in wait.

"I'm glad you're finding a new place," Randy muttered. What had Detective Jarrett said? *Be careful with these people. They're*

190

dangerous and you're vulnerable. I hated that he'd been right. But I *didn't* feel unsafe, not even with Viktor still in possession of my spare keys. That was strange.

"Who else lives in this new house?" Randy's question snapped me out of my reverie.

"Grad students, I think. The guy I talked to sounds Russian."

"Huh. Well, that's the neighborhood." Randy grinned. "Is he cute?"

"I haven't met him yet," I replied. "But I can assure you I'm done with all that — shitting where I sleep."

"That's an interesting way to put it."

I was on my way home from a ramen-noodle run the following evening when my flip-phone rang: Detective Jarrett. I cringed inwardly, but took the call. It wasn't like I had an overabundance of friends these days.

"Hi, Detective." I crossed West End Avenue in the middle of the block against the light. Living on the edge as always.

"Lane, how are ya? Long time no see."

"Yeah, I've been super busy with work and a lot of other stuff." I quickened my pace.

"Let me take you out to dinner." It was phrased as a command, not a question. Why was there always this layer of dominance whenever he spoke to me?

"I don't think that's such a good idea."

"I know a great place," he wheedled. "Best Veal Piccata in Brooklyn."

"Look, if this is about that confidential informant thing, I have to tell you my answer's not changing." I hopped over a pile of curbside frozen slush. "Sorry to be so blunt. I just can't do what you're asking me."

The line went silent for a moment and I wondered if he'd hung up. "I understand," he finally said. "I wish you'd reconsider on dinner, though. I'd love to take you out. The C.I. discussion's off the table."

Shit. "Like on a date?" Now I regretted not setting him straight with the bouquet of roses.

"Yeah. Don't sound like it's so crazy. You're a beautiful girl."

"I — I don't know. I'm not feeling totally ready to date anyone right now."

"You're not the first girl to fall for Viktor's type, you know. You're better than that." I'd reached my building, so I pushed through the glass door and into the slightly-warmer vestibule. "You made a mistake," he went on. "Don't lump all of us together. Not all guys are like him."

"I'm sorry, Detective. I can't go out to dinner with you." I ended the call and took a deep, cleansing breath to clear my head. I didn't want to hear any more from Detective Jarrett about Viktor's type. Nor was I interested in his opinions on my psychological motivations where dating was concerned.

And as I descended the stairs to the basement, I realized something else. I *didn't* have the world's greatest judgment when it came to men. And I had few friends at the moment. But if Detective Jarrett were the last man on Earth and he showed up with a plate of Veal Piccata, I'd just have to embrace the celibate lifestyle and starve.

24

"Lane!" Emily's voice rang out through the hallway. "Mason's being a turd." It was one of the rare days when neither of the Waldrop children had after-school activities, and now they were engaged in an epic battle over the TV remote. "He won't watch anything except zombie stuff on Netflix."

"Why is this suddenly a problem? I thought you guys had eight different screens to choose from." I wrestled a turkey breast from the oven and set the roasting pan across two burners of Cynthia's Viking Professional range.

"Mom said no zombies." Emily padded into the kitchen, grabbed a small bottle of San Pellegrino from the fridge, and sat down at the counter.

"Mason!" I called. "No zombies!" The instant-read thermometer was nowhere to be found, so I said a silent prayer against Salmonella and moved the meat to a Williams-Sonoma cutting board that I'd had to season with food-grade mineral oil when Cynthia first brought it home. "Mason," I repeated louder, warningly, and the TV sound switched off.

"I heard you the first time," Mason grumbled as he slouched into the kitchen. He turned to his sister. "Why you gotta draw aggro?"

Emily smirked.

"Homework, both of you," I directed, and I dug the scale out of a drawer. Lately, Cynthia wanted everything measured to the tenth of an ounce.

Mason grabbed a bottled water and joined his sister at the counter. "When's Dad coming home?"

"I don't know, hon." Since my poker-face was for shit, I pretended to be fascinated with carving the turkey. "Have you tried texting him?"

"Yep." Mason fiddled with his iPhone. "I know what we need," he announced, and a familiar song started playing through the speakers mounted above the breakfast-bar.

"What's this?" Emily grabbed Mason's phone.

"Lane's playlist that her *friend* made for her." Mason looked over his sister's shoulder while she pecked at his phone.

"Very funny," I muttered. "I didn't say you could keep that."

"You didn't say I couldn't," Mason pointed out. "Anyway, it's cool."

Emily's eyes flashed. "Which friend made you a playlist? Is it the guy you're always texting with?"

"Never you mind." One of Cynthia's turkey portions was coming in on the heavy side. I wondered what two-tenths of an ounce of turkey breast looked like, then decided the correct answer was *I don't give a fuck.*

"Ooh, Lane's boyfriend," Emily teased, and she swayed back and forth to the song that was playing. "He likes indie rock." She and Mason exchanged conspiratorial looks. I pretended to ignore them, but I had to smile: they were bonding, even if it was nominally at my expense.

"Homework," I repeated, and both kids groaned in unison. Now I was their common enemy.

"Okay, but we're gonna keep listening to this," Emily proclaimed. "I can find meanings in all the songs and tell you if it's, you know, meant to last forever."

Yeah, right. But I had to admit that hearing Viktor's playlist again brought out some warm fuzzy feelings. Or maybe it was just hanging out with the kids while they were enjoying each other's company so much. "Lots of electronic stuff," Emily mused, chewing on her pencil. "Maybe he's the modern type."

"Not likely," Mason scoffed. "He doesn't use Spotify."

"That's 'cause his girlfriend's phone is so lame," Emily pointed out. She looked to me for confirmation.

"I refuse to participate in this conversation," I told her, and she and Mason both giggled. Then the front door opened and slammed shut, signaling Cynthia's arrival. I went to the fridge to grab her evening meal. But as soon as I saw her face, I knew something was wrong.

"I need to speak to you alone, Lane." Cynthia's voice was trembling. *Fuck.* I knew it: I was going to get fired.

I followed Cynthia upstairs with a creeping dread in my stomach. I fully expected her to turn foul-tempered on me, but when we got to her office, she collapsed into a club chair and burst into tears.

"Cynthia. What happened?" All I could think of was Brad. That bastard!

"It's Hugh." Cynthia wiped at her eyes and I handed her a tissue. "He fired me."

"Hugh?" I repeated stupidly. "How could Hugh fire you?"

"For non-compliance," Cynthia sobbed. "I was sloppy. I wasn't following the program." She blew her nose. "I told you, he only works with winners!"

I was privately relieved that this termination-of-employment hadn't hit closer to home. I sat down in the chair opposite Cynthia and waited for her to collect herself. She went quiet for a moment, then resumed sobbing even harder. "I'm a fuck-up," she wailed. "I fail at everything I try."

"No. No," I told her softly. "You're not a failure."

"I'll never lose this weight. I'm a pig."

"You're not," I insisted. Where was this self-loathing coming from? "You're a size twelve, almost a ten now. That's below average for American women." I handed her the box of tissues. "I would never look at you and think: She's fat."

Cynthia hiccupped. "Hugh says I'm not ready to do the work." Her voice was barely above a whisper.

"Hugh is a fucking idiot," I replied, and when that seemed to pique Cynthia's interest, I doubled down. "He fires anyone who has the slightest difficulty following his cockamamie starvation diet. Of course he only works with winners — he cherry-picks them retroactively. Anyone who actually needs his help gets the boot. It's survivorship bias." I peeked at Cynthia: Was I going too far? Being too uppity? But she seemed visibly calmer.

"You have a point," she said.

"You look thinner," I insisted. "How many pounds have you lost since you started?"

Cynthia hiccupped again. "Fourteen, not counting the two I gained back yesterday."

"Don't quit before the miracle happens," I reminded her. She nodded, but she still looked uncertain. "And don't let that bastard vandalize your success. You're not perfect and neither is anybody else."

"Gwyneth Paltrow," Cynthia countered.

"God, I hope you're not being serious."

Two days later, I left work an hour early and paid a visit to the house on Brighton Fourth Street. As advertised, it was clean and quiet. Dmitri, the fellow I'd corresponded with online, explained that he was a graduate student at Brooklyn College — as were Lev and Angela. They seemed normal, more or less. I assumed that all three were from Russia, although I didn't have the nerve to ask outright. The other housemate, Irina, wasn't there. She was a nurse at Mount Sinai Hospital, Dmitri told me, working second shift.

I followed Dmitri up two flights of stairs. "It's unfurnished," he said while we climbed. "Bathroom is shared with Irina." The bedroom was Spartan, but marginally more cheerful than my current arrangement, and it had a window with cheap aluminum blinds as well as a small closet. An ugly linoleum floor would need to be covered with a rug the moment I could afford one. I peeked in the shared bathroom. It looked like it had new fixtures, and it was tidy.

"It's nice," I told Dmitri, and he led me back downstairs to the shared kitchen and small living room. "Electricity and heat are included in rent," he said. "We share the cost of Internet service. It's an extra fifteen dollars a month."

"That sounds reasonable." I glanced around the kitchen — nothing special, but at least you could stand in it. Even with the WiFi add-on, I'd be saving a couple of hundred bucks a month if I moved in here, and the housemates seemed unlikely to annoy me overmuch. "What about laundry?"

"There's a laundromat two blocks away." Well, nothing in life was perfect. "It's a one-year lease," Dmitri continued. His glasses were so thick that I could tell his face would look completely different without them.

"Anything else I should know?"

He scratched his chin. "It's quiet here, not a party house. No drama. Just pay your rent on time every month and clean up after yourself, and it'll be cool."

No drama! I could see the appeal, as someone who'd eaten, slept, and breathed drama for the last several weeks. Time for a break from all that.

"I'm absolutely interested," I told him. "What's the next step?"

Walking home afterwards, I sent a serious request out to The universe that the credit and background checks I'd signed off on wouldn't disqualify me. And that this new arrangement would be a happy one. Sharing a living space with other people was a risk; I acknowledged that. I didn't know them any better than they knew me. But getting out of that basement was something that needed to happen.

My flip-phone rang as I was crossing West End Avenue. I answered without checking who it was, foolishly.

"It's Mike Jarrett, Lane. Please don't hang up."

Oh no. Not him. Not now. "You have ten seconds to redeem yourself."

"I acted like a jerk before. I'm sorry."

"Okay."

"Will you forgive me?" He did sound contrite.

"Look, I'm exhausted right now." I'd arrived at the door to my building and all I wanted to do was fall into bed. "Can we revisit this another time?"

"Have coffee with me Saturday. At Starbucks. Ten o'clock."

"I'm working Saturday." I never thought spending the day with Cynthia would seem like I was getting off easy, but life was strange sometimes.

"Sunday, then."

I sighed; it still sounded more like an order than a gentlemanly request. But I would have agreed to almost anything to get off the phone.

"Fine, Mike. See you Sunday."

By Friday afternoon, I was consumed with worry over the credit check. I hadn't heard anything from Dmitri and each passing hour seemed to further seal my doom. Still, I had to hold it together; both kids had an early dismissal from school. Emily had invited her friend Isabella to accompany us home for a playdate, and Mason seemed just as surprised as I was when Isabella's younger brother Kamran tagged along.

"You guys both play Minecraft all day and night, so you might as well play it together," Emily said. Isabella looked up from her phone and nodded emphatically.

"How do you know I want to play Minecraft?" Mason snapped. I shot him a warning look and he scowled down at the sidewalk. Kamran didn't react; either he didn't realize Mason's fury was partially directed at him, or he didn't care.

Well, this was gonna be awkward.

The moment we arrived at Chez Waldrop, both girls stampeded up to Emily's room and slammed the door behind them, leaving me with the two boys. I looked at them with feigned nonchalance. "Do you want a snack or something?" *Please,* I implored Mason telepathically, *act friendly.*

Kamran shrugged. "Sure." He slid a small laptop out of his backpack and set it on the counter. "Want to see my under-water house?"

Mason remained silent, so I piped up. "I'd love to see it. Do any creepers live there?"

Mason snorted, but he didn't say anything. "Wash your hands," I told them, and then I busied myself getting a snack together — no easy task now that Cynthia had banished everything tasty from within these four walls. Eventually I found some pretzel rods and organic lemonade, which I set out on the counter as the boys returned noisily from the powder room.

"I made a trading post," Mason said, hoisting himself up onto the stool. "It has a pig parking lot." The timbre of his voice had changed completely. I pretended not to notice or care about their conversation.

"Cool," Kamran replied through a mouthful of pretzels. "I can show you my lava moat. The only way to cross it is to right-click on a secret block. I'd show you my TNT planet but I already blew it up."

"I made a TNT elevator and it blew up my house." Mason poured two glasses of lemonade, sloshing it all over the counter in the process.

"Cool." Kamran grabbed another pretzel rod and shoved it into his mouth.

"Yeah, it worked better on YouTube," Mason said as they headed for his room, their arms full of snacks and drinks and Kamran's laptop. They left a trail of crushed pretzel-crumbs behind them.

I wanted to cry with happiness and hug Emily and do a dance of joy. At the very least, I had to tell Cynthia that Mason was socializing. Just as I took out my phone to text her, it rang. Fabrizio.

"Any idea where Cynthia is?" He sounded agitated.

"I thought she was with you." Cynthia's agenda had included a morning hair appointment, lunch at some restaurant, and the gym.

"It's her second missed workout in a row," Fabrizio told me. "Yesterday she texted me and said it was an emergency. Today, nothing. I texted her but she's not answering."

That was odd. Come to think of it, Cynthia *had* been strangely quiet in the texting realm lately. "Thanks," I told Fabrizio. "I'll raise the alarms and let you know when she turns up."

I texted Cynthia, then Brad. Neither one answered. Calls went straight to voicemail. Shit. Where were they?

Then my flip-phone pinged. A text, from Dmitri:

Your credit and background checks are good. When can you move in?

Well, hallefuckinglujah.

Cynthia finally turned up, texting me at five-thirty that she'd be home around nine. *I'm meeting a friend for drinks,* she wrote, and I was left scratching my head. I remembered to text Fabrizio, but I'd been so absorbed in trying to track Cynthia down while getting dinner ready for the kids that by the time I called Brighton Realty it was already closed.

"Whatcha doing?" Emily asked. "Texting your boyfriend again?"

"I'm setting an alarm to remind me to call my landlady tomorrow," I informed her. "Little Miss all-up-in-my-business."

"Huh." She tossed her ponytail. "I didn't know those old phones *had* alarms."

"Every time I use it, it's a journey into the distant past. The phone itself is coal-powered."

She rolled her eyes. "And you say *I've* got a fresh mouth."

My first thought when I awakened Saturday morning was overwhelming relief that I didn't have to have coffee with Detective Jarrett for another 24 hours. Followed by giddy anticipation: today was the day I'd give notice to Mrs. Pasternak!

Cynthia was in bed and barely responsive when I arrived at work, so I roused the kids and made them breakfast — organic whole-grain waffles with fresh berries and a dusting of powdered sugar. Then I told them to get dressed and agree on a movie, because we needed to get out of the house.

Tiptoeing up the stairs, I knocked softly on Cynthia's door.

She'd already slept in an extra hour and a half; between that and the missed workouts, I was starting to worry. No answer. I peeked inside. "Cynthia?" The pile of blankets twitched. I ventured a few steps into the room, taking care to make my footfalls as soft as possible. "Are you okay?" I whispered. "I'm taking the kids out and I don't want to leave you alone if you're—" Crazy? "Sick."

The blankets shifted position. "Go out," Cynthia's muffled voice came from somewhere inside. "It's fine."

I hesitated. "Do you want me to—"

"Just *go*, Lane."

I backed out on tiptoe and shut the door.

25

"You should be getting hazard pay dealing with that woman." Randy broke off a piece of the corn muffin we were sharing at our usual diner on First Avenue.

"The staying-in-bed-all-day isn't even the worst of it," I mused. "I mean, who hasn't done that?" Randy arched a doubtful eyebrow at me: tumbleweeds. I plowed on. "What worries me most is the radio silence. She's hardly texted me in the last few days, and today she didn't even text me once."

"I take it that's unusual for Cynthia?" Randy took a sip of coffee.

"It's unheard-of for Cynthia. Normally she can't get to the corner drugstore and back without texting me at least twice. I'm worried she's lapsing into some kind of catatonic state."

"Enough about the crazy lady," Randy said. "Let's hear about Lane."

I snorted. "There's some overlap there, I'm afraid."

"Well, let's hear it."

"First the good news. I gave notice to my landlady today — I'm moving into a new place. With housemates."

"Fantastic!" Randy fist-bumped me across the table. "Shall I assume there is some not-so-good news to go with it?"

"Remember who you're talking to, Randy." I fidgeted with my

coffee mug. "I still miss Viktor."

"I'd be surprised if you didn't miss him." Randy pushed the muffin towards me, but I wasn't hungry.

"I want to forget about him and move on. God knows I've done it before." The diner suddenly felt chilly. "I used to be good at that — cutting people off."

"Why would you want to be good at that?" Randy asked. I shrugged, and she studied me for a moment. "Have you heard from him at all?"

"No. It's like he's dropped off the face of the Earth." I clasped my hands together on the table in front of me. "And I'm worried about him. I'll wonder — is he okay? Is he in trouble? Is he sleeping at night, or having those nightmares all alone?" Randy nodded, but she didn't say anything. "Tell me I'm being an idiot," I finally blurted out.

"You're being human." Randy gave me a rueful smile. "You can't turn this stuff on and off like a microwave. It takes time."

"It blows." I drummed my fingers on the table.

"Any other romantic prospects on the horizon?" Randy asked. "Nothing like a new paramour to ease the pain of lost love."

"You have got to be kidding. But I *am* having coffee with Detective Jarrett tomorrow morning."

"You're not!" Now Randy looked shocked.

"He wore me down. He's quite persuasive." Randy wrinkled her nose. "But you're right, I'm probably wasting my time with him," I conceded. "And I've decided he's got to be on steroids."

"So why have coffee with him?"

"He really wants to see me. He keeps calling." I rubbed my forehead. Why *had* I agreed to have coffee with him, anyway?

"Pfft. Cops." Randy drained her coffee cup.

"What do you have against cops? I still haven't heard that story." Probably because we always talked about my drama whenever we hung out.

"My sister was married to a cop," Randy sniffed. "Briefly. When it went south…"

I waited, but she was staring down at the table, lost in thought. "What happened?" I finally asked.

Her eyes met mine. "Things got physical."

"Shit."

"Yeah." She sighed and shifted in her seat. "That blue wall of silence, though. It's no joke. They never rat each other out. Ever."

I thought about Detective Jarrett. Would he lie to protect a wife-beating colleague? I wouldn't fall over from shock if it happened, but then again, it felt like an unfair generalization. The fact that he was a cop didn't automatically make him a bad person. "There's nothing wrong with the good detective on paper," I said, thinking out loud. "He's got a legitimate job. He makes an honest living. It's way more than I can say for Viktor."

"So what, Lane?" Randy said it loud enough that a few people sitting nearby glanced over at us. She flared her nostrils, but lowered her voice. "Just because he's not Hitler doesn't make him The One."

"I never said he was The One. It's just coffee."

Randy leaned back. "Okay. I won't deny you your caramel latté. Just think about something for me, if you don't mind."

"What?"

"Ask yourself if you feel safe when you're with him."

I felt haunted by Randy's suggestion the following morning, even as I reassured myself again and again: it wasn't a date with Detective Jarrett, it was just coffee.

"You seem distracted," he observed once we'd sat down at the table. He'd gotten coffee and a slice of the marble loaf again.

"I've got a lot going on." I sipped my iced coffee without elaborating further.

"Well, you weren't too busy to give me another shot." He gave me a lopsided grin.

Shit. He still has the wrong idea. "About that."

"I know I'm not your usual type, Lane," he said softly. It caught me off guard and I wondered if that was intentional.

"I wasn't aware that I had a type," I finally said, to break the silence. I so didn't want this to turn into another discussion of Viktor.

"You seem to be working really hard," he observed. "Getting back on your feet financially."

"I'm trying."

He nodded. "What I want to say is, you don't have to live this way."

I had no idea what to make of this statement. "Which way is that?"

"Hand to mouth. Never sure if you're going to run out of money before the next paycheck. Hiding out in your shitty little basement apartment."

I bristled at that last item. "Assuming all that is true — which it isn't — what exactly are you proposing?"

"Let me help you," he implored. "Let me in. I only want to take care of you." I stared at him. "Come on, Lane. I don't bite."

"Is your offer back on the table?" I asked him. "Is that what you're saying?"

"Forget the offer." He placed his hand on top of mine. It was warm. I flinched and pulled my hand away. "Come on," he repeated. "Give me a chance. I only want to make you happy."

"You make it sound like you're coming to my rescue." Could anyone *make* me happy? Certainly not him.

"And what's so bad about coming to the rescue of a beautiful girl like you?"

"Nothing," I muttered. "I just don't want or need to be rescued."

"That's not the tune you were singing a couple of months ago," he reminded me, and that stung, hard. I felt my face flush. "And then you fell in with all that mess. It's not right." He reached over and tucked a stray piece of hair behind my ear. I instinctively drew away from him. "Come on," he wheedled. "Why so glum?"

"Every time I talk to you, I end up regretting it," I said, and even as the words tumbled out I knew that I'd hit on the truth. "That is just a huge flashing red danger-sign in my books."

"Every time, huh?" He leaned back in his chair, frowning.

"Yes. Somehow you manage to piss me off at every single opportunity." I stood up. "This isn't ever going to work."

"Sit down," he ordered. There was a hardness in his voice I

hadn't heard before.

"No. I'm done." I walked away from the table. Then I heard the angry scraping noise of metal on flooring. I picked up my pace, eager to get away from him.

"Lane." He caught up with me on the sidewalk outside. "Don't be stupid." When I kept walking, he stood in front of me, blocking my path.

"You're in my way," I said, suddenly grateful for the pedestrian traffic and bystanders. *Do you feel safe when you're with him?* No, not at the moment.

"You're making a mistake." His voice was low, intense. "If you're back with Viktor, I have to warn you—"

"Excuse me." I darted around him and hustled away, my heart pounding the entire time. I didn't look back until I'd crossed Brighton Seventh Street. And I *didn't* feel safe — not until I was back in my shitty basement apartment with the deadbolt locked.

For once, the prospect of going to work Monday morning was reassuring: I could leave Brighton Beach and its cast of weirdo characters behind for the day. The Waldrops were scheduled to fly to London Friday night, and I needed to make sure that the family vacation was awesome enough to compensate for Brad and Cynthia's crappy marriage and complete lack of interest in their kids. The only wrinkle: Cynthia wouldn't leave her room.

"Are you in there?" I called through the closed door. "I brought tea and toast." The kids were safely off to school, and it was just Cynthia and me in the apartment.

"Leave it by the door," came her muffled reply, followed by total silence.

"Okay," I called out with false cheer. "It's right here for you!" Then I shuffled off towards the kids' rooms and started setting aside clothes and toiletries to pack for London. What else could I do?

My flip-phone rang when I was inside Emily's closet, sweating buckets and digging through an improbably vast stash of skinny-jeans. "Yeah?" I answered, fumbling my phone open with one hand and wiping my brow with the other.

"Miss Haviland? It's Mrs. Pasternak. From Brighton Realty." I could almost smell the cigarette smoke through the phone.

"Oh! Hi. Is there a problem?" I emerged from Emily's closet and promptly tripped over a hot pink fake-fur bolster pillow.

"There is no problem. I have news. You gave notice to move out, but we need apartment sooner. You will move out next Monday, if that is acceptable."

"A week from today?" My mind was racing. Dmitri had told me I could move in anytime — the sooner, the better.

"We will pro-rate your rent. This is acceptable for you?" Mrs. Pasternak sounded none too upset that I was leaving.

"Sure. That's great. Thank you."

"Fine. One more thing," she barked. Now I was sure I heard her puffing on that cigarette. "Your security deposit."

"Yes?" My worst fear from a couple of months ago had come to pass, only now it didn't make any sense. What could she possibly want with a security deposit at this late date?

"Yes," she huffed impatiently. "Do you want it, or should I just give it back to Viktor?"

I stood there stunned. Checkmate! Mrs. Pasternak exhaled into the phone.

"Give it — give it back to Viktor," I finally stammered. "I'll tell him to, you know, expect it."

"Fine." She hung up. At least she'd given it a rest with the Russian insults.

With great effort, I managed to set aside the bombshell of Viktor having paid my security deposit. I would deal with it, but later. For now, arrangements had to be made, and fast.

While cooking lunch for Cynthia that she probably wouldn't eat — and fending off concerned texts from Fabrizio — I confirmed a Monday afternoon move-in with Dmitri and arranged for a "Man with Van" on Craigslist to help me move my stuff. Then I headed up to Cynthia's room.

"You in there?" I called softly. "I have lunch." No answer, so I tried the door. It was unlocked.

I peeked inside. Cynthia was sitting on the bed in her bathrobe, her hair a stringy mess, her face streaked with tears.

"Oh, Cynthia!" I set the tray down and rushed over. "Are you okay? Should I call the doctor?" She shook her head. Her face was scrunched up in an awful grimace. The tears started flowing again.

I sat at the edge of her bed, which felt soft and plush compared to my lumpy futon mattress. "Is there anything I can do? Someone I can call?" As soon as the words came out, I regretted saying them: Cynthia threw her head forward and began bawling.

"No, there's no one you can *call*," she spat, and I handed her a box of tissues. "Nobody wants to be around me unless I *pay* them." She glared at me, then blew her nose into a tissue.

"That's not true," I protested. Weak.

"If I didn't pay you, you wouldn't be here," Cynthia insisted. "I mean, you act all nice and friendly — but you wouldn't *choose* me as your friend." She heaved another great, quavering sob. "I bet you think I'm—" *Sob.* "Needy." *Sniff.* "And annoying. Be honest!"

How honest, I wondered? Honest in an 'I need this job' way, or brutally honest? Brutal. That was the word Viktor had used to describe prison. *A brutal place,* he'd said, and why the hell was I thinking about him? I should be directing all available resources towards not getting shitcanned. Cynthia needed reassurance.

"I've never used the words 'needy' or 'annoying' to describe you," I said quietly.

Now she drew her knees up and hugged them to her chest. "It doesn't matter," she moaned. "Just leave me." She rocked back and forth a little and buried her face in her knees. Her overly theatrical behavior was actually a relief — at least she was talking — but something felt different. Wrong.

"Listen, I'm legitimately worried about you right now," I told her. "I don't want to leave you alone like this. I'm going to call someone." She didn't look up. "Tell me who to call."

Cynthia turned her head to one side so that her cheek was resting on one knee, but she didn't say anything.

"Fine," I said. "I'm calling Brad." I got up.

"No! Don't call Brad." Cynthia leaped out of bed and lurched towards the door, blocking my way.

"Cynthia, this is ridiculous. You shouldn't be alone. He's your husband!"

Cynthia burst into fresh tears. "No, no, you can't call him. Please don't. Lane. I didn't want to tell you."

"What?"

"I hired a private detective. Brad's having an affair."

.

26

I knew it! What a damn douchebag. As I walked, fuming, to collect the kids from school, it occurred to me that Mason's birthday trip to London was now in jeopardy, and I hated Brad for endangering it. But what could I do? Nothing.

I delivered Mason to his shrink appointment and got Emily home. She ran up to her room to finish a book report and I checked on Cynthia again. The lady of the house was in bed, asleep, at three-thirty in the afternoon. I wandered down to the kitchen and sat down at the counter. As long as I was already miserable, I might as well do the deed I'd been dreading. I pulled out my flip-phone and texted Viktor:

I'm moving out. Mrs. Pasternak has the security deposit for you.

I stared at the phone for a few moments, but received no reply. Wasn't that always how it had been, with Viktor? Days without a response, then *'you around tonight?'* Had those been booty-texts, technically speaking? I didn't want to think about him anymore.

I sent him one final text:

Thank you for paying that. I didn't know. I haven't forgotten that I still owe you money and I will pay you as soon as I can. Which would be soon, assuming the fucking bank ever came through with my refund.

Radio silence from Viktor. Maybe he was balls-deep in some

bordello-related situation. I flipped the phone shut and headed out to collect Mason.

"Is my mom still in bed?" That was Mason's first question when I picked him up at the psychiatrist's.

"She was when I last checked on her," I confirmed.

"She does that sometimes," Mason mumbled. My heart ached — for Cynthia, for Mason, for myself. It had been a difficult day. Mason shoved his hands into the pockets of his Yankees windbreaker; there was a chill in the air, now that the sun was lower in the sky. He looked so small with his overstuffed backpack hanging on his thin shoulders. I reached over and gave him a one-armed squeeze while we walked.

"How's Kamran?" I asked.

"Fine. We're playing Minecraft on the same server now."

"How about in real life? Do you see him at school?"

"Minecraft *is* real life." Mason gave me a side-eye. "We eat lunch together."

"Well, that's clutch. That's the best news I've heard all day."

"Lane, don't take this the wrong way, but you sound pathetic."

"Says you." My iPhone pinged: Cynthia. I stopped to read the text:

Brad just bailed on London. Hurry home.

"What is it?" Mason asked me.

"Your mom. Let's pick up the pace."

Cynthia was sitting at the breakfast bar when Mason and I returned home. Her hair was damp, so she'd showered — a good sign — and she was eating one of the meals I'd prepared, with apparent gusto.

"Hi." I wasn't sure whether she wanted to discuss Brad's latest douchebaggery in front of Mason. "I got your text."

"Mm hmm." She finished chewing and swallowed. "Mason, honey, would you mind excusing us for a minute? Lane and I need to talk."

"Sure." Mason plodded up the stairs. I watched him go, hunched under the weight of his backpack, before turning my attention back to Cynthia.

"So here's the deal," she said. All business. "Brad bowed out of the trip. Work commitments. Which we both know, of course, is fiction. And that's putting it charitably." She seemed a different person than she'd been earlier — determined. Functional. Awake.

"Of course, I can't possibly handle both kids on my own in London," Cynthia continued. "I've never been much good with traveling."

"The kids are old enough now that they're hardly any trouble," I said. *Careful now, don't talk yourself out of a job.* "I mean, they're pretty self-sufficient for short periods of time."

"No, Lane." Cynthia shook her head. "I'll need help. That's where you come in." She pushed her plate to one side and dabbed at her mouth with a paper napkin. "Do you have a passport?"

"Me? Yes," I stammered. "I mean...I think so. I'm not sure. Don't they expire?"

"Every ten years." This from a woman who couldn't even do her own grocery shopping. Somehow she'd managed to dig up this information at lightning speed.

"Oh. Then yes, I have one." Of course I could see where she was going with this, and I already knew it was going to be an offer I couldn't refuse.

"Then you'll come to London with us? For Mason's birthday." Cynthia had turned on the puppy-dog eyes again. But Mason was the reason I said yes.

Possibly more stressful than the prospect of flying to London with the Waldrops — and taking on complete responsibility for the success or failure of Mason's twelfth birthday — was the fact that I had to move house several days earlier than expected. Not that I owned a tremendous amount of stuff, but I did have just enough to make it annoying.

On hold with British Airways Tuesday morning, I texted both Dmitri and the Man With Van a pre-emptive apology for being a pain in the ass. But could we agree on an earlier move-in day that worked for all of us? Unfortunately, Dmitri was busy and working late most of the week, and he couldn't immediately get hold of the other housemates to ask if one of them could deal with me — and I didn't have their direct numbers yet. *I will get back to you,* he texted me, and I was left drumming my fingers.

Next up: British Airways. Brad's ticket was transferable, for a fee that Cynthia covered. And I'd found my passport, so that was another small victory.

Victor-y. Viktor hadn't texted back yet; I wasn't sure why I'd expected him to. Detective Jarrett, on the other hand, had texted me four times in three days to apologize and beg forgiveness. I fervently wished he'd lose my number.

Cynthia was quiet, busy with mysterious appointments. I suspected she was meeting with a psychiatrist or a divorce lawyer or both, but I didn't press her for details and she didn't volunteer any. It was almost as though we'd finally achieved that elusive professional relationship I'd always yearned for, except for the part where I had to accompany her and the kids to London and unilaterally save Mason's birthday.

I did what I could to psych myself up for the trip. I told Mason and Emily how excited I was to see London with them, which was true. I deflected all questions about their father to Cynthia, because I didn't know what else to do. And I packed up everyone's suitcases, including my own.

As it turned out the only moving day that worked for everyone — Dmitri, the Man With Van, and myself — was Friday afternoon. Our London flight would depart JFK at seven o'clock that evening. It was going to be tight.

"I still don't understand why you had to schedule your move for today," Cynthia pouted. It was Friday morning, Cynthia was putting others first as usual, and I was struggling to remain patient as I laid out the Waldrops' travel documents.

"The car will pick you up at three o'clock," I told her. "Then you'll get the kids at school. They already have their carry-on stuff in their backpacks." I'd packed those as well, doing my part to help create another generation of helpless Waldrops.

"Devices too?" Cynthia seemed almost hopeful that I'd forgotten something.

"Yes, and their noise-canceling headphones." I took the pile of documents off the table and presented it to Cynthia. "All three passports. And printouts of your entire itinerary, in the incredibly unlikely event that I miss the flight." At this, Cynthia flared her nostrils in alarm. "I will not miss the flight," I repeated for what felt like the tenth time in two days. "I just want you to feel secure in case, like, a crack in the Earth opens and swallows up Brooklyn in the next few hours. You and the kids are still good."

Cynthia sniffed her disapproval at that notion, but she accepted the passports and papers and put them into her carry-on. Then she walked over to the door and touched each piece of checked luggage: Mason's, Emily's, and finally her own. All TUMI, all exquisite, and all picked up by yours truly from Bloomingdale's the previous week. I already knew how terrible my own battered suitcase would look sitting next to them, but nothing could be done about that. As it was, I felt fortunate to be flying transatlantic on Brad's business-class ticket.

"Are you sure you can't put this off until after we get back?" Cynthia asked. "I'd feel better if we all stuck together."

"I really tried," I told her. "It was literally the only time that worked. And I have to be out of there before we get back from London."

Cynthia heaved a sigh, a smallish one considering all that this was costing her emotionally. "Fine. Text me constantly."

"Of course." What choice did I have?

I looked up and down West End Avenue. It was three in the afternoon, the temperature had soared to a summer-like seventy degrees, and my Man With Van was nowhere in sight. Fifteen minutes ago, I'd been annoyed; now I was starting to get nervous. I texted him again:

Waiting for you on West End Ave in Brighton Beach. You were due

15 minutes ago. Pls call or text me!!

As I hit SEND, I felt a vague Cynthia-like quality creeping through my consciousness. Then my iPhone buzzed with an incoming text from her:

Car came! En route to school now.

Great, I texted back, and I looked up and down the street again. Where was he? I felt a twinge of desperation-tinged-with-disgust at my return trip to Craigslist hell. It really shouldn't have surprised me this much that a Man With Van who advertised there was turning out to be unreliable.

I went inside and brought up what I could by myself: my suitcases, my pillow and comforter, the spool-table, and two boxes of miscellaneous items. Then I sat on the front stoop and checked incoming texts on the flip-phone: Nada. Missed calls? Nope. The iPhone buzzed. Cynthia again:

Everything okay???

Fine, I lied. Then I switched to my flip-phone and texted Man-With-Van:

If you're not coming just tell me. This is ridiculous.

The flip-phone chimed. Man-With-Van had texted me back!

Flat tire. In Sheepshead Bay now.

Well, what the ever-loving fuck did *that* mean? I hunched over my phone and texted him back, cursing at how long it was taking me to input the letters. Morse code would have been faster.

Are you coming - yes or no? If yes I need an ETA.

I glanced at the time: 3:20. Incoming text from Man With Van:

Chill…I'll get there when I get there

His blasé attitude was beyond irritating, but the ellipsis shook me to the core. It took every ounce of self-restraint I had not to hurl the phone into orbit. Of course Man With Van was flaking on me, the one day I couldn't be late! Right now Cynthia and the kids were en route to JFK in a luxury SUV that I'd booked for them, and I was sitting on a dirty stoop in Brooklyn waiting for a guy who wasn't coming. "Just fucking perfect," I muttered to myself.

Well, I could get a cab. It would haul most of my stuff over to Brighton Fourth Street, and then I could go straight to the airport. I'd be giving up my futon, possibly. *Probably,* I corrected myself:

with Mrs. Pasternak I couldn't be optimistic. But at least I'd still have a job.

3:24. I stood up to hail a cab, and that's when I saw Viktor.

27

Predictably enough, my first reaction to seeing Viktor was to drop my flip-phone. Down it toppled, onto the sidewalk, and the flimsy metal battery-panel popped off. I bent to pick up the pieces and hoped my face wasn't turning tomato-red.

When I stood up, there he was, squinting down at me with some measure of curiosity. He was wearing coveralls with the sleeves rolled partway up. A few locks of shaggy black hair had fallen over his forehead and he had a couple days' stubble. Of course he looked effortlessly sexy.

"Hi, Viktor." Suddenly I felt sweaty and frazzled and dry-mouthed.

"Hi." That impossibly deep voice. Save me! He looked from me to my meager possessions laid out on the sidewalk.

"I'm, um, moving out," I told him.

"Today?" He looked up and down the street, then back at me quizzically.

"Yeah, well. My Man-With-Van is a no-show," I grumbled. I tried snapping the battery-panel back on the phone, but it wouldn't stay in place. "Shit."

"Let me see," Viktor said, and I handed him the phone without thinking. He tried to press the piece into place with both thumbs, but it popped back out stubbornly. "Warped," he pronounced, and handed it back to me. "I have duct tape if you want."

"Thanks." Why did he have to be so dadgum nice?

He still had that curious look on his face. "Where are you moving?"

"Brighton Fourth Street." I wondered briefly whether telling him this was a good idea, then realized I was being stupid. If he'd wanted to stalk me, he'd have done it by now.

Viktor dug out his phone and glanced down at it. "I can take your stuff there, if you want. Truck is parked around corner."

My eyes went wide. "Will the futon fit?"

"Sure."

Somehow, Viktor and I got the futon frame and mattress up the service stairs and into the back of his pickup truck with the rest of my belongings. It was a dirty job, and by the time I climbed into the passenger seat of the truck's cab I was a sweaty mess — hardly fit for a Greyhound bus, much less Business Class on British Airways. Possibly a candidate for the cargo hold.

Then the truck's engine wouldn't start. *Here we go again,* I thought, but then it caught and we exchanged relieved smiles. I sat back and tried to relax for the short ride to my new home.

Stopped in traffic on Neptune Avenue, a thought popped into my head and I voiced it without thinking: "I've missed you."

Viktor continued to stare straight ahead, but his knuckles went momentarily white on the steering wheel. "I am surprised you said that," he murmured once traffic started moving again.

"Well, so am I," I told him. "But it's true. I've thought about you every single day."

Viktor looked like maybe he was going to say something, but he remained silent and drove on. "I don't know if you got my text," I continued. If this was going to be a monologue, I might as well get it all out. "I owe you thanks for the security deposit, which I only found out about this week. You can pick it up from Mrs. Pasternak whenever's convenient."

Viktor smiled. Eye crinkles! "She will deduct minimum two hundred dollars for poster you threw away. It was collector's item."

"Put it on my tab." That got me another half-smile. I missed him more than ever. "Why are you being so nice to me?"

He inched forward in traffic and glanced sideways in my direction. "Should I act like jerk?"

"No." Dammit. We were talking in circles again.

"I can grow mustache and twirl it." The Russian twang around the word *twirl* was really something. "If I am villain, I may as well look the part."

"Your English is improving." I looked out the window at a man walking his dog.

"Your phone," Viktor said as we turned left onto Brighton Fourth Street. "Look in armrest for duct tape."

I turned the roll of silvery tape over in my hands. "It's the blue house on the left up ahead. Do you have scissors?"

"Just tear it." Viktor double-parked the truck and killed the engine. "Here." He tore a short length of tape off the roll and handed it to me — a regular Mister Fix-It. Seeing him again felt wonderful. And awful.

Viktor got out of the truck while I taped the phone together as best I could. It seemed to still be functioning, so I texted Man-With-Van and told him to forget it. When I looked up I saw Dmitri standing on the front porch, so I hopped down from the truck. As I waved to him, I heard the truck's tailgate drop with a dull *thud.*

"Hey," Viktor called out to Dmitri. *"Ti mozhesh pamoch?"*

Dmitri looked surprised, but he recovered quickly and jogged over. Together he and Viktor hauled down the futon-frame and carried it over towards the house. I held the front door open for them, then retrieved stuff I could carry and headed back inside. The two men's voices rang out down the stairs as they negotiated the bulky frame around tight corners.

"Poverni liveya."

"Okay."

"Yesho chu-chuts. Vso harosho."

Stop eavesdropping on Russian conversations you don't even understand, I scolded myself as I carried one of the suitcases and my pillow up the stairs and left it on the second-floor landing. Next I brought up the table and the comforter, and finally the boxes of random belongings. I didn't have a prayer of getting the

futon mattress out of the truck by myself, so I checked the time —
4:15, not bad — and lugged the suitcase up to the third floor.

Viktor and Dmitri passed me on their way down and I got a
chance to see the bedroom again, this time with the futon frame
in one corner. I set the table down beside it and looked out the
window onto the street below. Viktor had jumped up into the
truck bed to wrestle the mattress into position for Dmitri. They
both seemed so determined. I smiled — it felt good to have help.
Then my iPhone buzzed. Cynthia.

What's going on?? We are at the airport!!!

Everything's good, I reassured her. *Almost done here.*

Come straight to the BUSINESS CLASS LOUNGE!!!

Will do.

Viktor and Dmitri brought my mattress in, dropping it down
onto the frame with a satisfying flop. I thanked Dmitri and gave
him a bank-check for my first month's rent. Then he vanished
down the stairs.

Viktor gave a satisfied nod at the futon. "Looks nice," he said,
rolling his sleeves down.

"Thank you." I handed him my house keys. "You saved my
ass today. Again."

"You're welcome." He looked around the room once more. "I
must go. I'm double-parked."

"I'll see you out," I told him. "I'm headed for the airport."

"Where are you going?" he asked on our way down.

"London, with Cynthia and the kids." I grabbed the suitcase
sitting at the bottom of the stairs. "It's a big fat family crisis. You
don't even want to know."

He smiled down at the floor, then at me, and we went outside.
I looked around for a taxi. I'd seen a few go by here, but there
weren't any at the moment. Secretly I was glad for a few more
minutes with Viktor. I looked up at him. Damn his handsome face
and beautiful bone structure! "Is this goodbye?" I asked.

"I guess." He hugged his arms around his middle and looked
up and down the street.

"I was a bitch before," I said. "So yeah. I apologize."

Viktor frowned. "You should not apologize," he said, just as a lime-green taxi turned the corner. I hailed it. Then I turned back to face Viktor again. I'd thought of this moment so many times. I knew I'd regret it forever if I didn't clear the air between us.

"Yes. I should. You've never been anything but a gentleman to me." Viktor looked like he was about to argue a counterpoint, but he just swallowed. "You know something? I still think you're a good person. Yeah." I shook my head. "Good luck figuring that one out."

The cabbie popped the trunk open, but he stayed in the car, so I grabbed my suitcase and headed around to the rear of the car. Viktor took my suitcase before I could object, deposited it into the trunk, and closed it.

"Safe travel," he mumbled. Then he turned and walked back to his truck without another word. I stared after him until the cabbie got annoyed with me and laid on the horn.

I made it to JFK and got through security with time to spare, but that didn't stop Cynthia from having multiple hissy-fits — first via text message, then by phone call, and finally in person upon our reunion in the British Airways Terraces Lounge. "Thank God," she gushed. "I was sure you'd miss the flight and *then* what would we have done?"

Emily and Mason, glued to their respective screens, seemed indifferent to my late arrival. Cynthia looked me over, and her expression reminded me that I still looked a mess from the afternoon's activities. "I'm going to wash up," I told her. "Can I get you a glass of wine on my way back?"

"Might as well." Cynthia sat back down on the plush lounge chair and examined her new manicure.

"Red or white?" My plan was to get her relaxed enough to sleep on the plane. The last thing anyone needed was Zombie Cynthia disembarking the red-eye at Heathrow.

"White. It's so hot today."

"Excellent choice."

Wiping the day's dust and grime from my face and neck in the ladies' room, I considered the afternoon's events and decided that the glass was half-full with respect to Brighton Beach. My new living space was a definite improvement, and my friendship with Viktor might be salvageable. *Focus,* I reminded myself: my continued employment with Cynthia might very well hinge on the success or failure of this trip. Still, I couldn't help taking out my taped-together phone and texting Randy:

Saw Viktor today. He doesn't hate me so that's good.

I had one unread text, from Detective Jarrett; I didn't open it. Meanwhile, Randy responded faster than I'd thought humanly possible:

Be careful!! I still don't like him.

I will, I texted back. *Back from Blighty in a few days. Let's catch up then.*

Right-o, guvnah.

What had I ever done to deserve such a good friend?

Following dinner at 30,000 feet, Mason fell asleep quickly in his lie-flat pod. I tucked him in under the blanket and plugged his phone into the charger.

Emily yawned. "Tuck me in too?" she asked.

"I'd be honored." I pulled the blanket up around her shoulders.

She smiled up at me. "I'm glad you're here, Lane."

"So am I." I smiled back, a real one. "This is gonna be fun." I thought about the Australia trip I'd taken on a whim — wholly unplanned, and probably overpriced. I'd started drinking on the outbound flight and hadn't stopped until the wheels touched back down in New York. With the benefit of hindsight, the once-in-a-lifetime Great Barrier Reef snorkeling excursion might have gone better if I hadn't had a raging hangover.

It all seemed so long ago and far away. I didn't want it anymore, I realized. I'd rather be here now — on a family trip. Even if it wasn't with my own family.

Emily yawned again. "My mom was freaking out that you'd be late and miss the flight."

I kissed her forehead. "My mom would've done the same thing."

28

"I don't *want* to go to a boring museum," Mason groaned. I was pretty sure that the walls of our hotel suite were closing in on me. My head ached. Cynthia had already taken to her bed complaining that her eyeballs hurt; I sensed that the kids and I were on our own for the next couple of hours. Belatedly it occurred to me that the coffee they'd served us on the plane had been woefully underpowered.

"I *have* to go," Emily whined back. "It's the Alexander McQueen exhibit!"

"It's not my fault you're lame," Mason muttered, and Emily's face turned pink.

"Let's talk about this," I suggested to Mason, and I led him to the adjacent sitting area. "What's going on?"

"I just don't want to go to a stupid museum for a stupid fashion show or whatever," Mason pouted. "It's *my* birthday trip. Emily shouldn't get to decide everything."

"Well, where would you like to go instead?" I couldn't suppress a head-splitting yawn that came over me all of a sudden. "Sorry," I added. "Jet lag."

"I don't know. McDonald's." He ground his heels into the carpet and scowled.

"I'm happy to take you to lunch at McDonald's," I told him.

"I'm sure there's one nearby. But that would be in conjunction with the museum visit, not instead of it."

"I don't *want* to go to a museum," Mason repeated, louder this time. His jaw was set stubbornly.

"Mason." I chose my words carefully. "I'm not going to sit here arguing with you all day. I'll take you out to lunch and then I'll bring you back." I stood up. "You can hang out with your mom while Emily and I go to the museum. Then we'll come back and you can choose our next activity."

"I don't *want* to hang out with Mom!" Mason scowled.

"Then come with me and your sister," I replied, making sure I kept my voice steady. "But I must warn you now that whining is not on the agenda."

"Everything okay in there?" That was Cynthia's voice, coming from the adjacent room. We were being too loud.

"Fine," I called back to her. Then, to Mason: "Pull yourself together, buddy. Let's all have fun."

Mason made a rude noise. But he came with us.

In the end, Mason wasn't thrilled with the Victoria and Albert Museum. But he liked the gift shop well enough, and afterwards we feasted on Big Macs and fries as promised. Then we took a taxi to the Earl's Court Tube station.

"It's the TARDIS!" Mason shouted when he saw it, and indeed it was — a purple Police Box standing on the sidewalk by the Tube entrance as though that were the most normal thing in the world. Mason was officially over the moon. I snapped a few photos of the kids, and a nice lady took a picture of all three of us. Perhaps Mason could digitally insert his mother later on.

"Anyone want a disco nap?" I was losing the battle against jet lag, but I'd keep going if that's what they wanted.

"I do," Mason said, and he leaned in against my arm.

I gave his shoulder a squeeze. "Emily?"

She shrugged. "I'm fine. Me and Mom can go shopping."

"Mom and I," I corrected her automatically as I hailed a taxi.

Emily stuck out her tongue at me. "Whatever."

Back at the hotel, both kids headed upstairs together. I dawdled in the lobby until I was sure they were gone, then introduced myself to the concierge.

"Miss Haviland. Delighted to meet you at last." The concierge, sharp-dressed and impeccably groomed, came around the side of the desk to shake my hand. "George Thwaite. I believe we spoke on the telephone."

"Thanks for all your help so far," I said. I felt like such a yokel.

"It has been my pleasure." He pronounced *been* like *bean*. Even considering that whole British thing, this guy was a little over the top. Then again, hospitality was his entire job and I could probably learn a lot from him. "I have some information for you and Mrs. Waldrop," he said, and he offered me a large envelope.

I arrived upstairs to find Mason already asleep. Emily was checking her phone on the hotel WiFi, and Cynthia was either getting ready to go shopping or having a nervous breakdown. "I don't have cell service," she fretted. "What if I need to get in touch with you?"

"Um. Find a WiFi signal, I guess?" I yawned so hard my jaw practically came unhinged, reminding me that professionally speaking, I still had a long way to go before I reached George Thwaite-level servility. "I'll check my e-mail," I added lamely. "Or you could call the front desk. They'll put you through to the room." Well, what had people on vacation done before cell phones? Used smoke signals?

"Mom, come *on*. We won't need Lane," Emily insisted. "I already know where to go. Harvey Nicks is across the street and Harrods is a few blocks away."

I had to smile at Emily's navigational derring-do. "Can I talk to you both for a second before you go out? About Mason's birthday."

"Yeah!" Emily whispered, and she gave me her full attention. Where on Earth was she getting her energy? I could barely sit upright.

"Okay, the concierge can arrange for a really cool birthday cake for Mason," I told them. "But we need to get the order in. I was thinking a chocolate TARDIS cake."

"Perfect!" Emily squealed. Cynthia knitted her brows in confusion, but didn't say anything.

"Are you okay with that?" I didn't want to push Cynthia too hard, but time was of the essence and I couldn't exactly proceed without her blessing.

"I don't know what a TARDIS is. If you say that's what he likes, then it's fine." Motherly duties complete, Cynthia glanced at her watch and stood up. "We should probably go."

"Have fun," I whispered to Emily. I said a silent hallelujah for babysitting duty and phoned our cake preference in to Mr. Thwaite. Then, unsure of where I was actually supposed to be sleeping, I crashed out on a fainting couch in the sitting room.

When I woke up, the sky outside had darkened. Mason was sitting in a chair next to me, his eyes glued to his phone. "What's happening on the Internet?" I asked him. My voice was scratchy with sleep.

"We can install an app," he mumbled. "Then we can text each other over a WiFi signal."

"Great." Some family vacation! I'd actually been enjoying my European break from Cynthia's constant barrage of text messages, but anything to put her mind at ease. I sat up and tried to rub the sleep from my eyes.

"Lane?"

"Yeah?"

"Why isn't my dad here with us?"

Shit. "Did your mom talk to you about that?"

"Yeah." He put his phone down.

"Well, what did she say?" Our conversation was creeping into dangerous territory.

"She said Dad had to work, and he's trying to figure some stuff out. And that I shouldn't be too hard on him, even though I'm probably disappointed."

"Oh." Astonishing! Who'd have guessed that Cynthia was capable of such diplomacy? "Well, what do you think?"

He stared at me. "I dunno."

"Come here," I urged him, and I patted the space next to me on the couch. He didn't move, so I got up and sat down next to

CLEAN BREAK

him. "I don't know much about what's going on with your dad," I said. "But I'm here if you want to talk about it."

He shrugged. I reached around and gave him a one-armed hug. "You okay?"

"Yeah."

I hugged him tighter. My poor Mason.

I ended up spending the night in the sitting room after all, on a roll-away bed I had to request myself. Not sleeping: I lay awake in a wide-eyed jet-lagged disquiet, alternately thinking about Viktor and castigating myself for thinking about him. I was such a cliché. What kind of moron flies halfway around the world just to waste time mooning over a man's attention?

I could only conclude that seeing him on Friday had weakened my resolve. It would have been so much easier if he'd acted like a jerk. But no — he'd been kind, like always. Maybe that was Viktor's purpose in my life — to teach me what being with a kind man felt like. Even if he'd been the wrong choice in the end.

Yes — wrong, I reminded myself. He'd been advancing prostitution, for fuck's sake! Or, at the very least, he'd been consorting with people who were. I hadn't wasted much thought on his cryptic "I didn't expect you to understand" routine. Human trafficking doesn't leave much moral wiggle-room.

So why did I still miss him so much? Okay, the sex had been glorious. My mind longed to drift off into that delicious smutty territory. But for the sake of argument, I forced myself to consider Viktor as a whole human being. Setting aside his prowess in the bedroom and his sleazy job, what was left?

Well, we'd talked — a lot. Not exactly my favorite pastime these past few years, but somehow it had worked. We'd even got past the language barrier — and now that I thought about it, Viktor's "not so good" English had turned out to be entirely adequate. Better than that: he'd had a way of excavating the truth from me, even when I wasn't aware I was trying to hide anything.

Like Detective Jarrett? No, not at all. Jarrett had interrogated and intimidated me, constantly chipping away at my self-esteem,

227

always pushing me towards his agenda even when I'd asked him to back off. My conversations with Viktor had felt safe — never adversarial. An exchange between equals. He'd opened up to me. And he'd never seemed to have any particular agenda. Maybe he was an exceptionally skilled manipulator, but even after everything that had happened I couldn't quite believe that was true.

I was mulling that over when Cynthia padded out into the sitting room wrapped up in a fluffy Mandarin Oriental robe. "You're up," she observed, and she flopped down on a wingback chair. "I slept all day. What's your excuse?"

I sat up and yawned. "Jet lag, I guess. How was shopping?"

She yawned too. "Very good. We have more yet to do, but now we know the lay of the land."

"I wanted to run some more birthday plans by you," I said. "If now's a good time."

Cynthia sighed. "It's as good a time as any, I suppose."

So Cynthia's personal involvement in her son's birthday preparations to this point had been less than Pinterest-worthy. At least she gave me a blank check to pay for everything. Emily ended up accompanying Mason to see *Matilda* the following afternoon, and after the show all four of us went out for dinner. The TARDIS cake was a hit. Mason loved the 3D-printed *My Neighbor Totoro* cookie-cutters I'd got him on Etsy, and Emily surprised me by presenting him with a crocheted Minecraft pig she'd commissioned. Cynthia got emotional when Mason unwrapped her gift — a fancy watch. Then she told him he could go to computer and robotics camp this summer, and Mason jumped out of his chair to embrace her in a bear-hug.

"Let's not make a spectacle of ourselves," Emily said, mock-mortified, and she and I exchanged satisfied looks.

Our final day in England was spent playing Zombie Laser Tag at a venue Mr. Thwaite had personally recommended. Not our most culturally relevant excursion, but I'd never seen Mason so happy, and even Cynthia seemed to have fun with it. We feasted on steak pie and bangers and mash at a cozy pub, and finished the night with the latest James Bond film at the Electric Cinema.

"Definitely the best birthday ever," Mason mumbled when I tucked him into bed at the hotel. "Thanks for everything."

"I had a lot of help," I told him, and I winked at Emily, who was in her bed and obviously hiding her phone under the covers. "Your sister and your mom played an equal part in this madness." I held out my hand for the phone and Emily stuck her tongue out at me.

"If you say so." He turned over onto his stomach with a satisfied sigh.

29

Once our New York-bound plane was airborne and Cynthia and the kids were situated, I slumped down in my seat and took out my flip-phone. I'd been afraid to turn it on since leaving the States — I had no idea what the story was with my mobile plan as far as international roaming charges, and I hadn't had time to look into it before our departure. With my luck, I'd turn the phone on for five seconds and it would suck my account dry downloading texts and voicemails from Detective Jarrett. But part of me — okay, all of me — wondered if Viktor had been in touch.

Again with the brooding over a man. Well, at least now I was stuck on a plane with nothing better to do. I was willing to concede that Viktor's friendship was important to me, perhaps even more so than the romantic connection if I had to choose just one. And I'd meant what I said to him the other day — he *was* a good person, even if I hated his job and the people he worked with. It still didn't add up. But he was a person, not a balance sheet. And he'd always been there when I needed him.

"No mobile devices allowed," Mason reminded me from the adjacent seat. "Phone's looking good though. Is that duct tape?"

"Yes. Cheeky."

He took the phone and examined it from every angle. "How soon can we expect it to go full steampunk?" He'd twisted his leg into what looked like an impossible position underneath him. Both shoelaces were untied. I turned my attention to Emily, who was beckoning me over to her seat.

"I've been listening to that playlist," she told me as she removed her earbuds. "Whoever made it for you is definitely intense. And conflicted."

I took a sip of bottled water. "Then I'll have to assume he was an intense and conflicted guy."

Emily frowned. "Is he, like, dead or something?"

"No. Why would you say that?"

"You're talking about him in the past tense." Damn, this girl didn't miss a thing.

"Lane." Cynthia had roused herself from her magazine and was shuffling into the aisle. "A word?"

"Sure." I followed her back to the galley. For once I wasn't paranoid about being fired, but that didn't mean something bad wasn't about to happen.

"I wanted...to thank you for everything you've done," Cynthia began. She looked uncomfortable. "For Mason. Both kids, really." She glanced around the cabin nervously. "He's made so much progress."

"Hey, it's my pleasure. They're both great kids."

"They need you," she murmured. "This trip would've been a disaster if you hadn't come."

"They need *you*, Cynthia," I said, and she gave me a look of surprise. "Well, you're here, aren't you?" When she nodded uncertainly, I went on: "It's important. It's important every day. Not just birthdays."

"I've been a mess," she admitted. "Sorry for being overly dependent on you."

I wasn't sure how to respond to this, so I gave her a noncommittal nod.

"You're right, though. They need me." Cynthia chewed her lip. "Soon enough they'll be grown and gone."

"Not *that* soon," I reassured her. I still had rent to pay.

"Brad wants to start Couples Therapy," she said suddenly. "He sent me an email last night. He's ended it with that woman.

He says he wants to try to make our marriage work."

"Is that what you want?" I asked her.

"I think so." Cynthia wiped away the beginnings of a tear. "Is that pathetic?" Her voice was barely audible above the hum of the jet engines.

"Absolutely not," I told her, and I gave her a hug.

The moment our plane touched down at JFK, Emily started teasing me in a sing-song voice from across the aisle: "Lane's got texts from her boyfriend!" I rolled my eyes at her and waited for my flip-phone to find a signal. Come *on,* I silently urged it, willing the electrons to move faster through space.

Finally, the phone came to life, showing six new text messages and two voicemails. Every single one of the texts was from Detective Jarrett, spread over the four days I'd been away:

I'm sorry.

You need to give me another chance.

Where are u? I'm worried.

I can still help u but u need to call me before it's too late

Swung by ur apartment & they said U MOVED OUT?

Are u back together with that sleazeball??

A coldness settled over me. My heart was thudding in my chest.

I checked voicemail. The first one was from the bank, informing me that they'd refunded my certified check — minus a cancellation fee — and deposited it into my account. The other one was from Detective Jarrett and it chilled me to the bone: *You're making a mistake, Lane. You're hitching your wagon to a piece of trash. Call me when you get this...stop messing around.*

"Are you okay?" Cynthia had paused in the middle of stowing her reality-canceling headphones. "You look pale."

"I'm fine." I couldn't shake the terror I was feeling about Detective Jarrett. "I'll just make sure your car is here," I added, glancing down at my iPhone.

"Thank God," Cynthia breathed as she settled back into her seat. "I don't think I could face a taxi right now. But feel free to take one home and charge it to my card."

I slept late the next morning — Cynthia, in a moment of mercy, had given me the entire day off. By the time I was up and showered, it was after two o'clock and I was starving.

The weather had cooled substantially, so I put on a jacket and set off towards Brighton Beach Avenue in search of sustenance. On the way, I marveled at how familiar everything seemed — huge, lumbering American cars on American streets, driving in good old American traffic patterns. Those British vehicles barreling down the wrong side of the street had been deeply disconcerting. I consciously avoided Starbucks, stopping instead at a small Russian bakery where I ordered a coffee and a *pishki* — a Russian donut.

"You buy two *pishki*," the proprietor barked. "I give you good price."

"Just one today, thanks." He grunted his displeasure but completed the transaction. Viktor had told me that haggling was part of the culture. Where was he? I'd texted him a brief hello before collapsing into bed last night, but so far, no reply. Now that I'd gotten my money back, I was eager to settle up the rest of his loan, but I also felt something else pulling me towards him. Was it affection? *Friendship,* I admonished myself. I would not jump in the sack with him just because I was feeling lonely.

Out on the boardwalk, I sat on a bench overlooking the water and called Randy. She picked up on the first ring. "You're back. Tell me everything."

"Well, Detective Fuckface is officially stalking me. I can't believe I ever thought he was worth a second of my time." I told Randy about the text messages.

"What a psycho! Did he call you too?"

"A bunch of missed calls and a voicemail. More of the same."

"Lane, I so didn't want to be right about him."

"I know," I muttered. "Thank you for not saying 'I told you so.'"

"You do need to get a restraining order."

"Seriously?"

"Seriously. And don't you dare delete those texts or voicemails. They're evidence that he's harassing you."

"Shit." I let my gaze wander out towards the horizon. Water and sky were greenish-gray. The coffee wasn't agreeing with my stomach and I sincerely hoped I wouldn't puke.

"What about Viktor?" Randy asked.

"I feel like we left things on a positive note," I told her. "Haven't heard from him since getting back, though."

"Did you get any clarity in London?"

I heaved a Cynthia-level sigh. "My heart and my mind are at loggerheads. But I think I'm rooting for my heart to win." It was too complicated to explain over the phone. "I'll fill you in next time I see you," I concluded.

It was already dark outside when I started walking back home. Noticeably colder, too, I thought as I hugged my inadequate jacket around myself. Both phones had gone eerily silent — I was half-tempted to text Cynthia just to see if she was still alive.

Walking up Brighton Fourth Street, I didn't even register the car sitting at the curb outside my house — a shiny, dark-colored Nissan Murano — until Detective Jarrett opened the door and stepped out. *Shit.* I stopped walking and looked around, but the sidewalk was otherwise empty.

"I just want to talk, Lane." He took a tentative step towards me.

"I think you've said enough." I was so beyond freaked-out by this asshole. "Please, just go away and leave me alone."

"Not until you tell me what's going on with you and that dirtbag."

"I have nothing to say to you." I felt surer about that than I'd ever felt about anything, but that didn't stop me from being afraid of him. Just how far was he willing to push me? And if he did go too far, what then? Who do you turn to for protection when the one stalking you is with the law?

"Then hear me out," he said testily. I wondered if I could get to my front door ahead of him, and decided that I couldn't. "I know you and Viktor were hanging out on Friday afternoon." My mind continued to race — how did he know this? Was he having me followed? I edged towards my house, but Jarrett stepped squarely between me and the porch. "I'm only telling you this because I care about you," he said, and I felt a chill run down my spine. "Are you back together with him now?"

"I'm not with anyone!" I shouted. A light went on in one of the upstairs windows of the house directly across the street. I was shaking all over, but my voice came out firm: "I will ask you one more time to leave me alone." Now the front porch light at my house went on and a short, curly-haired dude came out. Thank God. Shit, what was his name again? Lev? He was wearing a striped sweater and a puzzled expression.

"Hey Lev," I called out to him. *Please, let that be his name.* I gave him a look I hoped he would understand meant I really, *really* needed him not to go back inside and leave me alone with Detective Jarrett again.

"Lane?" he asked. "You okay?"

"Detective Jarrett was just leaving," I said pointedly, feeling deep gratitude in my heart for housemates and nosy neighbors.

Jarrett shook his head. "Unbelievable," he muttered. But he let me pass by unmolested.

"All units." Some device on Jarrett's belt was crackling with staticky output. "Ten-forty-four. Rego Park. Sixty-Third Drive and Alderton Street."

I spun to face him as he hooted with laughter. "This is perfect!" he exclaimed, and gave me a hard look. There was a dark kind of joy in Detective Jarrett's eyes that made me want to run. "Now I get to go arrest your boyfriend," he said in a stage-whisper.

He's not my boyfriend, I wanted to yell back, but I knew that engaging Detective Jarrett further was unwise. It had to be Rego Park! The prostitutes must be back in business. I hugged my arms around my middle and wondered what the hell a ten-forty-four was.

"I'll say hello for you," Jarrett called from his car. He got in and started the engine.

"Lane?" Lev's voice was low. "Come inside?"

I took one more look at Jarrett's car before going in. Lev

followed, and he closed and locked the door behind us.

First, I tried to contact Viktor. My call went straight to voicemail and two frantic texts went unanswered. Lev clattered around in the kitchen, tending to something he'd had heating on the stove. "You want some tea?" he asked.

"Sure, thanks." I paced back and forth by the door. I had no idea if Viktor was even in Rego Park right now, but what would happen if Detective Jarrett found him there? I tried to tell myself the worst case scenario was that Jarrett would arrest Viktor and that was it. But it felt so much worse than that. Recent days had revealed a side of Detective Jarrett that terrified me. I was afraid to think what he was capable of. I knew the smartest thing was to stay as far away from him as possible. And get that restraining order.

But what about right now? What if he directed that psycho crap towards Viktor? If something happened to him, I'd never be able to forgive myself.

I took a deep breath. *You don't even know if Viktor's there.* He could be cozied up in his apartment, wherever that was.

But, a dark voice in the back of my head insisted, *what if he's not?*

"Here you go." Lev held out a mug of tea. I accepted it and took a gulp. At least Dmitri wasn't around; I'd already broken the no-drama rule and I'd lived here a grand total of twenty-four hours.

And if I followed the crazy impulse knocking around in my head, the drama was only about to get worse.

Calm down. You don't even know if Viktor is over there.

"Are you okay?" Lev asked. "You look super freaked out about something."

"I — yes, I'm fine," I told him.

I gave Lev a fake smile, and stood to leave. I ignored the fear that my self-destructive tendencies were making yet another appearance. Ridiculous or not, I couldn't just sit here wondering if he was okay.

I slipped out the door, jogged down towards Brighton Beach Avenue, and hailed a passing taxi.

"Rego Park," I told the driver. It was like someone else was saying the words. Someone braver than me, or more foolish. "Sixty-Third Drive and Alderton Street."

30

What followed was the longest taxi ride in the history of the universe. I continued texting Viktor from the back seat, praying to hear back from him. If I could just know he was okay, I could turn around and go home.

Maybe that's what I should do anyway.

Then I thought about Detective Jarrett and the way his behavior towards me had been steadily escalating. I didn't think that was over. If Lev hadn't shown up when he did, I felt in my gut that things could've gotten very, very ugly. A wave of nausea came over me. I had to lower the window to let cold air blow on my face. How did I get into this mess?

I heard the *chop-chop-chop* of the helicopter before I saw the flashing lights further ahead. Whatever was happening, it was some kind of a big deal and the street was blocked by a metal NYPD barricade. The taxi could go no further.

I exhaled in frustration. I could hardly see anything, let alone enough to know if Viktor was here. "Right here, I guess. Thanks." I paid the driver and walked up to the barricade. The noise of the helicopter was even louder now. Emergency lights were flashing all over the place on the next block, but there wasn't anyone here, just a barricade to keep the traffic away.

Well, let them send me back if they wanted, but for now there was no one to stop me from getting a closer look. I gathered up my courage and walked past the barricade. I knew I probably wasn't supposed to, but technically there was nothing preventing an average citizen from walking down the sidewalk. Nothing except common sense. Which I'd left back in Brighton Beach, apparently.

I walked past four shiny black SUVs with tinted windows, which looked like part of a Presidential motorcade. On the far side of this group of SUVs, a couple of uniformed cops were clustered together with a man and woman wearing FBI windbreakers, shouting to make themselves heard over the noise of the helicopter. I kept close to the building and away from them, hoping the SUVs would keep me mostly out of sight.

I rounded the corner and saw three NYPD EMERGENCY SERVICES trucks parked haphazardly in front of a brick building farther down the block. The helicopter hovered overhead with a deafening roar, shining a searchlight down towards the rear of the building. And a few guys who looked like part of a SWAT team were standing behind one of the trucks. They had helmets, body armor, and very big guns.

"Hey." A barrel-chested uniformed cop came out of nowhere, causing me to jump. "You can't be here."

"I'm trying to find—" I began, but the cop shook his head and indicated the area I'd just come from. One of the cops I'd seen earlier was headed towards the barricade, apparently deciding to stand guard — probably because a small crowd had begun to gather there.

"Go down there," the cop told me. His tone brooked no argument. I complied, disheartened.

Maybe Viktor's not here, I thought to myself for the umpteenth time. *And if he is, he'll probably just get arrested. No worse.*

But in my heart, I didn't believe a word. As I walked back in the direction I'd just come, I kept thinking about the hard look I'd seen on Detective Jarrett's face when he said he was going to arrest my boyfriend.

Once I was behind the police barricade, I checked my phone for texts — still nothing. I finally broke down and tried calling

Randy. She didn't pick up and I didn't leave a voicemail. How could I possibly explain that I was re-enacting scenes from *Les Misérables* outside a whorehouse in Queens in hopes of finding Viktor before Detective Jarrett did? None of this made sense anymore, not even to me.

"Excuse me," I said to the young uniformed cop guarding the barricade. "Can you tell me what's going on?"

"I don't know, ma'am," was his stone-faced reply. Right. I jammed my numb hands into my pockets and strained my neck to try to see what was happening closer to the area with the SWAT team. What the hell was I still doing here? I couldn't see anything. Being shunted off to a lousy vantage point seemed like an ignominious end to the night. Still, there was activity happening over that way. I could hear it, and I couldn't manage to tear myself away from it, even if I couldn't see anything much besides the side of a police van and two empty cruisers with flashing lights.

"Hey. *Hey!*" The young cop was waving a gloved hand at a man and woman jogging down towards the action. The man was holding a camera with EYEWITNESS NEWS lettered on the side. "Stay back," the cop ordered them, and they settled next to me, close to the barrier. I checked my phone again compulsively: still no word from Viktor. Was this crazy, my being here? Yes, it was.

A light drizzle had begun to fall, rendering my fleece jacket even more inadequate against the elements. I assumed the woman in the news team was a reporter — she had the impossibly well-coiffed hairstyle of a television personality. She pulled up the hood of her windbreaker and I managed to catch her eye.

"I got really close to the scene," I told her in a low voice. "They made me move back here, but I saw a SWAT team. There are three big Emergency Services trucks."

"You're sure about that?" She and her cameraman exchanged a glance.

"Yeah. I was down there maybe ten minutes ago."

She turned to the cameraman. "Could be the Haz-Mat team. Scanner said ten-forty-four."

"Could be." He was busy fiddling with a dial on his equipment.

"Excuse me, officer!" The reporter got the young cop's attention. "Are we dealing with a bomb threat?"

"I don't know, ma'am," he replied, touching the brim of his hat. "You'll have to contact Press Relations."

She whispered something to the cameraman, who hoisted his rig up onto his shoulder and started panning around. In spite of the increasing rain, a few more people had joined us behind the barrier — curious bystanders, from the looks of it. Why would anyone in their right mind choose to be out here tonight? Excellent question.

Up ahead, I saw movement on the sidewalk near one of the police vans. I squinted through the darkness and falling rain. There was a person — a man — walking. He was wearing what looked like street clothes. Another man followed. And another. All three had their hands behind their backs. I could only see the barest glimpse of faces, but none of them looked like Viktor. They disappeared from view behind the van and I let out the tiniest sigh of relief. Maybe Viktor wasn't here after all.

But no. There were more people coming out of the building. Damn, this rain. I tapped the reporter on the shoulder and pointed to what was happening. "Can your cameraman zoom in over there?" I asked, but she didn't respond. I craned my neck for a better view. Two more men were walking, hands behind their backs. They were handcuffed, I realized. Then a third man followed behind them.

Viktor!

I felt immense relief at seeing him in one piece, even if he'd been arrested. Detective Jarrett was nowhere in sight. I turned to the cameraman again; he was a good head taller than me, and he had a zoom lens. "Can you see anything?" I asked loudly, not wanting to be ignored again. "Those guys look like they've been arrested."

He squinted into his viewfinder. "There're two plainclothes officers guarding a group of men sitting on the curb. Seven, eight guys. Hands cuffed behind their backs, looks like." He looked down at me and shrugged.

I hadn't noticed, or maybe I just couldn't see any plainclothes officers. I wished I could make sure they didn't include Detective Jarrett. "One of the guys they arrested is a friend of mine," I told him.

"Oh yeah? Which one?" The cameraman squinted back into his viewfinder.

"He's a white guy. Tall with black hair. Thirty-four."

"Wearing a black leather jacket?" The cameraman seemed very absorbed in this new task.

"Ty," the reporter said warningly. "Enough."

"Yeah, a black leather jacket," I said, a little too loud. "Is everything okay?"

He squinted into the viewfinder again. "Someone just came over. Another plainclothes cop." He leaned slightly to one side. "Now he's grabbing your pal. Damn. That's pretty rough."

My blood turned to ice. Detective Jarrett.

"Shit, I can't see them anymore," the cameraman told me. "Looks like they're headed over that way." He pointed to the second group of police vans, parked across the street behind two empty cruisers. I strained my eyes trying to see something — anything — through the rain and darkness and inadequate street-lights.

Suddenly I knew with terrible certainty that Viktor was in mortal danger.

What happened next was essentially an out-of-body experience. I didn't think. I pushed through the crowd and ducked around the barrier at its farthest point from the cop. And then I ran for it. I felt my legs pushing me forward, heard the soles of my boots thudding down on the wet pavement — but it was as though someone else was running and I was a spectator. Cold rain spattered onto my cheeks. Behind me, I heard the cop hollering — *Stop!* — but it barely registered, and I didn't look back. I ran first past one van, then another.

I was vaguely aware of someone else shouting at me to stop, but up ahead I heard a shuffling, and a commotion, followed by a heavy *thud* and then what sounded like a howl of pain. "Mother-fucker!" My heart kicked into higher gear. That was definitely Detective Jarrett's voice! I rounded the corner of the last van.

There they were: Viktor and Detective Jarrett, both on the ground. Jarrett was kneeling, facing away from me, crouched with a gun in his right hand. Viktor was lying on his side a few feet from Jarrett. His hands were still behind his back and I couldn't see his face.

"You fucking piece of shit!" Jarrett bellowed down at the prone Viktor, and he stood up — partway; he was still hunched over — and kicked Viktor in the ribs. There was a horrible *crack* and Viktor made a sharp gasping sound. I was just about to run forward and — hell if I had any idea what I was going to do — when the young cop from the barricade came barreling towards me with his gun raised.

"Down on the ground!" he shouted. When I opened my mouth to inform him of his grievous error in judgment, he hooked his leg around my foot, grabbed me by the collar of my jacket, and shoved. I dropped to the wet ground like a stone.

"Wait, I'm just trying to help my friend!" My appeal fell flat — not surprising, considering I'd just rushed onto a crime scene. But even now I couldn't seem to calm down. "Please, he's hurt. He's lying over there—" I thrust my chin in Viktor's direction, but no matter how I strained my neck, I couldn't see him from where I was lying.

"Hold still," the cop barked, a little breathlessly. "You're under arrest." He was holding one hand painfully behind my back. Cold metal closed around that wrist. He wrenched my other hand into position and finished the job.

"Good work, officer." Oh shit, Detective Jarrett. Adding to my fears for Viktor was now fear for my own safety. God, what had I done? "That was a textbook takedown." I heard Jarrett's heavy footsteps coming towards us.

"Thank you, Detective."

"That motherfucker over there attacked me," Jarrett panted. "He went for my gun."

"That's bullshit!" I wailed, realizing even as the words came out that this wasn't going to help my case.

I felt a hand grab my upper arm and then the uniformed cop pulled me up to standing so fast it took me a second to get my bearings. But then I saw him: Viktor! He was still lying there, facing away from me and unmoving. I wanted to call out to him, but I couldn't form the words. Jarrett was giving me a look so cold I couldn't speak.

"You, shut your mouth," Jarrett warned me. His face was so dark, I felt as terrified of what he might do as I had when we'd been alone on the street earlier. He turned to the cop. "Put her in the squad car. I'll call the paramedics to come take a look at this dirtbag." But I didn't think that's what he was about to do at all. I suddenly realized Viktor was in danger again.

"No, don't leave him," I pleaded with the cop. A whisper of doubt passed over his face as he looked from me to Detective Jarrett — maybe he'd seen Jarrett's dark side before too — but it was short-lived.

"Come on," he muttered, pulling me back towards the street by my arm. The smirk on Detective Jarrett's face made me want to commit violence myself.

"You can't. Please," I begged the cop as he pulled me, slipping and stumbling, towards the parked police cars. "That man over there, he can't defend himself!"

"Quiet," he snarled, but he stopped where we were, short of the police car, and — was this on purpose? — still in sight of Detective Jarrett and Viktor. The cop took off his hat and wiped his forehead. The rain had slowed to a light drizzle, but both of us were soaked.

Detective Jarrett noticed the delay and scowled at us. I didn't want to wait for him to order the cop to keep going. I started looking around for backup. Weren't there any other cops around? They were all busy elsewhere — with the other men who'd been arrested, and further down the block where there was yet more action — but I was determined to get someone's attention.

Before I could holler for anyone, I heard footsteps, hard and fast on the slick pavement, and I turned back to find Detective Jarrett right in front of us. He grabbed my arm and yanked me in towards him with surprising force. "You're interfering with police business," he growled. "Lock that guy up," he ordered the cop, and then he turned to me. "A word in private, Lane."

He pulled me around to the side of the van.

"Where are we going?" I asked. He didn't respond. Instead he dragged me up near the front of the van and pushed me face-first against the hood.

"Let's get these off," he said, and I felt him yanking on the handcuffs. For some reason that made me even more afraid — why was he doing this? Before I could complete that thought, the cuffs came off and he leaned in. So close I could feel his breath on my ear. I wanted to vomit.

"Do you have any idea," he hissed, "how much trouble you're causing me?" I tried to wriggle away, but he still had my arm and now he twisted it. Hard.

"Shit! Please stop," I begged. Dear God, it hurt.

"You shouldn't struggle," he whispered. "That's how innocent citizens like you can accidentally get hurt."

I froze, my heart pounding.

He drew back and relaxed his hold a bit until I was able to breathe almost normally again. Then, without a word, he twisted it again, harder.

"Stop!" I cried. The pain. It had just intensified a thousandfold. "You're hurting me!" But I knew he didn't care.

He waited an agonizing few moments before letting up. When he finally did, I choked with relief and tried to stand upright but he was still holding me pinned against the hood of the truck. "Why are you doing this?" I asked him.

"You're trouble," he replied, and his voice was oddly calm. He twisted my arm again, as hard as before, and that's when I heard myself whimpering. It didn't sound like me. He leaned in and put more pressure on my arm than I'd ever felt in my life. A sharp swoop of fear captured me. *He's going to break it off,* I thought, but I couldn't speak — my arm and my shoulder were a blazing torrent of agony. CRACK! The sound was terrible, gruesome. But it was nothing compared to the pain — searing, white-hot, snaking in every direction — until finally everything was swallowed up into darkness.

31

My first thought when I opened my eyes was *too bright.* Fluorescent lights. White walls and a white bed with white rails on the sides. It even smelled white. Medicinal. A hospital.

My second thought was *I need to puke,* which I promptly did. A nurse came gliding over. She was talking. I couldn't put the words together — her voice was loud and then soft, spouting words and random nonsense-sounds. I blinked and saw double. Triple. Woozy.

"Are you speaking English?" I asked the nurse. My mouth, dry as sand, was on a three-second time delay from my brain. "Can you talk slower?"

She patted my shoulder and said something I couldn't quite make sense of, then she poked something in my ear. A cuff tightened around my left arm, stayed tight, released with a *hiss.* I looked down at that arm and made a great effort to lift up my hand to scratch my nose, because it itched like crazy. Despite the brain-hand time delay, I eventually succeeded.

Good.

My eyelids were heavy.

"Lane? Lane, honey. It's Randy."

I forced my eyes open. My head ached and my mouth was horribly dry. "Randy?"

"Yes, it's me. How are you feeling?"

"Okay, I guess. A little sleepy." I shifted slightly in the bed, trying to sit up a bit, and felt a stab of pain in my right arm. "Fuck! I can't move my arm."

"It's immobilized," Randy said. "It's broken. Don't try to move it."

I let my head sink back onto the pillow. The pain in my arm subsided slightly, but not by much.

"You want some water?" Randy offered me a cup with a straw, and I drank greedily. Nothing had ever tasted so good. I leaned back and closed my eyes. *Water.* Rain, falling down steadily in the darkness. Running — where? To Viktor.

"Where's Viktor?" I asked.

"I don't know." She looked around the small, too-bright room. "I only just got here. I can't find anyone who'll tell me what happened."

I looked down at my right arm and shoulder; they were encased in what looked like a cast. Everything itched. "That cop you warned me about," I mumbled. "He did this to me. On purpose."

"Fucking prick." Randy's eyes were bright with tears. She took my left hand and squeezed it. "What can I do, Lane?"

My gaze wandered up to the drop-ceiling tiles. Squares! All lined up, neat in a row. God, I was high on something. Already I could feel the black void tugging at me. *Sleep,* it whispered.

"Call Cynthia," I told Randy. My head felt like it was sinking deeper and deeper into the pillow. "And find Viktor."

I woke up to a stab of pain — my arm! I must have moved it in my sleep. I was about to press the button to summon the nurse when I heard a familiar voice in the hallway.

"I'm not interested in his schedule." It was coming from right outside my door. "I want that doctor in here right now."

"Cynthia?" I called out in a thin voice.

"Lane!" Cynthia swept inside wearing her Burberry crimson quilted jacket. "I can't believe it. I just had to demand to see your doctor! Randy told me he's nowhere to be found." She sat down in a chair next to the bed and peered at me. "Water?"

"Yes. Thanks." *Awkward.* "Randy told you...?"

"Randy called and told me you asked for me," Cynthia declared, taking the cup after I'd finished and setting it down on a small table. "Of course I came right over." She shifted in her chair and looked around the small room. "To Queens." The word sounded alien rolling off her tongue.

"Wow. You didn't need to...I mean, thanks," I mumbled. Even in my morphine euphoria, I had enough sense to withhold the fact that I'd only meant for Randy to tell Cynthia that I wouldn't be coming in to work. But her interest in me was a surprise, as was her willingness to venture to the outer boroughs. "Who's with the kids?" I remembered to ask.

Cynthia waved away my concern. "They're at school. Don't worry, Lane, just focus on getting better."

Randy walked in holding two cups of coffee. She handed one to Cynthia and pulled up a chair. "Hey. How're you feeling?"

"Hold on. Forget about me for a minute." My brain felt hazy. "What happened with Viktor?"

They exchanged a look, and my heart sank. "No, Lane, don't despair," Randy urged. "We still don't know anything. We've tried—"

"What's his last name?" Cynthia interrupted.

I closed my eyes and tried to concentrate. "It's Viktor with a k," I told her. What the hell *was* his last name? Also something with a K. "Koz-something? Kozlowski? Kozlov." I remembered! Cynthia nodded at me and disappeared into the hallway pecking at her phone.

Randy scooted her chair a little closer to my bed. "I charged your phone," she said. "No new calls or texts came in."

"Thank you." I hadn't even thought of that; thank the heavens I had Randy on my side.

"I've called the city's information line to see if someone named Viktor was arrested," she went on. "All five boroughs, just in case.

248

Nothing." She scratched her head. "Maybe Cynthia will have more luck with his last name."

"Did you call hospitals? I'm sure he was hurt."

"Yes," she said quietly. "I asked here and called all the others nearby. I also called the morgue — Manhattan, Brooklyn, and Queens divisions." She sighed. "No Viktors. And no 'John Doe' males matching how you'd described him."

A question formed in my mind. "How did you know I was even here?"

"I called your phone and a nurse answered. And I called your housemate too, filled him in. Dmitri, right?" I processed this information while I tried to ignore the rising pain in my arm. How could I ever thank Randy for calling the fucking morgue on my behalf? Or Cynthia, for coming all the way out here? The mere fact that the two of them were here with me right now was astonishing. Somewhere along the line, despite my worst efforts, I'd managed to forge friendships.

"Eyewitness News," I said slowly. "There was a reporter. And a cameraman. Maybe they saw some of what happened."

"Did you get their names?" Randy took a pad and pen out of her bag.

"The reporter was female. Young." I closed my eyes. *Think!* "The cameraman was a big, tall guy. I don't know their names."

Cynthia swept back into the room. "No one named Viktor Kozlov got arrested. And there weren't any close matches or alternate spellings." She scowled down at her phone. "This is bullshit. I'm calling David."

Randy and I exchanged a quizzical look.

"Lawyer with the D.A.'s office," Cynthia continued, scrolling through the contacts on her phone. "He'll get to the bottom of this, or he'll put me in touch with someone who can." She put the phone to her ear and glided back out to the hallway.

I looked after her. A big aching lump was forming in my throat. "What am I even hoping for?" I whispered. "That he's in jail instead of dead? That he gets deported back to Russia?"

"Don't give up hope, Laney." Randy's face was etched with worry.

"I won't."

I wanted so much to be telling her the truth.

After much pestering from Cynthia, or perhaps despite it, Dr. Sullivan finally showed up. He had coffee-colored skin and retro plastic-framed glasses. "A spiral oblique fracture of the humerus," he pronounced, placing an X-ray image up on a wall-mounted light box. "With radial nerve involvement, I'm afraid. Hence the need for surgery. I used a plate and screws to secure the bone."

"Ah. Okay." I was still stoned out of my gourd on pain medication, so I felt extra-fortunate to have Randy and Cynthia there with me.

"Will it heal?" Randy asked.

"Yes." Dr. Sullivan beamed at me. "She's young and active and healthy. I'd say the outlook is very good."

"How long until she's back to normal?" Cynthia demanded.

"Tough to know for sure." He squinted at the X-ray. "Four to six months is my best guess. Of course, that's for a full recovery. You'll get passive range of motion quite a bit sooner, as long as you don't lift heavy items up over your head." He indicated something on the X-ray with his pen. "The bone actually heals in eight to ten weeks. From there it's just a matter of strengthening it up."

"Physical therapy?" Cynthia seemed so confident and capable. Like an entirely different person.

"Yes, absolutely." Dr. Sullivan checked his watch. "I'm discharging you tomorrow morning, Miss Haviland. You'll need to continue taking antibiotics to prevent infection, and I want you to follow up with me in ten days. Of course, call my office if you have any questions or concerns."

"Thank you," I told him, "for putting me back together." Sometime during this conversation it had occurred to me that I didn't have health insurance. I'd never be able to pay this wonderful man who'd been roused in the middle of the night to come save my arm.

"You're very welcome. Now, you're going to need some help

in the next few weeks. Getting around and all that. Do you have friends or family in the area?" He peered down at me. "Some type of support?"

I opened my mouth to respond, but Cynthia beat me to the punch. "Of course she does," she informed Dr. Sullivan. "Lane is coming home with me."

As much as I longed to be the fiercely independent tough girl, I had to admit that Cynthia was right: I couldn't possibly take care of myself for the next few days. I could barely make it to the bathroom and back without help from the nurse on duty. Still, the thought of staying overnight at Chez Waldrop was causing me minor unease. "Promise you'll come visit me," I begged Randy once Cynthia had left for the day.

"Of course I will, silly." Randy sniffed. "Do you think I'd pass up a chance to see how the fabled One Percent really live?"

"Just tell me when you're coming so I can hide the good silver." I picked at a blueberry muffin on the dinner tray. It was way too sweet and tasted terrible, but I was starving.

"I meant to tell you," Randy said. "I called Eyewitness News and talked to a producer. She was very interested in what I had to say."

"Did she connect you with the reporter I told you about?"

"No, but she wasn't working last night. She's gonna talk to the News Director and get back to me."

"Reason for hope." I took a sip of apple juice. "Randy, I don't have health insurance."

She snorted. "That's the last thing you should be worried about right now."

"Well, when should I start worrying? When I'm drowning in medical debt and hunted by bill collectors until the day I shuffle off this mortal coil?"

"Focus on getting through the next few weeks," Randy advised. "If that sleazeball cop did this to you, the City of New York is on the hook for your medical bills. Plus pain and suffering," she added pointedly, gesturing towards the hulking apparatus that encased my right arm.

"Shit, you're right." I turned that prospect over in my mind and decided that freaking out over medical bills was premature. "I guess I need legal advice."

"I think Cynthia's got that covered," Randy deadpanned, and we both laughed.

Morning came, and I wolfed down a breakfast of gooey flavorless oatmeal. The nurse removed my intravenous line and reminded me that I hadn't been discharged yet — they needed the attending doctor to sign off. And said doctor was very, very busy. So I lay on the bed, watched *Judge Judy,* and waited for Cynthia to arrive.

Half an hour later, after I'd offered thanks to the universe that the iPhone's battery was dead and thus Cynthia couldn't text me, my in-room landline rang.

"Lane. Sorry I'm late." Judging from the background noise, Cynthia was in transit — in the back of a hired Lincoln Town Car, probably.

"There's no rush, honestly. I'm still waiting to get discharged—"

"I visited David at his office," she interrupted. "He wasn't returning my calls in a timely fashion and I know we need answers on what happened to your friend."

"Wow." Words seemed inadequate. "I'm — I'm touched, Cynthia. Thank you."

"Don't thank me yet," she warned. Then, very urgently and muffled a bit, she barked: "Take the F.D.R. Drive!" I heard a man grumbling in the background — the driver, I assumed. "Just do it!" Cynthia snapped. "Sorry, Lane."

"Did David tell you anything about Viktor?" *Please, please, please,* I chanted silently.

"Here's the thing," she said, and she dropped her voice to a near-whisper. "David called his contact at the NYPD — and this is an important guy, very high up."

"Go on."

"There's no record of anyone named Viktor Kozlov being arrested. Anywhere. Ever."

"Never?" My mind flipped back to a well-worn card in its Rolodex of Shame — the Advancing Prostitution incident. Not to mention the Russian prison record, although I wouldn't have expected that to come up anyway.

"Nope, never. Now here's the really strange part. I asked about the whole...situation you told me about. The helicopter, the Haz-Mat truck, the SWAT team. In Rego Park — the night before last. Because even if they don't have Viktor's name in their arrest records, they'd have a record of everything else that went on there, right?"

"Right." I was impressed with Cynthia's sleuthing skills and badger-like persistence. From the sound of things, she'd marched into David's office and refused to leave — all on behalf of her kids' interim nanny and a person she'd never even met.

"Well, he couldn't access any information on it!" Cynthia squeaked. "It's locked down. Confidential. He said he hadn't seen anything like it since 9/11. He said it must be — and I quote — 'some *Zero Dark Thirty* shit.' That's what he said."

"Zero Dark Thirty," I repeated. "Wasn't that a movie?"

"Yes, Lane! The CIA. Military intelligence. Something like that. Anyway." She took a breath. "David's going to try to get some information through other channels, but he has to be discreet. It might be a while before we hear anything." I wondered what the odds were on David entering the Witness Protection Program rather than having to deal with Cynthia. "I just couldn't wait to tell you. I'll be there soon and I have clothes for you to change into."

The call disconnected. I looked up at the TV screen: Judge Judy was rolling her eyes at a hapless plaintiff.

What the fuck was going on?

253

32

I was breakfasting at Chez Waldrop the following morning when my flip-phone chimed: Randy! I swallowed the piece of thick-cut hickory smoked bacon I'd been chewing and took the call.

"I have two questions for you." Randy-over-the-phone was always all business. "First, how are you feeling this morning?"

"Living the life. Zero complaints." I was lounging on the daybed in Cynthia's second-floor office. Mason had personally delivered my breakfast — eggs, bacon, and orange juice with a Percocet chaser.

"Good. Second question. Are you up for some visitors?"

"Sure." I yawned. "Just tell me if I have to change out of my pajamas."

"That's a yes. The Eyewitness News reporter and her cameraman want to see you. They said they can be there in an hour."

The reporter's name was Andrea Gonzales and her cameraman was Tyler Morse. "I'm just so glad you're okay," Andrea told me. "We were frantic. Everything got so chaotic afterwards and we didn't know where to find you." She looked from me to Randy to Cynthia. "The police detained us. We had to get the station's lawyers involved."

It was a lot to process at once, and I wasn't sure what to make of it. But before I could ask for clarification, Cynthia invited everyone into the living room and we all sat down.

Might as well cut to the chase. "Do you know what happened with Viktor?" I asked Andrea. "The guy lying on the sidewalk."

"The paramedics came," Andrea said. "They got him into an ambulance pretty quickly." She took out a pad and pen. "What's his last name?"

"Kozlov. And it's Viktor with a K." I leaned forward in my chair. "Was he okay?"

"I couldn't really see anything," she said. "I didn't want to get in the way. They were working pretty hard on him."

I looked over at Tyler. "How about you?"

"I heard you shouting and I ran over. Then I saw —" He paused.

"My arm?" I asked.

"Yeah."

Randy spoke up. "Did you get what happened recorded? On camera?"

"I did." Tyler was steely-eyed. "Crystal clear."

I felt my eyes go wide with shock. This was unexpected.

"And?" Randy prodded.

"And," Tyler said, exchanging a disgusted glance with Andrea, "that memory card is now with the FBI."

"The station's lawyers are on the warpath," Andrea added. "They've filed a motion to compel the return of the card."

"Shit." I turned the FBI angle over in my mind. It lined up with the information Cynthia's friend had uncovered, but I didn't feel like it was my place to share that information right now.

Andrea was looking intently at me. "Tyler was an eyewitness to Detective Jarrett's actions that evening. We're both going to testify at the motion hearing tomorrow morning. Now that you're out of the hospital, they're going to want your testimony too."

"Forgive me for asking an obvious question," Randy said. "But why hasn't this already been on the news?

"Or on YouTube?" Cynthia looked scandalized.

Andrea and Tyler exchanged another glance. "We're under a gag order from the judge," she said quietly.

"Are you kidding me?" Randy looked like she might explode. "After what that monster did?"

"I wish I could give you more information." Andrea reached into her bag. "I wanted to give you my contacts' names at the FBI and Internal Affairs. And the station's legal team — they have a liaison." She handed me a slip of paper. "If you haven't hired a lawyer, now would probably be a good time."

I looked over at Cynthia, who seemed deep in thought. Randy was fuming and Tyler looked like he wished he were someplace else.

"I can promise you one thing," Andrea said. "They will not bury this. Not if I have anything to say about it."

Andrea, Tyler, and Randy all left together. Cynthia saw them out and returned to the living room fairly brimming with purpose. "She's absolutely right, Lane. You need a lawyer."

"That's probably true." I thought about my net worth, which fluctuated wildly depending on how I timed the purchase of my weekly MetroCard. But Cynthia was already swiping her way through her phone contacts.

"Brad's fraternity brother works at a firm that does a lot of civil rights work pro bono," she announced. "They were bragging about it at a charity thing. We won a silent auction — a romantic weekend at a partner's ski house in Vermont. It rained the whole time!" She walked towards the kitchen, phone glued to her ear. And by the time the kids arrived home from school — Emily escorted Mason and they both did just fine — I had acquired a lawyer.

"Lane, you should always stay here overnight." Dinner was over, and Mason was finishing up his homework at the kitchen counter while I fixed myself a cup of tea in an extremely maladroit one-handed fashion.

"The commute is pretty sweet," I admitted. "How's school?"

He frowned down at his French textbook. "I don't talk about school after three o'clock."

"Well, *pardonnez-moi.*" I tore open a sugar-packet using my teeth. I was hoping to get through the evening without any Percocet, and so far it looked promising with just over-the-counter medications. My brain-fog had cleared, at least.

"Who's the guy who was here earlier?" Mason asked.

"Patrick Van Heyst. My lawyer." Saying those two words together felt strange. "Your mom convinced him to take me on for free. She's a superstar."

Mason seemed to mull it over. "Have you found your friend yet? Viktor?"

"No." I sighed. "We're hitting a lot of dead ends so far."

"Then you should keep trying."

I carried my tea around the breakfast bar and sat down next to Mason. From the looks of things, he'd been tasked with some heavy-duty irregular verb conjugations. "The lawyer's filing some kind of motion. It's the first step in a civil rights lawsuit. The truth will come out, I hope."

"Mom said a cop did that to your arm." Mason's gaze moved from his textbook to his worksheet, then to me.

"Yes." I wondered where Detective Jarrett was at this moment. Hopefully locked up somewhere, although I doubted it. Trying to find that out had been another blind alley for Cynthia and me. I hoped Patrick would be more skilled at extracting information from the NYPD and the FBI. Both agencies seemed to excel at the art of obfuscation.

Mason yawned. "I'm going to bed," he told me. I gave him a one-armed hug and kissed his forehead. "You should go to bed too," he observed as he headed up the stairs. "Your arm heals faster while you sleep."

"Thank you, Dr. Waldrop." Mason was right. I'd texted Randy an update, not that there had been much new information to share. *Take care of yourself first,* she'd texted right back. *You're still recovering. Let the lawyer do his thing.* And I knew that she, too, was right. My plan was to head home to Brighton Beach tomorrow afternoon and do a test-run solo subway commute.

But first I had business downtown. I'd been subpoenaed. There was a motion hearing regarding the news crew's memory card. They were expecting me in Federal Court first thing tomorrow morning.

The Honorable Judge Owen T. Spencer looked like he'd just stepped out of an episode of *Law and Order*. For one thing, he was seated behind an imposing desk that was at least three feet above everyone else in the courtroom. And he was wearing that black judge robe you always see on TV. The whole effect added significantly to my feeling of having been sent to the principal's office.

Somehow I made it up to the front of the courtroom, and the bailiff showed me to the witness box. Then I had to swear to tell the truth, the whole truth, and nothing but the truth. Patrick had told me this probably wouldn't take very long. Easy for him to say. My mouth had gone completely dry.

The judge looked over the top of his glasses at the lawyers assembled behind two tables at the front of the courtroom. In front of each table stood a podium. "Whenever you're ready," he said to a silver-haired lawyer wearing an expensive-looking suit. He looked like Anderson Cooper's metrosexual older brother.

"Miss Haviland," the lawyer said. "I want to draw your attention to the evening of April 24th of this year."

"Okay." My voice, amplified by the microphone, sounded wobbly.

"Can you tell me where you went that evening?"

"I went to Rego Park. In Queens." I was already sweating. The scratchy black wool slacks and blue cowl-necked sweater I'd borrowed from Cynthia's aspirational closet were sticking to me in uncomfortable places.

"What time did you go?"

"I think around seven."

He nodded. "And why did you go to Rego Park that evening?"

"Detective Jarrett had told me he was going there and I was afraid he might hurt my friend. Viktor."

"Viktor Kozlov?"

I nodded. *Was he alive, or dead?*

"Please answer the question out loud, Miss Haviland."

"Yes. Viktor Kozlov."

"Can you describe the type of relationship you had with Mr. Kozlov?"

I wondered if there was a time limit on answers. "We were friends. We'd dated romantically but — but that ended a few weeks ago. So we were just friends."

The lawyer led me through my version of the evening's events. I answered his questions as truthfully as I could, occasionally glancing over at Patrick for moral support. Only one other lawyer had questions for me; the rest declined. I wanted blood where Detective Jarrett was concerned, but everything about this hearing felt overly civil, anticlimactic.

"They know who Viktor is," I whispered to Patrick in the hallway outside the courtroom.

"Yes. It would appear so." Patrick was checking his phone. "You're getting a restraining order against Detective Jarrett, by the way."

"Good." I pressed the Down button at the elevator bank. "Don't you think that's a potentially good sign? That they know who Viktor is, I mean."

"I don't know what to think about him." Patrick shoved his phone into his pocket. "Every time I think I'm getting close, we hit a dead end. It's almost like Viktor doesn't exist."

"Well, those lawyers in there seem to think he exists." I tightened a strap on my arm sling. "Have you spoken to the FBI?"

"Yes." The elevator doors opened and Patrick motioned for me to go in first. "The problem is that they're not speaking to me."

Later that afternoon, I trudged up the walkway to the house on Brighton Fourth Street and turned my key in the door. Being there felt strange. It was as though a line had been drawn between Rego Park and everything that came before.

The house was quiet; if anyone else was home, they were

behind closed bedroom doors, and I was glad for it. *Tell me if you have any issues,* Cynthia had texted during my commute to Brooklyn. *I'll send a car.* And yesterday she'd given me a pay advance. "Don't argue," she'd said. "I don't want you worrying about money. I already feel bad enough that you're going through all this without health insurance." Apparently she'd begun arrangements with her accountant to make my employment above-the-table — another surprise. Cynthia was full of them these days.

My room was as I'd left it, futon unmade, and I lay down on top of the comforter fully dressed. Every inch of me was exhausted, my arm was hurting, and the day's events were clattering around in my head. I wondered briefly where Viktor was. *Is he even alive?* I shoved that thought down deep. *Don't think. Just sleep.* I closed my eyes and drifted off.

"Lane?" A sharp knock came on my bedroom door. "Lane, are you in there?"

"I'm here," I groaned. What the hell? My eyes were slow to focus. "Come in," I added.

Dmitri poked his head inside my room. "You're back."

"Yeah." How long had I slept? I moved to a sitting position on the side of the futon and glanced out the window to the darkening sky. "What's up?"

"There's a guy downstairs," Dmitri said. "He wants to see you."

33

I raced downstairs, heedless of my appearance and the fact that my arm-sling had come unfastened and slipped most of the way off my shoulder. I was hoping against hope that the man here to see me was Viktor. Belatedly, it occurred to me that it could just as easily have been Detective Jarrett. But the guy standing on the porch wearing a tan trenchcoat was wholly unfamiliar. He looked me over. "Lane Haviland?"

"Yes." I looked him over right back. Average height, broad shoulders. Dark hair and a neatly trimmed mustache. "Is this another subpoena?"

"No, ma'am." He flashed a badge at me. "Hector Vargas. FBI."

"Oh." How I wished Randy or Cynthia were here! Or Patrick, I realized. "I should call my lawyer," I mumbled.

He shrugged. "Feel free. I'm not here to ask you any questions."

I took a step back from the door and waved him inside. He walked towards the sofa while I took out my phone and pulled up Patrick's number. But instead of calling, I eyed the FBI man. "What do you mean, you're not here to ask questions?"

"I'm not here in any official capacity. I just have a personal message to deliver."

I forgot about my phone and Patrick. "What message?"

"It's about Viktor," he said, and my heart soared into the stratosphere. *PleasePleasePlease don't be dead.* "He asked me to tell you he's okay." I must have been staring gape-jawed, because he quirked an eyebrow at me. "He was injured and now he's recovering."

Finally — hope! "Have you seen him?"

"Yes."

"Where is he?" I demanded. "I need to see him." He shook his head and I felt my hands ball up into fists. "Why not?"

"Look, this whole situation is…" He looked around the room, searching for the word. "Unusual." He scratched the back of his neck. "Officially I shouldn't be here. I'm doing someone a favor."

"I don't understand," I said. "Is Viktor in trouble? Is he getting deported?" The FBI man's face remained irritatingly neutral. "When can I see him?"

"I'm sorry I can't give you more information right now," he said softly.

I had nothing to say to that. Another dead end. But Viktor was alive and he was recovering. That was good news, even if he was in trouble. Too many emotions were hitting me at once.

Dmitri's voice sailed out from the kitchen. "Is everything okay, Lane?"

"Yeah." I turned to the man in the trenchcoat. "Is it, sorry, is it Officer…?"

"Agent Vargas."

"Thank you, Agent Vargas. I do appreciate that you came out here."

He nodded. "I'll see myself out."

I watched him go and clumsily tried to adjust my sling one-handed. It was impossible. Dmitri walked over. "Want help?"

"Yeah. Thanks."

He examined the sling apparatus for a moment and quickly adjusted it to the correct position. "What happened to your arm?"

"A cop attacked me," I told him. "Long story."

Dmitri just looked at me, speechless.

"Remember how you said you didn't want drama?" I asked.

"Yeah."

"Well, you might want to consider putting that in writing next time."

I made it into Manhattan the next day with minimal fuss, although the struggle was real when it came time to swipe my MetroCard at the subway turnstile. A kind fellow commuter assisted me with that task and I arrived at Cynthia's in plenty of time to get the kids to school — only to find out that they'd already left.

"Emily's plenty old enough to walk Mason to school," Cynthia declared as she helped me out of my jacket. "Don't trouble yourself about that, Lane. Patrick will be here in a few minutes. Rest. Put your feet up!"

I complied, although inwardly my mind was racing. What if the Waldrops didn't need a nanny anymore? I wasn't doing much in the way of personally-assisting Cynthia lately. Just as I was considering a polite way to ask about my prospects for future employment, the doorbell rang and Cynthia ushered a jubilant-looking Patrick into the living room.

"Don't get up," he said. "I have news."

"What is it?" Cynthia squealed. She lowered herself down next to me on the sofa and clasped her hands together.

"The FBI has offered to cover all of your medical bills. No questions asked, just a blank check. Hospital, surgeon, physical therapy, everything. Plus compensation for any missed work." Patrick beamed.

I frowned. "No questions asked in either direction?"

Patrick and Cynthia exchanged a look. "They still haven't said anything about Viktor," Patrick said. "The only information I've been able to get is that it's classified. It's a brick wall at the moment."

"That's not fair," I began.

"Listen to me, Lane." Patrick's voice was steady, like when I needed to calm Cynthia down. "Accepting their offer doesn't put us any farther away from finding Viktor than we are right now. It just means you won't get sued into oblivion for unpaid medical bills."

"What about that psycho detective who did it?" Cynthia demanded, and I nodded my agreement.

"This changes nothing in regard to Detective Jarrett except that you don't need to sue the NYPD to cover your medical bills. I've already got you a restraining order against him. The Department of Internal Affairs wants your statement," he added.

"That's all good news," I said slowly, letting the information sink in. "But I don't expect the NYPD to take this seriously. Cops here kill people all the time. Guilty, innocent, and everything in-between."

"Shouldn't he go to jail for what he did?" Cynthia demanded.

Patrick held up his hand. "One thing at a time. For Detective Jarrett to go to jail, the D.A. has to bring criminal charges against him. That would involve a grand jury. It might happen and it might not. The process is frustratingly secretive."

I exhaled. "He's going to get away with it."

"But," Patrick added, "There is nothing stopping you from filing a civil rights suit against Detective Jarrett and the NYPD. Even if you have no medical damages, there is still your pain and suffering to consider, plus the fact that your civil rights were violated."

"Will that get what happened out in the open?" I asked. I was almost afraid to hear the answer.

"I can't say. The judge issued a gag order on the TV station's case, right?" Cynthia and I both nodded. "Well, there you go," Patrick said. "I can't predict the future. But either way, I still think you have a good case."

I locked eyes with Cynthia, who nodded. "Then let's do it."

The next few days were a bit of a blur. Patrick accompanied me downtown to give my statement to Internal Affairs and it was, as expected, a dreary business. Randy visited with a basket of homemade cookies, which I shared with Emily and Mason while conspiring to keep them a secret from Cynthia. I'd been keeping Randy up-to-date on everything by phone, because texting with my left hand was too difficult; she'd been stunned by the FBI agent's visit. But if she had any new theories on Viktor, she was keeping them to herself. "Don't give up hope," she advised.

Brad still worked long hours, but he seemed to be making an effort to come home for dinner every night. Cynthia's mood had improved. The kids continued walking to and from school together; nothing terrible happened. I signed the Waldrops up for a grocery-delivery service and found that I could prepare meals as long as I gave myself extra time and didn't lift anything heavy out the oven.

Life was starting to feel normal again, sort of. I thought about Viktor constantly, but I resisted the urge to plague Randy about it. She'd been through enough. Patrick was working hard on all the legal stuff. I'd told Cynthia about the FBI guy's visit, but I was afraid to ask her for more information from David lest the black government helicopters come for both of them.

It was the first Tuesday in May — a chilly afternoon — and Emily and I were giggling over a YouTube video when my flip-phone chimed. It was a text from an unknown number that looked funny, like it was coming from overseas — a too-long series of digits beginning with 01144. Probably a Nigerian Prince scam. I opened it up anyway:

Naaaa naaa naaa na na na na

"What?" I squinted down at the screen.

Emily paused the video. "What's wrong?"

"I don't know. Wrong number, probably." I snapped the phone shut. Then another text came in:

Hey Jude

My heart may have officially stopped just then.

"Lane?" Emily's voice pierced my afraid-to-be-hopeful bubble. "Are you okay? You look like you've seen a ghost."

"I am definitely not okay." I stared down at the phone. "Can you do me a favor? Send a text for me." My left hand was so not up to this monumental task.

"Sure." Emily took the phone and frowned at its lack of a touchscreen. "Um. How?"

"The number buttons have letters on them. Press 2 once for A, twice for B, three times for C. You have to do it quickly."

She pushed a few buttons experimentally. "Oh, hell to the no. All right, fine. What should I write?"

"Write, *Who are you?* and send it," I said.

Emily bit her lip in concentration. "This is insane. I found the space! Punctuation?"

"Forget the punctuation. Just send it."

"Okay. Done." She handed the phone back to me. "I can't believe this is how you text people. It's like the Stone Age."

I stared down at the tiny screen. Emily had shortened *who are you* to *who r u* — smart girl.

In came a reply:

Who do u think? Would add a smiley emoji but that might break your rubbish phone.

"Oh my God," I breathed.

"Lane. What?"

"Reply," I commanded Emily, and thrust the phone at her. "Write: *Where are you?*"

She pecked away at the keypad. "You might as well just write a letter, you know," she muttered. "Buy a stamp and mail it." She handed the phone back to me and I stared down at it, my heart pounding. Then it chimed.

Look outside.

I ran to the Waldrops' front door and yanked it open. And there, standing on the sidewalk with a phone in his hand, was Viktor.

I don't remember how I made it from the Waldrops' doorway down to the sidewalk. Somehow — a miracle? — I got to Viktor without falling on my face. And it really was him. He was thinner, and paler, wearing a jacket I hadn't seen before. It had lots of pockets.

"Your face," I said stupidly. A scabbed-over cut on his forehead was surrounded by angry bruising. Below it, another, smaller scab bisected his eyebrow. The area below that eye was smudged purple that had faded in some spots.

"I think it's an improvement." That voice! He pocketed his phone and crossed both arms in front of him. "It's really too bad they could not fix the nose. I guess I'm stuck with it."

Something was wrong — he was moving way too slowly. Deliberately. "Are you okay?" I whispered.

"I will be." Viktor looked down at me, his head cocked slightly to one side. "How about you?"

I glanced at the bulky cast on my arm, then turned my gaze back up to him. My control was slipping and resistance was futile. "I look really stupid every time I try to swipe my MetroCard," I managed to say in a strangled voice. Then the dam broke and a wave of ugly crying commenced.

"Come here." His long arms pulled me in and I buried my face in his chest and wept. We stayed there for a minute. I felt his hand, gentle on the back of my head. If anyone passed us on the sidewalk, I took no notice. I wouldn't have noticed a grand piano crashing down to the ground ten feet away.

"I'm sorry," I finally mumbled, suddenly self-conscious. I scrubbed at my face with my good hand. "I must look like hell."

"We have an audience," Viktor murmured, pointedly looking over my shoulder.

I looked back towards the Waldrops' stoop. Emily was standing there gawking at both of us, and Cynthia was beside her, looking — frankly — a little bit desperate. "You okay, Lane?" she called out.

"Yeah." I waved to her. Then I turned to Viktor. "Want to come in?"

"We need to talk in private." He motioned to a shiny black Suburban parked illegally in front of a fire hydrant. When I balked, he added, "It's important."

I peered at the Suburban. A man I'd never seen before was sitting in the driver's seat, wearing dark sunglasses and a trenchcoat. My stomach lurched. I took a step back — away from the truck and away from Viktor. "I'm not going in there." Not even for him. No way.

"All right." Viktor studied me, his face imperturbable. "In the house, then?"

I nodded, but I didn't move. The Waldrops' front stoop was a stone's throw away. It occurred to me that I still had a lot of unanswered questions about Viktor. About this whole situation, really. And Emily was in that house. Mason and Kamran, too, up in Mason's room. Probably eating contraband potato chips and binge-watching *Doctor Who.*

"Lane?" Viktor's low voice drifted through the fugue state I was slipping into.

"Yeah."

"The guy in the truck is with the FBI." Klaxon alarms were sounding in my head. "I'll tell him to circle the block." Viktor thumped on the passenger-side window and made a motion with his hand. A moment later, the truck's engine turned over and I watched it slowly pull away. Viktor's eyes were on me and I felt my unease curdling into dread. I tried to form a coherent statement, but my mind had suddenly gone blank — so I stood there, staring at him like a colossal dope. "We can talk here," he said in a measured tone, "if it's more comfortable for you." His eyes caught the sun for a moment and they looked preternaturally blue.

My heart was thudding in my chest, hard and a little too fast. "Who are you?" I asked him. I wasn't afraid of him being around the Waldrop children anymore, but I also wasn't entirely sure I wanted to know the answer to the question I'd just posed.

"That's what we need to talk about."

34

"Lane, you'll catch your death of cold!" I looked up to see Cynthia hurrying towards us, still dressed in her yoga togs and holding out my jacket in front of her. "Here," she clucked, and she made a show of draping it over my shoulders. Then she faced me and straightened it out so it was even. "Everything okay?" she whispered.

I glanced at Viktor; he was trying to keep a straight face, with mixed success. At least he hadn't greeted Cynthia by name. "We're good," I said, and I locked eyes with a very-amused-looking Viktor. "Cynthia, meet Viktor."

"Finally," she announced. Then, before Viktor or I could respond: "Now both of you come inside and we'll exchange pleasantries in the house. Lane can't just stand out here in the cold."

Viktor offered me his arm, and we followed Cynthia inside to where it was warmer. We passed Emily on the stoop, and I tried to catch her eye but couldn't manage to. The way she was staring at Viktor, I thought her eyes might pop out of her head.

"Good!" Cynthia closed the front door behind us. "Let me have your coats." I handed her my windbreaker as Viktor started to awkwardly extract one arm from his many-pocketed jacket.

Emily, still staring at him with rapt attention, piped up. "Allow me!" She got him out of his jacket so he didn't have to reach around too far or twist his midsection, both of which seemed difficult for him. He was wearing a well-fitting olive-green sweater underneath, another item I hadn't seen him in before.

"Thanks," he muttered to Emily with a grateful smile. She was so busy beaming back at him that she bumped into the closet doorframe.

I caught Cynthia's eye and motioned her over to one side of the foyer. "Is everything okay?" she whispered. "Should I call Patrick?"

"No. I mean — yes, everything's okay. Don't call Patrick."

"Okay." She glanced over at Emily and Viktor. They seemed to be exchanging pleasantries, as it were. "I can't believe he just showed up!" This came out as more of a stage-whisper.

"Can you do me a favor?" I asked, and when Cynthia nodded vigorously I took a deep breath. "I really need to talk to him alone."

"Of course!" she whisper-screeched. "The TV room. Take all the time you need."

I squeezed her hand. "Thank you," I said, and I really, truly meant it.

I excused Viktor and myself from the Waldrops as gracefully as I could manage. Emily wasn't keen on having her getting-to-know-you chat cut short, but a stern look from Cynthia had her rolling her eyes and slouching off to the kitchen. Cynthia gave me a knowing look and disappeared after her. I led Viktor into the TV room and shut the door gently behind us.

"Please, sit," I offered. He looked from me to the 52-inch LCD flatscreen mounted on the exposed brick wall, then lowered himself onto one end of the L-shaped leather sofa with a small grimace. Moving around, even at this slow and sedate pace, was costing him. He watched me intently as I sat down.

"Who are you?" I asked again. At least now I was pretty sure I wanted to hear his answer.

"My name is Douglas Griffiths," he said, and his voice sounded oddly formal. "I was working for the FBI," he continued. "Undercover. It went on a lot longer than anyone expected."

"Is that a British accent?" My voice was way too high-pitched.

"Yes." He didn't break eye contact.

"You're not Russian?" Dumbest follow-up question ever.

"No, I'm not."

The walls of the room were suddenly closing in on me. I got up and made for the Waldrops' wet-bar. "This — this is fucked up. It's like a movie or something." I ran my good hand through my hair. *"Fuck."*

"Lane," he said, and I chanced a look back at him. He'd stood up and navigated his way around Cynthia's Japanese-shrine-inspired coffee table. He was looking at me with a contrite expression — whatever that was worth for a goddamn liar. "I am very sorry I could not be truthful with you."

"Yeah," I said, because I didn't know what else to say. I looked around the bar. "Do you want a drink? Whoever you are?"

"I can't," he said mournfully. *Cahn't.* "I'm on twelve kinds of medication."

"So have a San Pellegrino." I pulled one out of the mini-fridge and set it on the bar. For myself I took a bottle of Brad's fancy craft beer. "You're going to have to open these. I can't do it."

He hesitated a moment, then walked to the bar and got both bottles open. He took a sip of mineral water. He'd definitely lost weight; his face looked gaunt beneath the cuts and bruises. The one strategy Cynthia hadn't tried — getting the shit kicked out of her. The Food Coach would have to revise his program to include it.

"You have every right to be upset," Viktor said. Douglas. Whoever he was.

"I know." I took the bottle of beer in my good hand. "Is sitting more comfortable for you?"

He nodded.

"Then let's sit."

* * * *

271

"So. Douglas Griffiths." I set my beer down on the coffee table and looked levelly at him. "Is that what you go by? Not Doug?"

He shook his head. "Griff."

"Seriously?" It sounded wrong. He just looked at me with a confused expression. "Okay, Griff. It appears you're an international man of mystery. Would that be double-oh-seven James Bond, or Austin Powers?"

He smiled almost shyly, and his shoulders relaxed a bit. "It would be neither."

"Well, if you *were* James Bond, would you tell me?"

"I don't know." He leaned back on the sofa, grimacing a little as he did so, and considered the question. "Bond is MI-6. They're a load of tossers," he added with a smirk.

"So who do you work for?"

"No one, at the moment." He studied me. "Do you reckon Cynthia's hiring?"

"You mentioned the FBI," I insisted. "That guy in the truck. And the guy who came to my house, to deliver your message."

"Right," he said. "This was a temporary assignment. It's over now." I squirmed around on the sofa, trying to squelch down the million and one questions that were bubbling up to the surface. "I'm sensing that you want to know more about it," he added. "Though I'm certain to disappoint you with what little I am able to share."

I considered my line of questioning. "What was going on in Rego Park when — when everything happened?"

"Rego Park." He sighed.

"It was a big deal," I insisted. "Unless the FBI just happened to be meeting the SWAT team for afternoon tea."

He shook his head drolly. "Far too late in the day for tea. Ah, there it is, the eyeroll." He scratched his forehead. "Are you asking as a concerned citizen, or for your own personal—"

"Personal knowledge." I answered before he'd even finished asking the question.

He cast me a doubtful look. "Consider this off the record, then."

"Fine."

"Roman Maksimov," he said, and I nodded. "He was coming into possession of — let's say some stolen items." Griff sounded like a Shakespearean actor compared with Viktor's guttural Russian-accented English, not that I'd ever had any complaints. "He had a mind to sell these items to an interested party. Buyer and seller were meeting in Rego Park to inspect the merchandise. I had a very small window of time to request help," he added. "Hence it going tits-up with the police. Sorry."

"So did the FBI and everyone else rush over there mainly to get its hands on that merchandise? I mean, as opposed to arresting Maksimov and the buyer."

"The FBI got all of the above." But he acknowledged my point with a tilt of his head.

"What was it?" I demanded. "What was he selling?"

"That," he said, "is classified."

I took another drink of beer and tried a different angle. "Who was buying it?"

Another head-shake. "Someone who wanted to do bad things."

"All right." I chewed my fingernail. "You said it was stolen. Where was it stolen from?"

"Moldova." Griff's eyes betrayed the barest hint of amusement. Even gaunt and bruised and scabby, he still managed to look devastatingly handsome.

"Okay." I pondered this scrap of information. Where was Moldova again? Definitely Eastern Europe, but I couldn't place it on the map in my head. "Did the stolen stuff happen to rhyme with fluke-lee-ar?"

He set down his water, then turned mock-stern. "I didn't know you cared about current events."

"Sometimes I read *The Guardian* on the subway." When I'm not swooning over my handyman. *Who is not a handyman.* Shit! What had just happened to my life?

"Then it looks like you're all caught up," he murmured.

I waited for him to elaborate, but he seemed finished with the subject, so I shifted gears. "Where did you come in?"

"The FBI needed someone close to Maksimov. But he's a clever fellow — he doesn't trust outsiders. They couldn't get a suitable informant and they didn't have anyone who could go undercover. They reached out to my former employer. MI-5. That's the U.K. Security Service."

"Why you?"

"I was a trained agent. I spoke fluent Russian. My street Russian was passable. I had the tattoos." Lord, don't remind me. "I could pass for a fresh-off-the-boat criminal and not raise any alarms." He paused. "I was available."

This gave rise to a whole slew of questions I wanted to ask him, but I shoved them aside for the moment. "How did the FBI know that Maksimov would come into possession of — whatever it was?"

"They didn't know," he said. "I wasn't the only source they placed. There were others. Not just undercover agents — informants, assets." He was gazing at some indeterminate point in the distance. "I was a long shot. What do you call it? A Hail Mary."

"What's that like?" I asked him. "Working undercover for so long."

"Tedious. But you can't let your guard down. You build trust and you wait patiently."

I wondered which role I'd occupied in that scenario. Someone to pass the time with? "You could have told me, you know," I said. "I wouldn't have betrayed you."

"That would have been a mistake," he replied. "But I didn't have to involve you in this, and for that I do apologize." He looked like he wanted to say more, but he just shook his head. I felt like I'd been effectively dismissed.

"What about Detective Jarrett?" I asked, swallowing my wounded pride. "Was he part of this whole investigation?"

"No. He was investigating some of Maksimov's more mundane criminal activities." Griff looked at me for a long moment. "When he wasn't violently attacking innocent civilians."

"What's gonna happen with him?" I asked softly. Internal Affairs had been cagey about that.

"I've no idea." Griff leaned back against the sofa-cushion. "My

FBI handler says it's a legal quagmire. I heard you've got yourself a barrister, though. Loosed the hounds on him." He gave me a small smile. "Well done."

"Cynthia deserves the credit for that. And you're tired." I had so many questions for Griff, but the exhaustion in his eyes was unmistakable. I knew too well how it felt to be in need of a soft bed and healing sleep. "When did you get out of the hospital?"

"This afternoon." He rubbed his eyes.

"You came here straight from the hospital?"

"Yes."

I felt a twinge of satisfaction, hearing that. Maybe he really did care.

Don't be dumb. He's a liar.

But he'd sent someone to tell me he was okay.

Fine. He's a thoughtful and attentive liar. I couldn't do this to myself anymore. "You should rest," I muttered.

"You're right." He took out his phone and tapped something on the screen. Then his eyes met mine. "We're not done talking yet, you and me, yeah?"

"Of course not." I got up and offered him my good hand; he took it and stood up, again more slowly than I'd expected. My heart lurched sideways in my throat. *Please,* I begged the universe silently, *don't disappear again.* He might have abused my trust, but I wanted — needed — to come closer to understanding what had happened between the two of us.

Griff gave me another long look. "I'm free tomorrow after five. My flat's in Midtown. Would you pop over?"

Well, this was a shocking development. "You have an apartment?"

"No," he sighed. "Just a place to stay. It's quite temporary."

Tempr'ry. How long would it take me to stop thinking of him as a Russian guy doing a really good Benedict Cumberbatch impression? "Text me the address and I'll come."

He nodded, and then we retrieved his jacket and I walked him out. He'd gone suddenly prim and proper, asking me to thank Cynthia and Emily for their "kind hospitality" before climbing into the passenger seat of the black Suburban. Once its taillights had disappeared into the night, I turned and headed back inside.

I expected to find Cynthia lying in wait in the kitchen, but she and Emily were playing cards at the dining room table. "Well, finally," Cynthia said when I walked in. "I was getting ready to send a search party in there." Emily chose a more direct approach, throwing her cards down in a scattered heap and running over to me while emitting a high-pitched squeal.

"Emily!" Cynthia warned. "You'll scare the poor man away." She craned her neck. "Where's Viktor?"

"He had to go," I said, and I couldn't tell who looked more crestfallen at this news.

"But he just got here!" Emily wailed.

"I told him to leave because he needs to rest." My statement was met with twin looks of disbelief, so I plowed on. "He said to thank you both for your hospitality. Also his name's not Viktor." I was starting to feel the effects of Brad's beer, or maybe it was the fact that my life had just been upended. "Do you mind if I make myself a cup of tea?"

"What do you mean, his name's not Viktor?" Cynthia demanded. She'd risen to her feet and was standing next to Emily now, arms akimbo.

I swallowed. I felt stupid trying to explain something I barely understood myself. "Come on into the kitchen, both of you."

Over tea, I told Cynthia and Emily an amended version of what Griff had revealed, leaving out the parts he'd said were off the record. I also managed to text Randy a two-sentence version of events and requested some time with her tomorrow, either in-person or over the phone.

"Unbelievable," Cynthia murmured, and I couldn't argue with her. I'd fallen in love with a guy who didn't exist.

"He's an undercover spy," Emily said dreamily. "Lane, it's like a movie! Could you die? And that Belstaff jacket!" The pathetic part was that I couldn't argue with her either. I was still drawn to him. Randy's words haunted me: *How many excuses are you gonna make for this guy?* Too many. I had already made too many.

"It totally ties in with the playlist he made you," Emily concluded. "Hashtag just saying."

Cynthia gave Emily a sharp look. "How do you know he's telling you the truth?" she asked me.

"Mom," Emily groaned. "Sad trombone."

"No, she's right," I admitted. "I'm still trying to wrap my head around this. I need to talk with him some more."

"You need to get confirmation of who he is from someone trustworthy," Cynthia pointed out. "Not Griff," she added, and that was like a knife twisting in my guts.

I fiddled with the handle of my mug. Cynthia recommending a reality-check was the last thing I'd expected, but she had a point. "We could ask Patrick to make inquiries. The FBI hasn't been very forthcoming with information so far."

"I can ask David," Cynthia said. When I looked up she had a gleam in her eye. "Now that we have more to go on, I bet he can at least confirm or deny what Griff told you."

"Yes," I murmured. "That's a good idea."

A text came in — Randy.

WHAAAATTTTTTT???? LANE!!!!

I know, I texted back.

"You should crash here tonight," Cynthia said gently. "It's been a long day."

It had indeed, and I was sorely tempted. But some part of me needed to go back to Brighton Beach. Clear my head, sort out truth from lies, sleep.

"Thanks," I said. "But I need to go home."

35

I walked both kids to school the following morning, just because I wanted to. Mason, in particular, seemed clingy, and Emily was full of non-stop chatter about spies and secret identities and Belstaff jackets. I didn't mind. It was a welcome distraction from the sinking feeling I had that I'd fallen in love with a specter.

"At the risk of being a total buzzkill, please don't discuss this with anyone outside the immediate family," I reminded Emily.

"Fine," she groaned. "For once something interesting happens in my life and I can't even talk about it."

"Talk about it with me," I suggested. "How're you doing, buddy?" I asked Mason, who'd been shuffling along silently. "Hey, tie your shoes, please."

Mason bent down over his shoes but didn't say anything. He still looked comically small with his overstuffed backpack. I dropped down to his level. "Everything okay?" I asked him softly.

He finished tying the laces and we stood up together. Still he stayed silent, and the three of us started walking again before he spoke up. "Are you leaving?"

"No. Why, what have you heard?" I was painfully aware that I was adding very little value to the Waldrops' household of late. At least Emily looked appropriately alarmed at what her brother had said.

Mason shrugged. "No, I'm just thinking. You and James Bond will ride off into the sunset together. You don't need us anymore."

"Mason!" Emily thumped him on the head like any loving sister would, and he responded by kicking her in the shin. "You brat!"

"Hands off," I ordered both of them. We'd arrived at the front doors of the Weatherly School. "Griff and I are not together," I told them. "Right now I have no plans to change my employment status, and neither do your parents, that I am aware of." *Please let that be true,* I added silently. I'd been sending out a lot of requests to the universe lately. Maybe there was some kind of unlimited data plan for cosmic favors.

"But you're not going to need a nanny forever," I went on. I looked from Mason to Emily. When had they become more to me than means to a paycheck? Had it happened when I was distracted by Viktor, work, paying the rent?

Mason sniffed audibly. "So then you'll leave?"

"No." I placed my good hand on his thin shoulder. "We're friends now. And we stay friends no matter where we go or how old and gray we all get." I caught Emily's eye and she nudged her way into our little circle. "Okay?"

"Fine," Mason groaned. He gave me a half-smile, then turned and headed inside.

"Pick us up later?" Emily asked. Smart girl.

"I'll text you," I told her.

Back at Chez Waldrop, I continued to stress over how much longer the kids might require a nanny. Griff texted me; his *flat* was on a street I'd never heard of. Cynthia was so absorbed in hearing back from David that it had become a day-long project, and she seemed pleased to have something to do with herself.

Once I'd finished prepping Cynthia's meals, I headed up to the master bedroom suite. It was long past time to deal with the storage of her winter wardrobe.

"Lane, I forbid you to set one foot inside my closet," Cynthia called up after me. "You're in no condition to do heavy lifting."

279

She was right, of course, but I didn't want to hear it: my prospects for continued employment were looking dim. The kids didn't need me — not Emily, at least, and Mason was closing in fast on the age when he'd master the city.

I slunk back downstairs to find Cynthia on her iPhone. She motioned excitedly to me and mouthed "David." At least that was something. I put the teakettle on the stove and got down one mug, then another.

"Well, *you're* a hard one to get hold of," she purred into the phone as she sat down at the breakfast bar. "Yes, I am persistent. Guilty as charged," she tittered. Then she went mostly silent, apart from the occasional "uh huh" and the odd "oooh." I placed a teabag in each mug and waited for the water to boil. Yep, definitely earning that $12 an hour.

Suddenly Cynthia's side of the conversation became active again. "David, you're a rock star," she gushed. "I owe you dinner." Then she laughed. "Silly. 'Kay. Smooches. Bye!" She turned to me with a smile that frankly would have scared me if I hadn't been so desperate to hear her news.

"What?" I squeaked.

"He's telling the truth!" Cynthia crowed, and we both screamed in unison — at once marking the high and low points of my Personal Assistant career. "David went so far beyond the call of duty with this," she added. "Probably because I turned up the annoying-stalker dial and left it there all day!"

"You're a true friend," I told her. "Promise not to turn that dial up on me without a really good reason."

"Oh, stop," she insisted, but she looked more pleased than I'd seen her in a very long time. Maybe she'd keep me around for the moral support. I felt a pang of guilt, probably because I was a terrible person. Adding to this confusion: my mind was grinding itself into hamburger thinking about Secret Agent Griff. I wanted to talk to him so badly. And punch him in the nose.

"What the hell thought just popped into *your* head, missy?" Cynthia poured boiling water into both mugs and grabbed two packets of artificial sweetener. "You went from happy to miserable in about half a second."

Shit. In all the excitement, I'd forgotten about my poker-face. "I'm feeling a little insecure about my employment situation," I confessed, feeling like maybe a half-truth wasn't as bad as a bald-faced lie. "This isn't me putting you on the spot," I hastened to add. "You've been more than generous. But Mason asked about it this morning and I don't — I don't know. I guess I'm just looking for a — um, a general idea of what to expect in the next three to six months."

"Do you want to stay?" Suddenly Cynthia seemed so calm, so together. And I was drifting, scattered, insecure. Our roles had reversed.

"I do if there's work for me." I left out the part about the precise number of hours I needed to work in order to pay my rent plus expenses. And taxes, now that my employment was going legit. My stomach felt like it was tying itself into a Gordian knot.

"Okay. Here's the deal." Cynthia blew on her tea. "If you want it, there's work for you at your current rate." My heart swelled. "Magda thinks she'll be back in the next couple of months, but I'm thinking about getting back into the workforce." She emphasized this last statement with a small eyeroll.

"What will you do?" I asked. Cynthia with real-world responsibilities was an exciting and terrifying prospect.

"It's early days," she pronounced airily. "When I know more, I'll share. But it's highly entrepreneurial. One way or another, there'll be work for you to do. And as of next week, you're on the books officially. My accountant says you'll qualify for subsidized health insurance."

"God…that sounds wonderful." My relief was palpable. I wouldn't lose everyone in my life all at once. "I hope I can still see the kids a bit?"

"Of course. They need you just as much as I do. We'll figure something out."

"Thank you." I didn't know what else to say.

"You're welcome," she said. "Now go see Randy. She's probably dying from the suspense. I know I would be."

* * * *

281

Randy was waiting for me in our diner on First Avenue. "I want to hear everything," she told me. "And I do mean every fucking thing."

So I told her everything, including David's confirmation of Griff's role, and — after some minor hesitation on my part — the off-the-record information. "That part's sensitive," I whispered. "Not to be repeated outside our circle of trust."

"Do the Waldrops know?" Randy asked me.

"About the weapons of mass destruction? No way." I took a gulp of Coke. "Can you imagine the panic if something like that got out? Besides, he wouldn't even say if I guessed right. It was more implied. But really, it makes sense. It was either nukes or biological warfare."

"Why didn't I think of an undercover agent?" Randy muttered. "In hindsight it seems so obvious."

"Yeah, well, let's not linger there too long or I'll feel like the world's biggest idiot. I was having hours-long discussions with the guy *and* sleeping with him, remember."

"Indeed you were," Randy said, and she gave me a sly-fox look across the booth. "So will you be rekindling your romance?"

"Doubtful." I drummed my fingers on the Formica table. "I feel like I hardly know the guy. For all I know, he's got a wife and two kids at home in some quaint English village."

"That would suck royally." Randy picked up a fried mozzarella stick and dipped it in marinara sauce. "Eat," she reminded me, and I took one. It was greasy and delicious.

"He looks good," I admitted as I brushed crumbs off the side of the table. "A little high on the vampire scale for my taste. I hope he gets some color back in his face soon."

Randy finished her iced tea. "This whole situation is so far beyond ridiculous, Lane." I shrugged in silent assent as she studied me. "A couple of months ago I would've been worried about you. But I'm getting the feeling you'll muddle through it okay."

She was right — it *was* ridiculous. And I would muddle through. What had changed? Nothing. Everything. I had loved Viktor, or the man I'd believed he was. This Griff person was a mystery. I doubted he'd be a part of my life going forward. And that broke my heart a little. Okay, a lot. Even so, I wanted to see what happened next.

"I'm due over at his flat in half an hour." I turned Griff's invitation over in my mind: *My flat's in Midtown. Would you pop over?* "Why does everything sound so suave when a British guy says it?"

"Because he's James Bond. You want to do a bit of the old rumpy-pumpy."

I gave her a withering look. "Do you know where Tudor City Place is, or do I need to launch Google Maps?"

She smiled wickedly. "Please. Allow me to escort you."

Tudor City Place — an appropriate address for a visiting Englishman, I thought — was perched above First Avenue on a hill that started somewhere north of 40th Street and continued up to 43rd. It leapfrogged 42nd Street rather improbably with a small park. I gawked at the lovely prewar Tudor-style apartment towers, all brick exteriors with casement windows. "How did I live in Manhattan for so many years without knowing this neighborhood existed?" I asked Randy.

"It's one of those hidden gems," she replied. "I catered a party in one of the penthouses over in number five." We'd reached the top of the hill, so we headed for Griff's building past a shiny black SUV with tinted windows parked out front. A doorman greeted us.

"Apartment sixteen, uh," I said, and started digging my phone out.

"Sixteen-oh-four. He said go right up." The doorman motioned to the elevators.

"Oh." I turned to Randy.

"This is where we part ways," she said. "Here." She dug into her bag and produced a small paper-wrapped package. "Homemade cookies. You don't want to show up empty-handed."

"Shit, you think of everything." I took the package. "And come up with me! Lay eyes on the man, at least."

"Really?" Randy whispered. The doorman was busy with something at his desk, but I was 100 percent sure he was getting every word.

"Really," I said, and I pulled her towards the elevators.

36

Griff didn't open the door to his apartment to greet us — an unsmiling bald man wearing a security earpiece did. His hulking build reminded me of Detective Jarrett and I immediately disliked him. But once he'd ushered us inside, I saw Griff standing there and remembered my manners.

"Griff, this is Randy. She's my — my best friend and she, uh, she walked me over here."

"Pleased to meet you," he said smoothly, and he and Randy shook hands. The bald man lingered near the door; Griff introduced him as Andrew. I must have been the only one who felt awkward, because Randy immediately commenced ooh-ing and ahh-ing over the apartment's living room, which I'll grant was nice — in a utilitarian, utterly nondescript way.

"May I take your coats?" Griff was wearing a charcoal gray sweater over a black T-shirt. His black trousers were about the farthest you could get from Viktor's coveralls while still being men's apparel.

"I'll leave you two alone," Randy demurred. "I have somewhere to be. I just wanted to check you out for myself, Griff. I'm very protective of Lane."

He nodded, a faint smile on his face. "I understand completely."

"Don't forget the cookies," Randy reminded me, and then she left. Andrew closed and locked the door behind her.

"I suppose I'll have her to deal with if I get on your bad side," Griff said. He handed me a plate; I unwrapped the cookies and arranged them. "Would you like a cuppa?"

"Sure." I didn't know if he meant tea or coffee, but I didn't care. Some reckless part of me wanted whatever he was offering. At the same time I was dying to ask him if everything he'd ever told me was a lie. "Whose apartment is this?"

"It's a colleague's. He's abroad at the moment." Griff was fiddling with an electric kettle as he said this. I looked from him to sour-faced Andrew and realized that his professional sphere was far weirder than I'd imagined.

"It's nice." God, the small-talk was suffocating. I set the cookie plate down on a console table and looked out the casement window at a patch of still-blue sky.

"I prefer it to the hospital." He took two mugs from a tiny cabinet and spooned some sugar into them, then dug into an apothecary jar and plucked out two foil-wrapped teabags. "Is English Breakfast all right?"

"Yeah." I looked him over. He was wholly absorbed in making tea. "What happened to you, anyway? No one ever told me. Were you shot?"

"Yeah, in the abdomen." He handed me a mug.

"I never heard a gun go off," I said, and then I felt stupid, so of course I kept talking. "Isn't that always fatal, getting shot in the stomach?" I held the mug in both hands to warm them. "In movies it is, I mean."

"I suppose it depends on what gets hit and how long 'til it's treated." Griff looked over at Andrew, who nodded and disappeared into what must have been the bedroom. Then Griff motioned to the living area, which consisted of a love-seat and an ottoman arranged around a glass-topped coffee table. "Do you want to sit?" I must have been too lost in thought to answer, because suddenly the plate of cookies was hovering under my nose. "Earth to Lane," Griff whispered.

"I'm here," I told him, and I walked over to the ottoman and sank down onto it.

I knew, going in, that it was a fool's errand, trusting myself to exercise caution or good judgment where Griff was concerned. I'd never managed to do it before. The only sensible thing to do was walk away. What was I hoping for — clarity? Closure? Did it even matter? I suppose it did.

"There are things I need to tell you, Lane." Griff's deep voice cut through the chaos in my head.

"Yeah." I took a sip of tea. It was perfect. I dared a glance at him — he was looking at me with a strange kind of expression, a combination of sadness and concern. Was it pity? I looked away. As much as I wanted to have this conversation, I was dreading it in equal measure because I knew that whatever I found out about him was something I could never un-learn.

"I am so sorry I could not be completely truthful with you," he began.

"Completely?" I shook my head. "That's rich. Was any of it true?"

Griff held my gaze and I knew what was coming: the wife, the kids, sorry sorry sorry. I shut my eyes.

"Just tell me," I said. "Do you have someone waiting for you? At home in England?"

"I do."

I felt all hope inside me shrivel and die as he took out his phone and tapped it a couple of times. Then he held it up and I saw a photo of a yellow dog who looked for all the world like it was grinning, with a pink tongue lolling out of its mouth. "Her name's Lucy," Griff said.

"Lucy," I stammered. "Just the dog, though? No wife, or girlfriend?"

"Just the dog." He put the phone down on the table. "Would it be all right if I told you a bit about myself?"

"That — that would be fine." I was ready to burst with more questions, starting with whether he'd really been in prison. "I feel like I don't know very much about you," I added in a strangled voice.

"You know more than you think." I had no idea what to make of that. "Do you want to ask questions, or shall I just tell you the story of Griff?"

"I would like very much to hear the story of Griff." *Don't you dare hope,* I thought, but there it was again, the merest spark. "I'm going to move to the floor if you don't mind," I added, and I sat down, leaning my aching back against the ottoman.

"Feels like old times. I wish I could join you but I'd never get up," Griff murmured.

"Just do what's most comfortable." I took a cookie for good luck.

"I think I already told you that I used to work for MI-5," he began.

"Yeah." I searched my memory for what he'd said about that. "Security Services."

"I was a field agent," he told me. "In domestic counter-terrorism."

"So you *are* sort of James Bond."

He gave me an amused look. "It wasn't anywhere near that glamorous."

"All right. Sorry. Continue."

"They recruited me out of university," he said, and he fiddled with his mug before setting it down carefully on the coffee table. "I was good at it. We were doing good work." His eyes had fixed on that point in the distance. "It was a cracking team."

"Sounds exciting," I said softly.

"It was," he sighed, flashing me a sad smile. "Nothing gold can stay, yeah?" He picked up a felted-wool throw pillow. "I was assigned to a case—" He closed his eyes. "Eight years ago." His eyes popped open. "Crikey. I'm old. I had to go to Russia to meet with an asset. It should have been a quick in and out. I was careful. I still don't know how they got me."

"Who got you?"

"The FSB. Russian security service. It's basically the equivalent of your CIA."

"Shit."

CLEAN BREAK

"Yeah." He shook his head. "Eighteen months at Lefortovo prison in Moscow and then another four and a half years—" He dropped the pillow to one side. "At a labor camp near Kirov."

Holy shit. "What you told me," I stammered. "It was true?"

He gave me a long look. "Yes. But that doesn't make it right, what I did. Getting you involved in this. I put you in a shit position and I'm sorry."

I didn't know what to think, much less say, so I nodded numbly.

"I'm not going to sit here and pretend that telling you a bunch of half-truths is the same as being truthful," he went on, and he looked around the room before his gaze finally settled on me. "It was wrong. I was…" He shook his head. "I wasn't thinking straight."

"Are you telling me the whole truth now?" I asked.

"Yes." His voice was barely above a whisper.

I didn't believe him. But there were other, less-direct angles I could try. "Why didn't the British government do something to get you out of prison?" I asked.

"That's not how it works when this happens." His voice was tight. "You're pretty much on your own."

"Then how did you get out?"

He looked down at his hands. "I never had a case or an official sentence, so I didn't know what to expect. I wouldn't say I'd given up hope. Not entirely." He met my gaze. "One day two FSB agents showed up and told me I was being transferred."

"Was that a good thing?"

"Not necessarily. The FSB might transfer you into a shallow grave, or out of a helicopter at a thousand feet. Or back into solitary confinement." I shivered. How could he be so blasé about this? "I woke up," he continued, "in the boot of a car and when they opened it up there was London. An industrial park. They did a prisoner exchange."

"Jesus." I thought about London — those adorable taxis, Mason and Emily going bananas over double-decker buses. "Did you get a hero's welcome?"

"No," he said evenly. "To be fair, I didn't expect one."

289

"Well, what then?"

"A week in hospital." He took a deep breath. "Then debriefings. Medical tests, psychological evaluations. Five didn't want me back."

"What's Five?"

"Sorry. MI-5."

"Why didn't they want you back?"

"I was unfit for duty. They medically discharged me."

"That's bullshit," I observed. "After everything you went through for them?"

"It wasn't bullshit. With the benefit of hindsight, it was the right call. I was a mess, even though I didn't want to see it at the time."

"Well, you seem fine to me." I took another cookie and turned it over in my hands. I wasn't hungry.

"Your loyalty is showing," he murmured. "This was almost two years ago. You've had a little taste of what was happening. But it was worse. Not just the nightmares." His eyes were clear and somber. "Flashbacks. Panic attacks. I wasn't—" He paused, and my heart broke for him, thinking back to how he'd looked that morning in my apartment — asleep on the cold, hard floor. "I wasn't feeling quite human, then," he finally said. "I don't know if that's the right way to put it. It was difficult." He glanced off to one side. "Yeah. Grim."

"So what happened?" My tailbone had gone numb. I climbed back onto the ottoman and abandoned the cookie to the coffee table.

"I left London. They moved me out to the countryside. I need — I needed to be someplace less crowded." He swallowed. "I cooperated. Took my medicine, saw the shrink twice a week. Until they were reasonably sure I wouldn't go mad."

"Yeah, I know how that goes." Did he know that he was the only person in the world I'd ever willingly shared that part of my life with?

"Right." He gave me a gentle smile and I resisted a sudden and foolhardy urge to fling myself into his arms. "I had back pay to live on," he continued. "So I didn't have to find a job straight away."

"What did you do?" *Stop pining away for Viktor,* I ordered myself. *He doesn't exist.*

"I ran a lot. Read books, went to the cinema, caught up on years of politics and pop culture. I saw my sister whenever I could. I got a dog."

"Lucy." I smiled at him. "And then?"

"And then everything was going well for a while. I'd got a very boring part-time job. Let's see, Lucy and I were binge-watching *Breaking Bad.* And I got a visit from my old colleague at Five. The Americans needed someone and I fit the bill."

"Why did you agree to take the job?"

He gave me a strange look. "Why wouldn't I take it?"

"Well, they weren't exactly loyal to you when it counted." I'd imagined he was loyal, once, this cipher of a man sitting in front of me. "They left you in prison for six years."

"It wasn't personal," he said, and I wondered what kind of a person could really believe that. "Anyway, this job was a chance to prove myself. To prove I wasn't damaged goods."

Damaged. "You told me this," I heard myself say. "I mean, you told me..." I tried to recall what Viktor — Griff — had said weeks ago in my apartment. Who remembers entire conversations word-for-word? But he'd told me so much of his story. Confided in me. In his own maddening, purposefully vague way — half-truths, he'd called them.

"I recall that you were interrogating me about it," he said, and there was a faint smile on his face. It occurred to me that the story of Griff was turning out to be a revelation, just not in the way I'd expected because I already knew it. In a strange, backwards kind of way — a parallel-universe version. But still. I knew.

It hadn't just felt real — it had *been* real.

I stopped beating myself up just then, the moment I recognized and named it. Exactly that fast.

It was real.

"I hated lying to you," Griff murmured. "It's the worst part of this job, I think." He was fidgeting with his fingers but then he turned his gaze towards me. "Lying to the people you care about."

291

My heart skipped a beat.

"You once asked me why I helped you," he went on. "I'm afraid I gave you an incomplete answer."

"Was it my legendary beauty?" I smoothed my hair and tried to remember if I'd bothered with makeup this morning. "I get that all the time, you know."

"You are lovely." Yeah, right. His eyes lingered on me a little longer than necessary. "But that's not why."

"Why then?"

"After I got back from Russia." He wore a serious expression now. "I told you I'd changed. And not for the better."

"You said your sister helped you," I recalled.

He shifted on the love-seat and nodded in agreement. "She saved my life, I think. Having someone there who'd known me since...before I'd even known myself. She was a beacon at a very dark time."

"I'm glad, Griff. That's a good thing." I ignored the lump in my throat, reached over, and squeezed his hand. "I do know something about sisters."

"Yes. You do." His gaze was suddenly intense. "I saw something so brave in you. From the first time we met. Something so..." He shook his head. "Indomitable, stubborn. You were reaching out for something you'd lost. I didn't know what it was, at first, but I recognized it. And it drew me to you."

"All right." I cleared my throat. I didn't want to think about what I was reaching for. I knew I couldn't ever get it back.

"You kept on fighting for it," Griff added. "You're fighting for it still."

"And that's somehow admirable?" I felt so flustered all of a sudden. "Whatever I'm fighting for, it doesn't matter. It's pointless."

"I can understand why you'd think that."

"Can you?" I could hear the bitterness edging into my voice. I hated myself for getting emotional over this with him. Again.

"I knew I could never be the same man I was before Russia," Griff said. "Confident. Successful. At ease in any situation." He clasped and unclasped his hands, looked around the room and then down to his lap. "I believed," he said softly, "that I could take whatever they threw at me. Beatings. Torture. But it changed who I am. It hardened me." He met my gaze. "The man who went to Moscow — I don't even know who he is anymore. Just that he was naïve. He was blissfully unaware of what was about to happen."

I didn't know what to say to this, so I nodded silently.

"But you. Lane. You got into my head." Griff looked so earnest. "At first, I fought it. I had a job to do. Getting involved with someone on a covert op — it's not encouraged. Especially when you're already a bit of a mess, like me." He paused. "But when I was with you, even just sitting and talking — I felt more like myself — *really* myself — than I'd ever been since Russia."

"Maybe your real self is a Russian handyman," I offered.

He smiled. "It's as likely as anything else, at the moment. But I never felt that way with Sergey and we spent untold hours together."

"Touché." I smiled back. "And this is very nice of you to — to say."

"I'm not saying it to be nice." He stood up slowly and walked to the window. The sky had turned orange. "Being with you brought me closer to whatever it was I'd lost."

I got up and walked over to him. He was so tall. "What had you lost?" I was almost afraid to hear the answer.

"You once called it—" He chuckled. "The soft and squishy part." He looked down at me. "I'd thought it was gone." I mulled that over while he fidgeted with his sleeve. "There's something I need to tell you," he muttered.

"What?" That sinking feeling again. *There's something I need to tell you* rarely portends good news.

"I saw the video."

"The — wait. What video?"

"The news crew shot a video in Rego Park."

"Oh." That video. I'd almost forgotten it existed. "What about it?"

"It was difficult to watch." He gazed at me. "You put yourself in grave danger."

"It's the least I could have done." That got me a look of complete disbelief. "It was my fault to begin with! That psycho Detective Jarrett. He had it in for you because of me. He thought you and I were back together and he went apeshit. I was…" I trailed off. Had I even known what I was doing in Rego Park? Not really. "I was trying to help," I finally said.

Griff crossed his arms over his chest and stared out the window for a moment. Then he looked down at his shoes. "I saw what you did," he said. "You were brave. You had no thought for your own safety." He finally met my gaze. "You saved my life. Thank you for doing that."

"You're welcome," I mumbled, suddenly uncomfortable. "I haven't seen… I mean, I guess I'll have to take your word on that."

His eyes were locked onto mine. "You could have been killed. When I saw what you did, my first — my only thought was that I could never deserve you."

"What the fuck?" Goddamnit, I had to see this video! "You're talking like I saved the world from destruction or something. I only did what anyone would have."

Now Griff looked like he was in physical pain, so I waited. "From the moment we first met," he said slowly, "all I have done is lie to you. One lie, and then another, to cover for the first one. That's how it goes." He looked pleadingly at me. "I am so sorry, Lane. Maybe it went too far."

"Too far for what?" I demanded. He didn't answer. "Do you hear me complaining, Griff? About our friendship, or relationship, or whatever it was? About the sex?"

He winced at the mention of sex. He actually looked ashamed! "What happened," he finally said, "was not supposed to happen. It was unprofessional. Inappropriate. I am sorry."

"Well, I'm not," I told him. "But I was wrong about you. You're not James Bond. You're Batman. Saving our city from a nuclear dirty bomb or some other equally fucked-up shit."

He seemed perplexed by my logic-pretzel, but he'd relaxed his arms. He no longer looked so tightly wound he might crack in half at any second. But that was beside the point, I realized. I didn't want to extrapolate and play guessing games anymore. I was done with half-truths.

"How much of it was real?" I asked him. "If it was all an act — if *we* were an act — then I'm nominating you for a fucking Academy Award."

"It wasn't an act," he snapped. His eyes held fast to mine. "Never."

"Then let's address two things." I took his hand in mine. "One, you had a bit of how's-your-father on the job. We both enjoyed it, so enough said about that."

He looked down at me with an expression so tender I thought I might melt.

"And two, you lied about stupid stuff because you had no choice, and you talked to me in a fake Russian accent for several weeks. I enjoyed that too."

"Lane, I shouldn't have—"

"Shh." I twined my short fingers through his long elegant ones and met his gaze. Those icy-blue eyes. *Now or never.* "I am taking both of these matters and putting them aside, for now, because I'm madly in love with you," I told him. "That's the truth. Both halves of it. And I need to know what your feelings are for me."

The look on his face was exactly the same as if I'd just sprouted moose antlers out the sides of my head. *This is it,* I thought, and I let my hand go limp and steeled myself for the inevitable rejection. At least I had a job. And friends, and a place to live. Griff not loving me back wasn't the end of the world, even if that's what it felt like.

"My feelings for you, right now," he repeated — and it sounded like a stall tactic — "are, first and foremost, that you cannot possibly be real."

My heart caught in my throat.

"And second." He cradled my face in his hands. *Do not die,* I counseled myself. "I love you, Lane Haviland. I have loved you for a very, very long time. And even though I don't deserve it, you love me back. Despite my many faults."

"You think I'd let you slip through my fingers twice?" A tear ran down my cheek — I didn't know if it was joy or relief or just general insanity. Furthermore, I didn't care.

"Hey." He caressed my cheek and brushed the tear away with

his thumb. "I believe this is a happy occasion."

"Yes." I looked up at him. I could gaze at his face forever and never get tired of it. "What's the over-under on you staying here with me in the former colonies a little longer?"

His arms encircled my waist and squeezed gently. "That depends," he murmured. "How do you feel about overly-friendly yellow dogs with abysmally low intelligence?"

"They're amazing," I answered honestly, and he leaned in and kissed me — slowly, exquisitely, with tingles. Afterwards I laid my cheek against his sweater and felt his heart beating as I closed my eyes. "You too, you know. You're amazing."

And he was.

Appendix I
Russian Words & Phrases

Chapter 3:
Ty chto? Ahuyel - What are you? Gone fucking crazy
Cho blya? - What the fuck?

Chapter 5:
Blyats - Whore

Chapter 9:
Gavno! - Shit!

Chapter 10:
Spasiba - Thank you

Chapter 12:
Privet - Hi
Shas budu - I'll be right there

Chapter 13:
Pristegnis - Fasten your seat belt

Chapter 15:
Zek - Prison inmate
Suka blyats - Fucking whore
Bozhe moy - Oh my God
Kuvalda - Sledgehammer
Spletnitsa - Someone who spreads rumors
Murashki - Goose bumps

Chapter 17:

Nyet - No

Ne nado - That's enough

Pozhalsta - Please

Ya ne ponimayu - I don't understand

Chapter 20:

Ya veryu tebe - I believe you

Ya tebe doveryayu - I trust you

Chapter 27:

Ti mozhesh pamoch? - Hey, can you help?

Poverni liveya - Turn it to the left

Yesho chu-chuts - A little more

Vso harosho - Okay that's good

Appendix II
Viktor's Playlist

If I Ever Feel Better - Phoenix
Someday - The Strokes
Circuit Breaker - Wildcat! Wildcat!
Lucky Man - The Verve
Houdini - Foster the People
Island in the Sun - Weezer
Been There Before - Ghost Beach
Letting Go - Saint Raymond
Waves - Blondfire
Always - Panama
There She Goes - The La's
No Stranger - Small Black
Dream the Dare - Pure Bathing Culture
Everyday is Like Sunday - Morrissey
Midnight City - M83
If It Hurts - Gallant
West End Girls - Pet Shop Boys
Satellite - Guster
Wake Up the Ghosts - Leisure Cruise
Scar Tissue - Red Hot Chili Peppers
Running Back to You - For the Foxes
Earthquake - Leisure Cruise
Something I Can't Have - The Jesus and Mary Chain
Strange Feeling - Panama
This Is The One - The Stone Roses
Here Comes the Sun - The Beatles
Hey Jude - The Beatles

Listen to it here: http://bit.ly/1HRD9js - and visit
AbbyVegasAuthor.com for additional discussion.

Acknowledgments

Writing my first novel felt, at times, like a classic blunder —
right up there with a land war in Asia. Many people helped me
over the finish line and I'd like to thank some of them here.

My critique partner, Kel O'Connor, and my intrepid first-round
beta-readers — Amy Cabot and Ana Tellado-Schiff. And my
amazing editor, Donna Cook.

My on-call linguists — Roman Frenkel, Darren Hickling,
and Laura Hickling.

My subject-matter experts — Brendan McFeely,
Shannon Reeves-Rich, Greg Roehrig, Peter Schultz, and
Lawrence Sullivan.

My fellow scribes — Anja de Jager, H.M. Graves, Liz Madrid,
Gary Shteyngart, and Matt Weatherford.

My youth group — Jake Grubman, Lily K, and Sarah K.
(Visit me in the senility home, please, and bring contraband.)

My husband — still the best guy in the whole wide world.

Readers: Thank you for taking the time to read *Clean Break*.
If you enjoyed it, please consider telling your friends or posting
a short review. Word of mouth is an author's best friend and
much appreciated. Thank you.

Abby Vegas
AbbyVegasAuthor.com

Made in the USA
Middletown, DE
12 April 2016